THE BIG WHY

ALSO BY MICHAEL WINTER

Creaking in Their Skins
One Last Good Look
This All Happened

THE BIG WHY

MICHAEL WINTER

ANANSI

Published in 2004 by
House of Anansi Press Inc.
110 Spadina Avenue, Suite 801
Toronto, ON, M5V 2K4
Tel. 416-363-4343
Fax 416-363-1017
www.anansi.ca

Distributed in Canada by
Publishers Group Canada
250A Carlton Street
Toronto, ON, M5A 2L1
Tel. 416-934-9900
Toll free order numbers:
Tel. 800-663-5714
Fax 800-565-3770

The quotation on page 360 from Premier Smallwood's letter to Rockwell Kent is
from Kent's chapbook *After Long Years* (Asgaar Press, Ausable Forks, NY, 1968). The
quotation on page 336 from Rockwell Kent's letter is from a draft of a letter he sent to
the Collector of Customs, St John's, NF, July 28, 1915, and its source is *Rockwell Kent:
The Newfoundland Work* (Dalhousie Art Gallery, NS, 1987).

The woodcuts on the cover and endpapers are from pages 123, 21, and 52,
respectively, of *N by E*, by Rockwell Kent (New York Literary Guild, 1930);
these woodcuts are reproduced courtesy of the Plattsburgh State Art Museum,
Plattsburgh College Foundation, Rockwell Kent Gallery and Collection,
bequest of Sally Kent Gorton.

08 07 06 05 04   1 2 3 4 5

NATIONAL LIBRARY OF CANADA CATALOGUING IN PUBLICATION DATA

Winter, Michael, 1965–
The big why / Michael Winter.

ISBN 0-88784-188-0

1. Kent, Rockwell, 1882–1971 — Fiction. 2. Brigus (N.L.) — Fiction.
I. Title.

PS8595.I624B44 2004   C813'.54   C2004-903273-9

Jacket design: Bill Douglas at The Bang
Jacket woodcut illustration: Rockwell Kent
Text design and typesetting: Brian Panhuyzen

**Canada Council
for the Arts**

**Conseil des Arts
du Canada**

ONTARIO ARTS COUNCIL
CONSEIL DES ARTS DE L'ONTARIO

*We acknowledge for their financial support of our publishing program the
Canada Council for the Arts, the Ontario Arts Council, and the Government of Canada through the Book
Publishing Industry Development Program (BPIDP).*

Printed and bound in Canada

For
Hogarth, Jr

That day will mark a precedent
which brings no news of Rockwell Kent

— *The New Yorker*, 1937

BEGINNING

THE NAKED MAN OF BRIGUS

A man goes to sea here as one would depart from the earth for the moon or Jupiter. They are map-makers. The largeness of the Newfoundlander's field of labour is so apparent — I've become more intimate with our little round earth since I've been here than in all my life before.

— Rockwell Kent
letter to Charles Daniel, 3 June 1914

1

I have been loved. I can say this. But back then, before it all went wrong, I did not know enough to consider the question. I had married a woman with one facial gesture. Kathleen Whiting. A kind smile. When we made love, that smile. I knew I was wrapped up with goodness — if I kept close to this woman a good life would accrue. But there is something about goodness — I associate it with acquiescence, and I'm repulsed by compromise. I wanted to see Kathleen serious. If I caught her rinsing out the coffee cups, her face concentrated and her set mouth. I loved her then. What are you thinking about. About the children. About you. If you are faithful. Her firmness a blend of grace and warding off heartbreak.

Kathleen had said, as a resolution to our leaving New York, I want to make my life less complicated. And my friend Gerald Thayer had leapt at her. Kathleen, he'd said. If your life got any less complicated, the heart would stop right in your chest.

Gerald was the one who'd told us to leave the city. He was a writer and a son of the painter Abbott Thayer. Kathleen was his cousin. I told Gerald how I was angry about the New York painters and my reputation. I was mad at what the buildings were made of and the heat in the buildings. I felt anger was blotting out my love, and I wished to instigate a challenge to this anger. Youre tempted, Gerald said, by too many women, and youre in fights with men you used to respect.

He was alluding to a rift with his father. We were having a show and I had refused to include any art by someone already exhibited by the Academy. Abbott Thayer protested this: it's a labour union method. I called Abbott a crass sentimentalist. I guess the pettiness I felt made New York a little poisoned. I hate, I said, how small I've made the city feel. And I do not like to be exposed.

Gerald Thayer, on our way home: It's not the movement, I hope. He said, Everything is movement these days, and I'd hate for you to be persuaded by it.

Gerald thought about his own movement.

Did you know I'm originally from Buffalo, did you know that?

Pause.

I'm proud to be from Buffalo.

Me: Well. It's a finely situated city.

Oh go fuck yourself.

In the morning I watched the grocer at the corner pluck the wooden pennants that held the prices of the various cheeses. He plucked them like flags of nations. As if cheeses were nationalities and they were shifting. I saw him lift out the flags and rearrange them. All is movement, Gerald had said. It's movement for the sake of making something new.

2

We were folding my shirts. Kathleen was pairing up socks. How many socks did I need. What kind of weather will you endure. Wool, she said, is better than cotton. It will keep you warm even when it's wet.

I loved Kathleen's posture, the curve of her instep as she forced her fingers to judge the fabric of socks in the light of our bedroom window. She said, It is a terrible thing not to know how to love.

Me: Yes, even now I wonder if I am truly loving.

Kathleen: What is the impulse that drives love.

Me: Is it a good thing.

Kathleen: This is what I believe: when you make love, you are funnelling the world through the beloved.

You make love to the world through the one body. Yes, Kathleen, and making art is the same.

But what if you wind up on the wrong side of the art that lasts?

Me: I'm convinced our side will win.

You have become monogamous to that idea.

Yes, Kathleen, but it has left me wondering, now, if I've led a true life.

This reflection is steeped with opinion. It is important to note that during the time Kathleen and I packed my clothes for a life in Newfoundland, I had not yet come to this opinion.

3

I was thirty when I finally buckled up my pigskin suitcase, selected a box of paints. I entrusted my wife, in the months to come, with shipping off my tools and our worldly goods. In the spring, Kathleen would follow with our three children. This was our second attempt at a life in Newfoundland. Our first try, five years earlier, had ended before Kathleen set foot there. This time I promised her things would be right. Turning thirty had made me panic, but panic is not something I worry about. Panic incites me to concentrate. It was the age my father was when he died, so I was my father. My father had died away from home. The idea of being foreign appealed to me — I had lived most of my life in New York, and suddenly, with thirty rearing itself, the man-made surfaces bored me. But all sudden things come from a deep study of conversion — they are sudden only on the surface.

That Christmas, Gerald Thayer had taken me to seven parties. We had drunk a lot and were vulnerable to awe. But the things we saw were all glitter and no substance. A store was shut and a sign said,

CLOSING SALE
UP TO

As though they hadnt decided what percentage to mark off. Then I saw: the percentage was there, but it had faded. It had been marked in red, the most fugitive of colours. The store, Gerald said, was closed. It's been closed a long time. This shocked me, this realization that what could have been a fresh thought (closing) had been an old act (closed long ago). I want, I said to Gerald, to avoid that predicament. I want a thickness to pour into me, like honey or cement.

You want, Gerald said, to slough off the baubles.

He said you can get that only if you move to a small place, to the periphery, to a community that is one organism and does not change. That loves itself.

So that is why we moved.

And Newfoundland? In my early twenties I had gone to a lecture given by Captain Bob Bartlett. Bartlett was a ship's captain who would steer Robert Peary to the north pole, and I had been seeing a woman then, Jenny Starling, whose father, George Crocker, knew both Peary and Bartlett. Jenny's father was a sponsor for these expeditions, and he was hoping for a coastline to be named Crocker Land. In those days we were all interested in the Arctic. It was a novelty, going to empty, dangerous places. We loved hearing about men starving or freezing to death for the sake of a technical achievement.

Bartlett said these things. He described a fire on board the *Roosevelt*. Whale meat from Turnavik went rancid and seeped into the *Roosevelt*'s timbers all along the main deck, and a pipe ignited it. He spoke about the death of young Marvin. How they backtracked for his body and had to chop it out of the frozen sea. He mentioned the trouble with women, how he never married — for what woman could live with a man who spent years trapped in polar drift ice? I was holding Jenny Starling's shoulder when he said this. The exuberance of Bob Bartlett, the generosity of his laughter coupled with my own contempt for

New York, made me want to go to his country. His country was
Newfoundland.

Bartlett had just returned from the pole to New York with
Peary and Matthew Henson. I saw them from Gerald Thayer's
apartment on the Upper West Side. I was married to Kathleen
now, a new father and a disenchanted painter — all in five
years. The city opened its windows, and women hiked up
their knees onto sills to look down upon the flurry of white
tickertape. There they were: an early motorcade of smiling,
victorious, saluting men, Jenny Starling's father in amongst
them. Gerald's wife, Alma, leaned out with a paper sack. She
tore the side of it and let loose a flurry of narcissus petals. Some
landed on my hand. It was like a wedding, or the spreading of
ashes after a cremation. One or the other, it had that much
meaning to her.

There were cocktail benefits for the Peary Polar Club. Gerald
and I went to one, a cheaper one that just had Bob Bartlett. A
room of green leather and billiard tables. George Crocker was
there but refused to speak to me — he did not like how I'd treated
his daughter. But this is where I first spoke to Bob Bartlett. He
was not tall but a well-packed two hundred pounds, with a long
face, a well-shaved face. A little stiff in the face, but jocular. I
was taken by him, his sheer joy and good-naturedness. Bob
Bartlett was heading back home to Newfoundland. He had a high
voice, like some boxers have after theyve been punched in the
throat. I'm missing it, Bartlett said. He missed it more than any
man I'd ever seen miss home. It made me think he must come
from a wonderful place. As if returning to childhood. Perhaps
missing anything is always childish. I had no sense of home.

I'm signing up, he said, the young sons of rich Americans. For a trip into the Arctic Circle. You have a son?

Yes, I said, but he's only a baby.

Oh we'll take him, he said.

I'm not rich.

When theyre that young they come free. We've got a hundred thousand rounds of ammunition, rifles galore — he pushed my shoulder — we've got fishing rods and reels, all the gear.

You think there'll be anything left alive when you come back.

Possibly. I hope it's us.

What if, I said, I came aboard.

Your wife won't like it. But I can tell right off, he said. You'd love it.

Bartlett had a manly, physical presence that was coupled with a daintiness. He was physical and yet not sexual. He did not like to hold a wine glass — he kept setting it down. He was very well dressed, but it made his face red. He looked like he wanted to be in shirt sleeves. He wanted to throw open the windows and turn off the radiators. Bob Bartlett had a furnace in him. In his neck and belly.

But he did not believe me. He was humouring me. That I would come.

During the intervening years I met Bob Bartlett several times. He was often in New York and stayed in the Murray Hill Hotel, near the Hudson River. We would meet at his Explorers Club, a club I liked very much, for it felt incubated, or padded, as if sound diminished when you entered those rooms. Bartlett was looking for fresh expeditions, more young men, but the pledges were harder to come by. He knew I was connected to money, and that was part of what he tolerated in meeting me. The poles, he said, had been discovered, and no one wants to send their money out to the regions, not even George Crocker. There was talk, Bartlett said, of a European war. He was looking a little desperate. I too felt desperate. How to make a name when it seemed we had come to the end of things. Abstraction was the avant-garde, and I loathed it. An abstract painting is like a cat that ignores you and says, smugly, I am the reason for living. Art, I told Bartlett, should encourage life. Bob Bartlett liked my spunk and he aggravated my drive to come. I've got a house for you, he said, in Brigus. Neat as a pin.

I almost ended up, I said, in the town of Burin.

He looked interested.

Your prime minister, Morris, told me about Burin. But a family matter caused me to withdraw.

I did not tell him about the troubles I'd had with Jenny Starling.

So why not Brigus?

I talked Kathleen into it. I was twenty-nine, tossing the house keys to her, and she caught them nonchalantly. She had these beautiful big hands and she could catch things.

I'll try anything twice, she said, if it makes you happy.

What did I feel about that. I felt I could be myself. Here was a woman who did not want to curb me. For years I ran on that fuel. Having one's will done, my wife's will bent to my industry. But Kathleen's response was not as altruistic as it seemed. The thought of leaving New York appealed to her. Kathleen was a

small-town girl inside. The big city made her shoulders stiff —
she grew up in a rural setting in Massachusetts, where she had
access to wildflowers and the seasons of insects. She was formed
more of nature than of plumbing and electricity. And why
couldnt she say that. Okay, so she couldnt say it — it should
have been enough that I could sense it. The reason she wanted to
leave New York was to avoid meeting women I'd slept with.
Having to hear, Yes, I had an affair with her. I'm a man who
likes things spoken. At least when those things are in my favour.
The truth is, I played against this reluctance in Kathleen to say
things. And in this case of moving, I wanted her to blurt her feelings. Bringing our family to a small island country off the coast
of Canada, did that make her nervous.

4

I was working as a draftsman for the architectural firm Ewing
and Chappell. In order to leave my job I had to raise some
capital. I made a deal with my agent, Charles Daniel, for a
monthly stipend in exchange for everything I would write
or paint for the rest of my life. Everything: drawings, sketches,
paintings, books, travel pieces, ceramics, woodblock prints,
colophon design, illustrations. I said two hundred and fifty
a month, Charles. What do you say. He was kneeling at a
bookcase, his shoes off. His socks did not match. He chose not
to wear matching socks — he was quietly defiant in the face of
uniformity. He studied the spines of his books, almost solemn,
but he was looking for something. He said sixty-five, to the

books. Charles Daniel could read the spines of books without twisting his head to the side. I realized he was bargaining. Sixty-five dollars. He said it very quickly, as if he really had totted up my future work and thought it worth sixty-five a month. He was sucking on an apricot. He had the whole apricot in the side of his mouth. I sank on my arches. The sixty-five made me realize he was being generous. It had not occurred to me that I wasnt worth at least two hundred and fifty a month. I understood that my worth was outside of myself. There was the bowl of apricots on his desk. I thought, That's two dollars and fifteen cents a day. I divided that among myself and Kathleen and three children. Okay, I said. Do I need to sign something. Yes, he said.

Charles Daniel knew signed things cemented friendships.

I asked my mother. I visited her with the children. The children liked visiting because my mother had a greenhouse with a sunroom, and in the sunroom was a glass box with a very heavy black-and-yellow snake. Her inheritance had come through, so she said yes. She could send us fifty a month.

Gerald Thayer said, I want to give you fifty dollars. A present.

Me: Forget it.

Gerald: No it's hard to forget.

Me: It'd be a nuisance.

Gerald: You could get something with it. Blow it on something. Something cooked.

Me: I'd spend it. Then I'd spend it ten times over. I'd be in the hole five hundred.

Just spend it once.

Me: I'd do something lavish. Then say, That's Gerald's fifty gone. Then another thing will come up. Say we need a stove. Say I pass a foundry in St John's and there's a brand new shit-kicking stove. Well that's a permanent gift from Gerald sitting in our kitchen. Say the stove is a hundred. I'll think, It's half-price. If we put Gerald's fifty to it. Then there'll be I dont know.

Gerald: I'll get you a stove. Lug a stove to Newfoundland.

Me: Get me a drink. A hundred drinks.

I saw my friend Rufus Weeks. He was a socialist, an active one. He made his living as a vice-president of the New York Life Insurance Company, but he was one of those bankers who think profits increase during times of peace. He was peeling an orange. Let's walk, he said. Rufus was a man who liked to see things as he talked. He ate oranges because, as a child, he'd had an older sister who was ill. The doctor had prescribed fresh fruit. Oranges were imported and expensive, and he was not allowed one. Now he ate them with a vengeance, with bitter-ness. He was that kind of socialist. Rufus said he believed in character. In upholding morals. But only in public.

Manners, he said, are most important in a politician.

He was peeling the orange in one long spiral. What you expose should always be consistent and proper. Respectful to the times. But privately, character could and should be damned. Have you ever read *Mansfield Park*?

A long time ago, I said. In school.

We have buried Fanny Price and Edmund Bertram. The modern world, he said, is Henry and Mary Crawford. I want to be a devil, Rufus said. We all do. I want everything, but to be a public man means one must do everything in private.

I did not talk to Rufus about Kathleen. Marriage for Rufus was a domestic arrangement. He divorced the emotional life from his political one, and so in his presence I did the same. The private I disclosed to Gerald, it was the public I wished to discuss with Rufus Weeks. I wanted to organize men, to have free medicine. With Gerald I would say that Kathleen's character was thoroughly consistent from the public through to the private. It was her consistency that drew me to her. She had no different disposition once the door was closed. I never noticed her change, except for an occasional surprise. I hardly ever caught her in a private moment that embarrassed her.

I want to discuss labour issues, Rufus. I'm leaving for Newfoundland.

Newfoundland? He lifted the peel of his orange, as if the pith contained an answer. I know a man in Newfoundland.

I know the prime minister, I said.

No, no, Rufus said. William Coaker's your man. You must befriend him. He is a man for the people, and he can help you.

Rufus Weeks would write me a letter of introduction.

5

I went ahead of Kathleen and the children. It was February, but a rare warm day. They walked me down to the train station. Kathleen threw on a coat over her nightdress. She was in her slippers. I liked how there was something in her dress that was still indoors. It made her more intimate while outside, as if she carried no veneer. I stared at her naked profile, and she leaned her eyes my way. Her eyes said, Dont let anything happen. Her eyes were alluding to my last trip to Newfoundland. When I'd met up with Jenny Starling, by accident, in Boston. Kathleen was refusing to smile or to tell me how much she loved me. But I knew I was loved. The meanness in me she forgave. Every five days or so I was floored by how generous she was to my small-mindedness. She made me better, I was a person whose fingernails were flecked with the glitter of her even temper. I kissed her and I kissed my children. I shook hands with my son, Rocky. He is such a polite boy. He was polite because of Kathleen. I sat on that train and thought how open my life was. I was mustering up the forces of goodwill, angling my choices towards the life I thought was an ideal. I believed in the existence of standards and in marshalling the drive to attain them.

The train brought me to Halifax, and from there I took the Red Cross Line to St John's. The ferry was rimed with ice, the hawsers stiff with frost. It was brutally cold. I had asked for steerage, but they gave me a private room. We wouldnt put you in there, sir. Steerage is just for shipwrecked Newfoundlanders and theyre filthy, just like animals. The steward was not aware he was being judgmental, only pointing out the obvious. And you'll eat in the officers' mess, he said. The kitchen was well designed, with roll bars to catch the pots and a metal basin to hold the soap.

I wrote Kathleen a letter and I caught myself. I caught up with my true emotions — they rode over me just as the wake of a ferry comes abreast when the ferry slows down. I knew that I loved her. I had an urgent need to be with her.

William Coaker was not in St John's, and neither was my friend Bob Bartlett, but I did meet the prime minister. I dropped in, unannounced, at his office on Military Road. An American visitor could do that. Rockwell Kent, he said. Well, well.

I had met Morris five years before. On my first trip to Newfoundland. I'm going to try it in Brigus this time.

Well good luck to you, he said. And if there is anything I can be handy to, just shout. He offered me lunch. And then invited me to a hockey game. Halifax against St John's. Any plans, he said, for an artists' colony?

Not this time, I said. Only my family. I am a family man.

Why not stay here, he said. A bit more culture in St John's. We're even learning the tango.

He was genuinely pleased to see me, though I could tell he was itching to ask what had happened with Burin. He had the class to refrain from inquiring.

I spent the afternoon walking around the city. St John's was dirty with soot, the houses small and ill built. It had not changed since the first time I'd been there. That ill-fated journey to Burin. I was the only one, it seemed, who wanted to be in St John's. I stayed the night at the Prescott Hotel and then boarded the train to Brigus. I'd decided to move right into Bob Bartlett's backyard of Brigus. He had a man there, a Robert Dobie, who was to show me a house. Brigus was a merchant town that had been the headquarters for the annual seal hunt. A rich town on the decline. I wanted to see the hunt. Plan: Fix up the Dobie house, take in the hunt, and then call up my family. I will make love to my wife and paint hard and build a garden.

This here land is my outpost, and from here I'll make my name. We'll visit New York as a treat, and blend into Newfoundland life. I'd be a people's painter. Yes, I wanted to raise a brood of Newfoundlanders and honour my wife.

I say this, but I am incorrigible. It's true I did not think of Jenny Starling, but on the trip up I'd stayed in a Halifax hotel and flirted with the manager's daughter. I coaxed her down the hall to my room and sketched her sitting by my window. I left the door open, but I used my position as an artist to hold her shoulders, to move her hands in her lap, to tuck her hair around an ear. I held her earlobe and I bent down and kissed her. I felt her waist under her arm. I traded this drawing of the daughter for room and board. When the manager saw it he loved it. He reached into his pocket. You have to take this. Real money. I did the same thing in St John's — but this time a young widow. I did not try to kiss her, but I enjoyed moving the weight of her chest into the light. The woman took the painting without even a thank you. I mention this because at first I judged it a sign of the Newfoundlander's lack of gratitude. It was only later when I realized that the Nova Scotian does not like to be beholden to favours. He wants to pay for things and be paid. A Newfoundlander expects neither. He gives a hand and he gets a hand, and hardly a nod of the head to either.

Yes, St John's looked defeated, with squat wooden houses rammed together in the snow. Parts of it still burnt down from a tremendous fire years before. Charred wood covered in ice. I felt embarrassed for it. It was a city that would always be burning down. It had rivalled New York a century ago, but the systems of economy and climate had caused it to grow like a plant in the dark. Strength here lay in the rural.

6

Before I left New York I got a call from Gerald Thayer. He was drunk and it was late. His wife, Alma, had left him. He said, I need you to help me.

How.

Well, (a) you have to say you love me. So that's (a).

Me: What's (b)?

Could you please answer (a).

Gerald I love you. I'm crazy about you. Youre a swell guy. Youre my best friend and I'd do —

Okay, that's good. I thank you for that, Kent. Now. I'm gonna fill you in. Somewhere there is a glasses case. And until then the whole house is slithering. Pact: I'm there for you, Kent. And until . . .

Me: Until what.

The truth of the fact is, Kent. Is (c). Okay, if Alma wants to fuck some bizarre someone, that's for her to, that's. Kent, what do you want from me.

Me: I dont want anything, Gerald.

Gerald: I dont know what you want from me, I have no idea. But on an artistic level. I completely believe in you, and I'm there for you, and you and I are on a narrow path, a complicated path only few can negotiate, and youre coming to an opening and I'm there for you. Youre my friend and I deeply need you, and New York is a city of concrete monstrosities. I deeply need. There are so few things I need, but youre one of them.

There is a pause. He wanted to say that he needed me in New York, but he knew he'd spent a long time telling me to go.

Gerald: Should I throw up? I came into the kitchen sober. I was looking for my glasses and I ended up drinking a whole bottle of whisky. Kent I am wildly drunk. And I have to get up with a three-year-old. I gotta describe to you. I'm leaning over the sink in the kitchen. My wife's off with some mechanical engineer. It's not her fault. I told her I was in love with someone else. And she thinks now that maybe all men are assholes.

What does vulnerability mean to you, Gerald.

It's a good thing. You can change only when youre vulnerable. You can't become vulnerable, you have to be ready for vulnerability to descend upon you.

You think that about everything. Whenever I say what do you think about x or y, you say you cannot become x or y. You have to be ready for x or y to be bestowed.

Maybe. Life is so insubstantial. In a way I thought children. I need your advice, Kent.

He gripped the phone receiver so hard that I could hear the handle in his palm.

There's one inch of whisky in the bottle. What I'm doing now is sitting on the kitchen counter. I'm after pulling the cork out of the bottle. It's a — did you hear that? A full glass.

7

His wife, Alma. She is five years older than Gerald. Alma Wollerman was a model for Gerald's father, Abbott Thayer. That's how Gerald met her. She was naked, perched on a stool with angel's wings sprouting from her back, and Gerald stepped into his father's studio and was transfixed. Had his father slept with her? It was something Gerald had never asked. Before he met Alma, Gerald was with a woman who was eighteen. Gerald felt eighteen was too young. But since then he's seen her. She is twenty-four now and he can get along with her. I've heard, he said, that she's great at sex and she isnt boring.

Are those the things, I said. The three things to a great marriage.

What.

To get along, have great sex, and not be bored.

Gerald: Yes those are the things. Youth is a good one too.

So youth is a piggish fourth.

Who's counting. The thing is, Gerald said, I've loved younger women. And younger women, forgive me, are not as smart as older women. But Alma hung out with older, smarter men.

Like your father.

She's older than me, and smarter than me because of her tastes.

Alma Wollerman liked how hairless the back of Gerald's neck was. It was the first thing she noticed about him: she was sitting beside him in a theatre — she was with his father — and

Gerald leaned forward. There was that clean bit of neck to the shoulders, exposed.

Gerald: Thing is, you have an idea about marriage. That having children will make you pull up your socks. You believe in the system of marriage.

Me: Rather than.

Gerald: The not framing of the experience. Letting it receive meaning after it's lived. Right now you imagine living chunks of your life. Youre seeing them exist out there in front of you. There is an incipient promise.

Me: This year, this one coming up in Newfoundland, I will have no commitments. I will have no promises to keep. No one to meet. It will be the first time in my life that no one expects me. There will be no expecting except the duties of marriage and children. I want, I said, to be a good husband. I want to focus on hard work and my family. I want to be faithful.

Gerald: If you disappear up there no one will notice. And if it doesnt work out, if you come back to New York, this will be your last time in a disappeared state, so enjoy it.

This has turned out to be true.

8

I boarded the train to Brigus and was again bumped up to first class. So far I had been good. I had been flirtatious, but nothing outrageous. The carriage was not half full. I had four seats to myself. I rode through the snow out of the life I was living. There is the life you lead, which contrasts with the desire for a higher conception. On that train to Brigus I thought I was heading towards a supreme excellence. I admire this goal. In my art too. That seems to have been my downfall.

I was wondering all this on the slow train to Brigus. The corners of the houses packed with snow for extra insulation. I was excited but wondering. I was mediocre, true, but I was romantic as well. I was vainglorious, holier than thou, a king of pigs. I was all of that. But all of that was about to face a challenge. I sat in first class, happy in my aloneness until three boys ran in, wrestling one another and fighting for the window seat.

We just sold our rabbits in St John's, one said. And then, Who are you?

I am Rockwell Kent.

They were delighted to hear I was on my way to Brigus.

We're from Brigus, they said. Youre that American painter.

They were Tony Loveys, Stan Pomeroy, and Tom Dobie.

I was told, Tom Dobie said, to keep an eye on you.

Who told you that.

Rupert Bartlett.

Oh yes, I said. And your name is Dobie. A Robert Dobie was to show me a house in Brigus.

That'd be my father, Tom said.

He's gone now, Stan Pomeroy said. He's dead.

Tony Loveys: Look.

He pointed out the window to some men in an open tilt, shoeing ponies.

I'm sorry about your father.

Tom Dobie chewed on his finger. He had fair hair and blue eyes.

There were men hauling wood with fresh sleds made from the same wood. Their arms and backs bent to work.

Was it recent.

It was last year.

Stan Pomeroy: It was down the Labrador.

I didnt know what else to say. They were turned to the window. What are they preparing.

Theyre in collar, Tom Dobie said.

In collar?

The men are sealers, Stan Pomeroy explained. Theyre cutting firewood and logs for spars and punts.

The air was clear and the snow ten feet deep. Often there was nothing to see, the snow from the railroad's right-of-way ploughed so high on either side. So then you were reduced to looking at the window itself. There was a bright green mould on a leather flange where the thick glass met the wood. A bead of condensation on which the mould drank. I can love even that. Back then objects were made from living things. Nothing was inert.

The coachman came by. Are these boys causing a havoc?

Not at all.

To them: Youre not supposed to be up here.

Neither am I, I said. And ordered tea for the four of us.

I was five days away from my family now. It's true that I had mixed feelings about my escape, but for the moment I was delighted. No event is simple, however, and I missed my family too. I have the skills to make friends anywhere, but I do get exhausted by the constant newness of solitary exploration. I was northeast of everything. Everything is all youve walked past and witnessed and smelled and touched. I was proud of the strong pigskin suitcase that rode in the baggage compartment. I felt good in a wool coat. It was a good coat — I had found my chest size.

The tea arrived in two pots to share with the boys. It came on a wicker tray with the coat of arms of the country of Newfoundland — a caribou. The tea service was pewter and the milk rich and white.

Some good to be drinking tea on a train.

It's a treat all right.

Me: Apparently youre not used to treats.

I had created delight. This milk has come straight from a cow, Tom Dobie said, and then chilled with a block of ice sawed from a lake. It's as though products in the icebox, I said, grew cold from the fear of the ice block crushing them. The boys laughed at the novelty of that thought.

9

Tom Dobie: It's beginning to snow a perfect smother.

The train turned and sank and lifted and stopped to have drifts shovelled away.

Is this the stop?

You could see nothing but snow.

Let's have a look, Stan Pomeroy said. We got out: there was a white horse on the tracks. It was walking in front of the train, pure white. It was as if the horse was the source of the snow, the snow leader. A man ran after it, and the horse bolted ahead.

Then the train moved, but it had to brake, for the horse had slowed down.

What'll we do about this horse.

Let's dart in the woods, Tom said. We'll go up ahead.

He and Stan put on snowshoes and walked into the trees. They were gone a minute. Then they appeared in the distance, trudging up the grade out of the woods, ahead of the horse. They walked back down towards it. The horse hesitated. The train pushed the horse along, and Tom and Stan Pomeroy snagged the horse by the neck and led him off the tracks and down into the trees. The train passed and then the boys ran up and got back aboard. The horse watched.

Good work, I said.

It snowed harder then and you could feel the train ploughing through drifts. I ordered tea biscuits, and as I buttered one I saw the flash of my face in the polished steel of the butter knife. I was thirty-one, the age I had wanted to be all my life. It is an age when important work gets done. But now I was anxious that I wasnt doing the correct work and being praised. I was a smart, educated city boy used to riches who, through bad luck, had become poor but refused to appear impoverished. I supported labour unions. I read Darwin. I was a socialist. I did not, outwardly, believe in God. I believed that if He existed, He'd forgive me.

I passed around the tea biscuits. With jam on.

It's funny but true that we always feel old, except in retrospect. I was very young, I realize, but I felt older than I wanted to be. My hair was thinning, but I kept it short and I prayed that it would thin in a graceful manner. I loved my wooden paintbox, which I had under my seat. I had pride and I was chuffed. This would be my time. I kept pressing my heel to the box and feeling proud of it.

An hour later and the train shuddered to a halt.

We all got out to have a look at the snow. There were about thirty people on board, all men. A vast hurl of snow. The stokers passed out shovels. Tom Dobie, as we dug out the choked wheels, pointed at the bright moving blur of a ginger fox. The stoker said okay and we got aboard again. The engine ran furiously, trying to grind through the snow. The drifts became worse. The driver jammed her into a field of powder.

We got out again to look at the front of the train.

Tom Dobie: That's a lost cause there.

It was buried. The whole side of the hill just a white slope, no sign of a track. Snow whipping past us horizontal. There was no edge to the snow where your eye could rest.

Tom: We'll make Brigus before the train if we start walking now.

He pointed to the trees, but I didnt see Brigus, just the tops of trees. The boys were to snowshoe there, at least get into the woods.

Isnt it a little treacherous out there.

Tom: If you start in snow you'll have fair weather for the rest of the trip.

May I join you?

Yes boy you can come along.

The driver had an extra pair of bear paws, he called them. Oval snowshoes with no tail. Made by someone unhandy to make a wooden bow, Tom Dobie said. I took a satchel with chocolate and an extra pair of socks and a roll of canvas I thought might be useful. I'll pick up my suitcases in Brigus. The driver laughed: I'll race you. The boys each had a pack with a tumpline over the forehead. The driver wished us luck.

We left the train in the storm and I followed the backs of the three boys. They were entering a whiteness, a flat and bright canvas. We crossed a fluorescent slope and ducked into the white trees. When we were among the trees the wind died down. I tugged an evergreen by a branch, just to see its coat of snow slip off. Bright green needles underneath. We shoed through some small valleys of plump snow. There were no shadows.

Lift your racquets like this, Tom Dobie said. Pretend like youre a partridge. He called the snowshoes racquets. I was sweating from the exertion.

They were cousins, Stan Pomeroy and Tony Loveys. Tom Dobie went shares with them on a cod trap.

So, I said, about your father. Bob Bartlett gave me his name.

You were talking to Bob Bartlett.

He was in New York.

We havent seen him now in two years.

He's on his way. But your father.

Yes, that was my father and Bob Bartlett probably dont know he destroyed himself last winter. But that house, I know that house, she's run into cruel hard times, hey boys. The Georgian one by the Pinch, he said to Tony and Stan.

They said, No sir she's all broke up.

Tom Dobie was quiet and smouldering. He was dressed the way the men dressed, with a muffler and a peaked cap. But he was wearing old seaboots that fit a man and were meant for summer. They were his father's. Such was the fate of the son. There was the doomed whiff.

Arent your feet cold.

My feet are all right.

I said that my own father was dead. That he'd died when I was seven.

It was just last winter, Tom Dobie said. We had a rough time of it down the Labrador. We couldnt make a go of it. It's just me and mother now.

We had a boil-up in a droke — a sheltered bunch of trees. We walked for another hour. At the edge of a frozen bog they pointed to a grey-and-white caribou stag. He sniffed the air and the weight swivelled in his chest. Gone in a second. We walked over to his tracks.

Tom Dobie: How about here, boys.

Yes, good as any.

Then I realized they planned to camp overnight.

Perhaps, I said, we should have stayed with the train.

No sir we'll get to Brigus faster than you ever went directly.

I was not happy about this. But there's exuberance for you. I had left the train and now it was getting dark in a woods I did not know with these three strangers.

They made a bivouac, chopping small trees for a lean-to, limbing the boughs and making a floor of them. The boys had spent the winter doing this, catching rabbits in central Newfoundland. They had made a trapline and boxed the rabbits and shipped them into St John's aboard the train. They had each cleared a hundred dollars from T. J. Edens and now they were heading home to go sealing.

I put the canvas over us — a canvas I would later paint on — and we slept together. I slept well. I woke up with Tom Dobie's arm over my shoulder. His young, relaxed face. It was sweet. I could hear dogs.

In the morning they fried bacon. Stan Pomeroy had caught a rabbit in one of eight slips he'd set overnight. The slips were not wire but made from sail twine. The rabbit was in one they called a hoist, a snare at the end of a sprung branch. He's pretty to see, Tom said, a rabbit hung in its hoister.

Stan Pomeroy chopped through the back legs with an axe and pressed the front paws off with a knife. He tugged the white fur off like unrolling a sock and then jointed the purple body and fried it in the bacon fat. They shared it out.

No thanks, I said.

They looked at me.

I dont eat meat, I said.

You dont eat meat. Boys he dont eat meat.

Give me some of that bread. I'll be fine on bread.

Tom: Is it like a religious thing?

It's a belief. That we're better off when we dont eat animals.

You mean youre going to live out here and not eat anything.

There's grain and vegetables and beans and rice. There's a lot you can eat. I'll eat fish. I'm not opposed to fish, and I confess I like eggs. I'll even eat a chicken.

Too bad we never snared you a grouse. All year round. Boy youre gonna starve on that.

They ate into the rabbit and bacon with some bread and tea. I shared out my chocolate, which they all admired, and I noticed

they did not eat but saved. We drank the tea stark naked —
without milk or sugar. Tom Dobie poured the bacon fat into
his mug and gulped it down. The enamel mug was caked with
the fat. It was becoming a smaller and smaller volume for anything to be poured into.

What'll you do when it fills up.

I'll just ream her out, he said, and start over again.

It was a raw clear day, the snow packed down, the day after
a storm.

I opened my eyes to this. Another day of snowshoeing. I
prepared to march. I am a man of acts, but I tell you, each act
begins like exercising a stiff muscle.

Lift your legs high, sir, Tom Dobie said again. They were
having a good laugh at my struggle.

We made it into Brigus that afternoon and Stan and Tony
kept marching — they were on their way to the north end of
the harbour. The train, said Tom Dobie, will be along shortly.
We had been hearing it through the morning, straining in the
distance.

We sat there at the station with our snowshoes. I took out
my pencil and sketchbook.

I accept inertia and I can live within it for a long time.
Travelling is pleasant because you can assuage any guilt at inac-
tivity with the excuse that you are moving. As though you had
anything to do with the forward progress of a train. Well, this is
the whole pleasure of capitalism, to pay for the efforts of others.
To jockey yourself into position to make your skill prized and
worth the attention of others.

The train hauled itself out of the hills. Pried through the mat of spruce up by Thunderbolt Hill and curled and sunk away. A few townspeople were walking up to the station. I knew their names, for Tom Dobie was there to tell me. Jim Hearn a pharmacist. Bud Chafe he's got a shop.

The train sounded and then it was seen and heard sandwiched together. The horror of its brakes, the joints freezing up, the panic and patience of its Clydesdale stance and exhaust. The freezing breeze caught up with the train like a cloud shadow. The canvas mail was thrown off and crates marked CHAFE rapidly traded for the crates Chafe sent back. I found my bags. Men climbed down the perforated steps clogged with dirty snow, snow jammed into the works and yet the works still working.

I thought, What the hell. What the hell am I doing. Where the hell is this and what is a place like this all about. Several times a day I checked myself. What are you doing, my son. What's it all about. If I were to offer anyone advice, it would be to ask yourself that question. Or never ask. If you dont want to inspect the creak in your soul that's okay. Go ahead and die unaware. I'm not being facetious.

My yellow suitcase in the flat snow. I took out a small map that Bob Bartlett had given me. As I said, it was because of Bartlett that I was here. Because I happened to meet this ship captain at a lecture five years before and mention my interest in Newfoundland, because of that spur I was in his hometown. Life's occurrences arrive both through determination and through chance. I looked at the map. Then up. Tom Dobie was at the suitcase.

Sir, he said.

I was concentrating on becoming the man I wished to present. I wanted to look focused and not self-conscious. I had held an abstract of the land in my mind and was stepping, it seemed, for the first time into its geography.

Sir I knows where you wants to be going.

Call me Kent.

Okay, Kent. You be wanting the Bartletts I reckon.

I want to go to that Georgian house that your father was going to show me. It's marked here on this map.

Kent, she's all stove in.

I'd like to see it. And to myself: He underestimates my endurance.

We followed the postman who had come on his old pony to collect the four-oclock mail. Swift, they called the pony. With the toe of each seaboot Tom Dobie smudged the wheel tracings in the snow. All the houses had ladders on their roofs.

We walked to the Pinch. We came upon the Georgian house that Bob Bartlett said I could have. The house he hadnt seen in two years.

The roof had broken from the snow. The windows and the spine of it had all gone. She had exhausted herself.

Well that is very welcoming.

You'd have to be as foolish as Bud Chafe's dog to live in that house.

So I guess.

I was disheartened.

Like I was saying, Rupert Bartlett he's just over there.

He pointed to a very bright, merry house billowing with woodsmoke. So much for endurance.

10

Rupert Bartlett: So youre the painter.

I am the man.

It was not the right thing to say to me, but I understood this is what is thought of me. It wasnt that I was embarrassed by the honour, but I preferred sometimes to be a human being on a quest for the good life, and not a painter.

Get in, he said, and hapse the door.

I said so long to Tom Dobie and shook hands with Rupert. His grip and arms were strong. He was a man who kept his sleeves rolled, even in winter.

Rupert said, When you meet someone youve heard so much good things about, you dont want to meet them.

Or like them, I said.

Yes, there's that too.

He pushed my suitcase up against the foot of a grandfather clock. It was a new clock, with a pair of stuffed grouse, half white, nesting on top. Rupert had this ginger moustache. He was in his twenties, a svelte man used to doing lots of work with his forearms. He was like me.

No, leave them on.

There was a split chimney that arced over the hallway and pushed fireplaces onto either side of the house so you could walk under its heart. Mother did that, he said. One year when father was down the Labrador, she was tired of walking around the hearth, so she blew this hole right through the middle of it.

I followed him into the dining room. It was hot. There was a red sofa and a big family album. There were evening lamps and books, a piano. There was a good coal fire on.

I took off my coat.

No one was there, just an open book of essays by Emerson. A set of brass binoculars in a leather cover flung on the chair cushion. What Rupert had seen us with and then flung. Rupert was a flinger of things. Effeminate but physical. A marathon runner.

A maid came with a tray of tea.

This is Emily.

Pleasure to meet you, Mr Kent.

She was lovely, a pale young face and green eyes. I was in a place where they introduced the servants.

You wouldnt have, I said, anything to eat?

Youre hungry my goodness yes.

A piece of cheese would be fine. I'm a vegetarian.

Oh really. Well then you must be hungry. What is it to be a vegetarian?

As long as it's not a mammal.

Some of that turre, Emily.

Rupert sent her off to make me up a plate.

The name Emily made me ask him about the Emerson.

I like, Rupert said, to read work by men my own age.

And this was a young Emerson.

I prefer Thoreau.

Yes, the lover of life.

Rather than your professional dreamer.

And he quoted Thoreau: I went to the woods because I wished to live deliberately.

That's me, I said.

Welcome to the woods.

Rupert pushed two fingers into his red moustache. He explained that his brother, Bob, was returning from a failed venture. A ship, the *Karluk*, had sunk under him, men were stranded on a Russian island in the Arctic. But his last telegram said he would be home in a month.

Rupert was here for the winter. He was dormant. His father was upstairs in bed. The fact of this made him realize he had a story. He livened.

Father was washed overboard, Rupert said. He was going through the water like a duck. They hauled him up like a wet seal, put him in bed. Said his back was awful sore. He'd lost his false teeth. Mother turned him over and found his teeth dug in his back.

We went up to see him. His wife, Mary, was there reading to him. The Bartlett parents both snug in bed. It felt odd to be so intimate, as if they were my children and I'd come up to tuck them in. William Bartlett was in fine shape, big wrists. He laughed about the teeth.

Yes if the lads hadnt pulled me out I'd still be in cold storage.

William Bartlett was arranging a ship for the seal hunt. Forty years he'd captained a ship — he would captain one for fifteen more. Yes, he said, he could remember Brigus when you were either a Bartlett, a Pomeroy, or a sheep.

Rupert was staying out of the seal hunt. He was gearing up for the Labrador fishery later in the year. He was the younger son and yet he seemed older than his father. Less exuberant. I could tell he was in a funk. He was restless and almost sooky about it, to use a Newfoundland expression. They had been expecting me for weeks.

I was more than welcome, the father said. To bide as long. I could have the run of the. His son Bob's room or the.

He did not know I was here to stay in Brigus for the rest of my life. I told him about my family. How I'd come ahead to secure a house.

Well there are other houses. We'll find you one. My daughters have one across the.

He pushed his arm to the side.

Rupert and I went back downstairs to the red sofa. There were biscuits and cheese, cooked potatoes and carrots, and a sweet pickle. There was a dark meat.

That's bottled turre, Rupert said. A seabird.

It's fine, I said. It tasted very gamey. I picked up the binoculars and applied them to the Head, as they called it. Just a quiet arm of land.

How come no one's ever built out there.

There *is* a house, Rupert said.

There's nothing out there.

She's well hidden. In this light you'd never see it. Halfway to the lighthouse. Out by the naked man.

Pardon?

There's a pile of stones near the headland. We call it the naked man.

There are no lights on.

No one lives out there. Is it just you and your wife?

We have three children.

It's a little tight, Rupert said. And a little out of the way.

I like out of the way.

It's a snug little house for all that, he said. I'll look into it. He wiped his hands on his trousers. He was nervous. Youve arrived, he said, during the hungry month. You'll be wanting friends around you. That's how we get by.

Rupert had liked how I smiled at that youngster. The Dobies are good people, he said, and it was tragic what happened to the father. It should not have happened, that. What a mistake. I am a man, he said, who believes the world belongs to children. Though I dont have any children.

Rupert was a stiff man with that fastidious moustache. It could make you nervous. The Bartlett lip. Representing everything formal and unfeeling in the world. But the Bartletts were not cool men. They had been handed a stiff, severe lip and did their best to work around it. Rupert's shoulders were tight and this was a Bartlett trait too, something Methodist, and I knew the word *methodical* applied and that was Rupert to a tee. Struggling to rid himself of Methodism. True. He did not press his pants. He had two years to live and we were both oblivious to it.

11

I stayed the night in Bob Bartlett's bed. The sheets were fresh and rough. There was a big hardcover book on the night table:

Warren's Household Physician. On the shelf Hudson's Bay scotch whisky, seven volumes of the classics, skate blades, an enamel cup, leather skates. There were crates on the floor of baking powder and Sunshine Biscuits (USA). Maxwell House tea, Prince Albert tobacco. They used this room for storage.

I missed my wife beside me. Kathleen became most herself in sleep. I loved it when, nearly morning, she'd push me. Then she'd tug at my head. She was deeply asleep, but aware too. She wanted me. She'd haul my neck to her. Nuzzle her face in my shoulder, tug on my cock. That demand of me, almost unconscious. The reason she could do it, to be selfish.

There was a toilet across the hall, and I got up in the dark to use it. The toilet was a new thing for the Bartlett house. The first to have it in Brigus. But someone was in it. Then out came a woman carrying a kerosene lamp, her dark hair down, in a nightdress. It was Emily. I stepped back. The lamp lit up her wrist. Light poured down the inside of her arm.

Pardon me, she said.

So she slept here.

In the morning the sisters, Eleanor and Emma Bartlett, came over. Emily brought in porridge, eggs, toast and coffee, and a jar of English marmalade, and I told my story. I knew the gesture I gave was Gerald Thayer's: it was a way of pushing the hand out as though dealing cards. I didnt know what I was telling the Bartletts, but I laughed at the fact that I was even speaking in a Thayer sort of manner about New York. My strength was devoted to noticing my push into the world, rather than the content of what I was saying as I pushed. I saw that Rupert was impressed by the New York material, in a way that I did not deserve. I was coated with the success of the city, as though I had built every brick of it. I was my own man, but these gestures appropriated from others kept rising up. I doubted at that moment whether Rockwell Kent even existed. And what made me laugh was knowing that other people were left thinking me such a strong character, when no character existed at all.

It made me miss Gerald. It made me think of that last night with him, when he said, If there is one thing I wish, it's that Alma were younger.

He was referring obliquely to Kathleen, who was eight years younger than me. If he had a Kathleen. Often Kathleen looked at me, and while she admired my ambition, I could see she thought of a fixed plan. Fixed plans stifle me. She thought of growing old with me. She saw the plan of her life decided, and she did not have enough interest in opportunity. She was not attentive to the avenues of venture we happened to be walking past.

I said to Gerald Thayer, Perhaps Kathleen's not enough.

Gerald: Enough is asking too much. Then he said, Is she lazy?

No.

Then there's something. There will be something in her that's praiseworthy. She will have a talent. If there's a — no, find the talent and you will love her.

I thought it was good sex, getting along, be unboring.

No, it's talent. And avoiding laziness. No one is enough. That's why you have friends.

12

Tom Dobie said that house on the Head belonged to the Pomeroys. They had closed it up for the winter. We walked into Irishtown, past the Stand where the two churches stood, around Jackson's Quay and Grave Hill and down through Pomeroy's fields, where Stan Pomeroy and Tony Loveys were cutting firewood on a sawhorse. They did not wave. Ice at low tide passed through the footing of the bridge. And was slit up by it. It was slit in two. Seagulls sat on the rocks and on the ice. Low tide, Tom said. The low water revealed twelve feet of dark wet rock and then the bright snowline, like a receding gum. Tom Dobie named every place we came to because I asked. Up Rattley Road, which narrowed to a cart path, the snow had collected in the corners of the path. Youre going to need your racquets if youre to push through this, he said.

We left Brigus outright and the path widened to an arm of soft white land between the rough rocks. Printed in values of grey, white, and black, as though the land were an engraving done in zinc. There was no colour, except for the blue of the sky. Pointy tips of fir sticking off the horizon of hills. It's a landscape on a human scale. We crested this and now the cottage that I'd spied with Rupert's binoculars, snug and rough, in behind a screen of young juniper, their limbs coated in fresh snow. The house was quite to itself, the windows boarded up. There was not one footprint near it. There was snow here beneath the trees, and it had moulded itself and hardened from the prevailing wind.

We stood at the gate. It stank of creosote. I was overjoyed. That house have seen a better day, sir.

It will see even better, Tom.

The little house stood on a sheltered terrace that had been dug from the steep hillside on the north side of the bay. It was just one and a half storeys built into the side of the hill. What you saw of the roof through snow looked sound and the foundation solid, and on these straight qualities I trusted. I was right to trust.

That house, Tom said, havent been lived in for a generation. But whoever built her was thinking about grandchildren.

We walked to it.

Dont know who'd want to live in her, though. Youre closer to Cupids than to Brigus.

He said the glass had been taken out of the windows and stored under the stairs so it wouldnt bust.

There was four feet of level ground in front of the door before the hill began again its tremendous descent to the bay. The house seemed like a predicament, a toehold.

What a spot.

There was a stunted tuckamore, the nest of a gannet.

If meagre, I said.

I paced off the house and it was thirty-seven feet long.

Tom on the side called out, Fourteen feet wide.

Your feet or my feet?

Just regular twelve-inchers, sir. I made an allowance.

Fourteen feet, then.

Pointing to a hollow, You can do your nuisance over there until we fix you up an outhouse.

There were two chimneys. A wealth of chimneys. I turned back to town.

Dont you want to have a look inside, sir?

I'm used to the insides of things, Tom. And I'll tell you, the outside of a thing will inform you a lot of its innards. Now let's go meet the rest of the world.

13

I hired on Tom Dobie. What William Blake wrote: He whose face gives no light will never become a star. I subscribe to this, though it's not the entire story. If you are full of light then you must be aware that smaller lights are intimidated. Light attracts but also makes people close their eyes. And so it's never enough to be large and generous. A star must permit smaller lights to shine. This is something I did not know until I was in my forties. I was a brash young light who read Blake.

We spent the days shovelling the house out, removing some hay the Pomeroys had stacked in there. The ceilings were an even six feet. Lucky I'm a short man. We pried off the boards and caulked in the windows. I got one fireplace working halfheartedly. We stripped the walls and glued on muslin and walked to Chafe's to pick out some pretty paper. Tom Dobie nodded to Chafe.

How's your mother, Bud said.

Thanks Mr Chafe. She's fine.

You'll be needing salt pork.

We're all right.

Havent come in for anything in a while.

How's the credit.

Youre all right, Tom.

I chose colours I knew Kathleen would like.

Jas Kelly came in and asked for some flour. A butt of pork. Some molasses. Chafe took up a ledger and marked it down. Jas pencilled in an *X* and took his supplies.

As we walked back I asked Tom about it. So you dont pay for it.

Chafe tots her up.

And when do you pay for it.

He lets us have it on credit until the fall. Then takes off what our fish brung in.

You sell your fish to Bud Chafe.

He has a culler. What come in and tells him the price.

So you dont know the price.

Chafe is good. He gives us what is fair.

So he pays you and you pay him?

There's no money as such.

Does Jas Kelly know what that flour cost him?

It's all in the ledger. Chafe got it in the book.

Does it matter if he buys it today or next month?

I guess the price changes. Yes, she do change. Chafe writes her down, the provision and the date.

So youre saying Jas Kelly doesnt know what he spent today.

Fishermen usually just get the provisions they need. It's there in the book. Chafe keeps her all written up.

It sounds odd. It sounds feudal. So you dont know what you owe Chafe.

He says our credit is good.

But youre reluctant to get some provisions.

We didnt have a good year last year, okay? Chafe's been good to keep us supplied. Mother doesnt want us to be too beholden.

I slept at the Bartletts'. I asked Rupert about how Chafe deals with goods. The truck system, Rupert said. Fishermen in debt to merchants. There are worse than Chafe.

But you deal with fish.

The Labrador fishery, yes. And we set a price after St John's. We keep it competitive. Now a young man like Tom Dobie, he's to his gills in with Bud Chafe. Been with him now so long, through his father. Can't get out from under him.

So you could call him an indentured servant.

The system, Kent. It works.

To whose benefit.

Well, men like Dobie and Jas Kelly get grub and supplies when they have no money. They'd starve if not for Bud Chafe.

But theyre at the mercy of Chafe in the fall. Chafe can set his own price for fish.

There's no other way to do it, Kent. Unless youre angling to have a fellow like William Coaker move in. And that's bad news. A union. All that'll do is create another level of bureaucrats. No it's best this way.

After a week I moved into the house. I borrowed a green tent from Rupert. I set the tent up in the main bedroom above the kitchen. I did a romantic thing. I lit three stout candles and took out my father's flute. It's a silver flute that my mother gave me. I dont really like the flute. It's a bit ethereal and tight-assed. But

I wanted to learn how to play it. I knew playing the flute was the opposite to how the main waters of my character flowed. In the tent with the candles and the window's three little panes of glass over the frozen harbour, it sounded good.

I woke up in the morning. I woke up to light filtering through the fabric of the tent. But I had forgotten about the tent. I was looking at the effect of the canvas. My father took me once on a train for a weekend in the Adirondacks, and a snow had fallen. We were staying in a cabin. Snow had caked against the cabin windows. I remember waking up to the pattern of light breaking through the snow on the window.

I braced myself to the cold. The stove was out and I could easily roll over for another hour. But I flipped off the blankets and pushed my feet into socks, untied the tent flap, and wrestled on a shirt and sweater. I walked down the stairs and pissed on the snow near the front door. I had a brown wool hat. I took to wearing the same clothes.

The floors were frozen. Frost on the coffee pot. A pair of gloves I'd left on a chair surprised me for a pair of hands. I love the cold. It was the reason I had come here. Discomfort had become an obsession. Or it may be that I hated discomfort so that I got a kind of exultation from the effort of overcoming it. Truth: I had wanted to live the rest of my life in Newfoundland. But it turned into sixteen months. It was enough to consider love and heartbreak and commitment and humour in the face of the crushing ache of being alone in the world.

There was snow in the firs, and the branches were heavy and solemn. There were valleys of trees, with arms of snow frozen up into the valleys. If you must have it all culminate. If you insist. It came down to a small chunk of time that broke me. It formed me. It pried apart my backbone and left me beached. It shucked me. I will tell you of a desire to live with a rural people, to love them and be loved.

The mornings were bright and clear. I had kindling and I shivered until the stove was hot. I had ordered seven tons of coal and a collier was on its way — Rupert told me that his brother, Bob, was captaining it. But I laughed at my cold bones and I kept opening the stove door to see the orange faces with their grey noses in the flames. I love being on my own.

Tom Dobie had learned a lot from his father. He had his father's tools and the fate of the father was a story I pieced together from Bartlett and the Pomeroys. It was a story of starvation and a rifle in Labrador. But I could not ask Tom about it. It would come, I thought.

My own tools — my father's tools — were on their way from New York. Kathleen was sending them. And so I made do with the Dobie tools. I ordered wood from St John's and then found out that the Pomeroys had a pit saw just over in Cupids.

Why didnt you tell me, Tom.

I thought, Tom said, you wanted wood from town.

I imagined a large enterprise, instead a shed with Stan Pomeroy and Tom Dobie inside. A hole in the ground and Tom in the hole wearing a veil of crepe, sawdust on his shoulders. I had plans to build on to the south end and also shore up the sills and footings. A studio and an extra bedroom for the children.

Each morning at eight Tom arrived carrying half a pie or a large piece of cake or some fresh bread wrapped in a cup towel.

This was from his mother. I made coffee, and if he had cake we broke into it for breakfast. The brook was my fresh water and the outhouse was at the north end, near the trail to the naked man and the lighthouse. If it was cold out Tom suggested we split some wood.

He'll cleave better if it's frosty and it'll warm us up.

The birch was fragile under the axe. The cracking echoed off the hills. I am the only one on this side and I wanted them to know I was at it.

We know youre at it when there's smoke coming out of your chimney.

From here you can see the cup of the cove, but they can see me too. The landscape changed depending on the snowfall.

The axe over Tom's head, hovering. Then whipping it down on the junk. Sometimes he'd lay the wood on its belly, to split in through the stomach.

It was hot work, and Tom stopped to take off his jersey. He pulled the jersey and shirt and undershirt all over his head and down to his wrists. And he stood there, a boy of sixteen, letting the sweat on his kidneys evaporate in the cold February air, his wrists chained by the bulk of the shirt and jersey.

14

As Tom and I rebuilt the house I had time to think of Jenny Starling. I like to ruminate on past lives when I work, to see how my life could have been different. I had known Jenny before Kathleen. I'd lived with her for six months. She had this angled forehead and she spoke quickly. I was going to marry her, but she was already married. Jenny was getting a divorce from her husband, Luis Starling. But did I ever truly think I'd marry her? I thought about this as I hammered home a ten-inch nail. I enjoyed looking at Jenny's eyebrows. You wonder how much talent and mystery a person needs in order for you to want to live the rest of your life with her. And Jenny had a nervous tension. She had no children with Luis. Luis, of course, hated my guts. He wanted her back. Everyone wanted her to return to Luis. Jenny's father, George Crocker, disowned her.

We lived in Monhegan. I taught at the artists' colony there. I built a house, a house a bit like this one. But I was not convinced by Jenny. There was something unruly about her, something in her I couldnt contain, and it worried me. So when I met Kathleen Whiting in New York, I decided to leave Jenny Starling.

15

Tom Dobie had this manner. Of holding the back of his head when he talked, and he spoke to the floor. When he came by in the morning, my greeting to him was one word: Coffee?

I wouldnt mind, he said, checking the soundness of the windows, a coffee.

He would, occasionally, cast out a brightness. He was bright. He was honest. He was shy. He was oblivious to how he projected himself in the world. And this is very attractive. Tom Dobie was strong but seemed to motor around in first gear: it was the potential for strength. But in moments of panic, when I needed force, he would exert himself. There were flashes of power, and then he was marked by power. Tom Dobie possessed it yet it rarely surfaced. And this was true of both the muscle and the temper of the young man.

Thought the boo-darbies got you.

Me: Pardon?

The fairies. Heard your flute last night. Came right over the water. Awful nice.

Occasionally, when the wind came up, I stayed at the Bartletts'. I had dinner with Rupert, his parents and sisters. Once, Rose Foley came over. And she sang afterwards. She was a big woman, full of life, and her breasts rose as she belted it out. Can I walk you home, Rose. Of course, Mr Kent. She was my age, a widow with two children.

They said Bob was on his way any day now, the collier iced in at Holyrood. Tom would meet me at the Bartlett gate, Emily Edwards waved to him, and we'd walk over and I'd put on the coffee. I loved the sounds of ritual. The coffee pot clunking onto the cast iron, the sizzle of water droplets evaporating on the hob. I loved that more than the coffee. It was early March now, calm and pleasant.

It's strange to be over here so much, Tom said.

And looking at the cottage, Boy, youre roughing it.

When we entered to put on the coffee he'd stamp his feet and say, every morning, She's all a chunk of ice!

There was enough sun and the work was hard, so you did not want it warm. But when you stopped it was freezing. I put in the stove. There was some dry wood, so dry it was hollow and hard. I had ordered coal and I thought about the coal so often that it became a steady image on the floor of my brain. I hung my socks on the stovepipe, and they burnt like toast. They went stiff like toast.

It was the domestic moments that made me think of Kathleen. I remembered the sound of her skin. When I brushed her bare arms.

Sometimes in the dark outside, on my way to the new outhouse. If I stepped on a branch. I said, aloud, Scary. I pronounced it in a childish voice, a lisp on the *S*. I pronounced it as I would if Kathleen were present. We did those things. Scary, the young language.

I often spoke to my absent wife and children. When I made a meal. One should not cook too long alone. In the kitchen I spoke to Kathleen. And I'd laugh at myself, talking to her when she was not there. This, a clear sign of love.

Is love a realization that you love? You recognize that you are in love, and then you decide to cultivate it. It is an impulse you can wrap the hand of your mind around. But without that initial surprise — like finding a wildflower in your garden — no amount of wanting to love, of committing to the act of love, will generate it.

Soon there was so much snow and frozen rain that I was afraid the roof might buckle. We put in two posts to reinforce the peak. In some of the smaller houses in the cove the new weight cracked windows.

Do not commit during the bloom of youth. Wait until that initial flush subsides, or you will commit to the wrong partner. It is true that men who are monogamous marry often.

16

When I married Kathleen I promised her that my relationship with Jenny was over. And it was. We were friends. I was faithful to Kathleen, even though I'd told her that I might not be. I might find other women attractive. Kathleen knew this.

She didnt want to live in Monhegan, because of Jenny, so I convinced her to move to Newfoundland. The plan: sell the house I'd built in Monhegan, and get established in Newfoundland. This was five years ago. When we had the one child. I thought, We'll go to Newfoundland and set up a little Monhegan.

I went on a scouting mission. The ferry to Newfoundland leaves from Boston. Jenny was living in Boston. I thought, What's the harm in looking her up. I called Jenny. She was having dinner with her sister. Did I want to join them. So all we did was eat dinner. Then I went back to my room at the Essex Hotel, and I was happy with myself. I'd withstood desire. I wrote Kathleen a postcard telling her of the meal with Jenny Starling and her sister. I wanted to be honest with her and prove my resistance. I'd promised myself honesty and a bolstering of restraint.

The next day the ferry did not move. I was frustrated and worried about the expense of another night at the Essex. Then I saw Jenny. She had come down to wish me off.

The ferry won't depart, I said, until tomorrow.

Let's go for a walk, she said.

We talked about Bob Bartlett — she'd recently met up with him at a party. Single man, she said, but he's asexual.

Could be otherwise, just not acting on it.

Is there a difference, Jenny said, between suppressing your sexuality and being asexual.

I think there are only a few asexual people.

So do you live far? I asked. She was wearing a new red sweater.

Just down there.

Then I'll walk you.

You mean if I lived far you wouldnt?

Laugh.

I meant to take a cab if it was far, but youre stuck with me until your door.

Oh, youre not fickle.

Do you have a problem with fickleness.

I like consistency in people, she said. I dont like it when a person treats me well and then badly.

Jenny was talking about me. About how I'd dealt with her and Kathleen.

You have, I said, a dislike of fickleness.

Let's say I like people with ficklelessness.

We walked on like this.

I live in one of those flats, she said. It's nothing special. Luis thinks an ordinary apartment will make me come back to him. I didnt even see the actual apartment but another one that happened to be vacant. And I took it.

At the door. Well, Kent, thank you for the walk.

I leaned in and we kissed. A tender kiss, and she did not move away. This is how you know that you can kiss again. The lingering. So we kissed. And held each other.

Jenny: Are you fondling me.

I'm a little fond of you.

There was the sound of a metal door being roughly opened.

I said, I hope youre keeping an eye over my shoulder for anyone wanting in.

I can't see over your shoulder.

We kissed again.

I dont have anything to offer you in the way of a drink. I have champagne.

You dont have a cup of tea.

I have tea. Would you like to come up for a cup of tea.

I bent her hips. There was the cream ass. I lifted a leg. I felt the weight of her entire thigh in my hand. I immersed myself. It was the frustration at inaction that I drove into Jenny Starling. I pushed my optic nerve into the bridge of her nose. There was her head against the headboard. There was a hot fold of her with my fingers. I moistened my fingers. A heavy curtain flipped over beside the bed. You could hear a street. Things in a street.

Youre a wolf, she said, in sheep's clothing.

I put the wool in wolf.

17

What you must understand is that my wife knew. I told my wife this would happen. I will marry you, I said to Kathleen, but you must know this: I will be with other women. I was honest to her about this. We came to an arrangement. Kathleen said this:

If it must happen, dont let me catch you. I want no evidence.

Truth: She said it with an air of martyrdom. And when she drew a scent of an affair, she demanded to know. She did not want to know, but then she had to know. And I felt guilt. I felt the guilt of having wronged her. But that guilt was mixed with the honesty with which I had approached our union. I am a man with big appetites. I confessed to these appetites, and now I was being judged for them. But I understand the love of a monogamous woman. Kathleen wants to believe that I won't do it. She believes in the virtue of monogamy and that I am virtuous. My guilt was proof because I loved her so much. She was full of God, and I couldnt bear her censure.

But my desire for Jenny Starling. To exercise with her, to permit her muscles to flex and push my body, was to accept her influence over me, and Jenny knew it. Our fucking was personal, as though I were confirming myself in the world, or it was a spiritual proclamation intended to persuade the world. Intimacy created meaning. I had turned Jenny Starling over several times with just my hands. It's true that in those days I wanted to press against any woman if she allowed it. I had a gear I could reach called abandon. I wanted to be remembered. It was vanity, and my vanity about Jenny Starling lasted an evening and a morning. We were raw from the sex. It was not erotic now but a motion that united us. It was a farewell joining, a gentle but brutish thrust to assist us over the separation. The push was to be kept in the brain. And Jenny had no problem with my departure. We linked like insects that cannot unhinge. She came several small, unexpected times, and I pulsed in her and burned from the excess. It was not enjoyable but necessary, as we were addicted to it. For we knew the extent of our time — what little we had of it.

I remember her open closet door. Jenny had fabric hung on it with pockets, and in the pockets were pairs of shoes. I thought it interesting that someone had realized that doors werent shouldering enough work. It was only one side of the door. So you could shut the door and forget the work the door was always doing.

In the morning I heard her up. She showered. I smelled coffee. And she came in dressed. A black-and-charcoal top. Jenny bent down and kissed me. It's nine, she said. I'm late for work.

But it'll be okay?

Yes, but they'll know. Women know, she said.

On Jenny Starling's kitchen table was a white cup full of black coffee. The white was so unblemished.

18

I'd had this affair with Jenny Starling on my first trip to Newfoundland. I had promised my wife I was done with her, and, through a coincidence, I'd ended up spending a night and a morning with her. Then my ferry left Boston for Nova Scotia and then a train to St John's. I met the prime minister, Morris, on the train. He waived the duty on my sketch box. He listened to my plans for an artists' colony. He suggested Burin. Ice-free port, he said, solid storerooms on the water. I'll give free passage, he said, to artists and tax breaks for students.

I loved Burin. The birch groves and blueberry bushes and there was a marsh I sank in.

After seeing Burin I returned to New York. I did not tell Kathleen about staying with Jenny, though she knew I'd had dinner with her. I sold the house we had in Monhegan. I had my wife and son ready to leave. While I was in the middle of a set of push-ups with my feet on a kitchen chair, the postman came and Kathleen knelt down and laid the blue letter franked in Boston on the linoleum between my hands and oh she knew.

I finished my twenty repetitions, stood, and primly tore off one end of the envelope. Near the middle of the letter was a word with the tails of a *p* and a *g*. I knew the word before I'd even got to it; it was next to the face of my thumb. I knew the information contained in this word as though the word itself had impregnated the letter. I was shocked at how I had not thought of this possibility, how dumb I was not to connect. But I did not tell Kathleen anything. I held on to the idea of the way things were.

I said to Kathleen, I have to go to Boston.

That was it. It's hard to believe that Kathleen accepted this without any other words being said. We both knew it, and somehow not saying the words undid it.

I stayed with Jenny Starling three days. She demanded that I leave my wife, that I take up with her. She almost convinced me that I should. And perhaps a promise leaked out of me. I am a bad man for promising. There was my desire in the idea of being with a woman I could talk with, but there was something repellent in her now being pregnant. That the two should mix. It had begun with the letter: I did not like the handwriting. How could I be passionate with a woman who writes this way? But how is a man to relieve himself of repellent thoughts? I did not tell this to Jenny but resorted to the responsibilities I had to my wife. Yes, I would accept Jenny's child as my own. I would do all I could to take care of her and the child. But I would not leave my wife.

We did not sleep together. Jenny wanted it to be our last three days. Fucking is a declaration of just the two of you. It excludes the world. I refused it. I felt of all the things I'd done to Kathleen, this resistance could shore up some goodwill. I had sold the Monhegan house because it brought Kathleen memories of Jenny. That was where I'd slept with Jenny while courting Kathleen. So. These three days were the end and the end is different from knowing you have only a short time. I had the rest of my life with Kathleen, which makes you feel different. I am not a great man. I have fucked over those I love. I hurt Jenny and did very badly by Kathleen. I am a man of appetites and an inability to refrain from the most intimate act a man and a woman can do. I love the feast of fucking, the permission and the giving. It is a religious act. I am not religious, except for sex and art. They are my king and queen, and I do not mind lying to honour them. There is a greater honesty at work, or at least to hell with telling the truth. To lie does not betray integrity. At least, my definition of integrity.

When I left, when Jenny Starling saw that I was certainly to return to Kathleen, she relaxed. She began to smoke. She loosened up. She became herself because she had lost everything. In that becoming of her self I was glad to have chosen Kathleen. I wanted a clean woman. There was a fixed ideal in my head, and I recognized the hypocrisy of my own moral waning. But also there was a keen realization that I had not known Jenny. She had kept her self from me because she felt that if I'd known who she was, I would never have been with her for a minute. There was something strong in my character that made people act a role they hoped I'd admire. A strong character does not mean a champion of moral high ground. It is alluring but damaging. And here she was, drinking heavily, smoking, her stomach relaxed and big. Surprisingly, she became beautiful.

19

The train home to New York from Boston. Speed damaged the trees and small towns. Then dusk destroyed the world. I told Kathleen everything, except the fact that on Wednesday and Thursday and Friday morning I had not permitted this woman who had sent the letter to unbutton my sleeves and clench the back of my hair and lift me. That I did not lift her and turn my hips to search. This denial of sex seemed paltry, and I could not use it as a confirmation of my love for Kathleen. It seemed like a position, and if I had done that, it was only to use it as collateral against the guilt of previous misdeeds. I would admit to the child, I would accept him. But all Kathleen said to me was, You shaved.

What.

Youve shaved.

She made me throw out all of my underwear.

I remember the waste of that. She closed her ears to my plea for mercy. At my attempt to be good but the boat out of Boston was delayed. I said I'd had no idea that Jenny would come down to see me off. She hauled out my postcards from the scouting trip. Omissions, Kathleen said, are horrible. They are the worst forms of lying. For they harbour the scent of truth. About the boat's delay and Jenny's send-off she said, A coincidence is never that impressive to someone else.

Kathleen did not know what to do. We had a child, Rocky, and she was pregnant too. Kathleen hated the thought of another woman pregnant when she was pregnant. How can a man make two women pregnant at once? And claim to love? Does he think he is a god? She did not know what to do. At times it was only her goodness that prevented her from hating me.

I was frantic. I wanted her. I wanted everything about her. What I wanted was the form of life I was living. I wanted to be married.

She had to be away from me, she said. Would I book a train, upstate. Her parents in Stockbridge, Massachusetts. She was dragging her parents into this. But what did I expect. How long do you need, I said.

I dont know.

She was gone a week. I wrote and called her. Rocky had a fine time. He loves his grandparents. They have a farm. He was pulling up fresh new carrots clotted with soil.

We will give her, Kathleen said, the proceeds of the house.

She did not say her name.

Yes.

And our savings.

Okay.

I dont want you to have anything to do with her.

Agreed.

And youre emotionally stupid.

I admitted to this.

So that ended our first attempt at Newfoundland.

20

Was I relieved? I had salvaged things. I'd realized that my own ambition, let's call it Rockwell Land, was tied up not with a place but more with the idea of who I was. The primary things had been salvaged. The family. My son, Rocky, my pregnant wife. New York. I could live in New York. I did some drafting for Ewing and Chappell. I pushed my T-square away from the plans for a confident bank and exhaled. I worked for three solid years. We had two more children, girls. Jenny had her son, George. I was lucky. My friends were married. The frame of marriage. I needed the structure of it. I was a crazy man who needed parameters. A wife. I liked my wife.

Three years passed like this and my wife grew closer to me. But there was something in the new form of her closeness — she kept a veneer. I had hurt her and this was the result. It was not anything we spoke of, but it shone on her skin. Kathleen was self-conscious around me. A little formal. And then I remembered how she'd been when that letter arrived from Boston. She had laid the envelope on the floor while I did push-ups, as if she'd known of the affair all along. As if nothing I did surprised her and she was above it. She knew better than me. She had a good spirit, whereas I had the devil in me. She judged me but loved me for the devil. It was the one thing she was superior about, and I was a coward to mention it. I was glad she was the way she was. I did not want a confrontation. It meant rubble. A confrontation meant everything that we were would crumble. So I took it. I accepted it like a punch to the ribs to protect the face. Faces. I hated the way my wife's face remained steady, and I knew she had an ugly face when it fell into emotion (we all do) and she would not let me see her face ugly. It wasnt the affair or the baby but the way we dealt with it that made me think we could not be together forever.

21

I thought of all this after walking with Rupert down to the Bartlett tunnel. He was offloading a floater. The tunnel is about eighty feet long, through solid rock. At the far end is Molly's Island, and around it the green-and-white thrusting of the tide onto rocks, spraying up forty feet. We took a pony with us. The waves pushed in and rose, making the pony nervous. The men off the floater shook hands with us. Flour, roofing tar, new barrels, and pipe for a water pump. So, Rupert said, rumour has it you were in Newfoundland once before.

He had heard something. I tried coming, I said, to Newfoundland, yes. Four years ago. Soon after meeting your brother.

We loaded the cart and pointed the pony back at the tunnel.

You had plans, he said, for an art school.

I wanted to bring artists and students here.

You met Morris.

Morris. Yes, Morris, the prime minister. He loved the idea. How'd you know that.

Oh, I know Morris.

So it was Morris who'd told him. We were walking back through the tunnel, and the underground aspect of Rupert's questions made me feel like I was being interrogated.

I guess youve found out about me then, I said.

A thing or two.

I decided to be open with Rupert. He was being nice to me, so why not confess. Morris told me that there are good ideas and bad ideas, and that this one, to make a university in Newfoundland, was good.

Yes, Rupert said. That man's mouth never goes slack.

A promise, I said to Rupert, can shape you even when the promise is broken.

You went to Burin.

The prime minister suggested it. I liked the name. It's the name of an engraving tool.

Rupert: The bays are good there. Ice-free in winter. There are good storerooms on the water in Burin. Unlike here.

Yes, what is it with this tunnel.

We dont use it much now. But we needed it back when the fishery was good. Say fifty years ago. All this harbour was blocked with boats and wharves. Our claim was this here rock, and we got tired of lugging our gear around it.

He smacked the rock with his hand. You were ambitious.

To Rupert it must have been as if some external circumstance too chagrining had upset my distinct vision. And he would have been right. It was because I did not want to mention Jenny Starling in Boston. I did not, even now, want to mention it to you. I helped coax Rupert's pony with his heavy load up to Hawthorne Cottage. We unloaded her.

22

Even though I do not believe in God. Even though this. When I was alone in that house. When I was waiting for Tom Dobie to join me. While I waited for the coffee pot to heat. Even though I believed in experiences and objects and was a man who believed that a good, godless life can be lived on earth, even so I prayed to God. I knelt and prayed. I prayed to the fireplace, which was praying north. I asked God to make me strong and make me love the things that were good. I wanted to love Kathleen. I wanted her to be enough and to be a vessel through which all the things of the world could be funnelled. I believed in children and friends. The fact that we do not live on, I did not let this depress me.

23

I met up with Rupert Bartlett down at Chafe's. I was buying supplies: nails, oakum, food. Bud Chafe told me that people did not usually buy on a day-to-day basis. They bought provisions, stores. They bought barrels and sacks and tubs. They sold the same way. They sold nothing for eleven months and then on one afternoon in the fall they hammered out a price for their fish. When the fish ran good, Rupert said, the price fell. When the fish were poor, the price was a little better. Bud Chafe smiled. Just a little bit better.

Rupert said his brother was back in St John's on board the *Morrissey*.

I said, I thought he was captaining a collier. I thought he was in Holyrood.

Yes, but the *Morrissey* was put in dry dock to have her keel caulked. So Bob is there and soon he'll be captaining a collier.

You mean he hasnt left yet.

The news was wrong. He'll be here in a jiffy.

Bartlett would offload coal — I had ordered seven tons of the coal. When I made my order Bud Chafe's pencil stopped.

Seven tons. Let's see. Youve come in here and tried to buy four small potatoes, one onion, and seven tons of coal.

I said, I'm sick of being cold. My family is coming and by God I want to stoke that house like a furnace room. Seven tons, I figure, will do me a year.

I can sell a gallon of spuds. A gallon's as small as I go.

By the time Bartlett rounded Conception Bay the ice had come in. We saw the collier, black with soot, at the ice edge. I watched through binoculars. Men coated in coal dust, pointing out a direction for Bartlett to steam through. He was trying to make it to the Bartlett wharf and tunnel. You heard the stokers encouraging the engine, the steam pressure build, black plumes belching from the sole stack, and you knew he was ramming her through the ice. I passed the glasses to Tom Dobie.

Tom: He won't do it.

Men from Brigus were hired to help the crew punch through two hundred yards of ice. I got an afternoon at it. They used saws and pikes and poles to lever out the ice pans. They gripped ropes and tracked the collier through the cut channel. They were halfway into port when Bartlett got impatient. He waved them off. I had not seen him in action before. The men dropped their ropes and jogged away from the front of the collier. Bartlett guided the collier back to the mouth of the harbour and gave her full throttle. His momentum split the ice and carried him in a few boatlengths. A seam of black opened up ahead of him around Molly's Island. He was fine and skilful until he got about a hundred yards from the tunnel entrance. He could have set her there and towed the coal ashore on sleds and ponies. But he ground the collier deep into the pack and wiggled her furious arse. A pan of ice nosed up and pushed a neat, silent hole through the neck of the bow. The collier sat there on top of the ice, quiet now, with a wide wound plunged through the side of her. Then she slipped down to sea level. Bob Bartlett and three crew stepped over the side and walked ashore, as if that was that. The crew all slunking backwards, watching the collier lean to port and sink, heavy with coal. Bartlett refused to look, just walked straight to the Bartlett tunnel and got a hand up onto the wharf apron.

I watched the deck creak through the ice, the water curl over the bow and lick at the masts. I had ordered seven tons of that coal. Now on the bottom of the harbour.

24

I was out of wood and getting cold. I was still sleeping in a tent in the upstairs bedroom, the room above the stove. A green canvas, heavy. Just to keep the heat in.

Wet sleet was on the kitchen window. Night. It looked like a fringe of silver tinsel. This was a time when I thought I was a good artist. Before I knew for sure that I was mediocre. Or is it middlebrow. What is the difference. It is true that I wrote letters to cubists, telling them they were wrong. Art should make you interested in life, not in art. Art is a by-product of living. I was against many things, and I believed the way to be against them was to rant and argue and never be conciliatory. I loathed diplomacy.

I slept in the tent in a room on the second floor. Bad to worse, I thought.

25

I went over to the Bartletts' to see Bob. Rupert showed me in. The Newfoundland men were short, like me. Except when sitting down. When they sat down they appeared taller.

Bob Bartlett was talking to Bud Chafe. Bud's son Charlie was still missing in the Arctic. Bob was saying he was all right, he would be fine, Bud. He just needed to get a ship back to Wrangel Island. If the men kept their heads Charlie would be all right. Bud said, Is it money. I have money.

Bartlett came over to me. He had his mother on his arm.

My best girl, she is.

And we shook hands. His big tough hand.

So what made you come finally. Besides me. New York to Brigus is twelve hundred miles.

I've wanted, I said, more than anything to live on the ocean. Probably for no other reason than you were born inland.

He thought, when he met me, that my wish to come was eager rather than lasting. I told him of a bath I'd had. It was in Gerald Thayer's basement in Manhattan. When you dunked your head under you could hear the subway go by. It was the only time you heard the subway and I loved it. But all else about New York I could eschew. I wanted to explore the hem of the coat of a continent. It was the chunk-shunk of the subway underwater or this.

He said he had a bath coming to him. He was lousy. Almost always was on board boats. Lice, he said, won't go to an unhealthy person.

We stood in his Artic Room — the old way of spelling Arctic — which had green-and-gold wallpaper, but you could hardly see the walls for the congestion of framed photographs of Bartlett in the North. It was my first time in this room. The picture frames touched each other clear across the length of the wall. I wondered but did not ask if there was room for a brother's exploits. Or if Rupert considered exploits. I wondered later if this was part of why he'd signed up early, got commissioned, and threw himself into France and almost begged to be destroyed by a fresh young war and blown up in a new way.

Bob: You sure took the farthest house from town. Dont you find it a bit of a march?

Me: An artist must walk a lot.

Oh you'd like it down north, then.

The photographs of Bartlett glinted in square slants like a panel of windows in a ship. There was a photo of that first day of April, when Peary had forced Bob Bartlett to return to the *Roosevelt*. That was the morning, Bartlett said, that Peary betrayed me. He took the coloured man, Henson.

Betrayed you.

In small ways I can see the rationale.

It is a powerless moment, isnt it. When someone tells you what to do.

It has humiliated me. It's dampened my passion for other people's witnessing my deeds.

Bob Bartlett could not live in a world that had no audience, and when the audience was broken into individuals, he could not stand their accolades to his face.

I love printed praise, he said. I think the world of newspapers.

I stared at this photo of Bartlett's argument with Peary, an argument only because Bob had defined it as such — it was of two men staring at each other in the distance of a foreground of white, Peary's mouth open, a hand gesturing, while Bartlett stood at slouched attention, as if carrying a heavy bucket in either hand.

A photograph, he said, is much like the physical image of an inner, fleeting, unspoken moment. This one here, that's when Peary came back to Greenland with Crocker Land sighted. We discovered new land. It's the last land in the world to be found, and we found it.

Crocker Land. Named after George Crocker, Jenny's father. We leaned against the mantel and had a drink. Bob took coffee. I touched a soldier brick in the fireplace — called that because it stands on end. Bud Chafe said he had to go. Mrs Bartlett was seeing to dinner. Rupert was on the stair, his nose in Emerson. The middle brick is the keystone. It checks the gravity of all the others.

Bob Bartlett did not seem perturbed by the collier. It was as if that was the risk you took. Coal, he said, is a more intimate cargo than bananas. He had spent four years of service in the West Indian fruit trade aboard the *Corisande*. I hate, he said, to eat a banana. But at least it never got into your coffee. Coal gets into everything — it's like a woman in love.

Rupert said they were about to have supper and would I stay. They left me to the Artic Room. At the end of the photographs was a window and I saw Tom Dobie in the road talking to Emily Edwards. I watched them turn. I decided to speak a word just as Emily turned back for the door. I said the word *reckless*. It was a strong word, a word I could not say aloud. I was saying it to be a shit disturber. There was a politeness or restraint going on out there between Tom Dobie and Emily Edwards; restraint stood like a third figure between them at the Bartlett gate and then it pushed that beautiful young woman towards the house, she wasnt even looking back, and I felt Tom Dobie in the corner of my eye. I was impressed with how much you can see out of the corner of your eye. Then Tom went home and Emily stamped her boots by the clock with the white partridge nesting above midnight. Eleanor, the sister, was laying out silverware, placing the forks and spoons face down in the old-fashioned way, and

Emily Edwards ran in to help her. I walked into the parlour and sat myself in a chair with strong arms and listened to Rupert Bartlett, that quieter younger brother with two years left to live, speak to his older brother as though he were his father.

26

Jenny's father, the word *magnate* applies. Part of the allure of Jenny was her father. George Crocker financed dry docks and port facilities, had sunk a fair bit into railroads then sold the lot, and was now financing Peary's polar ambitions. And so the big circle of how I got to meet Bartlett and ended up bringing my family to Newfoundland.

They spoke, Jenny said, more since she'd returned to Luis. George Crocker's tastes ran through his daughter, and marriage appealed to him. Jenny called our son George, after him. He wanted heirs.

George Crocker had an aquiline nose and the same cliff of forehead he'd given his daughter. His shirts were English. George Crocker was an American with a European flair — the capitalist European. Once Jenny had become the wife of Luis Starling, he allowed me to design letterhead for his offices on the West Coast, San Francisco and Seattle. I needed the money. And now that his daughter was out of my hands he became fond of her, and me. George Crocker recognized a part of himself in Jenny, appreciated the daring. It was her lack of caution — she was living her life in a real way. He was encumbered by a love of money and he loved the Crocker name.

27

Gerald Thayer: Do you remember a distinct image from a book, or are you left with a general sweep.

Me: Definitely a general sweep.

See, that's the difference between you and me right there.

Gerald often exclaimed at a homecooked meal. He'd push back from the table and say, How much. How much would you pay to get a meal like this in a restaurant?

And if that restaurant had a flag hoisted after sunset, he'd walk in and tell them to take it down. Yes, he hated to see flags aloft at night.

Cocks, he said. Why dont you paint men's cocks.

Their penises.

Yes, their genitalia. All your men have bushes. They look like big strong women. They are made of wood and their cocks have all been whittled off.

Well thanks, Gerald.

Or you stick a thigh in front of the cock. Every time. Youve got a problem with cocks, I think. Tits you paint. Vulva and asses you reveal. Men's asses even. As long as theyve got a perky ass. I doubt you'd ever paint my ass. But the cock — what is it with you. Everything about you is grand and Greek except for the —

Just lighten up on me.

Gerald loved to bicycle in the snow. I have seen him cross a street and from his arms a barking. Then a set of ears. He was a man who liked to rescue dogs.

The problem with you, Kent. Is youre not swayed by the modern world. You like something, you do something. Your art, for instance. It is not really new art. It is not abstract. You dont like abstraction. And so you can't follow it.

What youre saying is, Gerald, an artist should follow the modern world, and whatever form it presents, the art should mirror it.

That's kind of what I'm saying.

But I'm a realist, Gerald. I'm ashcan. I see the dirt and yet I see the spirit behind the dirt. I'm a good drawer. Forgive me, but I can draw a straight line.

You went to a technical school.

You have a problem with that.

Let's not get into it.

I think it's too late not to get into it.

Okay, I want some cocks out of you. And filth. Youre no stranger. You speak of dirt, but there is no dirt in you. Give me snot. Give me a torn shirt. It's all starry nights and bowsprits and men hanging like Jesus from the crow's nest.

Me: Youre talking woodcuts. You have to reduce the real to its strongest elements in a woodcut. You have to have things lit from behind. That makes them monumental. As though you were looking at a slide photograph.

But the flaws are what are important. That's what's human. You draw gods.

So we got into it.

Art, I said, should be three things: full of sex, in a surrounding different from your own, and imbued with an unexpected intelligence. And there should be something unscripted in it.

I'll try anything once, Gerald said — he was ignoring me — I've even tried some things a second time. But you. You try only a few things, and you try them all the time.

I'd met Gerald through his father, the painter Abbott Thayer. When you lose a father early, as I did, you look for fathers. Gerald Thayer was working on a book about his father's theory of camouflage in animals. He wanted me to help illustrate it. I learned a lot about painting from Abbott Thayer, and not just technique, but reasons for painting. I lived with the Thayers for several winters. The extreme cold of their house that Abbott Thayer insisted upon — and we all had to sleep outdoors. Abbott Thayer believed temperature controlled the mind. Yes, he was a stoic, and his son, Gerald, while inheriting this stoicism, compensated for it with a lavish hand. Abbott Thayer led miserable hikes through the Adirondacks, and it was Gerald who packed the smoked salmon sandwiches, the Bordeaux, and the corkscrew. I can hear Gerald now: Leaving easy life behind, we turned the winter kind to us who faced its cruelty like men.

I love to see principles, especially unorthodox ones, get handed down from father to son.

28

What was I thinking. Was I thinking. I spent all day chopping through four feet of ice. To get to a pile of slush, the slush you get when youre ice fishing. To retrieve some old wet birch. And haul an armload of the heavy wet wood up the hill and into the house to dry. It'll take a week before you can burn it, Tom Dobie said. Sodden. The tiny house frozen and smoke from smouldering wet wood. It did not look good.

29

What is integrity anyway, except constancy in character. And what if maintaining a constancy is false. What if one assumes that the soul is not thoroughly unwavering. Why honour the man who does not change his opinion. Who does not alter his course. Who is methodical and predictable. Why praise the pattern. What if there is no accurate measure of a man's behaviour. A few things: the pulse of the world is always shifting between poles. I have become attached to the ontological. I believe in atheism and the power of the ontological. The reason I do not believe in God is because I am happy with this world. I believe in slim books. I believe in the shape a boat cuts through ice. Sometimes we need God. Our hunches are not intuitive, or they are a blend of nature and the absorption of cultural ways. The third is will to know a truth. This is my book, this will to know.

30

The wind was a solid thing. It lifted the house. Bob Bartlett came over to see my progress. He shook his head. If I were to build a house from scratch, he said, I'd leave off the eaves. Eaves are overrated.

He saw the tent I slept in and laughed.

You know where that tent's been?

He told me. Past the Arctic Circle. Dogs and seal blubber, rotten tins of pemmican have slept in that tent. At various times.

I feel a bit like an explorer, I said. In this house.

Bartlett: I'm going in the woods now where there's a blue bunch and cut me a dory. Game?

Sure, I'll come along.

There was a grain of snow in the air still and this snow got into everything. It was the opposite of coal and yet snow percolated in the same manner. The air bit and had a curl to it that got under your scarf.

When you entered the woods the wind died down.

There was a stand of dead spruce. The bark stripped the previous year. They'd used the bark as shingles on a store down by the water. Bartlett had left the trees standing to dry out. Fir, he said, is too greasy to cut in spring. There were a couple on a hill with their trunks bent up to reach the light.

Those, he said, where theyre not boxy. Are excellent for runners on a sledge.

We set to chopping out some trees.

Me: I dont want to drop this on your head.

Bartlett: Oh no not to worry.

We chopped out about forty logs.

Bartlett: I'll come in later with the pony. I'll squat the timbers then bring them over to Pomeroy's.

We hauled them together in the snow and made a brow by the trail. We sat on the wood and ate sandwiches. My feet were wet and cold. Bartlett started a boil-up with a sulphur match. We had trimmed the branches from the logs and with these, some old man's beard and strips of birchbark, we made a blaze. Just seeing a kettle on a fire in the snow, that pleased him.

Bartlett: You just fart?

No.

You always smell like that.

It was sunny and crisp and I asked Bartlett what he was wearing. What he was wearing? He stripped off a foot. He wore swanskin up past the knee. Below this was his sealskin boot. Under that three pairs of wool socks.

I said, Show me your foot.

His foot was pink and dry. It was, as he'd say, healthy. He noted the tired heels of my leather boots. We'll get you set up with some sealskin, he said.

Feet were important to him, as they are to all travellers. He had seen many toes lost to gangrene, whole sides of feet carved away like soap under a doctor's scalpel. The gangrene they got was from frostbite. Dry gangrene it was, not the gangrene you got from open, infected wounds. He was very proud not to have lost any toes in the North. I asked him about the *Karluk*, about what had to be done now.

The loss of a ship, he said, affects a seafaring man much like the loss of a loved one. It's hard to talk about it.

Then he seemed to relent. I'll tell you another time. That's a story, that one.

31

Bob Bartlett invited me iceboating up behind on one of the ponds and I took my sketchbook to make a postcard for Kathleen. They shovelled the snow off the pond, hooked sails on several punts. The punts had skate blades under each corner, with one at the back on a swivel. That was your rudder. They were catamarans and they flew. The pharmacist Jim Hearn had the best one. He let me try it solo and I nearly decapitated myself on the swinging sail.

Spill your wind boy.

Shove down your tiller.

He's gonna destroy himself.

He's on the hand of it.

They built a fire on the shore and boiled the kettle. Bartlett was in charge of that. A long line of boats, he said, had sunk under him. He seemed unperturbed in a business way by ship failure. He had carried the footless Peary into the Arctic Circle and then Peary had ditched him. I've been a miserable sealing captain, never a good haul like Father. The *Karluk* was money, he said. Otherwise I'd never have taken the job. The *Karluk*. The ship had sunk eight months ago. The men stranded on Wrangel Island. I'm raising money, he said, for a rescue. There's a Brigus lad, Bud Chafe's son. I watched him fall over the side and hit his head on the ice. He was unconscious but then came to. We lowered a sheet and he rolled in, like a hammock.

You okay?

Sure I'm good, Skipper.

How many fingers you see?

Three. Three fingers.

What's your name.

Charlie Chafe.

And what day is it, Charlie?

Sexday.

What did you say?

Sexday. It's Sexday, Skipper.

Charlie if you die in my charge I'll never forgive you.

They put him in a bunk and brought him rum and soup.

At the time I was not attracted to these stories of the North. I listened to them and enjoyed them, but I wasnt interested in other people's exploits. I wanted to have my own. I was a little envious of Bartlett: here was a man who, after a farewell to thousands on the East River, had tied up in Oyster Bay and been received by Teddy Roosevelt. Bartlett had marched about Sagamore Hill and told the president the strengths of the ship that bore his name. I was sitting with a powerful man who had guided Peary to the north pole, and now he was wanted and it was a surprise to hear him bad-mouthing Peary.

I left the iceboats and joined Bartlett by the fire under some spruce. He'd built the fire on rocks and the rocks had melted through the ice to the ground. There was a kettle hanging over it on a green pole. Bartlett wiped his nose on the back of his glove. The gloves were trigger mitts, with a thumb and index finger knitted in. He said the *Karluk* venture was to be a geological survey. What an outfit, he said. They left Victoria with their deck piled high: fresh meat, vegetables, snowshoes, skins, alcohol drums, and canoes. They had unmarked boxes and cases of equipment enough to stretch over this whole pond. It would all get sorted when then reached the rendezvous at Collinson Point. That's what the commander, Stefansson, thought. It was the worst-organized expedition ever bar none guaranteed.

Me: Vilhjalmur Stefansson?

That's the man.

I know him, I said.

I hope he wasnt in charge of leading you someplace.

I painted a mural for the post office in Washington. It was a letter being mailed in Alaska and arriving in Puerto Rico. I was impressed with the plight of the Puerto Ricans. So I painted a group of women receiving the letter from a mailman on horseback. One of the women was reading the letter. You could see the writing, but it was in a language no one could understand. The post office didnt like that. So they copied the letter out and sent it to a specialist in northern languages.

Bartlett: And it was Stefansson.

He knew the dialect.

It was an Eskimo language.

Kiskokwims. It said, To the people of Puerto Rico, our friends: Go ahead, let us change chiefs. That alone can make us equal and free.

Youre a strange bird, Kent.

They still paid me, which was nice of them. And I thought it good of Stefansson to figure it out.

I wish he'd stayed on dry land.

You didnt find him striking.

An empty craft, Kent, always looms high.

32

I realized that I did not know who lived in Brigus. So as we worked Tom Dobie told me. I credit him with an intimate knowledge of the community. He pointed out obvious ones to get me grounded. The Pomeroys next door. Stan and Old Man

Pomeroy, he said, theyre fishermen and woodcutters and Old Man Pomeroy he's a laugh and I used to steal tobacco off him and hide it under a bureau when I was small and he learned me how to catch rabbits.

Next to him, Tom said, is Miles Sweeney and he's a prate box who knows how to do everything except work. Amanda Sweeney she got a big mouth. That's Bud and Alice Chafe over there, you knows them pretty good. They had three sons. One got killed in a accident and the other one died when he was young and Charlie Chafe he be the third and now he's lost on the *Karluk*. Alice she's as big as a camp. They got a house with a downstairs built into her. Jim Hearn lives in that red house, he works in the pharmacy and he's always sniffing. Sniffles, that's what we calls him. Billy Cole he operates a shebeen I'll take you to, and next to that is Carmel Lahey she's old, black hair cause she dyes it. Dr Gill is after her, he lived in Boston for a few years and got a straw up his nose.

We worked and then took a breather. And in the breather Tom found a new house to speak about.

That one there's Rose Foley she sings good you knows that and she's a widow. She got two youngsters. Patrick Fardy next to her he got one leg. He's sensible though he lost all his hair and his head shrunk like a wet cat.

How did Fardy lose his leg.

I thought it was a boat hook. But maybe he was fooling around and got stuck in the leg with a prong and it got infected and had to come off.

Now beside him is Tony Loveys and he goes in shares with me and Stan Pomeroy. Tony's older than us he's married though his wedding was only a half-hour long cause they havent got any money. I suppose that's the reason.

Pause.

There's more, but theyre not all worth a mention. Except for me and Mom over in Frogmarsh. And Jas Kelly, he's up the droke a piece. He got a set of crabapple trees. Nice apples. People always rogues him and then he goes off his head. I works in the woods around Jas. I like Jas though he's a bit of a starve guts, he won't feed you.

And that girl I saw you with. The Bartlett maid.

That be the Edwards. Yeah, Marten Edwards is the cobbler, Mrs Edwards she died of a lung ailment and yes theyre all right.

And the daughter's name.

Emily. Emily Edwards.

You like her.

She's a cramp hand.

She's a what?

Like I said, the Edwards are all right.

33

Tom Dobie tapped the barometer in the Artic Room and Bartlett saw that.

Did you knock the barometer, Tom Dobie?

Yes.

Did I give you a hammer and say, Check the barometer?

Everyone, I said, is getting up earlier.

Tom: No I'm up the same time every day.

Youre at the door here ten minutes earlier than last week.

No I'm not, he said.

He's coming, Bartlett said, an hour after the sun rises.

Sun's the same, Tom said, every morning.

I often, Bartlett said, speak of time in reference to the moon. You haul your nets, he said, two hours before the tide, dont you Tom.

You work in front of the moon sometimes, instead of in front of the sun.

Me: So you think about when the moon will rise.

Tom: The time is always correct in the sky.

Bartlett said the sextant has three knobs to hold, so the heat of your hand does not affect its reading.

All of this I needed years later, in the wilderness of married life.

34

Tom Dobie: My mother wants to see you. Would you come over to supper.

Only then did I see the distance. How far Tom Dobie had to walk each morning to work for me. When I mentioned it he said, Dont worry, a man's got to think.

They lived in Frogmarsh, the south side of Brigus harbour. I was on the far northern end. We worked that day replacing a rotting sill. The loudest sound in March was the water in the brook sloshing against its ice cave. There was a young fruit tree encased in ice from a silver thaw, and the harbour was open and quiet. We walked across the stone bridge and down past the churches and the inner pond and around past George Clarke's house, where some boys were taking cock shots at a bottle on a fence. The mother at the door. I introduced myself.

I'm Tom's mother, she said.

Sorry what's your name?

My husband's name was Robert Dobie.

I waited. And so I called her Mrs Dobie.

Close the half door behind you, she said. To me: I thought you were from Torbay. They all speak like you in Torbay.

Tom here, she said, is a muddler in the head with little to say. He's shy as a horse, she said. And he can come to a fury and he's strong enough to make damage though I'll have none of it. He's stifled either way, arent you Tom.

They lived in a small saltbox with a linhay off the back. There was a cow in a shed and a root cellar and a northern ash in a field for the cow to stare at in summer. They grew hay. There was a compost and a wooden crate beside the compost with sixteen chicks in it. The heat off the compost.

Tom says you dont eat animals and I wasnt about to cook you fish so we settled on this goose.

Goose is great, I said.

Mrs Dobie was a bright woman. She had long hair and strong hands and she was confident in the little she had in the way of furnishings. She smelled a little. I was relieved she was not embarrassed.

There was soup and then the goose. Potatoes and turnip and cabbage, followed by doughboys in hot jam. It was all good. The soup was yellow and the broth was full of golden globes of oil. When the soup was hot the globes were alive and bright. I could see the oil was from pork fat, though there was no pork in it. I ate it. Tom held one forearm flat on the table. Mrs Dobie did not. If you swirled the soup a slice of carrot would rise and sink. There was barley.

There were just the three of us.

Mrs Dobie sat erect. When the soup turned lukewarm all its happiness sank to the bottom.

I said that I'd heard Tom was skilful with houses.

It's a far cry from a house, Tom said. A far cry.

The mother looked at her son. He had been all bone, this son, just a shovel with skin on.

Tom sat across the table and listened. Tom considered the bread and decided to say, You can have all you want of me.

Mrs Dobie: Now if ever there was a false consideration. Of paid work.

Tom: I wasnt trying to fool him.

He pushed the bread to his mother and Mrs Dobie held it to her chest and cut off a slice for her son and one for me, sawing towards her cardigan and clicking the blade on the buttons.

What a mother, he said.

As if it were all to do with passing judgment, she said.

I ate the goose. It was the best meal I'd had. Richer meals at the Bartletts', but this was the tastiest. I noticed that the floors were covered in sand, and that someone had passed a broom through the sand to create a pattern.

Mrs Dobie was the kind of woman who spoke her mind before all the information had been presented. She got to a con-clusion quickly, and while this may have been seen as presumptuous and ignorant, if you knew her you'd see how right she was and how her perception paid off. You would come to appreciate her honest sizing-up of a character or a predicament. There was a tortoiseshell barrette in her hair. It was the only thing pretty in the house.

She said to me, Tom said you looked like you'd walked off a coin. Like you'd just come round the world and studied us all before you got here.

They cleared the table and scoured the teapot. Tom opened up the door for a gust of air to wring out the tight supper smell. Want to have a walk around? She was embarrassing him. You could just see my cottage from their front door. It was getting dark. I'd forgotten to leave a lamp on.

We went to visit the cow. Tom fed her some hay. There was a three-legged dog keeping her company.

That's Smoky.

Hello Smoky. Where do you keep your geese?

We dont have geese. We had a goose.

Jesus, Tom. You should have served me fish.

Mom wouldnt cook you fish.

Smoky wagged his tail and lifted his head.

So youre doing all right here.

It's been a year, Tom Dobie said, since my father destroyed himself.

They were living in Labrador. Tom and his father had left his mother and the twins in their rooms in Turnavik.

There were twins?

I had two sisters.

My God.

His father carried a sack with a wood plane, a rifle, and a herring net. He carried them to trade for food. They were starved. The young twins had stayed with their mother while Tom went with his father. They were all getting pretty thin, Tom said, but the twins they were losing out. They walked three miles south in a blizzard to the Henleys' and Alphonse Henley had shown the Dobies his flour barrel, the tub with the pound of salt meat, and the Henley family was as destitute as his own and who, Alphonse Henley asked, needed a wood plane or a herring net this time of winter. The father and son walked inland to the mouth of Red Head and found the trapper Goudie, but Goudie had nothing either and showed them everything in his store to say he was not lying. It was this revealing of empty tubs that put shame in Tom Dobie's father, not the asking. It was the hollow sound of a wooden lid on a dry keg.

They walked north and came upon an errant caribou track and the father could not believe it. It was a fresh footing as snow was falling and the caribou, which are not known at this time of year, must have been some lost soul himself. They followed the track and crossed a frozen river and saw the deep punches through the snow crust as the caribou hauled himself up the shore and through the woods. They followed the deep trail up a hill to a crest where the woods fell away and they saw him now with his snout low and frozen on them. The caribou knew of them. The father shouldered the rifle and aimed and it was a long shot, just in range. The caribou lunged forward and stumbled to the side and plunged into the snow and treeline.

They ran after the point in the trees and there was a ribbon of blood in the snow. The father stopped and said, Remember this spot, Tom. Look behind you. They pushed into the woods and at first the trail was easy with the blood, but then the snow pelted down furious and hard and softened the trail and covered the blood. Or maybe, Tom Dobie said, the wound had closed over. Yes, there was less blood. They should have stopped at the first tracking and let the caribou run his course, but they were eager to get the animal down.

They tracked and retraced their steps all day and they confused their own footprints with the caribou's. The father was not a woodsman, he was a fisherman, and he cursed himself now for chasing after the animal.

Late that night they bivouacked under some fir and made a fire and boiled the kettle and slept on some boughs. In the morning Tom realized that he could not feel his feet. His father unlaced his son's boots and rubbed the toes. Tom remembers this as his father's last gift before the sad decision. Robert Dobie took off his own socks and gave them to Tom and they walked north some more. They passed back over the frozen river. The surface of the river had raised up high and fastened over and they walked on this. Near the centre the ice was rotten. They fell through. Tom was expecting to enter cold black water, but he fell through a hollowness. They plummeted ten feet to the bed of the river. They smashed into four inches of frozen water and hard stone. As they lay there, stunned, on the cold rocks, they looked up and saw the pale blue ice of the bright ceiling above them. It glowed blue with the light of the world. It was as if they had fallen into another one.

Dont breathe in too deep, his father had said. Or you'll sear your lungs.

They were hurt from the fall but full of adrenalin. They took small breaths. The air was charged with cold under this ice.

They were chilled to the bone.

The river was a long empty tunnel and the floor of the river was slippery but well lit. They walked along it, hoping to see a crack in the roof along the side where they might climb up and get through. They slipped on the rocks. They were getting colder. It was a glowing chamber. They got to a bend in the river's bank where it was less steep. The father chopped at the frozen rock and soil. Sparks flicked off the axe. He made footholds. They climbed up the side of the hollow riverbed to the ice roof above. The ice above them was eight inches thick. The father chopped away at it until he had a hole to pull themselves through. They re-entered the world. They were cold and wet in the raw wind, so they built another fire.

You know how long a stick like this will last, his father said. A burnt stick, he said. They find sticks like this in burial grounds. If you burn a stick, he said, and bury it.

He plunged the charred stick in the snow. Tom did not know what his father was saying. It had something to do with lasting.

They paced themselves over barrens and crushed through snowdrifts. They passed the ridges of spruce and found Drodge at his winter camp, by a brook that had not frozen. But Drodge was not there and there were no provisions here either. Robert Dobie laid his plane on Drodge's cutting board and wept. He wept for a minute and then picked up the plane and said, This is it. There seemed to be hope in the tone of his father. Tom hauled together the net and they bore up southeast for home. When they saw their own salt store, Robert Dobie said to his son that he loved him and that he was sorry. They walked in together and Rachel Dobie had snared a partridge the day before and they had a little soup with the twins and this cheered them. But then Robert Dobie told Tom to go with his mother and try to find some food at the Halls', he hadnt tried Hall and Tom said there is no point for Hall was known as useless and coarse and Robert Dobie said, I'm telling you now to go. None of them was thinking correctly any more. Tom asked if he was okay and the father said he was very tired or he'd go himself and maybe a woman would help the story, who knew, and he would take care of the twins and to see you noon tomorrow, Hall would have you over. The twins were five, hungry and screeching. They were all hungry and the boy said okay and the mother said yes she would go.

He must have taken up the axe and, with the back of it, tapped the twins on their heads soon after. That stopped them. He would have said, Forgive me. And the quiet crowded the room. Tom's father had sat at the table and fed some wood to the fire. Then he fished the wood out again, to save it. The father took up the rifle and sat himself in the corner. He was going to destroy himself. He would have done it in the woods, but they needed the rifle and he did not want to risk their not finding it. He would have used a rope, but he did not want them to see him hanging. His grandfather had hanged himself in a stone barn in Brigus and Robert Dobie was the one who had discovered him.

35

After this story I walked back around the cove of Brigus and along the Pomeroy headland. It was dark. There was a pony hauling itself into the light of the Pomeroy shed, and then I saw Stan Pomeroy. I waved to him.

You need a light?

I'll make it.

What, by feeling your way along? Let me get you a light.

I'll be fine, I said.

Suit yourself.

The snow was dark blue. I could see the sweep of lighthouse light over the water, but not the lighthouse. It lit up, intermittently, the pile of stones they called the naked man. The house is cupped into the land, so not even the lighthouse could help me find it. The walk was long enough that the darkness had begun to sink into me. Black sky and a dark blue acre of snow slanting down to the water. The sense of vision diminished and all became a crunching surface under my feet. I could hear the rut of the shore. The cold, fresh air on my face. But I felt with my feet and I put out a hand to fend off a wayward branch or cliff face. I walked slower. It was stupid not to have lit a lamp. I heard the ocean and then the hollow sound of the brook. I saw the naked man. I was near the house. The mass of the house blanketed sound in front of me. But I could not see it. I made my way in the black until my hand was surprised by the side of the house. I felt my way around the corner of it. There was a window, but I could not find the door. I brushed the side of the house. The house was longer than I thought. There, a sill. And now the door. But where was the latch. The latch was missing. I did not know where I was. I was losing my memory. I focused on the present. Was I where I thought I was? And where did I think I was? Who was I? I flattened myself against the side of the house. I was against something flat. That was for sure. But the sense of a particular place drifted away from me and I could not remember any place, not even my childhood home. Then my fingers felt the latch, the door latch of the house in Brigus, and that entire house reappeared in my head.

36

In the land of no refrigeration, the salted pig is king. I missed grated carrot, slices of cucumber. I ached for lettuce and a ripe tomato.

Bartlett's was the only home in Brigus with electricity. The power was a month old when I arrived. They had running water, and had a pump for a toilet. I had barrels of water and tins of kerosene and a woodstove and two fireplaces. I had a shallow outhouse and the iced-over brook four feet from the new corner of the house. The brook sounded different from month to month. Frozen over in March, like water rushing out of a bottle.

Each morning Tom Dobie walked the path through Pomeroy's. I watched him throw a stick at the cows and stroll along the road towards my yard. It seemed the walk altered him, as if my house was a transition from a life he knew to one that offered a better opinion of himself. The only times he'd been over here were to pick berries or walk out to the lighthouse on a

Sunday, perhaps with the boys. Berry picking, he said, meant time with a girl.

He assisted me with the front mullions. He kept remarking on the southern view, compared with the northerly he and most of Brigus had.

Brigus, I said, does not take advantage of the seascape. Youve got small windows in your houses.

We have to keep the saltbox warm. Lovely big windows make the draftiest of rooms.

But the view, Tom.

Why would we want to look at the salt water? When we're out on it all day long and that's enough of it.

This shut me up for a while.

37

Tom Dobie's foot brought up solid in the snow of Pomeroy's garden. He banged something free, a dark log. He tilted up the log and pushed snow and stiff grass from a face. We gouged soil from the eyes with our thumbs. A woman's face. A grey, tarnished head and shoulders and sweet waist. Her torso was sawed at a slant, from spine to navel. A figurehead. She had pointed a schooner out of harbours, Tom said. Had leaned her way across water and directed men into port. I turned the wet figurehead over and asked for it. And Mrs Pomeroy said of course, without a thought to it.

We carted her back to the cottage. I left her, elevated, to dry slowly in the woodshed. Then scraped her with a rasp and sandpapered her and doused her with preservative. I painted her skin white, with blush in her cheeks. I dyed her hair black. I gave her a necklace and daubed her earlobes with gold fleck. It was silly, and the whole time, while my skill as a craftsman showed through, I laughed at the joke. I'll set her up, I told Tom, where every man may look at her.

I let Tom varnish her once a day for three days.

We bolted her to the lintel over the front door.

Her breasts of hard wood, straining from the house. Shiny and wet. A bowl of goldfish and lava rock.

Tom: You know who she looks like?

I didnt.

Emily Edwards.

It was erotic. It was the first thing Tom had seen, the first artifact, that caused him to fall in love with made things. I could tell that he looked at a boat now and saw the work that went into making it sail. How a window let in light yet kept weather out and detoured the weight above it around the sills. I saw these notions revealed to him.

The Pomeroy cows kept us company. Their brown-and-white faces smudging the windows. I wanted a fence up for Kathleen's arrival, I said, and a gateway arched over with the rib of a boat.

We could put up a garden rod fence, he said.

I want pickets and posts. I want you and Stan Pomeroy to cut me a fence.

Tom witnessed my certainty and could not fully articulate the delight in his skin.

38

Lonely. I met Kathleen Whiting when Abbott Thayer was giving a talk on art. She entered the theatre late, as I had done. She was with Gerald Thayer. I was leaning against the acoustic wall and I saw them arrive. She stood at the open doors as we waited for Abbott Thayer to finish taking questions, the doors closing behind her on their pistoned hinges, her hands flat against the doors, slowing their progress. I want, Abbott Thayer said, everyone to get down on their stomachs. Please. I want you to approximate the viewpoint of a predator.

Some of us lay down.

Kathleen stared at the floor, shy, ears listening to Abbott Thayer, her hands flat in front of her as if in some eastern prayer. It was that consideration and grace.

Later, Gerald introduced us. She was his cousin. Abbott Thayer's niece.

Kathleen said, I like to think of people afterwards.

What do you mean.

You can admire them as youre with them. That's one thing. But then you can reflect on them. How people do things. Their consideration.

Me: I like realizing good deeds.

Kathleen: But also funny things. For instance, I heard this woman just now saying that this lecture was like the play the other night. And what she meant was that they were sitting in the back then too.

I didnt get it.

It wasnt the content, it was the environment.

39

We had a feed of bread and molasses, or loaf and lassey, as Tom Dobie called it. We sat on the front step under the figurehead and ploughed into it.

Captain Bob's clock, Tom Dobie said. You seen that?

The one with grouse nesting on top.

Tom: I saw it come in aboard the *Morrissey*. I was tying her up. Didnt know what it was, I was only four or five. Did a cleat hitch with the painter while the men carried it off. The clock come in a shipping crate, and when it hit the gangplank I thought a coffin. I tried to think who was missing, who could fit such a box. Then the crew tilted the coffin on end and a bell chimed and I realized its true nature. Even so, something of the coffin is still in the clock.

Me: There's something dead in the telling of time.

40

We dug out what Tom called the dung sink by the kitchen door. I was frightened to think that my children would have to live in this cold. Cool air had brought in the pack ice. You couldnt see the ice, but you felt it on your breath in the mornings. I wrote Kathleen, You'd better wait. Wait another month.

I woke up at dawn and punished the fireplaces and made coffee. I slopped the pot liquor from the night before into the dung sink and walked along the hill above the cottage with my portable easel, my box of paints, and a square of canvas. I looked at Brigus from the hill. The boys had pushed slub ice under the bridge and that allowed the surface to catch over smooth. Then they let her wait to mature like they were waiting for a crop to grow.

I painted a picture for the joy of painting.

The pans of ice in the harbour knit together. Now they could skate under the bridge and out into the bay. It was healthy ice. One boy skated with a chair. Pushing the chair along.

They skated past the spars of the sunken Bartlett collier. The spars stood out of the ice and one boy climbed up into the rigging. The boat was still carrying four hundred tons of coal on the bottom of the harbour. The spars sticking up out of the ice as though two different dimensions were merging into one, some kind of collage gone wrong.

Farther out the boys unlaced their skates and copied on the loose pans. When I say copy I mean they leapt from ice pan to ice pan in a game called steppy cock. Until they were in the strain of the Head, near the edge of what Tom called the blue drop, or open water. The ice cakes were big enough to hold one boy. They ran and hopped, sinking and tilting the pans until their feet were soaked. There were no seals here, the seals were thirty miles out, on fields of ice, and while most steamers were congregating in St John's, Tom Dobie was promised a berth on the *Southern Cross*, which would take on crew in St John's and then dip into Brigus before returning to the Gulf strait. Tom wanted the berth, but Rachel Dobie said she disapproved and I was urging him now to stay with me. They could sell the berth, she said. And Tom could work for that fine young American. Me.

The boys would lean their wet rubbers up behind the stove, the toes of the boots filled with hot dried green peas. And in the morning they'd be dry.

I delivered my worn boots to Marten Edwards. He thought they could be salvaged. And I want, I said, you to make a pair of seaboots for Tom Dobie.

It'd be easier, he said, to order a set from Bud Chafe.

I agreed to that. And also picked out a sealskin coat. For myself.

41

The last night I had with my wife. I did not want to make love and Kathleen said, I love you. She asked, Do you love me?

You shouldnt ask that, I said. You should just let me say it.

You can't even say you love me.

Those were my last words to her that night. And in the morning she rinsed the coffee cups with that firm mouth and this was before the children rose and I was thinning out my father's suitcase. I had an urge to tell her then. Just to melt the firmness. I wanted to take her shoulder and turn her to me, to lead her to the bed. I felt the urge in my chest, but I was late with packing and could not make the urge compelling enough.

When we met at that lecture of Abbott Thayer's she was seventeen. I moved to Monhegan and wrote to her. I met Jenny Starling and started having an affair. Through the fall I wrote

Kathleen. I wrote fifty-three persuasive letters and she wrote thirty-five encouraging ones back. At Christmas I convinced her to visit Gerald and Alma in Monhegan. But even then we were polite and shy and formal until the drinking began. Jenny was there — it was her birthday. There were several Monhegan artists there. I put my hand on Jenny's waist. Kathleen saw the hand and walked out of the kitchen. Jenny has an outrageous waist. Gerald was loaded and upset because the dog was gone. Tiff's gone, he said. He was reeling about the rooms in slow motion.

After blowing out her candles Jenny said, Thanks guys, for everything.

Speech, Gerald said. Say something.

Jenny, deadpan: Thanks, guys. For everything.

That repetition, said two different ways. She was saying, I've enjoyed fucking all of you.

We went out to the back porch to look for Tiff. Kathleen was not there. Jenny said to Gerald and Alma, I miss the sex. That's the main thing about not being in a relationship.

Gerald: Not that one-night stands arent an option.

Jenny: No, but you dont want to live on only that.

Gerald leaned against me with his forearms.

Me: Youve got New York hands.

So what are we gonna do, Alma said, about the aching void in Kent?

Me: Why can't anyone call me Rockwell?

Gerald: Because Rockwell sounds like a made-up name.

Rockwell is my secret name. It's my father's name. I will name my son Rockwell.

I wonder, Jenny said, if we should all be having illicit affairs.

She was talking about us. The thing we had was private and I could not promise her anything.

Gerald's finger in the air: Let's settle the question of Kent.

Me: I guess youre medics of the soul. Youre just gonna put your heads together.

Gerald laid his head on my chest. To me: She's the prettiest thing to piss through a lock of hair.

Who.

That Jenny.

Jenny and Alma both heard this. It made Jenny put on her coat.

Jenny: Can someone walk up the hill with me?

We were all standing in the kitchen. Wondering now what to do.

Gerald: Just stick your tongue in my mouth and everything'll be fine.

How long, Alma said, ignoring her husband, can Rockwell Kent go around idly having fun?

Gerald, slumped against my chest: Forever. I've seen guys —

But what's the best. Arent you becoming interested in some woman?

I shook my head. I looked at Jenny. Kathleen was in the living room.

There's no need, Gerald said, to be hasty.

He's twenty-five, Gerald. Do you think anything he does now will be hasty?

Me: Thank you, Alma.

Gerald: Oh where's my dog.

Tiff's around, his wife said.

No. He's run off. And now he's gone.

Have you checked upstairs.

Mournfully: No.

Me: I'll look.

Gerald had me pinned to the rail. Alma pried him off, but she couldnt hold him. A slump to the floor.

Get up, Gerald.

I'm comfortable. He said, I do not want to be medicalized.

He was gesturing to the ceiling like a Greek philosopher with a moral point. Only the tip of his finger sober.

Okay I'm leaving, I said. And as I walked down the hall Gerald tackled me. He lunged at my knees. I see the pinrails in the staircase fly past me. The floor smack me in the ear.

Okay, I said. Maybe I'll stay for one more.

I decided to go upstairs to check on Tiff. Kathleen in the front room. She was listening to a student of Abbott Thayer's. We have to find Tiff, I said.

Of course.

I held her hand and we took the stairs. Her hand was cold but confidently in my hand. The doors were all closed. She led me into a dark room. She hauled me into herself and shut the door with her foot. I can smell her now, the heat of her face. She said to me, Why is it that when you talk, people look over their shoulders.

Kathleen Whiting pulled the shoulders of her dress down. She tugged at my belt. I love my name, she says. My name is an old name. I like Levi as a name. Isnt that a sexy name, Mr Kent?

I'm half tempted to steal. You have to get someone pregnant, Mr Kent.

Who.

Some youngster, I dont care.

This shocked me into action. I lifted Kathleen Whiting's dress and pushed her to the wall. I pressed my hand between her legs and her head leaned back. I had my hand on her. I sunk to my knees and buried my face in her. She opened her legs. Her hand on the back of my head. She pressed herself into me, using her head against the wall as purchase.

Where the hell is my dog.

Gerald had swung open the door. He slumped against the moulding. We saw, from the light in the hall, that there was a baby in the room. We were in the baby's room. Gerald was careful getting to a chair. He was judging the air with his bent knees. He lit a cigarette.

Tiff sauntered in. Tiff old boy.

Then Gerald saw us for the first time. I stood up.

Kathleen was showing me to the bathroom.

Yeah.

We can't leave you here.

Gerald: I'm okay.

You might fall on the baby.

Jesus I'm okay.

You should go lie down, Gerald.

Naw. Gonna do something here with old Tiff.

Kathleen: Youre falling into everything.

You make it sound like I'm incompetent.

Gerald now come on.

And she convinced him to leave. He was convinced.

Kathleen: Isnt he great?

This was after Gerald left.

Me: A little bit too much Gerald. You know, here's Gerald coming at ya.

Youre not jealous are you?

When drunks arent drinking, I said fondly, theyre good company.

I slept on the Thayer couch. I was up early and put in a fire and heated water. I washed the floors. I did the dishes. The Thayers ginger on the stairs with their hangovers. Coffee, put some coffee on.

Gerald: I thank you for doing the floors. And for doing the dishes.

Alma: And what about for doing your cousin?

Me: I think she did me.

Oh, Kent. Kent you are so full of yourself. And a bad man. She's seventeen.

Gerald had sat on someone's guitar. It was Jenny Starling's guitar, I said. Gerald is pissed off about breaking it. I'm sorry all right?

I had seen Kathleen straitlaced. Then twelve hours later I had seen her shit-faced. She was the last up. She took me aside.

Kathleen: So. If we both enjoyed ourselves, I'm wondering. I mean, we were very drunk. And perhaps.

What.

We should see.

Okay, so what do you suggest.

When youre back in New York. You invite me to dinner.
All right, I said.

42

Five hundred wet starlings landed on the roof. I could hear
them clattering along the cavestrough as I worked. The rooms
were light. The percentage of wall devoted to window was
good. Across the water I heard poor sounds. Sounds of hollow
tin and hungry animals.

It rained and washed the snow away. Rain thrummed on the
roof. It was a thick sound, like the pouring of berries from a
drum. The rain on the snow was like torn sheets of paper.

Tom Dobie: The more rain, the more rest.

He watched me paint and he asked about it. Why I painted.
It is almost, I said, a religious activity.

You believe in God?

In the religion of Christ. A person's own beliefs. I believe in
the will of the vision of one, with laws to protect the rights of
many. I dont respect the authority of the book or the church, I
said. I support the work of a man. I believe in the work.

Who doesnt.

My wife believes in the man. That the man wasnt himself,
but an agent for God.

Well, Tom said, I just believe there's got to be something
after.

March was mild and I had hopes. Even when all of them
were saying the worst wasnt over, I had hopes. I didnt stop

erecting fences to keep the Pomeroy cows out. I cleared a garden and burned a heap of old wallpaper. I built, with Tom, the extension to the house where I put my easel, a maple desk, a chair, and above it a small bedroom. Tom pounded a coin into the sill.

That'll keep money in your house.

The extension was eight feet by twelve feet.

That's for the little ones.

They be coming soon.

In April.

We stood by the burning wallpaper.

43

Tom: So what'd you do today.

I walked around town. I spent all day at it.

Tom: You must have walked around it twice.

Walking home at night. The blue acre of my snowy land, the dark blind house. Inside on the flat kitchen table I pushed my hand around until it found the belly of a lamp funnel. There were matches in a nook above the door. I fed the embers in the stove. I went to bed in my Arctic tent in the upstairs room. I pressed my feet against the canvas side of the tent and held my arms above my head to let the blood drain out of them. I let the blood pool in my torso until my arms tingled with a helium quality that made it easy to imagine I was floating. Then I prayed the way I'd heard my father pray. At this moment I thought I too was a methodical man with no initiative who copied the ideas around me. Very good at emulating the nature I admired, but the life I lived was not my own. It was a construct of someone else's will. I was only seven when my father died. I thought this without forming the thought into words. It was a feeling I had, or a witnessing that I would, in later years, begin to pronounce on. If you were to look at me here you would see the muscles in my brow working and the facts accumulating between my outstretched arms, and you could predict that I might, if I were freed up to ponder, come to some true thought about my predicament at the age of thirty-one, some sad and wondrous realization that I was alone in the world and yet very lucky and loved.

44

The ground melted from behind the houses. The ponds were covered with sleepy ice, Tom called it. A field opened up beside Beaver Pond. The field was about the size of a tennis court, a flat field. Would it be good for tennis. Would it. I thought about this as we whitewashed the clapboard, painted the trim, and tarred the spruce shingles. Tom said, Let's go over and look at it for God's sake.

I paced it off. Whose land is this.

You better ask the Bartletts about it.

Tennis would go over well, Bob Bartlett said. The pharmacist Jim Hearn. He owns that land.

I approached him. Hearn was a character of suspicion. He walked about with just the fingers of his hands in his pockets. He was a big, tall, bald man with a red beard. It was as if all of his energy had gone into muscle, but he was unable to tap into it. It was a resource lost to him, and instead he devoted his strength to carrying around this girth. He asked questions to which he knew the answers. What else. He was the kind of man who wore all his money and it was not much money but he made it look like more money. So if you stared closely you saw that the watch was gold plate and the wool of his jacket was thin, if well cut. He stood very erect, to get all he could out of his six feet. Sniffles.

Jim Hearn was delighted. Yes yes of course. Pleased I had come to him. It's a field for making grass, he said. Not much lost to the ponies and he did not care to play, but yes, he said, go to it on the field.

Should I pay you for it. Or should we sign something.

No need for that, sir.

I realized I had judged him and then I remembered the iceboats and thought, How mean of me. Jim Sniffles Hearn, a good man.

He was very excited about the tennis court. Or perhaps that he could be handy to me.

He said a woman had just come in to see him saying her tata fell. He examined her. It was the worse smell he's ever. He wiped his nose. She was wearing several layers. He lifted up the skirts and saw tendrils of a potato creeping out of her cervix. Her uterus had dropped and she stuck a potato up to hold it in. It had rotted and fallen down.

Some things you'd rather not know.

45

I walked to the telegraph office. I needed to wire New York about a chest of tools. They were my father's tools and I was worried, for they hadnt arrived. The man before me was sending a message to a Mrs John Burns in Chapel's Cove.

He said, I have berth on *Southern Cross*, sail in four days.

The cable officer: Youre allowed one more word, Mr Burns.

And he thought about it and said, Then put *Goodbye*.

The seal hunt. I was next.

Please put a search on this parcel, I said. It is a chest.

Best talk to the shipping agent. George Browiny.

Where is he.

He'll be back now the once.

I waited. Then George Browiny came in with a load of trout. He'd been ice fishing.

Oh won't be long now sir, he said.

He did not even look at my receipt.

It's a big old black walnut tool chest, I said. Full of tools and it is late.

George Browiny: Won't be much longer.

Again, not a glance at the description or my insurance number.

They are good German tools. The Germans, I said, make the best tools on earth.

We'll send a boy over, Mr Kent.

On the way home I saw the *Southern Cross* turning the point into Brigus. Tom was chopping wood.

Look at that boat, I said.

She's not a boat, Tom Dobie said. She's a vessel.

What's the difference.

He held up a junk of wood.

A boat her rudder got to be out of doors.

And a vessel?

Encased.

He put his hand over the wood.

46

A lick of paint. I was pretending to be Kathleen, arriving at the house and appreciating the colours I'd chosen for the rooms. And now the cleanup of my brushes. The wild yank of turpentine in the nostrils. How old was I when I realized that turpentine is not chemically different from paint. Often a weak substance is used to dilute the strong: it's not opposites that annihilate but a weaker solution of what is powerful. The thrust behind vaccines. Same with character, or love. We hate to see a weaker form of ourselves. It reminds us of our faults.

47

Bob Bartlett invited me down to the wharf. It was busy with men.

The *Southern Cross*, he said. Last of the wooden walls.

She was anchored out in the frozen harbour. Men were gathering up their provisions, tugging on jackets made of sail canvas. A man stood patiently while his wife looped a tow

rope over his shoulder. Gaffs in hand, flagpoles, and sculp-
ing knives.

They call the hunt the swilery, Bartlett said, and Brigus
invented it. Ponies and carts of provisions and men's chests and
barrels of pork and sacks of flour. For three days she'll be in
port, he said.

Men were dragging their gear out in rodneys pulled over
the ice. Crew on the *Southern Cross* flung over oiled ropes to
winch up the works. We walked out on the ice to the wooden-
walled vessel and stood under the luff of her bow. She was tall
above us. She was one of the last to rely on wind. Fitted with an
engine just to round her out. She had three masts, and all her
sails were hoisted. Her decks covered with rough board and rails
wrapped in rope to keep her clean from the work of the sealers.

They take birch rind, Bartlett said, and lime. Shake around
the beams to keep the hold sweet and dry.

Why is she full of sail?

Dry her canvas. When theyre dry they'll brail her gaff
topsail.

These sealers were from Colliers and Cupids and Hibbs
Cove and Port de Grave and eight from Brigus proper.

Bartlett: Would love to go myself. The Gulf hunt is a useful
one. Usually a good haul. Can never tell, though. Never had a
good voyage. Swilers, they think they'll make fifty dollars. One
year, I think — one year there was a crew that made fifty dollars. So now that's always the feeling. Could make fifty dollars.
But they got nothing else to do this time of year. Come look,
she's full of coal.

He nodded at the men.

You need all that coal?

They all knew him.

This man, Bartlett said, wants some coal.

Seven tons, I said.

We'll ask, the man said, George Clarke about it.

That's as good as done, Bartlett said.

So youre saying George Clarke is captaining the *Cross*.

Yes, Father was supposed to, but he's not feeling number one.

All these men, Bartlett said, they come here last Christmas to sign up with Father. Some like Tom Dobie they got a secure berth they can sell it now. Tom Dobie got five dollars, did you know that?

So he's decided not to go.

Sold it to Rose Foley's youngster. Look at them line up for their four fathom of ratling. Watch that man cut it with an axe on a block. And see, theyre all wearing sealskin boots waterproofed with Stockholm tar. You could learn a thing off them, Kent.

For three days they loaded provisions and got the ship in trim. I went aboard to see George Clarke and he agreed to sell me the seven tons of coal. I hired four men off the *Cross* to help me sled it over. We used a block and tackle to pull it up the embankment. They dumped it off near the Pomeroys'. A castle of black rock stunningly majestic against the white snow.

What, Bartlett said, youre making your own naked man over there.

They said their goodbyes on the stagehead, and we wished the men luck. The younger sealers were delighted but wore the air of propriety. They had all shaved their faces that morning, and it would be the last time any of them shaved.

The seal patch was passing north to south about thirty miles out. But they were heading west, to the back of the island and the Gulf of St Lawrence. That was the herd the *Southern Cross* had drawn.

Bartlett shared around a bottle of port. He rose a toast, Bloody decks to em!

They all thought George Clarke a solid skipper.

Bob uncoupled his telescope and we took turns studying the *Southern Cross* as the men tracked her through the ice. The men had sawed chunks of ice from her prow, sang shanties as they sawed. Chunks were hauled up onto the ice as they were cut. So there was a wall of ice alongside her.

There is no excitement greater, Bartlett said, than sailing a sealer out of Brigus.

There used to be forty vessels in line, he said. Sixteen thousand men in parade. You could walk across the harbour from your house to Tom Dobie's and not get your feet wet. Well, those were the days.

The *Southern Cross* loaded up and hoisted mainsail but couldnt budge. She sat out there for the night, waiting for a swell to break the bay ice. That night we saw her forecastle lanterns, and by noon the next day she had tossed a kedge anchor to a passing ice pan. You could hear the men singing as they pulled in their mooring lines and slipped out for the ice-fields to the northwest and into the blue drop.

48

Bartlett: You better get your coal under wraps.

It's the end of winter, no rush.

He laughed. We got a long ways to go yet, Kent.

The cottage was deemed barely liveable by Tom Dobie and the Bartletts, and so I sent for Kathleen and the children. I had written all through February and March. I never called Kathleen a pet name, just Dear Kathleen, but I was warm and silly in the letters. I've never gone for pet names. I described vignettes of Brigus, always lighthearted and with hope. I described young Tom Dobie and what he thought of the figurehead. How Bartlett barely looked at her but said that I had indeed knocked together a rough likeness of Emily Edwards.

There was something Bartlett could not appreciate in the figurehead. But Tom, I could imagine him turning out figureheads a century ago for the bow of every schooner in Brigus.

It was interesting that I spoke of this wooden lady. That already my wife had a competitor.

Each day I'd try to appreciate something decorative, entirely without function. I said to Bartlett, Why is the trim on your house picked out in blue?

Just to ease the eyes, boy. Just for a bit of colour.

And all the gingerbread. For there was a heap of work in the eaves.

If I were building her, there'd be no gingerbread.

But you'll maintain it.

I'll hire two boys to paint it.

Bartlett could not make the leap. He thought my love for beautiful things extravagant, though he never spoke against it, and sometimes he would laugh at me.

Bartlett: Nothing useful can come of looking at what youre doing as anything other than a necessity for survival. As soon as you look at your work as something outside of you, then it's gone from you. Youre not part of it. You have to be a part of it.

This was a man who had driven a wooden boat through ice into the Arctic Ocean for nothing more than the illusion of being at the geographic top of the world.

Deep down, I said, youre an artist too.

Deep down I'm a survivalist. Nothing matches sailing out of Brigus in a sealer, Kent. That's the height of spirit. An explorer, he's going to achieve something. Soldier too. But a sealer is going to decide if his wife and babies will have molasses with their fish. Deep down, Kent, we're all for survival — even you.

Tom and Stan delivered a cartload of freshly sawed pickets and posts. The pickets varied in length. I asked about this. Tom said, Who owns the fence — the house or the hill.

The house, of course.

So the fence should stay level with the house, not the ground.

We measured the slope and made an allowance, and the railing along the fence stayed horizontal. It was true, the fence was part of the house now, instead of belonging to the hill.

But I differed with Tom on the arrangement of pickets, railings, and posts. I thought it looked smarter to have the pickets all flush on the inside, and to give the railing to the world.

You sir, Tom said, are always looking for beauty in things.
And why not?

Well what is a fence for?

To demarcate property.

Tom paused, and said deliberately, A fence is to keep things out.

I would agree with that.

Then why offer a railing to an intruder? Why make it easy for him to boost himself over your fence?

And so we built the fence with railings and posts inside.

49

Each day in late March the weather grew milder, the harbour a quilt of white acres stitched with blue. I woke up naked and stood at my door naked. The physical weight of sunlight shooting down the barrel of the harbour. The brooks were full, their shells of ice melting hollow. Blades of grass shot up through the snow. I reached up and smoothed the wooden breast of my figurehead. I scratched my balls, letting the sun hit me in the thighs and belly. I like walking around naked. I like seeing, in the hall mirror, my cock and balls hanging like fruit. I posed in a tennis volley stance. I dreamed of my tennis court. Maybe by April, I thought. I thought that, even though Tom reckoned on clearing Jim Hearn's land in June.

I walked, barefoot and naked, to the brook for a pitcher of water. My cock hauled itself up with the cold. A bumblebee flower pushed itself out of the snow and it was hard to believe men were swiling on ice pans just thirty miles north of here. The Pomeroys were letting their horses out. One was pissing near my load of coal. I was convinced that the old Norse story of finding grapes here was true.

I dressed and walked into town. Outside Chafe's, Mose Harris read the newspaper. He was in his shirt sleeves.

Nice isnt it, he said, when you can go out in your figure.

Pardon?

No need for a coat.

Yes, it's a relief. What's new?

The wireless messages, Mose said.

From the sealing fleet.

With so many of the men gone, Brigus was imbued with an absent potential. That it could continue without the men, yes, but only on the promise of their return. A sudden immense profit would then occur. The cove ticked over without them. The word *potential* seemed to fit the agitated state of the community. It was like a kettle boiled dry.

As Tom and I worked on the cottage Bud Chafe and Tony Loveys visited me. One brought a bottle of cow's milk and bread, the other had goats' skins for the floors. The rector came by and told me of his service on Sundays, and was I handy with pianos. They'd all heard I slept on boards, in a green tent, so Marten Edwards brought, on his head, a feather bed and a pillow wrapped up in a spare sail.

Nice hat, I said.

My Sunday best, for you and your wife.

You got a humour.

To match your own.

We pulled it up the stairs to the bedroom. They were happy to see a man receive a real bed.

Marten Edwards: We heard you slept in a tent, but we didnt believe it.

I should put it away, I said. It's warm weather now.

None of them was sure of that.

Marten Edwards: You been walking in your softs?

He noticed I was barefoot. I've been known, I said.

I'll get a move on, he said, fixing your boots. For the weather won't hold.

I'll miss the tent, I said. Sleeping in it reminds me of my father.

This was my old bed, Marten Edwards said. He's new. But when the wife died I couldnt sleep in him no more. Nothing wrong with him. Just memories.

I was glad for Marten's bed, if only for Kathleen.

But the weather. A southerly wind pushed the pans of ice out the bay, and it opened blue and calm. On a bright Sunday, the brook trickling madly, on my way to the Church of England, the church of my childhood, I passed Mrs Pomeroy.

I said, Lovely day.

She said, We'll pay for it.

What did that mean.

I walked over the bridge to the inner harbour and met up with Tom Dobie and Bob Bartlett on the Stand, past the United Church. They had no bell then, just the flag of St George raised up. The old men knocking their pipes empty against the step rail. I said to Tom, The rector called on me.

Tom Dobie: To claim you.

Yes, I guess he wants my number. With all the young men gone sealing it's a dull church.

Bartlett: But youre an atheist.

I like the story of Christ, the images. My wife is Christian.

And the architecture appealed to me. I love being inside churches. This one had a high ceiling supported by carved timbers, and stout pillars connecting Gothic arches. It resembled the framework of a ship's hull. As if we sat underneath an overturned boat. The church had recently been electrified, and there were oil lamps refitted with bulbs along the choir archway and over the organ console, bulbs with milk glass reflectors hung on long cords down the aisles. The English Bevington pipe organ was a beauty and forty years old.

On the walk home I exclaimed how profound the weather was, so beautifully clear. I had received a letter from New York, complaining of the snow.

That's a bad moon, said Bob Bartlett, and we all looked up. We're in for dirty weather.

I questioned him on this.

I never knew it to fail, Bartlett said.

50

On the last day of March big blossoms of snow fell softly. I met Bob Bartlett in Chafe's. The old woman is plucking her goose today, he said. On the walk home the blossoms turned heavy and the snow fell faster. Wind twisted the snow sideways.

Through the afternoon a storm invaded the bottom of the bay. I brought in a load of coal and got the heat belting. The wind piled up weather into the Head. It covered, in a rude minute, the bright fields of Brigus with snow. It bleached the barrens and dumped wet hail and wind up through the valley, a swipe of a giant white, brainless paw. Three feet of snow on the field I thought could be a tennis court. The evergreens by the brook were full of complaining sparrows. Through the night I listened to the house creak and buffet, the foundation groan. In the morning there was a calm and I could not hear a thing. Even the fire was out. It was colder without the tent. From the bedroom window I melted a patch of frost off one of the panes: the world was white and newborn. I was freezing. But at the top of the stairs I could tell something was wrong. The light reflecting up the stairs was different. It was a whiter light, as if an animal waited for me down there. I made my way down. Here was frost on the rug, the tabletop white, even the fireplace painted with snow. A drift four feet high at the open front door. A chunk of Greenland had pushed into the room. I put in a fire, but the chimney was clogged. I dressed and used a bucket for a shovel to make my way out to the doorway. I swept up the snow with a broom. A wind was picking up, a new storm. The sill and hinges frosted shut. I had to chop through the ice with an axe to get the door shut. A ragged flurry, the wind stronger. And so I abandoned my house for the Bartletts'.

I had to use the rock face to guide me into town.

On the path I met Marten Edwards, all hunched up with a package under his coat.

Can I ask, he said, what youre doing out.

I could ask the same question.

Thought I'd deliver them afore the weather got desperate.

He had my boots wrapped in paper tied in string.

Well, youre a diligent man.

It be my own sake I'm thinking of. He laughed. My reputation.

We moved into the rock face, let the slabs of rock take the brunt of it.

I explained the drafts in my stove. Why I was abandoning the house.

Oh yes, that be a cranky house you got there. At least you got a useful bed.

I might return to the tent tonight.

I understand. You got to get some coal. Get some heat into her.

We were standing next to the heap of coal. It was under three feet of snow. That, I said, is my coal.

Yes, we noticed you didnt settle that away properly.

We stood sheltered in the cleft of the rock face. Marten Edwards had my winter boots pressed to his chest for protection. We waited to see if there'd be a lull. We waited as though it were the storm's turn to speak. Then Marten Edwards took, deliberately, from his pocket a bent knife and cut the twine wrapping the boots.

I cut them down to the sole, he said, and replaced the heart and bottom. Then I put the uppers back on them. Theyre what you call fox boots.

He handed them to me and I put them on. I shoved my shoes in my pocket. The boots were smart.

He closed up his knife. I dented the knife in a fall four years ago, he said. Over the rock by Bartlett's wharf. When my wife died, it was a fall of grief. Landed on the knife. What made me turn to cobbling and smithing.

He rubbed the dent with his thumb.

What youre not a cobbler.

Fisherman. But nothing to cobbling. If you can open a fish you can close a shoe.

Marten, I am sorry about your wife.

I should marry again I'm sure.

It'll come, I said.

Marten assured me the wind would not abate, and so we buttoned up and steered towards town. We took turns in the front. The devil's blanket, he said.

51

Snow drove horizontally and slapped the windows white. It insulated the houses from sound. I made my way blind to the Bartletts', and they had tea and supper. I split some fresh boughs for the cow to sleep on. I could not believe the weather. I wouldnt take Bartlett up on spending the night in his bed. I'll be fine on the couch.

You won't be able to stay keeled on the settle.

I could have the maid's bedroom or the first-floor room. At first I thought he meant I could sleep with the maid. He said, I sent Emily home to Marten Edwards.

I laughed and Bartlett asked, What is it. And me: I'm just admiring your rose-coloured home-knit drawers.

You'll be begging for a pair.

I slept in Emily's bed. I slept naked, to have the sheets against me. I thought of her against me and dreamed of her. I settled down to enjoy this episode in her warm bed. If I'm ever in bed with a man, she said to me. On top of him. And lift myself up, press up with my arms and look down on him, it is then that we both get self-conscious.

I pushed her head into the floor. I twisted her head. I opened her legs, and through her open, familiar legs there's Kathleen, leaning against the doorsill of the kitchen. I move into Emily with my wife in the doorway, her arms crossed. There is a demon head in Kathleen's hair and the wire trap of my hand over Emily's mouth.

Morning. I am in a foreign room. My leg is twisted through the rungs of the footboard. Alone in a cold room, in Bartlett's house. I am glad to be alone. Glad that Kathleen is not around. So I dont have to hide anything.

I admitted, at breakfast, to pins and needles in my leg. When Emily arrived I could not look at her. I noticed her shape move around the room.

Sleeping in that bed, Bartlett said, I knew you'd get dunch. I hope you dont mind, Emily. We put him in your bed.

It's a very good bed, she said.

We walked over to the telegraph office, where half of Brigus had gathered for news. Marten Edwards was there. It felt awkward to have slept in his daughter's bed. To have had that dream that ended with his daughter.

Some storm, I said. I guess I said it cavalierly, for no one spoke.

Bartlett: All storms are ocean storms, Kent. And they are terrible.

Wouldnt they love, Marten Edwards said, an arm of land to tuck their schooner into.

I had forgotten that people were out on that. In ships. In that storm. I had forgotten that things happened beyond the skirt of vision laid before me.

That's what they got, boy. They got to St Mary's. For sure.

The telegrapher was excited. I got Dot and Dash, he said, right here. The *Southern Cross* has passed St Pierre and Miquelon.

Cheers.

She's rounding Cape Race the last they heard.

The *Southern Cross*, full of men from Conception Bay. The master George Clarke from down the road and the second hand was Jas Kelly of Frogmarsh and there were a hundred seventy-one others from all along the coast. All safe.

52

On April Fool's morning news came off the wire of the sealer *Newfoundland* in trouble. Its men were missing. A report leaked from the post office clerk that the *Southern Cross* had rounded Gallery Head and was holding up in Renews. Relief charged through the shoulders of the Brigus crowd. They could see all their men sheltering now in Renews. Renews was all right. The people of Renews would be useful to them. They were imagining the *Southern Cross* tied up and the men greeted, the seals aboard and the men waiting out the storm with a big feed of grub on the table.

But then that hope was met by a discouraging official report: the boat in Renews was certainly not the *Southern Cross*. You had to erase what you thought you knew. What was the last thing heard of the *Cross*. Actually, nothing. There was no report that stood up.

The *Nascopi* was fine at the icefields, and William Coaker was calling a halt to the season.

Bartlett: William Ford Coaker. He's a farmer, not a fisherman. And you know, Kent, Newfoundland has stamps for every kind of industry. Fishing, the swilery, woodcutting, mining, logging, but the one stamp theyve never made is for farming. You know why? Farming is useless. Coaker is a farmer from Green Bay and he heads up the Fisherman's Protective Union. Now tell me something queerer. First union in the New World. Now he's sticking his neck into the swilery. A farmer aboard to inspect the conditions of the men, and he has the gall to call a halt to it.

The union, Bartlett said so that everyone could hear, is strong around here. Too strong.

Then he changed topic, for he could be a diplomatic man. It was five years ago this very day, he noted, that Peary and Henson left me to make their dash to the pole.

And how was the weather.

At eighty-nine degrees? It was a clear, broad morning.

A boy thought Bartlett meant the temperature. He didnt know it could get so hot at the pole.

Latitude, son. Degrees of latitude.

I remained holed up with the Bartletts during these early days of April blizzard. It was frustrating. Mary Bartlett: You won't return to that drafty cabin. A rogue wind, she said, could funnel in off the lighthouse, recoil off Red Head, and come snatch that cabin up and dump it in the harbour.

It was a second chance to look on the town in winter.

53

We woke up to news on page four of *The Evening Telegram*, fresh off the train — news of fifty dead off the *Newfoundland*. Fifty sealers had frozen to death.

In our harbour we saw three small boats.

There's men in those boats, Bartlett said.

Open boats, Tom Dobie said. They look like rodneys.

Or a gunning punt.

Where they from.

Can they be from the seal patch.

Theyre not from no seal patch.

We went down to the government wharf and Bartlett pushed the *Morrissey* out. We steamed out through the young ice.

You can tell theyre in trouble, Tom Dobie said. Theyre barely rowing.

We got in amongst the three boat crews. Bartlett passed a looped rope down and each man pulled it over himself, and we hauled them aboard and gave them blankets. They were exhausted and cold. They were Carbonear men, and they'd been out for the day, one said. Just a mile out from home, on some swatchy ice, when the wind come up. No food or water or heavy coat, nothing on them.

Where's your breadbox.

Ate it out.

How long you been out.

Since yesterday last.

There was a butter tub in one rodney that the three crews had shared. They'd had hard tack and tea and two coconut shells with cork stoppers. One for molasses, the other for butter.

Bartlett: You men you all got the fiddlers.

Yes, we're beat to a snot. But happy now.

Sure that boat there is leaky as a flake.

She's a clever boat for all that. Kept up with the other two.

Yes, I suppose she's done you well.

The Carbonear men were like birds blown off course. The wind had driven them into the bottom of the bay. They knew that if they hung on they'd reach Brigus or Holyrood. Bartlett took them in and fed them pea soup and put them to bed aboard the *Morrissey*. They were frozen and hungry. Look at them eat, he said. Theyre face and eyes into it.

The next day, page six: seventy dead.

But no news of the *Southern Cross*.

Bartlett had to leave and I decided to go with him to St John's. He was on his way west, to the *Karluk* rescue. I needed supplies from town and I wanted to see the steamers come in. Bartlett kissed his mother and hugged his sister Eleanor and shook his father's hand and Rupert's. Then we jumped aboard the pony cart that had Tom Dobie at the reins to take us up to the iron horse for St John's.

I sat across from Bob Bartlett. Men were coming up to him. You know anything, sir? He did not. He said the prospects werent good, but we must hold our faith. Faith. I thought of Kathleen. She said once that faith is summed up by Jesus and Adam. She was reading a *pensée* from Pascal. Morality, she read aloud, is summed up by concupiscence and grace. You believe that? I asked, What is concupiscence. Kathleen: It is the inception of desire. Yes, Kathleen, I believe it.

St John's. Bob and I stayed in a hotel on Cochrane Street. Across the road a fire had burnt down three houses, leaving just their chimneys. We walked over and Bartlett leaned into a fireplace. If a chimney, he said, is tall enough you can see stars even in the middle of the day. Take a look. I stretched in and looked up. And yes, deep down the black telescope of the chimney I saw a pin of light. That single star so deliberate, it looked fake. It was the fleck of white one leaves on the black pupil in a painting.

54

Theyre coming in.

Bartlett was shaking my hip. He was barechested, his trousers on. It was six in the morning and freezing. He had an enormous chest. It was when he was sideways on that you noticed it, when he bent over to pull on his socks. The swilers, he said.

I dressed and followed him down to the harbour. The snow had melted and frozen again. Bartlett passed me a slice of bread with molasses, and the bread had chunks of pork fat in it. I ate around the fat. There were thousands of men and women lining the finger piers, the air damp and heavy, their hands in pockets. Boys with oversized caps, their collars flicked up at the neck. Behind us people were carefully trudging down the steep, white hills, the towers of the Basilica breaking the cold plain of the horizon, the sun coating the rock of Signal Hill with a bright, thin icing. The delight and fright of a city in the bare morning. Men recognized Bartlett. He repeated the same conversation:

It was the *Newfoundland*'s crew what caught the brunt of it.

The *Bellaventure* had the men and would be first in.

Yes, followed by the *Nascopi*.

It was the *Nascopi* what ended the hunt, a man said, because William Coaker was on board.

Bartlett put a hand on the man's shoulder. The hunt was over, he said, because it was the thing to do.

He took me by the wrist and we pushed forward into the men. He could be intimate, he knew when to be intimate. He waded into the men, offering support, and they recognized that this was the fate sometimes when sealers went to sea and I was getting upset that nobody seemed to be outraged. It was Coaker who'd ended the hunt and no one was telling Bartlett anything different, at least not persisting. There was deferral. And I thought, There is something to be said for persistence. They were too passive for me.

The flags were up on the hill, so we knew that they were coming in. And then quickly this black vessel steaming hard into port. It had all its flags flying. It felt odd, the speed and the flags. It looked joyous. It belched its horn, zipped through the cold blue water, and sidled up to dock.

Bartlett: That's not the *Bellaventure*.

It's Billy Winsor, a man said. What a cunt.

Billy Winsor had spurted past the *Bellaventure* portside. Billy Winsor flying all flags fast into St John's harbour with a full load of pelts.

Bartlett: You hear that?

What.

There are no cannon.

I dont get it.

You win the race home you get the cannon. There are no cannon for Billy Winsor.

The men and women were fifty deep against the stageheads and finger piers. Billy Winsor tossing out a hawser, but the men at Harvey's refused to tie him on. He slipped down the harbour apron. Past us and farther west. A couple of sealers jumped over the side to tie on to stanchions and they were pushed back aboard. They found a spot near the shipyard.

Perhaps, Bartlett said, Billy Winsor is a man who believes that in the face of a tragedy, it is best to maintain the structure of tradition.

The slow nose of the *Bellaventure* rounded Signal Hill. Arms began to point. She swung her bow towards Chain Rock and then slipped through the Narrows to Harvey's pier. Her flag at half-mast.

Look at her forehatch, Bartlett said.

It was heaped with seals under a tarpaulin. I was surprised there were any seals aboard her. Why do they have seals aboard?

Those arent seals, he said.

Well, there's one.

Men were pulling at the tarpaulin, rope had iced onto the deck. They levered the stiff carcass of a big seal with blunt hatchets. They carried the frozen seal to the side as the *Bellaventure* moored. But the seal was not a seal. It was the pelt of a seal, and inside the pelt was a frozen man. You could see a sliver of his body through the open belly of the seal. His hands together, as if in prayer. They handled this body with no more care than if it had been a seal, for the men knew only one way to offload cargo. It frightened them to touch this half seal, half man, they were nervous around unlucky things. The hard, buckled body slid from ropes and thudded to the apron with the shock of a hollow weight. It is wrong for all the majesty to be gone from the body.

He crawled in there, Bartlett said, to stay warm.

The *Nascopi*, with Coaker aboard, docked beside the *Bellaventure* and the crew tumbled over the side to assist. William Coaker was a big man but not very strong. He had a cane. Constables pushed back the crowd, and I realized we were part of the push towards the harbour. I was leaning into the men in front of me. Stretcher-bearers carried off the frostbitten, but they could not get through. A pulse pushed us back and there was room. George Tuff, Bartlett said. We watched as George Tuff was helped off, determined to walk, and there were men with white bandages past their elbows and knees who were crying with pain at the thought of touching their limbs. Their arms pointing upwards, as though still in shock at the empty horizon. We pressed the crowd back.

One survivor: I was froze for two days and now I'm on fire.

Another: I'm so tired my eyes are falling together.

The men were ready to talk. Their gaunt heads and white hands. They described the wind and snow lifting off the white surfaces of the ice. Two crews watching as Abram Kean's *Stephano* vanished in the squall. You could still see her smoke. Then they walked away from this ship, as ordered by Kean himself. To kill seals and get back aboard the *Newfoundland*. But where were the seals? And where was the *Newfoundland*?

The dead men were laid out in the basement of the King George Institute. The corpses were covered in sheets along theatre chairs and on the floor of an empty swimming pool. They brought bathtubs from all over St John's. Nurses were thawing the bodies in tubs of warm water. Their knitted caps still frozen to their foreheads. In one tub they were coaxing the thawed seal pelt away from the dead man. Yes, thawing allows the human to return.

And near them, in the seal-oil factory, men were skinning thick layers of fat from seal hide. Billy Winsor's catch of whitecoats and older seals — the ones buttoned up the back — and large adult hood seals. The hide, Bartlett said, is sent to England to be worked up into leather. The fat ground up, steam-cooked, refined, and then sunned in glass-roofed tanks until it becomes pure, white, tasteless, and odourless: oil for soap.

In my hotel room I read a special edition of the *Telegram*. Now the paper's first few pages were no longer devoted to the advertising of Smallwood's chrome tan wellingtons (light as a feather, tight as a cup) or Sunlight soap at T. J. Edens. The front page, under a large black headline, spoke of the *Bellaventure*'s arriving in St John's with the bodies of the *Newfoundland*, of

Arthur English's account of his time on the ice. There was a photograph of George Tuff being helped off the *Bellaventure*, and there in amongst the heads of the men, my own face, mine and Bob Bartlett's.

55

Bartlett was angry at Coaker. He should know better, he said. Coaker's blaming Abram Kean. Kean could do nothing. Kean thought the men were safe. The problem was not Kean's arrogance or his lack of thought for the men, Bartlett explained. The problem was that the ship had no wireless. Political, Coaker makes it all political.

But isnt that an indication of the captain's lack of concern for the men?

Wireless is an expensive addition, Kent.

And its main purpose, I said, is perhaps to notify other ships of the welfare and whereabouts of their men?

This is true, Kent. But to say it the way Coaker is, it's as though Kean meant to do harm to those men.

Negligence is the charge, I believe.

Then I believe Kean did what was right and is certainly following precedent. Misfortune is what it is.

I thought Bartlett was misguided. I waved him off, though, with a feeling of loyalty and deep affection. Bartlett could delay no longer. He had his own men to rescue, and he was leaving sunken and serious. I gave him fifty dollars. It was my mother's money. Put this towards something, I said. Youre a good man. His last words to me: Dont make a scene.

I got my own supplies (fruit, nuts, lentils, and vegetables from T. J. Edens; photographic film from the Likeliness Shop) and headed back to the train station. I was early, so I stopped into the Anglican cathedral. Men were at work on the steps, a rope across and one red word: DANGER. I stepped across the rope. Inside, the organ. I'd heard the organ, it was the reason I went inside. And, regardless of the danger and the men at work, because the door was open. I like accepting unexpected invitations. Why? To avoid what I think is to happen next and to move myself into the unforeseen.

Inside, some scaffolding and one iron ladder. The organ played "Ode to Joy." There was a horn player. It was a strange tune in the face of mourning, but it felt oddly appropriate. There was just one man with a boy sitting in the pews, and I recognized the man's profile. They were sitting in the front, the man's legs out past the kneeler, his cane hooked over the pew. Leaning back and taking in the organ and the horn. It was William Coaker. I sat over to the side of them. He turned and saw me and nodded. My appearance is one of a foreigner. His shirt was undone at the neck and he was holding his brown tie folded in his hand in front of him. As if it were on a plate. It's the horn what makes the organ beautiful, he said, turning around to face me.

I introduced myself. Yes, he said. I've heard of you. The painter out in Brigus. I told him I admired him, his organizing the fishermen. That I was a socialist too, and an atheist, and believed in the struggle for labour. He was pleased to hear it, except for the atheism. A little inappropriate to say that here, he said.

But this is not the place to discuss business either, he said. Not in front of the boy.

I stayed on an extra day and visited Coaker at the offices of the Fisheries Protective Union. I showed him the letter of introduction from Rufus Weeks. That did not impress him. He gave me pamphlets to distribute to the men in Brigus. There are many men, he said, to form a cadre. Get Marten Edwards and George Browiny. Talk to Tony Loveys and George Clarke's family. A grieving family is always useful. Even Patrick Fardy. A one-legged man adds depth to a movement, though I admit he's pretty useless.

A cadre. Coaker was harder than I thought, but I admired his resolve. As I took the train back to Brigus, even I felt exhilarated by this new responsibility.

56

I would wear red socks, if red socks were plentiful or cheap or readily available. I would buy them and wear them. I thought this as I happily pulled on my cream wool socks. I opened the door to the grey day, a man wearing nothing but a pair of socks. This is the thing about eccentrics: they do not spend time looking for red socks. They may decide to wear them, but they are absent-minded. I stretched up and stroked the wooden painted breast on my figurehead.

57

By the fifth of April the *Southern Cross* was officially given up for lost. Precisely one month before, she had left Brigus on her way to the Gulf. The harbour had been clogged with slob ice and a hawser was winched out and the men, like a tug-o'-war, heaved the ship through the ice. The men had given thanks and I remembered how I wished I could have been with them. I wanted to be with those Brigus boys. There was a good chance the *Southern Cross* would have been first home, and that was what had sunk them. They probably went down while George Clarke was figuring out how to fly her all flags. He gambled with the greed and pride of being first. Weighed down with seals they struck a hard storm.

The people of Brigus grieved for their eight lost men and boys, and then they exhaled and entered the world again. They opened doors and shook one another and tried to discover what could be done now with eight of their best gone for good.

58

One dead man did return to Brigus — Miles Sweeney. He had died from a fall on the *Nascopi*. Miles had hit his head. He was put in a rough coffin made of narrow spruce boards, the seams of the box caulked with oakum and then pitched. One of the crew had prepared the body. The body was washed and clean clothes put on it. Coarse salt was packed around it. The shroud kept the salt in place. Gauze was laid on the face and a pint of rum poured over it. Then the shroud was sewn up from head to heels. The body put in the box and this placed on deck to remain there until the ship reached St John's, when it was passed on to the undertakers.

59

There was an assumption that the big ships were permanent, like a hill. One man might fall off or break his leg or freeze or drown. Fishermen were used to men in dories and small boats disappearing, even a schooner. But a steamer, even a wooden wall like the *Southern Cross*, promised some kind of permanent rigging on the ocean. There was something urban in a steamer, something of the New World that shunned the savagery of small things run on human power.

60

I watched April pass in mourning. I wrote to Kathleen that the town seemed dumbfounded. The Dobie boy was treated as though it were not conceivable for him to be alive. As though people forgot momentarily that Tom had not been on the *Southern Cross*, that the rest werent back with him, that he had sold his berth to Rose Foley's son. There was resentment that he had stayed to help the American, even when he gave Rose Foley back her son's five dollars. It was unfair. The absence of the men was hard to fill in. There was no satisfying story to explain it. There were no witnesses.

Thomas Connors, captain of the *Portia*, was the last to sight the *Southern Cross*, off Cape Pine. He came to Brigus. There was a town-hall meeting. She answered the *Portia*'s whistle, Captain Connors said. She answered it and he figured George Clarke would head her into St Mary's bay. But the storm, the high bulwarks, the heavy load, and the low-mounted engine. An act of God, they called it.

I stood up. I cannot let that remark go unchallenged. Acts of God, I said, are often an excuse to explain away human disregard.

That made people listen. They turned to me. I stared at Captain Connors and could sense these white faces turning to see who was talking.

It is the nature in which this hunt is run, I said. That is the problem. The priority is seals. The priority is profit for the sealing captains. George Clarke was only following orders. He was beholden to the merchants here in Brigus and in St John's. He had to be first home. He disregarded the welfare of his men. If only there had been a telegraph system aboard the *Southern Cross*, but the reason is, it's too expensive. And the only reason to have wireless is to signal the state of the crew. This tragedy would not have occurred, I said, if the fishermen were unionized. If they had a say in how the hunt was run. I have pamphlets.

I shook my yellow leaflets.

This caused much muttering and confusion.

Are you calling George Clarke to blame?

The man is dead.

Butterfly wings, one man said. Referring to the leaflets.

Patrick Fardy stood up on his crutches and came over to me. His bald head was sweating. He put a finger to my neck. Just watch what youre saying. He looked ready to ask me outside.

Thomas Connors continued as though I hadnt spoken. The *Kyle*, the *Seneca*, and the *Fiona*, he said, were all out looking for her. The *Bloodhound* had spotted a mass of debris ninety miles off Cape Broyle, but all hope was not yet lost. He made it sound like this searching for evidence was an example of the care given to sealers. He wished all the grieving families his prayers and optimism. When he finished men came up to him to shake his hand.

Nothing else was heard of the *Southern Cross*. Later in the summer there were reports of planks, pelts, and wreckage off the coast of Ireland. But they were just reports.

61

I wrote to William Coaker and told him of my mistake. He wired me back three cryptic words: CHECK AND MATE. I got the message when I went to the wireless office for news of my tools. I felt bad inquiring about them in the midst of these deaths. I felt my resistance was frivolous and yet I would wake up at night and think about that box with my father's tools and realize it was the sole important object in my life. Kathleen had sent them steamer freight a solid two months before and now I learned from the shipping agent, George Browiny, of their demise. In the storm that had caused the deaths and disappearances of so many, the *Sydney* had run a reef in fog off Halifax.

Yes, so a delay. How long a delay.

George Browiny: I wouldnt call it a delay, sir. The freighter's sunk.

I understand that. I am interested only in my tool chest.

It is completely sunk. Everything on board gone. We have nine steamers and three wooden walls gone without a trace.

He was looking behind me at Niner Harris, next in line.

I dont want everything on board, I said.

All cargo is on the harbour floor, sir. It's been some awful bad weather.

If the cargo is on the bottom of the harbour, then it has hardly disappeared without a trace.

Oh they know right where she's to.

Well then I want someone to salvage it.

Look, Mr Kent. There are two hundred men lost at sea out there. The men and women in line here are looking for fresh word. There are small boats astray. There are cousins and uncles and children and mothers, all out of whack. Do you really want me to tie up the lines for a tool box.

They are my father's tools, with insurance.

Well, sir, you'll have to do without them I'd say.

Cable Halifax. Put up a twenty-dollar reward.

What a fuss for a box. Your insurance —

Good money for a box on the bottom of the ocean. They were my father's tools. They are of German manufacture. You dont find tools like that.

George Browiny: A man should not travel too heavy.

Just put up the reward and shut up about it.

When I left the wireless office, I regretted my rudeness. I had wanted to ask George about a union. I thought a man in his position, a shipping agent, could help be a leader to fishermen. When I turned around I saw Niner Harris and Tony Loveys and George Clarke's wife, all waiting for word on their relatives. But I had lost my tools — my father's tools, forged in a Stuttgart foundry from the hardest steel in the world. The tennis court was there, it just meant playing with snow up to your hips. My cottage was a sieve for drafts and my coal was under four feet of snow. Bartlett was gone. The monthly cheque from Charles Daniel was late. The food was bad. I was alone and damp and tired of winter. I wanted my family. My wife. My children.

EVENTS *TOO* BAD ARE GOOD

Events *too* bad are good. And one may some day learn, in honoring those factors that have made us men, to put the last straw first.

— Rockwell Kent
N by E, 1930

1

They had heard of my wife and they had heard of children. There were the other stories too. I had made my stand for a union, so people, naturally, had a desire to talk. These people had long lines of communication. Stories that had come from the post office and from the railroad station. But there was anticipation about the arrival of Kathleen.

Kathleen made my New York friends uncomfortable. She was a shy woman with a sensual presence. She looked about a room and sought out how she could help. She often did the chores she disliked doing, assuming that others disliked them as well. This is a strength of character. But in the long run, after a stay of several days, she bored my friends. Men are attracted to beauty and a sensual nature, but they do not want to be trapped by it. They appreciated her manners: she was a woman who made her bed in the morning, especially if she was a guest. Gerald said he hardly knew she'd spent the night. She left no evidence. She was an animal in that way, but out of politeness and embarrassment of her own functions. Kathleen was not a person to relax when a room was full of conversation. She seemed oblivious to silence. She was inward, but she held an enigmatic charm, an honesty that people wished to cultivate and preserve. People like the idea of the Kathleen Kents of this world existing as testaments to integrity. And there she was to answer for the greatest betrayal. I had asked her to decide for us. I had relinquished control of my future, this in the eye of a God I had rejected. But my God rested more on an ethical standard. I clung tenaciously to the desire to do good, and the only good was for Kathleen's will to be done.

It's true that the body will betray us and everyone we love will die. This was Gerald Thayer's big dread.

I never spoke a word of this. But a man and his acts cannot be separated for long. And Newfoundland possesses a circular wind that carries information. You can know a man in Newfoundland and never have met him. Men replacing men, men who have lived alone in tilts in desolate harbours. Alone in a cove for three generations. And if you slip by as a passenger in a one-handed dory the fisherman who is rowing will say, Never dodge in there, son. For that loner will take a shot at you before he looks at you. There are men alive today pinned to the stories of their grandfathers. They *are* their grandfathers, and in a sense the story of Rockwell Kent, the who of it, was being filled in by curious people. Who was this man who lived alone in that old Pomeroy house out along the far end of the harbour.

The private acts of an American cannot be silenced from the ears of a Newfoundland outport. He carries these acts in his eyebrows. They sift out of his trouser cuffs. They are as obvious as the acts he commits in public.

2

I hoped the weather would warm for Kathleen. She arrived with our three small children, after boarding a ferry to Port-aux-Basques and then the Red Cross Line to St John's. Rupert Bartlett had been in town and was pleased to chaperone her. They all came down the path to the house. It was a fine day, crisp air. Kathleen wore a pale blue skirt that curved out like a bell at the ankle. The skirt was printed with flowers. Or printed with the outline of flowers, for the flowers were white. I watched them stop at the Pomeroys' so Mrs Pomeroy could see the baby, and I could tell that Kathleen was polite about that but hungry to see me. She was enjoying the delay and I decided to meet them at the gate, not to go up to the Pomeroys'. The children ran ahead, the children we'd named after ourselves, throwing themselves at me and then Kathleen, who was holding a harness she had invented for Clara. Kathleen's body against me, her strong frame, the smell of the hair behind her ear. I love you. I love you too. Rupert with a tin of candies for the children and a pear for me.

What is it, Rupert said, about naming children after your-self. Rockwell and Kathleen.

He handed me the pear.

My wife and I have little imagination for names, I said.

Kathleen: The pear is from Gerald Thayer. He said you wrote about vitamin deficiency.

He sent me a pear?

There was a basket. The children ate the rest.

I held my wife. Kathleen is taller than me, with dark hair. She has a deep voice. I loved her so much and yet I did not love her. Explanation: I knew she was loveable. I knew she was good. I loved her body. I loved the privacy of knowing that I had, when she was breastfeeding Clara, tasted her. I loved making the goodness of her turn sexy. Of making her realize she enjoyed being carnal. She had virtue, and towards this I willed myself, even though I knew the outcome. I knew the outcome would be my sleeping with someone else and then the torment and exhaustion of fighting about it.

Rupert would be going. If ever, he said to Kathleen, you need anything, we're only across the way.

And oh —

He handed me a letter. It's from my brother.

Kathleen's bright, kind face. Her long hair. I loved her back. Let's take this letter for a walk, I said. We went out to the naked man with the children, to see the water and the Pomeroy cows. The cows were lying down. It's going to rain, Kathleen said.

Me: How many legs does a cow have.

Rocky: Four.

Me: Five. If you count their heads.

We were taking a little time to get used to each other. There was something stiff to Kathleen. Something unhappy that surfaced on her face, and then she managed to bury it. I did not want to point it out.

I remember walking down a street with Kathleen in New York. There was a new set of traffic lights, a man at the corner manually operating them. We held hands. Kathleen did not enjoy main strips: they were too noisy. I never noticed the noise — in fact, I loved the busy drive of intersections. So we were approaching the intersection, to cross over and enter a side street and the quiet. We had had bad luck. We had eaten a bad meal in a restaurant with bad service. I knew bad luck would linger. I held Kathleen's hand and I thought, If the light turns yellow I will leave her. And the light did turn. The man did not linger on the green for us. I could tell that Kathleen was blaming herself. We did not speak of it, but she knew what I thought. I was with a woman who cultivated bad luck and did not like loud avenues.

Rocky, the eldest: Where are the lambs and their mothers?

Me: Gone to slaughter.

And he gasped.

I rubbed my son's blond head and held him to my thigh.

Not all the lambs, sweetheart.

The Pomeroys kept lambs and we skipped over to the bottom of the garden. If youre up early, Rocky, you will see them etched in the new sun. They will all be baa baa black.

I loved my son. Years later, after the divorce, I took my son to Alaska. I was a man who liked to travel with his son. He was thirteen during Alaska and serious. He drew and he painted and he was careful to look at the world accurately. I did not teach him this. Or it was not a teaching of mine. I was reluctant to instruct my children on how to draw. I left materials out for them. There were pots of hard watercolours, lots of paper, crayons, and brushes. I let them mangle cheap brushes. But I would not tell them how to paint. If they asked a question I would be honest. I remember Rocky asking me once about the face. I said, Often people draw the face too big.

I opened Bob Bartlett's letter. I heard, he wrote, youve met Coaker. That youve spoken against Thomas Connors. He said, You know not what you do. Wait. Let me help you.

3

I stared at Kathleen, but she would not speak of it. I tried my child voice but she was reluctant. She set up her kitchen. She turned the rooms into family quarters. She dressed the children's beds. Something had happened to her and I decided to live with the silence. I can be patient.

Her feet were hot. I filled a basin with water from the brook. Sit down. There was a towel. I placed her feet in the basin.

Kathleen: I feel like I'm heating up this water with my feet.

Youre heating up my bathwater.

The snow melted off the black coal. Seven exact tons of it. I picked up a chunk. There is a glint to coal, it is built of wafers. To see the immensity of the load — these black blocks converted to heat, my children warm in their beds — it made me feel responsible and a good father. The Brigus men were puzzled by it. It was the only remnant left of the *Southern Cross*. The size of the order and that somehow I had robbed the *Southern Cross* of a power that might have saved it. Spring would soon be here, what was I doing.

It took three days to cart the coal over and house it in the shed. We started with pressed eggs of coal and then larger chunks on top. The heat made us happy. It surprised me. Tom Dobie told me this: You can be two of three things — hungry, cold, or tired. But if youre all three, youre doomed.

Kathleen had brought her guitar and sheet music, and she sang "Let Me Call You Sweetheart." I sang her a local song I'd learned from Rose Foley. I'd quote a verse here, but I dont like books with song lyrics. The one word in it I love is *pulverized*.

I told her she'd have to learn it — I'm so bossy. Though I didnt know I was bossy then. Something in my tone said her song was not enough. I was oblivious to this injury. I did not know that I was stifling her. I wished only to be unguarded.

4

I worked in the new little studio. I painted a picture of our house, the Brigus harbour in the background. I wanted to mark the occasion of our reunion. I could hear the children's footsteps above me. I ate Gerald's ripe New York pear. It was like I was savouring the fruit of the big city. That is so Gerald, to send me a pear. I saved the seeds and buried them in a pot on my studio window. They germinated. I'd plant them in the garden in mid-June, that's what Tom Dobie recommended, to avoid the last frost. The birches began to unfurl. All around me these buds of hope, but I knew there was something not right about Kathleen, and her mood made me despondent.

I had painted a picture of the house and was ready to put people in it. I had built a part of this house, had tarred the roof and painted the shingles. So it was odd to now be painting a picture of it. It was as if I were creating my entire world and then making art from it. I looked at the house in the painting. At the windows. I painted in Kathleen. She was leaning out the bedroom window — with despair, it looked like. Then me, slumped against the side of the house, head down. Boy, was that bleak. Was that it? Was that what I'd desired in coming here?

Her arrival was not fabulous. I did not know this fully until I started the painting.

I asked her to look at the painting.

What is it, I said.

It's upsetting.

Why is that.

It fills me with dread, she said.

I tried to say that it wasnt the full breadth of my feeling. Just on occasion. But I agreed it was a house of dread and I felt she was responsible. I was showing her the painting to make her confess. When I painted it, I said, it helped get rid of the feeling. Also, happy things are less interesting to look at.

Kathleen had nothing to say to that. She had three children to look after. It just made her sadder, that painting did.

I wrote letters to friends in New York. They were letters I did not show Kathleen because they were flirtatious and I didnt think she'd understand. I love to flirt in my letters, to men and women. Kathleen was trying to absorb Brigus. She had a camera, and she photographed the town. It made her seem less attached to the place. More of a witness.

She was a good photographer. She remained objective and she knew a good composition. She understood that the world appears smaller in a photograph. That grand things, like the shoreline and the horizon, appear thin and insignificant on photographic paper. She'd make sure to have a side of rock in the picture, or some substantial house in the foreground. When you looked at Kathleen's photos it appeared that you were looking at the land directly, and that you were in the land.

They were photographs with thickness. As though her eye encouraged a thickening, or strength. And something in the encouragement of thick landscapes informed me of her spirit. She was generous.

I realize now that I was judging her from the first moment of the day to the last, but judgment can often be a good judgment. She put up with it. Well, she put up with it for fifteen years.

Once I went for water and before I got to the brook I returned.

What is it, she said.

I just wanted to tell you I love you. I woke up this morning in love with you and I didnt tell you.

She did not stop clattering the dishes.

Do you love me, I said.

Yes, she said.

In an energetic way?

I love you throughout, she said.

I took the doors off to paint. I had a line of doors outside against the sawhorse. Doors outside, I said to young Rocky, appear very tall. They relax into a larger size of themselves, dont you think? If you build things outdoors that are meant for indoors, you have to measure very carefully.

He seemed to think about that. I did not know really what I meant. I liked talking about things I wasnt sure I believed. I preferred to speak of things as they occurred to me. Kathleen was the opposite. She liked to compose her thoughts, come to a conclusion, and then speak the full thought. I was often unprepared for a discussion, or too hotheaded.

We visited the Bartletts and the Pomeroys. Rupert liked Kathleen. I overheard them speaking of flowers. She made him comfortable, as they were both quiet people. I'm often anxious around quiet people. I want them to talk more. It was part of the reason I liked Newfoundlanders — for the most part they talk a lot, and conversation encourages more conversation. Kathleen and I read books and played music in the Bartlett parlour. We listened to Rose Foley sing. They had heard my flute and wanted me to play. We appeared at church and sang. I stood, upon request, to perform Schumann's "Two Grenadiers." I sang it in German and thought of my nanny, Rosa, who had taught me the language. Outside, after the service, I was applauded.

Rupert: You know German.

I learned it as a boy. But it has made me appreciate German culture all the more. They are quite a sophisticated people.

But the kaiser is a greedy throat.

Yes, I said. For him there is always more.

And speaking of more, we had little. Money. The allowance from Charles Daniel was always late. Even though I had lived much of my early life without money, I acted as though I had it. This comes from a privileged childhood. My father, a lawyer, was well paid. My mother was used to civic responsibilities. There was a strong house and my German nanny, Rosa. But when my father died the money went with him and we had to go live with my mother's sister. Rosa did not come with us. Losing Rosa was the worst of it, and it took me a long time to realize that her departure was not strictly a result of our lack of money. One afternoon I went upstairs because I heard my father laughing. I saw them standing by the mirror of my mother's dresser.

Rosa was bent over, her elbows on the back of a chair. My father behind her. My father was looking at himself in the mirror, and Rosa was holding her head in her hands, almost blissful, as my father pushed into her. It was the chair that my mother sat in to do her face. They were in their clothes, but it was Rosa I noticed. My father's hands were on her hips. I never asked my mother if she knew, but when my father died she fired Rosa immediately and we moved to my aunt's.

From then on we lived as though we had money because that was the only way we knew how to behave. I'm still this way. I dont own a wallet. My money is crumpled in my pockets. I dig into a pocket for money and the money is there. I've always felt money is my right, even though I had no cause to expect it. But I've learned that much comes to those who expect it should.

5

Tom Dobie had a few pots out for lobsters. It was early May.

Ever done that before?

I did. In a place called Monhegan.

Did I want to go with him. We have to leave early, he said. Before daylight.

I'm usually up, I said, before daylight.

It was still very cold. I went down to the stagehead. He'd brought the three-legged dog.

His name is Smoky, yes?

He's like a puff of smoke.

He's a beautiful dog.

Tom: He's all dog.

Smoky was a big black dog with white markings.

Tom Dobie threw a set of oilskins at me. I put them on, standing in the punt, as he rowed out to the dory moorings. The oars spattered with ice. They rubbed on the thole-pins. My oilskins went stiff from the cold. We reached the dory and Tom chopped ice off the gunwale, and then I helped him row out to sea just as the first light appeared. The dory's oarlocks were outrigged, which was unusual in a rural boat.

You got to go with a bit of technology, he said. He learned that from Bartlett.

We each took an oar, and then Tom told me to sit in the back and rest up. The shape of him rowing, against the dark water and the bright morning light, I knew it would make a good woodcut.

Cold enough for you.

I like the cold, I said. It's stimulating.

Yes, Tom said. It's nice to build a fire out of wood youve cut yourself to warm a little dory youve built yourself.

He had a stove under the seat, and wood in the cuddy.

We rowed out to the cork buoys for the lobster pots. Smoky sat behind me and licked the back of my head. The land being carved from the sky. The rub and sloosh of the oars. I was about to haul lobsters. I looked like a man of action. And yet the essence of me is a man of sloth. And I despise that man. I work against him.

I get up early, Tom. Because I want to lie in bed. And I work because I'm lazy.

That's a queer thing, he said. When there's a choice in the matter.

The dory was spruce, with maple runners and an oak footrest from a kneeling stool in a church. That's sacred, he said. We were still in low voices. Any place you pray in, they can't tear it down. Me and the Pomeroys we built her in February.

Who painted it.

I did.

It's a nice colour, the green.

Yes, it sets her off, dont it.

A cork buoy and a slanted rope down to the lobster pot. Hand over hand hauling it up, a wet wooden cage with three purple lobsters.

Looks, he said, like we'll have a good haul.

6

Kathleen had kept it to herself. She knew it was wrong, but she had to manage her feelings. I had to forgive her that. She had a letter and she was unsure of its contents. It was a letter from Jenny Starling. It arrived, she said, two days before they left. Its shape and colour and postmark of Boston struck her as hard. It made the first letter, from four years before, feel like a fresh incident. She was not happy to be the bearer of such a letter. She hated having it on her.

I would rather, she said, this woman dropped out of our lives forever.

Her entire trip had been clouded by that letter.

I had not heard from Jenny since we'd drawn up a settlement over the future of our son. This letter. I opened it.

Our son, George, had died.

I sat in the studio with the letter. Kathleen said I should be alone with it. I turned the painting *House of Dread* upside down. To make it less literal during this moment, but it seemed to intensify its loneliness. The letter was formal, brief, but tenderly inscribed. Jenny's penmanship, which I'd thought childish, now endeared her to me. That she had to tell me this. And how she must have looked as she wrote it. Where was her husband, and what did Luis Starling think. And had Luis Starling tried everything to save the boy. Yes, George's illness had been very bad.

I told Kathleen and she was sorry to hear it. There was peace in her face. She was kind to me. I was surprised by her sincerity. This boy had been an irritant to her, I understood this. But Kathleen was not flushed with any relief, only with regret at her tardy delivery.

Is there anything I can do, she said, in her child voice.

I'd like a bath, I said.

I'll heat some water.

The bath was good and it made me think of Gerald's bath, and how you could hear the subway in it. That made me think of Jenny. She was the kind of woman who, in the bath, turned off taps with her feet. When we returned to our Monhegan bedroom there would be coins on the blankets from our pockets. When she spoke. There was something rude in Jenny's face, yet she had a polished gait. I liked her shoulders, her big hands and wristbones, how they made her arms appear slender. Yes, there was something in the wrists, watching her open up a jam jar.

I'd met Jenny at a restaurant in New York. I was single then. I'd spent the day with Gerald Thayer. Gerald knew tricks that fascinated children. I watched him dress for his son and daughter. He had them sit on his bed: he was stripped to the waist after shaving, and he dried his arms with a towel then put on a dinner jacket. Just his bare chest and the jacket. He unhooked a blue shirt from his closet, held the shirt in his hands as though it caused a problem. It was as if he could not take the jacket off again. The children urged him, Take off your coat, Dad. No, he forced the shirt up the sleeve of his jacket. He bent his back, shrugged the shirt across his back, and then a blue cuff appeared at his other wrist as he buttoned up the chest. His children delighted. He did this nonchalantly, as if no one were watching him, as if they were watching a film of their father. I have seen him press his daughter's wrist and make her fingers curl. He was the reason I married and had children — the sadness of solitude is forgotten by those with families: they envy solitude, but only the peace of it.

Gerald had been dragging a finger down an open atlas. You want to get a piece of pie?

Me: I'm not hungry.

Gerald: What's hunger got to do with it?

Me: What are you doing.

Gerald: I'm looking up the Hellespont.

Did you find it.

What do you think.

He was staring down at the pale blue of the Mediterranean. It looked like a country.

What made you think to look in there.

Dont people go skiing at the Hellespont?

Me: People dont ski at the Hellespont.

It's something I've heard all my life, and three times this week — I'm realizing I dont know what it is, okay?

It's a part of the sea. Keats drowned there. Or Byron.

So it's Greek.

You got it.

He turned to me and saw my new coat.

You must think you look really nice in that.

I scanned his bookshelf and found a guide to classical literature. I tossed it to him.

Look it up in there.

He did and read aloud about Athamus and his children and his second wife, who was mean. The way he read from the book made me love him. Gerald was the kind of man who made mistakes often, but he learned from them. If he did not know the Champs Élysées was the same as Elysian Fields, and even what those fields referred to, he said so and asked about it. So it wasnt embarrassing to hear him mispronounce a word. Nor was it sweet like my wife, who might refrain or avoid having to face the word.

Do you ever think of the ideal woman.

I think of my inability to be satisfied.

But the ideal, Kent.

I've built up a list of qualities.

Gerald: What does that tell you.

It tells me we should go eat.

Youre not hungry.

Youve made me hungry.

I make people hungry.

No, Gerald, you only make *me* hungry. And not all the time.

I'm not a man who encourages hunger?

You are an exemplar of the appetite, Gerald. Jesus, let's go.

He put on his coat.

Gerald: Do you listen to what your body tells you to eat.

Yes, I said.

That's a form of. What is that. That's sort of mystical, isnt it?

It's hunch-driven.

Yeah, a person who follows his hunger, who tries to give the hunger a brain to think with. That's my kind of person.

You can reason with him.

That's what I want in a woman.

Me: A woman with a brain in her hunger.

You know what I mean.

I think youre misjudging your current wife.

I might be one of those men who marries the same woman he's just divorced.

You mean the very same woman.

Yeah. Not some twin.

Have there been men who do that?

It runs in my family, Gerald said.

Oh, it's in your blood.

My mother's brother. Also some cousins.

That I did not know.

And people leave each other. To return.

Without all the official divorcing and marrying.

Yeah, no paper trail.

Me: It's living a life more intricate than the record shows.

But I definitely want to get divorced. I mean, I'm happy now, but when it happens I want to have that experience, legal and otherwise.

You want to be able to say youre divorced.

It's the having something official.

You see it as like getting a degree.

You could look at it as a form of study.

You are a strange man, Gerald Thayer.

We crossed a wide road and the numbers, I noticed, were large: 1138 and 1140.

Me: Would you ever live in a house where your number was up in the thousands.

It would never occur to me to question the number of my house.

So that's the difference. Between you and me.

Go live in your number 3, your number 24, Kent. Go bake your bread and smoke your pipe and thresh your wheat and hew your wood. Go, for fuck's sake.

A horn sounded. It sounds like a tongue depressor, Gerald said, stuck up a cormorant's ass.

We sat outside a small restaurant and ate. We shared sour cabbage served in a cast-iron pan. We talked like this through the afternoon in the open air as traffic passed us. It was all theoretical. It was, Assume this. It was, Consider the following. It was analysis, but it was honest. Gerald said it's true you can't work when youre drunk.

But good work, he said, gets done six hours after waking up from a hangover.

Like me, Gerald liked to speak the truth as the truth appeared to him. He'd had such a good summer, he was tanned. When he smiled, a dimple on his cheek opened up and the skin was white.

He said, You know what Alma said? She said, What kind of life can I have with this Gerald Thayer. There's only two people my husband will eat with. And Rockwell Kent is one of them.

Gerald was broke before they were married. Alma said to me, I'm gonna take care of Gerald.

Me: I dont think love has to be like that.

It gave Gerald an anxious feeling. They lived hand to mouth. Alma had fifty-four cents. No, she said, money is coming in tomorrow.

They didnt have enough money for a marriage licence.

Me: Strange that you didnt have enough money.

Gerald: No it's not. We often dont have enough.

At the behest of his wife, Gerald had begun clipping his nostril hair. I knew him when his nostrils were abundant with hair. I liked him that way. This is what married life does to some men: it restrains them. Or they become conscious of scrutiny. Most women are aware of this without getting married. It ruins people, this reconciliation with majority perception. Later in life Gerald liked to carry a roll of dental floss.

We were so theoretical in those days. We thought we could control the heart.

As we ate it grew colder and we thought about going in. Gerald noticed a woman inside plunge her fork into a table full of yellow flowers — it was a pot of flowers outside the window that seemed to sit on her table. She was eating alone. Well, she was eating with a book.

Me: She knows how to dress for summer.

Gerald: She knows how to dress for all occasions.

We went inside for a drink. We stood at the bar. It had darkened, and Gerald Thayer watched the woman's reflection in the window — outside the yellow flowers, their stems pushing through her head as if attempting to rub out her poise.

Someone at the bar said, Did you say read the box score?

Another: I said read the Bible.

Gerald: What's your favourite bit of the Bible.

Me: When Jesus allows Mary to wash his feet. She dries them in her hair. And then she uses that expensive ointment.

How lavish, how decadent, yes.

I watched Gerald Thayer slam his hands against the bar and go over to her. She said to him, Good to meet you.

Gerald: We've met before.

I dont remember.

Gerald: You dont recognize me with all my clothes on.

Pause.

I'm joking. What are you reading.

The woman looked up and said, It's not that important.

Gerald was ordering the drinks. He looked old. He was less than twenty-five.

You love architecture, he said, with animals. Or figures with a lifted leg.

It makes them look more relaxed, she said.

Like the caryatids, he said. How they carry weight on their heads and yet have one knee bent, to make the roof light.

With lions it's a rampant gesture.

Her pale blue eye appeared between Gerald's lips. That was the angle I saw them at. So as he spoke, bent over to her, it was as if his lips were massaging her eye.

The rest of the night was the drink and my saying goo night to Gerald Thayer as he took Jenny Starling back to her apartment. He wiggled his eyebrows at me as they left. A bicycle ran over an empty cigarette package. He woke up, he told me later, with scratches on his face from her earrings.

7

Gerald Thayer could not take her on, could not take care of Jenny Starling. He was married, so he sent me in. Jenny Starling, the divorcee musician with a house on the island of Monhegan as part of her settlement with Luis Starling. It was an excuse to go there. I ended up spending a year on Monhegan, built a house, learned to lobster fish, and Jenny and I were together for two hundred days, though I could not promise her anything. It was this trust thing. I could not allow her to be open. My refusal to let her be open caused her anguish, for it closed her down and she grew weary. She was so smart to grow weary.

Then I met Kathleen Whiting.

It was her youth and utter devotion. It was the way she closed her eyes before she nodded her head. The way she played with children. There was no risk, really, and at the time life was a struggle to achieve grace. I knew there would be no war out of Kathleen Whiting. I could dominate her. I'm not sure I knew this then, but I learned my lesson. About being loved. How the worth is in the giving. The permission to be oneself.

The truth: one is erratic when one is of high hopes. I would say that if you were involved with someone who is on the cusp of exuberance, who feels the wing of inspired thought, my advice is to beware. But more: there is no one else to be with. Be with them. You may as well get into it as live a life of hesitation.

8

Gerald visited us in Monhegan. How he murmured at Jenny's description of an oar stirring a phosphorescent shoal. But it wasnt even an oar, it was a comparison to the oar. The thing was Gerald Thayer's fingers stirring up a trail on the inside of Jenny Starling's thigh. And Gerald murmured at that and I knew he would fall in love with her. He had slept with her, but I am talking about the heart. When a man lets out such a sound. It is a betrayal of the inner course, and that course will have its way even though he is unaware of it at that moment. I heard the sound of *mmm* come from his throat, hardly out of his mouth but through the skin of his throat, and I knew that body would be after her.

It felt like the final chapter in my life with Jenny Starling, now that our son was dead.

9

Kathleen: Tom Dobie looks like he's working hard not to do anything.

Me: It takes a lot of effort on his part to stop from doing something.

No, this is it — he looks like he's trying hard to stop himself from doing something bad.

I love you.

Kathleen: I love you too.

Would you say that out of a hundred times that I love you gets said, you say it first forty times, and then I reply, I love you too. And I say I love you first maybe thirty times, and you say back, I love you too. We each say I love you about thirty times without it being answered.

It's just a lone I-love-you.

Me: So, on average, youre moved to say I love you slightly more than me.

Yes, that's true.

It is?

Yes.

Youve noticed.

Well, you noticed too.

But I was assuming I was a little crazy.

No, I know what you mean.

10

The important thing is for change in belief to occur. If one is born an atheist, one should become spiritual. A person with no change is not searching. My wife was a Christian and she stayed a Christian. For the fifteen years she was with me she suppressed her feelings. But she had an underground river of Christianity that bubbled up in fissures through the years.

A death in the family can be an agent for change. I wondered what my son's death would mean. Would it renew my faith. My father's death had caused me to question my belief in God.

Kathleen peeled apples for a pie. You rotate the apple around the centre of the peeling. It is a motion I caught her doing, so as to keep the apple turning clockwise and the peeling to unravel counter-clockwise. There was something in this that explained how we peel away time and yet manage to return to it.

Kathleen was singing a song, over and over. Or maybe she was singing several songs. But it sounded the same. Until Rocky growled, How long is this song anyway.

Tom Dobie looked at Rocky's face: The eyes of him. He's just like a husky.

Me: He's just like you.

Kathleen said a dog had followed her. A three-legged dog. She paints a white mark down her forehead and nose. A beautiful —

Cape Shore water dog, Tom said. And smiled. Yep, a registered breed. I once had a dog, he said, with only two legs. One in front and one behind. It'd be like a bicycle. Every time he stopped he'd have to lie down.

11

Tom Dobie and Stan Pomeroy at the head of the wharf, their legs splayed, sorting through their fish. How theyre elbow-deep into fish. They were tossing crab into the water.

Can I have some crab.

Stan: You gonna eat that stuff. We'll set you aside a tub if
you stop sketching off pictures.

Then he wanted to see what I had of him.

Tom: He lines that off pretty good, dont he.

Stan: He marked out a likeness of me there.

Then they turned to watch a small boat come in.

Tom: Look at that skiff.

Dory.

She's a skiff.

She's a dory, boy.

Go on, you useless article.

Look at the rake on her.

Look at the side, the ramp.

Okay, a flat.

She's a dory, okay? A dory.

What about that *V* in the back there.

That's a little skiffish. But she's a dory.

What about —

Ah shut your face.

Go fuck yourself.

12

Kathleen boiled the crab. I laid newspapers over the kitchen
table. The children could see I was excited. There was pepper
and fresh bread and butter. I had them sit down to this. I gave
them each a large napkin. Then we tore into the crab. We
pulled the meat out of their shells. The children chewing on

the pliable hoses of their legs. We boiled another batch. We had enough for three boils. I got the water galloping and we sat there and ran out of bread. We were delighted with the work. Then I realized it was no work at all. It was pleasure. So often I mix up work and pleasure. It's true that I've hardly ever felt like I've worked. For me it's all about eating as much crab as you can.

I decided to get to work on the tennis court. There were six boulders on the Hearn field. Five I dug out with a pick and rolled to the side, and one I left to bury. I dug a hole to the side of it and pushed it in. I felt like a gravedigger. Tom Dobie and Stan and Tony Loveys were trimming logs nearby: shores, beams, and longers for their flake.

They might lose some brinkles, Tom said, but that makes them better.

They worked at their work and I worked at play. I filled a barrel with stone and rigged a set of handles from a grass cutter and pulled the barrel over the field. This is grooming. This is flattening a fallow field. Jim Hearn came over.

What are you doing.

Waiting for a train.

He thought about that. Now that's not very friendly.

I decided to stop. Youre right, Jim. You are correct. And I'm trying to change my behaviour. I'm trying to be gentle. In the way that gentle is meant. Truth is, I hate being asked obvious questions, Jim, but youre only trying to be neighbourly.

He said that there was an old seining net over at Chafe's, and that Bud Chafe had tennis racquets and gear better than what they had in town even.

I rolled my field. While Hearn watched. My children watched. I let my anger melt away. I did this for three solid days. I made a parcel of flat earth.

13

Me: Do you think we're good.

Kathleen: Yes, we're good.

Me: We're good and smart, arent we.

We're not bad.

We're smarter than most. We're pretty important, arent we. I mean, our friends think — theyre impressed by us.

I dont think we should be saying this.

We're just saying it to ourselves.

I'm not comfortable.

We're not boasting.

But it could lead to something. It could affect us.

I just want it said. I want it acknowledged privately.

I dont think anything stays private. It leaks out.

14

Kathleen: Theyre not an attractive fish, the codfish.

Me: A third of them is face.

After dinner we put the children to bed and then stepped out. You abandoned children in those days. We walked into Brigus proper while the moon rose and ate the clouds. You could feel the heat of the land come up and warm you. There were voices ahead. We turned onto a small road. There was an argument. A young couple beside Hearn's pharmacy. Their dark shapes slewing into each other. There were wrists being grabbed. We stopped. I held Kathleen's hand.

It's Tom Dobie, I said.

And Emily Edwards. But I did not say this. The door to Billy Cole's shebeen was open, light pouring out. There were men's voices. A man in the doorway spat on the ground. Emily was pushing Tom up against the boards of the pharmacy. Tom took it. Then the man stepped away from the light. The man laughed and I could see now that it was Stan Pomeroy. Tom said something. Stan Pomeroy bent down and took up a shovel. He tested the weight of it. He hoisted it back, very slowly, and swung the flat of it like a baseball bat. It swung through the air, and the face of the shovel flashed in the light, then it caught Tom full in the chest. It staggered him. He collapsed under a window. There was a scream, and it was Emily. She launched herself at Stan, pushing him off.

She said his name, Stan.

I could see the pair of them then and I thought, Theyve slept together. Stan Pomeroy. Emily was yelling at Stan Pomeroy to leave off. Then she hauled Tom up, but Tom pushed her away. Stop your screeching, he said. Stan watched them. Another man came out. Tom's knees buckled, then he put his hands on his knees to find his breath. Stan went back into Billy Cole's with the other man. The men inside were laughing.

Let's walk up to the corner, I said. Tom and Emily were wrestling now. Emily was rough with him. I realized they were the same size. He was tough and young. Emily, a bit taller. Get your can hooks off me. Youre as foolish as a hen, Tom Dobie.

He was grabbing at her.

Kathleen called to her, Do you want to come with us?

Yes.

Kathleen walked over to her and stood planted. Tom took this in — he stared at my wife as though he did not know her. He said, You can hear the ocean panting.

Kathleen, I realized, had not met Emily before. Emily was tucking her hair around her ears and then this happened: a goat sprang out of the open shebeen window and landed on Tom's shoulders. It knocked him over. The goat scrabbled up, stood there a moment to look at us, and then darted sideways into the dark.

Tom Dobie was perplexed and drunk, one hand in the dirt. He pushed himself up. I went to him. He leaned back against the pharmacy, rubbing his chest. Then he bounced off the side of the pharmacy and came at me, as if I'd been the goat. I tried to block his progress. I put a hand to his chest. He hung his arms down low.

I said, Are you okay.

Stay out of it, he said.

He reeled in to me and I could smell the alcohol. I thought his chest may have been broken, but he was only winded. He looked in pain but ignoring the pain. He said, One man stands downstairs, the other upstairs. In a pit saw.

You better get some sleep, Tom. And I'll see you in a few hours.

We had promised to go fishing. His arms were stiff and his fists ready to fight. You dont know who youre talking to.

It's time to go home, I said.

That's what we were going to do.

I'll see you at the slipway in six hours.

Kathleen walked ahead with Emily. Tom Dobie said, I've got you noted.

As though I was some kind of informer.

I leaned him up against Bud Chafe's store. He was so drunk. Kathleen and Emily doubled back. Emily said, Maybe I should go to him. He's not gonna like me now.

Kathleen: I think it's best to call it a night.

Kathleen held her and laughed to me at something Emily said into her shoulder.

It's not right to laugh, Emily said.

I wasnt laughing at you.

They were hugging. He should know he'll never do better than me. I'm too good for him.

You are, Kathleen said.

We had no sure idea what the fight was about.

She walked home with us. Emily would not talk about it. She just said that Tom Dobie was the sweetest thing, but sometimes when he's kegged he goes around like he's got three small dogs hanging off his elbows.

I had no notion, I said.

Yes, you see the good in him.

She looked away, as if a bit shy of showing me the difference in her mind between me and Tom. She stared above the hill. Look at the fox eye.

A ring around the moon.

This is how we had Emily Edwards stay with us.

15

Tom did not arrive at the slipway. I walked there the next morning and then back home. We ate with the blinding seven oclock sun on our faces, a beautifully sweet Emily Edwards fresh and young and Kathleen and I agog at her in a delightful way. Kathleen, I could tell, was impressed with how Emily had held her own. How she'd pushed off Stan Pomeroy and then corralled Tom. The children, too, all crazy for her.

I asked her again about what had happened.

I'm a slut for honesty, Emily said. But really, honesty is such an easy thing in this town.

She ate with her elbows all over the table. When she breathed she breathed with her belly.

Kathleen: I'm so sensitive. People are sensitive, dont you find?

Me: Not me.

Emily: No, me neither.

Kathleen heard this and wished she could be in league with us.

Stan was only trying to get a rise out of him, Emily said. Not get into a hammer and tiss. But he said too much. Said I was trying to jig him. It was just for badness Stan said it, a bit of devilment, but that's when Tom went and give him a bazz in the face.

She had slept on the chaise longue. Upstairs the night before there had been something in our trying to be quiet. It was realizing that a house guest is the same as your parents. I had mocked a cry to our quiet passion.

You sound, Kathleen had said, like the tenor in that opera.

Pagliacci. But I dont know the opera.

That is the opera. Yes, youre operatic. Youre a lot of instruments.

I'm not just some piccolo.

Oh youre a huge wind instrument.

I'm not too huge.

I mean youre symphonic, Mr Kent. Youre a voice surrounded by the symphonic.

Just let me know if I'm too huge.

All the instruments have their ears pointed in my direction.

Yes they are very much perked.

Now you have to wait for the crescendo.

Youre the conductor, Mrs Kent. Tell me when I can let rip with the cymbals.

Youre the cry of a large lonely bird in the copse of a larger forest.

That you come upon in a clearing.

A glade.

The greens and blacks of a glade.

What is an everglade.

Oh God, say it. Say *everglade*.

Ever. Glade.

I held Kathleen close. Maybe it's to do with evergreen. Perhaps the green never goes.

A permanent green.

That was very nice.

Wasnt it, Mr Kent.

In the morning, as I said, I had awoken early to meet Tom Dobie. As I left I saw Emily guzzling water from a ceramic jug. She needed to breathe, but she had to have water. The jug dropped off her mouth and she gasped for air. Then quick to the mouth again. She slugged at the water until the suction of her mouth slipped off the opening. She licked it. Dropped the jug to the counter with a ka-thunk. Exhaled then inhaled deeply. She is finished. She is tired. She would like to lie down on something larger than the chaise longue. Just the sheet over her hip, the blankets kicked and pushed to the floor. And as I stood there at the open door I thought we were in Italy. Maybe the windows shut with louvres where the sun is. I'm in Umbria with this woman. We will open only one side of the apartment at a time. In the middle of the afternoon we'll change sides.

Excuse me, I said. I'm going to see Tom.

I should be on my way.

Nonsense. Make some coffee or go back to bed. I'll be out of your road.

16

There was a note from Tom. Tomorrow morning, sun-up. I got up and was out the door in the dark. I met Tom at the slipway with Smoky.

We slung the dory out into the water and climbed aboard. Tom rushed to get the oars in.

Sit back, he said, in the arse of her.

How you feeling.

We were whispering. The dark makes you whisper.

I couldnt get out of bed yesterday, he said. I had the dawnies all morning. That drink at Billy Cole's will pure kill you.

You can row with your chest like that?

Stan caught me in the solar plexus is all.

I watched him row.

Dont go giving me a hard stare.

I was just wondering what that was all about.

Me and Stan, he said, we're the best of gear, okay?

So it was Emily.

It was about everything. For me it was everything, and there's no point in getting into it except to say that me and Stan, we got more nature than what we need.

The horizon arrived as a shade of blue. There was not a wag of sea. The wet oarlocks and the slap of the boat in the water. Tom rowed crosshanded for half an hour. The sun arrived and painted the land back in. I let the sun warm me. I let Tom do all the work. I had Smoky's chin on my shoulder.

Try the four-ounce minnow, he said.

I flicked out a line and caught a mackerel.

That'll be our bait.

It was six in the morning.

It was grey and overcast, a good day for fish.

Water's cleaner over there, he said. More tide over there. Fish swim against the current.

I took a turn on the rowing. Line up those two houses, he said. To keep you straight. Now hook up and you catch the water with your paddles. Yeah, that's a nice catch. Feather the oars. Ten minutes of that and your arms will feel it.

Tom leaned back and closed his eyes in the bow. He was listening to me row.

What's the most powerful thing on earth, he said.

Wind?

No.

Water?

The power of God, Kent. Next thing.

The sun.

Nature. You can't fight nature. You got to go with it.

He opened his eyes again. Fish, he said, meaning cod, is in a hundred and fifty feet of water. To jig proper, you got to have your line vertical. Some fishermen, they sit down. I find you got to stand. They never catch as much as me, that's cause they sit. You can't feel the fish sitting, I find. Youre vertical and you jig three times. That's when you get one. Never been as much fish in the bay my whole life.

We werent that far from shore. It was nice to be on the water, so close, and seeing the land you lived on. I could hear someone calling out, Here, chuck, chucky. Here, pig. There was a kingfisher in top of a fir. Chirping its sweet chirp. Three kerns coasted over the water.

They eat, Tom said, about ten pounds of fish a day.

I rowed out farther.

We'll get to the spot, he said, and then you keep her up.

The shoreline was opening up behind us. A smear of birds

on the water. Tom lined up the Head of Brigus with Bell Island behind him and said, Those are your marks.

Youre using triangulation.

No Kent we use no navigation whatsoever. You just line up the naked man over there by your house with the island at your shoulder, and when you can see Colliers past the Red Rocks then you know youre on the ledge.

Tom had pulled out two lead jiggers and line and handed one over. I watched him as he paid out line. He wore woollen wristbands to prevent blisters.

So you find some men are better fishermen than other men.

There is a trade in it, Kent. Some men will never make fishermen. There is a lot to learn in it. You have to know just where to go and how to get there.

I let my jigger sink until it touched bottom, then pulled it in a yard. Smoky watched me. He watched me tug on the line. He knew what I was doing. It was as if I was his hands.

I felt my line resist solid, as though I had snagged a sunken log. I pulled up the log, arm over arm, it took twenty seconds to haul in the line. A large white belly emerged from the water. A slow twist of codfish upside down that broke the water plane and gained weight. I yanked it over the gunwale. It twisted stiffly, waking up, and I released the jigger where it had gaffed the fish in the side.

Dont get your gear all tangled. Just throw your jigger over.

It seems rude, I said, not to catch them in the mouth.

Tom had one coming over the side as well. You, he said. Everything's got to be done in a beautiful way.

We left the fish to suffocate under the snout of a licking dog. He loves the salt.

Again the dull resistance of the line but now more understood to be a fish. I could tell by the weight on my finger that it was a smaller one, but still it rose big and white, about seven pounds, over the side, its gills stretching wide for water, its huge alarmed eye staring out. The fish looked brand new.

We're in for a good spurt of fishing, Kent.

We hauled about twenty such fish aboard. The floor of the dory filled with their grey, speckled sides. They looked like English setter puppies. There was a small metal box to make a fire in. Tom stoked in a fire.

Get me a pan, he said, from the cuddy.

There was a cabinet under the front seat. He cleaned a fish over the side, and herring gulls raced in for the floating guts. They fought for them and he cut the fish in chunks. The fish was full of pale roe, and he cooked these on the side. He had some potatoes already peeled in the pan, with pork fat and an onion. Tom covered the pan for ten minutes and then laid in the chunks of fish, the blue porcelain of thick fan blades. It was something solid and blowing. As we waited he scooped out the roe and split it in two and we ate it off our fingers.

The lady fish, he said, wears the britches.

I dont get it.

The roe, Tom explained, looks like a pair of pants.

Then the entire white meal wafted into me. I rinsed the enamel plates in the water. Tom served up the fish and potatoes. We poured on salt from a tin and ate joyously.

This, Tom said, is the best way to eat fish.

We sat there with our plates on our knees. The heat of the meal coming through the enamel, nice on our knees.

He felt he was saying things his father would have said. He had to say them now.

I do the same thing, I said. Say things I know my father said.

Tom nodded to this.

It's not fair, he said. But enough's been said about the dead.

The fish held together in chunks, which you could flake apart. It was the sea itself you were eating, a fresh, pure, thriving taste, elusive as the taste of water.

I love this, Tom said. Again, he was being his father.

So this is what you find beautiful.

This is correct.

Sitting here after a feed of fish and potatoes on the water. This feeling, I said, is what I paint.

Youre good company on the water.

Me: I feel I'm home.

I love it here too.

I looked back on the land. Do you love the woods?

I love being on the water more. Can't swim a stroke, but I love it.

My family was waking up. Kathleen fetching water from the brook. I waved but she did not see me. She was just a chalk mark of white.

I suppose it would be difficult to keep more sheep in Brigus.

No, it would not be very hard.

Tom talked about the fish and the work. He was manly. Physical. And yet he did not talk about Emily. He spoke of who had a berth aboard what vessel. Who had sixty quintals or fifty quintals yesterday.

Quintals, I said.

That's a hundred and fourteen pound.

He talked about the trap. He worried over it. If his was right. He asked himself, not even speaking to me, because the day before he and Stan Pomeroy had only perhaps five quintals out of it. I wonder, I heard him say, if we got the leader right. I wonder has a whale gone through it. And then, Ah, we'll go over all the leader tomorrow and see what's happening.

And then, as we're jigging: Who's that going up there?

And we watched another crew with a load.

There were three more crews behind him, each with a load. And Tom looked to see where they'd come from and how long it'd taken and how sunk down was their gunwale. All day long that's what he talked about.

17

The church organized a drive to raise funds. I had the children help me make puppets. It would be a Punch and Judy theatre. But what would our characters be. The children were often asking questions, and so I thought to make a question puppet and an answer puppet.

Rocky: How about a bird that wonders and a cat that answers.

So little Kathleen made a bird and we called him the Wonderbird. He flies under things.

He gets to the bottom of things.

The underbelly bird.

No, it's Wonderbird.

Rocky made a cat and called it a panther.

He answers to the Wonderbird.

He's the anther panther.

The Anther Panther and Wonderbird.

Those, I said, are terrific.

I built a portable theatre that folded and we marched down to the Stand, where there were booths for cookies and punch and a spinning wheel. Men were gambling at a crown and anchor. I sat under the theatre and had Wonderbird ask every question it could think of and the Anther Panther solved the world's problems in no less than ten solid hours, until every loose penny from every pocket was collected and donated to the Methodists' worthwhile cause, whatever it was.

I should have been easier with the children. But I did not want to have children with bad manners. Kathleen was much more generous, and it was the only thing she'd get mad about, my judgment. My attempts at laxity were strained. I was not easy about letting them be the way they were or even playing with them. I had opinions. I was quick to warn them if they almost knocked over a glass. I'm too proscriptive. But maybe that's a good thing, Kathleen said.

They were outside, pitching buttons at a stick.

Well, theyve made me pull up my socks. Theyve forced me, I said, to be responsible.

Youre serious about the painting.

About making a living at it. We should have Emily Edwards over more, to help with the children.

A few hours now and then would be good.

Kathleen was exhausted.

Have you seen Tom Dobie?

I havent seen him all day.

I went over to the Pomeroys'. To talk to Stan. But they were gone, his father said. Stan and Tony Loveys and Tom. Off mending the nets and getting the cod trap set up, and theyve been gone since dawn and he wouldnt see them again before nightfall.

18

It began to rain and Emily Edwards made my son a sandwich. Rocky said he liked how Emily made food. She makes it look real tasty. Even brown rice. But especially apples and sandwiches. He said, Emily says things like, When I'm eighty I'm gonna live in an apartment in Manhattan forty storeys up and smoke on the window ledge and look out on all the people walking past.

I heard her say, Let's open a window. The wind will help us clean the table.

Every action Emily did she spoke of aloud. She'd say to Rocky, I'm taking off my shoes and hanging up my coat. She'd say, Let's get the kettle on and let's put a piece of fish on to soak and cook him and eat him. I heard her say, If you go to the Pomeroys' for eggs, Rocky, you have to wash your hands after. All this through my studio door.

I found myself thinking about her. I was trying to paint but I was writing a poem in my head. Or a poem that is like an equation. That she is round but has an edge to her, like an eye is round but has a corner. People say she is round, but I've found an edge to her. There is nothing I have given her. She has found it all in her roundness. Every edge, every corner of the room she's found me with something other than her.

I had Rocky and little Kathleen eat before we left for dinner at the Bartletts'. They had big appetites and I didnt want them embarrassing us.

19

We hadnt seen Tom Dobie, so I walked over to Frogmarsh. They were out checking the trap, Rachel Dobie said. Tom and Stan Pomeroy and Tony Loveys. I hate it when theyre late.

She was by the root cellar with a piece of watersoaked fish — that was the kind of fish they kept for themselves, fish they could get only a number-two price for. She'd decided they hadnt caught much. Had I seen anything. I hadnt.

Me: Can three men handle a trap?

Rachel: Yes sir they got to.

Tom had got up, she said, in the dark with a hangover. She could smell it. He's been on a square bender, that one.

The boy had marched past his mother and into the porch and flung his boots on the oilcloth. Then he laced them on. He filled the black kettle with water from the dipper and placed it, dripping, on the back hob and they both listened to the branding sizzle. That was the last she saw of him.

I walked back to Kathleen. The sky had darkened and it was windy. Where there's a break in the houses you blew away. This was their first excursion of the season, I said. So we stayed up and played cards. The wind abated.

Kathleen: There's a light.

A quiet lantern rounded the Head. A lone trap skiff rowed into the bay. We went outside. Once you saw the skiff you could hear the rub of the oarlocks. There were two figures at the oars. Tom Dobie and Tony Loveys.

I'll go down, I said. They must be exhausted.

Rachel Dobie was there to tie them on. They were prying a large fish from a sheet of canvas on the floor of the skiff.

Tom: I need a hand, Kent. My handwrists are all worn away.

I hoisted myself down, and from there the fish turned into the stiffened body of Stan Pomeroy. He was white and frozen flat, with a gaff mark in his jaw. He was dead and half-naked in the shaky light. He looked like he'd been dead all his life.

Tom Dobie said not a word, except, quietly: One two three. Together we cracked Stan out of the frozen canvas sheet. Strands of unmixed blood swam in the sea water in the bottom of the boat. We hauled him to the stagehead. I was at the feet. Bare cold feet.

Tom: What do you think, Mother.

As if she had a plan to revive him yet. To dip Stan in warm water. Thaw him alive again, gently. Tom hadnt seen our faces. We were trying our best to stay calm.

Pass up the gear, boys.

There seemed to be no urgency in the situation. Items were passed up. Then we climbed up the wharf side. Tony Loveys: I'll go get Old Man Pomeroy.

Tom Dobie stood guard with us, the corpse of the barefooted Stan Pomeroy rimed in a crust of ice. Stiff. The wharf was a cold wooden water. What a good kid, I said.

Tom Dobie took off his jacket and laid it over Stan's bare cold feet.

That's about all I can do now.

He knew, at least, that the bare feet were wrong and needed protection from the elements.

He was leaning over the cod trap, Tom said. You could hear the fish chopping on the surface when they rowed near the trap. Stan had one foot up on the gunwale and it was icy. That's how we went at it. We had the haul ropes hooked and the doorways shut off and Stan was checking the spy bucket. Trap's crammed with fish, he said in a soft voice. Fish were thick, their mouths full of kelp. The walls of the trap were straining and Stan was drying up the twine. So he got full up on the gunwale and he almost capsed her, but then he fell over.

He slammed into the icy water. Just melted into the crowd of fish. I saw him wrestle over onto his back. It was like a jelly of bodies crowding him. His hands they came up very white. None of us can swim, me, Stan, or Tony. So he just sank beneath the fish.

Tom Dobie was telling us this when Tony Loveys came down the path with Mr Pomeroy. I'm disgusted, he said. Mr Pomeroy looked over his dead son and waited.

Tom: We hauled in the trap, sir, to save him, but the catch was heavy and there were only the two of we.

Mr Pomeroy nodded at this. He knelt down and touched Stan's face.

We poured the fish into the skiff, trying to get at Stan. But he was smothered. We had fish up to the gangboards. I saw his hand rise out of the fish, and I made a grab for it to haul him out of the fish, but he was — sir, there was nothing.

Tony: He was gone.

So we kicked out all the fish to make room in the skiff hey Tony, and we started to rub him down. We rubbed his arms didnt we and pulled off his boots and Tony had a go at his feet. We tried to coax the air into his lungs.

Tony: His eyes were out of his face.

He didnt drown I reckon. We just couldnt get any air to him.

Tony: He suffocated for the success of the fish.

This is the story Tom Dobie reported to us that night. He told it once again, to Stan's mother at the Pomeroy kitchen table while Stan's body lay over it, before Mrs Pomeroy covered him in a tablecloth. Go home, Tom Dobie, she said. And take Stan's gear and store it in the twine loft. I'm lonesome, she said, to have it in the house.

Mrs Pomeroy didnt say anything else to us but went up to her room with her husband. We saw off Tony Loveys, and then Tom and I walked over to Frogmarsh with his mother. He went up into his room, he told me later, and all the whites of the bedroom were lit by the moon, even his own feet at the heel of the bed, numb and strange to him. The birch ribs of the bunk bed, the same wood as the skiff and the wharf, the stage and the house and even what they burnt for heat. It was all connected: home, boat, stagehead, fish.

I lay in bed with Kathleen and thought of the image of Stan Pomeroy amongst the fish, in the dark, while the far wall of the bedroom shone a blue light. The wall was a pale cream in the morning — what was it with colour. Everything seems to depend on circumstance. But I had seen a large fish at first in the bottom of the skiff, and ever since all I've seen is Stan Pomeroy. So in truth a thing is a constant thing, though we may believe it to be something else occasionally. Yet here was the wall changing before me and what did it mean? To say sunlight versus moonlight or artificial light?

20

Sad, sad. They kept Stan's body packed in brine and on a warm day in June they took him from the root cellar and laid him barefoot on the kitchen table again. They had a wake. Rachel Dobie bought a dozen clay pipes and spread out a cloth full of tobacco. The men walked in and filled the clay pipes and stood and smoked. I was among them. Stan had whitened and his flesh was of an old fish. Where they had held him the flesh stayed pushed in. The brine ran off his cuffs and trousers and ruined the tablecloth. The wound on his jaw was grey. There was a grimace on his face. On his chest was a white square made of ribbon with the letters IHS. I Have Suffered.

Tom Dobie and Tony Loveys dug a hole at Grave Hill and they lifted Stan Pomeroy off the table and put him in a box. They did not carry the box — instead, the pallbearers escorted the box on a cart. They did not have a lid on the box. The pallbearers wore white bands around their caps. They carted the pickled corpse up Grave Hill and lifted him out of the box and lowered him in the hole with the tablecloth wrapped about him. I did a sketch of this. Mr Pomeroy had taken some of the soil and warmed it in the oven. They spread handfuls of this warm soil on the tablecloth. Then Stan and Tony Loveys shovelled over the cold soil. It still had ice crystals. It was hard earth they dropped onto Stan's body.

I stood at the graveyard gates and drew a picture of Stan's burial. Kathleen and the children among the mourners. Curved lines on the hill and the drift of weather. I would send this to Charles Daniel. See what he thought of this life in Brigus.

Later, we went home and I spread molasses on slices of bread. We ate them while I fixed more, cutting them in half. I brought a slice to bed and laid it directly on the sheet beside my head. I did not use a plate. I ate the bread and molasses and did not fall asleep. Instead, I got up again and walked to the field across from the house and ploughed and set out a garden. I could plant everything, Tom said, except the potatoes.

21

My tools arrived, my father's tools. The big walnut case was at the station. They had salvaged them. The wood had bulked out and the hinges on the box were caked with rust. The lock busted off. I asked George Browiny about that.

Accidental, he said. Looks it. Probably when the freighter went down.

More like vandalism, I said. And I thought there was more to it than he was letting on.

I had Swift the pony lug the box home on the mail cart. The hills were full of dandelions. I opened the box and the tools jiggled on their little ledges, tucked in alcoves, hung on nails. The tools too were lined with rust, but a bit of oil and steel wool and they were fine. Behind each tool lay a painted shadow of the tool on the wood. So you knew where it belonged. All that was missing was a table clamp and a vise. It wasnt so bad. Perhaps George Browiny was right. The woodcarving tools were wrapped in cloth and leather and the cloth had oil on it. The carving tools were marvellous. My father's tools. When my father died there was a field of dandelions. There was sun. It was a day like this day. It was before I knew that the sky wasnt always blue and bright. There was the news and there was a letter from him. And my mother folded the letter, unopened, and pushed it into the wastebasket. As though the corpse had lifted a finger, or inhaled, as if the gasses of my father had mustered in his lungs and infected the letter with decay and the roil of illness. And when his ashes came home, there was a funeral and Nanny Rosa was not invited.

My father used to open his mail with a pocket knife. He believed a man should keep a knife on him. He was a man who could do two things with his hand at once. He could hold a bottle of wine with his thumb and forefinger and gesture with the rest. Splay up with those three fingers.

22

Me: Can you cut me a cross?
      Tom: I can make you two lengths.
      Cut me two lengths and I'll make a cross. I'll carve Stan's
name on it.

I realized that part of the reason why I had moved to such an
isolated place was that I was losing my ability to feign interest in
boring things. I was becoming a loner. If you want to get along
with people it's important to be polite. Or to cut people off
nicely and feign an excuse. New York is full of idiots.
      Kathleen had not tired of being polite. We spoke about this
after Stan's funeral. How removed I looked, sketching pictures
of the mourners. How she and the children had accompanied
the family to the graveyard. She said, Youve even forgotten how
to mask indifference.
      Was I indifferent?
      I felt I had been politely tempering my emotions. For thirty
years I'd done that, and now my face was betraying me. There
was something to profit from the death of Stan Pomeroy, and
I was not about to show false emotion. I was excited to draw it.
And yes, perhaps there was something boring in the fatalism of
accepting death.
      Kathleen: We all know when we're being boring, but we
appreciate the polite gesture, the kindness of someone's
responding with class and respect.
      Yes, I said. We like people who tolerate us, and they feel
liked and like you back for it, even if you are boring them.

But you look like youre afraid you'll be stuck with them.

Is it that plain on my face?

When you said that to Mr Hearn, about waiting for a train.

You were there for that?

You told me about it. As a joke.

This was depressing me. I felt like a bad citizen. Kathleen tried to revive me. When I say these things, she said, about your bald honesty, it's not that I'm judging you. I'm saying that youre more open to your own nature, and I tend to cut myself off from that kind of experience. I'm impressed with your free attitude. But it's also scary to realize I'm hitched to this.

Me: I feel youre judging me.

Kathleen: Perhaps part of me is.

Me: Which part. I touch her thigh. This part?

Kathleen: I'm trying to make light of my jealousy. I'm trying to speak of it so it doesnt fold into the secret life and go on growing without either of us speaking of it.

Jealousy is an odd word.

Envy, then. I envy your zest, even if it is nasty. So forgive me if you feel like I'm chastising you.

You think every possible thought, dont you, Kathleen.

I think every thought. Yes.

23

The women were making fish along the shore. The older ones wore slouches to protect their faces from the sun. Flies were on the fish so thick that sometimes the fish looked blue.

Tom Dobie and Tony Loveys had built a flake out along the Battery trail.

Tom Dobie: You put flat boughs on the flake and you spread the fish on the boughs fair in the list and when the leaves drop off and the wind blows up underneath, up through the boughs, well then that is what makes excellent fish.

With Stan buried and the cross planted they turned to Marten Edwards, and he had gone in with them. They were getting good fish in the trap, just trouble drying it with the poor weather.

24

Rupert Bartlett was heading to Labrador for the season. He asked his sister Eleanor if she could recall where the tulip beds were. He didnt want to coil rope on the tulip beds.

I'm going to count on your memory, he said.

I helped him with the ropes. The flies were bad and he was using a dried-out branch from an aspen to kill them. He held the branch over his head and flicked it back and forth, the sharp twigs of the branch killing the flies. He was loading up a cart to take down to the *Morrissey*. The Bartletts had a station in Turnavik. Youre more than welcome to come down with me, he said.

But I wanted to get work done here. I mailed off my *House of Dread* to Charles Daniel. I didnt like the mood of it infecting my family. I had recovered from the friction of the seal hunt. I was making my wife happy. I wanted to paint something hopeful.

We waved off Rupert and the *Morrissey*. I did as Rupert had suggested. I watched the women work. Rachel Dobie and Emily Edwards with Rose Foley and Amanda Sweeney. Their backs bent all day.

I took to watching Emily. To see a young woman hard at work. I tried not looking at her, but I liked to see the strain on her face. Exertion in the young is sensual. I imagined myself behind her, I held her as she bent over and turned the fish. That's it, Emily. Now put your hands down. You dont even know I'm behind you.

Rachel stacked the fish to press the water out. You got to keep it off the ground, Emily said, or the damp will take out the pickle.

Rachel Dobie: Let nature do work for you is what I says.

After a night in waterhorse the fish were ready to spread on the flake.

The fish is in the woman's care, Emily said, stretching. Leaning back. Now let me just put a leg between yours. Let me push you apart with my knee. How she stroked a strand of hair out of her face. The flies drove her crazy.

A man catches the fish, Emily said, and the woman makes it.

Rachel: We mind the children, flakes, house and gardens. All the men mind is the fish.

Emily: Except for that one there.

Yes, but he's an artist.

And they have a laugh at that. A really good laugh.

25

I sawed wood and sometimes I borrowed the Pomeroys' dory and rowed over to Frogmarsh. The flakes extending off houses covered with fish. You had to spread the fish like they were your babies, Rachel told me. She wouldnt allow Tom to lay out fish. He isnt careful enough, she said. The most delicate stage of making fish, when it's put abroad on flakes.

I had become vegetarian in New York, but I ate the fish. Fish were triangles of white protein. Rachel showed me some lightly salted fish from last year. It was the colour of teeth.

Rachel: What makes a beautiful fish is the amber colour. It looks like it's flecked with flour, with no blood spots. No mark from the liver. A good nape, split down through the tail, with a thick, smooth, dry feel.

Then I walked along the shore, to where Emily was. She smiled at my lack of industry.

A good piece of salt fish, she said, you could hang on your wall. And hard. You could slice a man's hand off at the wrist.

She made a motion to slice off my hand.

Tom Dobie thinks that's you I've put over my door.

Emily: It's not much of a likeness, I'd say.

I painted, with ink on cardboard, a picture of Emily Edwards tending the flake, a sheep in silhouette behind her, the jaws of black land surrounding her. Sheep and black jaws. I gave it to Tom Dobie.

Sure I'm never making fish.

That's to remind you of the work the women do.

Theyre always reminding me.

Tom hung the drawing on the wall behind the stove. He studied it.

He'd loaned me a half-ton vise that was used by the railroads. He'd brought it over in his wheelbarrow. A block of maple in the mouth of the vise. I was carving a picture of Tom in his dory. Everything you do not want in the picture, I said, you carve away.

I peeled away shavings of light from his head and arms. How planned a woodcut must be. The ideal form present behind the wood. The emergence of dark and light — that it must be one or the other. The carving tool and the wood grain. It is important to consider the tactile joy of the work.

26

Kathleen pinned her hair up. Then she bent over to dig. She was planting a perennial in the rock garden. She checked a crevice to make sure it was connected to the earth by soil. Otherwise it won't last, she said. The frost will kill it.

The tomato flowers with six white petals. The seeds from Mary Bartlett. Her son Bob loves a good tomato. What was happening to Bob. No word. No one knew.

Kathleen sat back and cut a slice of apple with a knife. She ate it off the knife. She was sitting back on her own legs. To save her dress.

Could you live here?

Kathleen: Let's give it five years. It takes five years to decide anything.

Okay we'll live here five years. We'll pretend we've been elected to office.

She passed me a slice of apple on the blade of her knife.

When you do that, I said, it looks so elegant.

I could be in love with her. I was in love with her. The way she worked, I could funnel all the work of women into her bent frame.

The original reason, she said, why people cut slices of apple with a knife is not because it's elegant. It's because they have false teeth. But I'm doing it because I've got lipstick on and I dont want to spoil my mouth.

As I watched her eat this apple Kathleen became aware of me watching. She was uncomfortable with it. I wanted her to act a little now. Assume an air, work her wiles, seduce me. But she was a woman unable to totally lose herself, even in sex. She could not shake the stiffness of self-awareness.

27

I woke up to a sunny day and I was thirty-two. The hay was white and leaning. A chain of icebergs floated across the mouth of Brigus. I planted three of Gerald's pear seedlings on the shelf of garden sloping down to the water. A Pomeroy pony came over to the fence, strong, stout, and blowing green snot on my shirt. A wild happy eye, bright and game. If we lived here ten years we'd be able to stand at the front door and pick fruit. I noted that it took seven hours for an iceberg to appear and vanish beyond Red Head. Growlers drifted up to the bridge. The bergs were strays, having calved from glaciers in Greenland, drifted south on a Labrador current, and taken a wrong turn, entering the dead end of Conception Bay. They will sail into Holyrood, grind on the bottom and melt.

The caplin were sighted in Harbour Grace, Tom Dobie remarked. We watched a seiner on the horizon shooting out its nets. A seiner has a glass window in the floor so you can see the fish. The men of Brigus prepared cast nets at Jackson's Quay, and Tom Dobie walked over in his new seaboots to say tonight was it.

28

They built three bonfires on the landwash at Jackson's Quay. Fire to guide the caplin in. It was dusk. We brought the children over. A group of children were passing a burning stick around. Kathleen spotted Tom Dobie with a wheelbarrow and six empty barrels he'd rolled down for the caplin.

Kathleen: How's everything, Tom?

Oh, the best of gear.

The sun had sunk over the woods, and they were cooking a feed of pork and beans on the shore. They cut hanks of bread and we drank rum, our faces orange from the blazing fires. We raised a glass to Stan Pomeroy, for he loved the caplin. And the caplin were coming tonight.

Tom Dobie: They will look like a force of bad weather. And they will strike fast and roll.

Nine dories prowled around the caplin nets. And beside them ponies and carts in the water up to their axles. Twilight drawing the outlines of things. They will scoop up enough caplin to fill a thousand barrels. They will pull the carts up to the gardens, the ponies and the carts turning the long grass silver as they drag themselves up the hill. Some of the caplin for breakfast fish and some to the horses in hard days when fodder is scarce.

The men were wading in a little with their cast nets. I lifted little Rocky onto my shoulders and searched the water.

When you sees em, throw the net to the back of em.

The water was black, the shoals green and blue. There were boulders and kelp fanning in slow motion, and I spotted a flounder sitting passively in the dark green, as though dark green became it.

The green pitched to black. It swarmed black, then beat into a soft grey curve and then a slick of silver pins as the curve darted and separated around my feet.

Theyre here.

Tom Dobie slung his net and allowed it to sink in front of us. The black was filled now with slits of silver as the net bulged and caught around a heaving, independent bulk.

Put your son down and offer a hand there if'n you dont mind.

I handed Rocky over to Kathleen and lay hands on the net. We floated the mass to shore, caplin squirting free through the mesh, busting their silver guts to squirm out and spawn. What an image of chiaroscuro. We dragged the heaviness up on the apron, the delighted mad haul while the sea cleared its throat.

Now that's enough for the gardens.

The high tide arrived and the caplin crested and tumbled in the surge of ocean. So many fish just snapping there, trying to touch their tails while the children ran to the lip of the sea to gather up the shocked caplin, the small gash of their gills blinking like eyelids. The children scooped these frantic deaths into their arms and dumped them into carts and barrels, leaving behind a beach stained with custard-coloured eggs the texture of grit, a wave retreating, clicking the pebbly shore.

We took our caplin in a tub on a gully stick across our shoulders and walked up the shore and over the path to Frogmarsh, Tom Dobie's oilclothes gleaming with water and sweat, and as we walked Tom said, Okay change over. We walked on in the dark while groups of men around us did the same. All right change over. And at the top of the hill we stopped and laid down the tub and shared a cigarette and then, Okay, let's go.

29

I mowed the grass with a hand roller. I hooked up a seine net between two spruce posts. I gathered my friends. I had made friends and now I was presenting them with a tennis court. I served Dr Gill — he was wearing his suit and hat and standing well behind the baseline. He returned and I missed his volley. The Bartlett sisters cheered us, their arms around each other. I had invited the fishermen and their families, and most of them had laughed and said, politely, that they'd have a go in October — when they had time to play.

Dr Gill served out the game. I blamed humps in the green, the net leaned in his favour, there was a wind in my face, the sun in my eye. The weave of my racquet was loose. I hadnt the proper footwear.

Me: I am not the best at racquet sports.

In fact, Dr Gill said, youre a poor loser.

I shook his hand over the net while the audience of the Bartletts, Tom Dobie, and Kathleen and the children gave us a hearty clap. Marten Edwards and Bud Chafe came over and I offered my racquet to Marten and they carried on. Jim Hearn watched from his pharmacy door. Despite my poor performance it was a fine colonial afternoon.

30

We played tennis in the late afternoons. The hard ponk and swing. The thrill of a rally. Exerting yourself against a foe some distance away. Being friendly. I arranged a sign-up sheet — some of the fishermen got into it. Both Tony Loveys and George Browiny had a match. George Browiny, Tom told me, was always looking for a reason not to go to the wireless station.

During the working hours I walked the fields and made sketches and studied landscape and seacoast. I watched children picking snails on the shore rocks. I went down to sketch Rachel Dobie and Emily Edwards still laying out the fish. Drawing allowed me to look. Tom Dobie and Tony Loveys were there too. Marten Edwards was mending the trap. They were worried. There was trouble with the fish drying. Tom thought it was flies, but Tony Loveys said it was the slime. The mixed weather was causing the fish to get a mould. They were scraping it off as they turned the fish.

Tom: We threw a bit of salt on it, Kent, but he got in because of the bad weather. Havent been able to lay out the fish fast enough. It's bacterial.

Tony Loveys: Got to salvage what fish.

We'll re-salt and then wash him all again.

If you see dun on him, Tom said to me, then you got to scrub it off or the fish will get dumb, wet, and broken. If you clean him he'll be good, but some of it got the fly spits. You got to scrub that too, with water, and salt him and you got to kill the maggots, but my God what a bad grade we'll get when it comes to cull.

He showed me a fish with maggots. On the edge of the fish, where the edge doubled on itself. He pried that open and seven white maggots twisted slowly awake.

Emily: And then if the sun comes out too strong sure you got to double up the faces of the fish, same as if it were spilling down rain, keep the sun off the faces, too much it sunburn the fish. Yes, if it's not raining then the sun burns you. Got to put quilts up on the longers to shade the fish or bough it over.

They share their concern with me the way theyve shared everything else. The men watching the women work. The rock slabs on the shore are worn. Covered in mats of blue mussels, periwinkles, kelp.

31

How's the fishing?

Tom Dobie was catching trout in the brook that runs through town. Smoky lying in the shade. Tom wasnt sure what I was asking.

You mean the trouting. Theyre clever fish, Kent.

He was putting them in a butt of water. I got a little hole up farther, he said. Dammed over. Raise these youngsters in it and catch them again in the fall.

We walked the brook to the dam. We passed a horse, a shy one that moved behind the trees. Smoky went over to say hello.

He's got a hide on him, Tom said, that horse. Orstick.

Smoky left the horse and sat down.

What's that mean, *orstick*.

It's German for lie down.

I thought about that. No it isnt.

I'm joking boy. It just means, Or I'll get the stick. Orstick. Sounds German though, hey?

We walked up to a spot near the horse, under the trees. About six yards across, the swelled banks of the brook. It was August, sweltering, and the mosquitoes were bad.

You dont mind me taking a dip here, I said.

Tom shook his head and looked at the horse. I stripped. You coming in?

I'm not too smart when it comes to swimming.

He watched me cannonball in with a peel of laughter. He saw me enjoy myself.

Jump in, I said. I'll look after you.

He took off his clothes. He went over to where it was shallow. He was ginger about it. It was quite deep and it was true that he could not swim. I love throwing myself into cold water. He sat himself down in it. Smoky sat and watched.

Tom Dobie: It's lovely.

I could not touch bottom.

It's freezing.

He did a little dog-paddle.

We dragged ourselves out and sat on the bank in the half shade, our elbows on our knees, shivering in the heat. Tom fished a stick of tobacco from his trousers. Then he leaned back. I liked the hair. It was fine hair and it was lazy up his shins and the backs of his legs. Then the dense patch around his cock. I decided to stare at his cock a bit, I was thinking of Gerald's comment of my refusal to paint cocks. Tom's was tight but lengthening out now with the warm. Thick and healthy. It was relaxed, he was at ease. His knees opened. He was letting the heat of the sun get to his groin. I liked the length of his legs and the shape of his ass. The hair merged in a line up to his navel. And that was it for hair. His bare, clean nipples and the circle of pink around them was small. It was the smallest of pink. The lines in his torso and arms were slender curves, not hard muscle, just gentle and strong. There was not a straight line on him. His complexion clear, his skin pale. Then I saw his eyes. He was looking at me the same curious way. He had, I realized, a body like my own, but more idealized. At least, more like the body I'd like to have, the potential of my own body.

I should pour those trout in now.

32

Tom Dobie at my door. Jim Hearn, he said.

Pardon me?

He's after having a conniption.

A conniption.

I was cutting the grass down on the tennis court, and he won't allow me in no more.

Is that right.

I walked into town, past the merry cows. Down to Hearn's pharmacy. I opened the door, but Jim Hearn would not look at me.

What is it, Hearn.

You can't have the field.

I decided to stare at his red-whiskered chin.

Is it because you havent played. If you want to learn I'll —

I've changed my mind.

Me: Hearn. You agreed.

Not in any writing I have not.

I took him outside. I beckoned him. Come here, I said. We walked to the field. I anchored the pick and leaned my chin on my hands.

Now make me move, Hearn.

Kent, I dont want to —

I'm joking, Hearn.

But he would not laugh.

There'll be no tennis court on my land. I'm barring you and I am going to St John's now to secure that legal entreaty.

There was something in how he carried his head. He held it back about two inches, as if he wanted the extra space to veer his head away from an assault.

Something had turned in him. Something petty and he would not say.

Tom Dobie used his hands when he talked. He'd stare you in the eye when he listened. Then look down at your feet when he spoke. He explained to me and Kathleen that Jim Hearn had no complaint towards me. His animosity was for Dr Gill and Mr Cantwell.

I looked at Kathleen, trying to figure this one out.

Tom: When he heard they was both members of the tennis outfit. He dont want Gill on his property. Hearn's not about to have the other doctor on his land.

But Hearn's not a doctor.

I mean Hearn's doctor. The doctor who uses Hearn, Dr McDonald. He dont play tennis neither. Hearn and McDonald. See, McDonald sends his patients to Hearn. But Dr Gill sends his to Cantwell.

And Hearn sees Gill and Cantwell playing tennis on his land.

Hearn can be small.

Me: A toad.

Well, there's not much to do.

Kathleen: I think it's understandable.

Me: Let's go talk to Gill.

I walked over to the doctor's office with Kathleen.

Gill said, We can frighten him.

Me: How's that?

We'll grab him at the railroad station. On his way home from St John's.

Kathleen: Love.

We'll take him into my office. We'll open up the cabinets. Nickel-plated instruments of torture. He'll sign his house away.

Now that would get a rise.

Gill: Hearn's a lamb when he's cold. A lion when he's hot. There's nothing to worry about.

And so that was the plan, the ill-conceived, foolish thought.

33

Hearn was away to St John's for supplies and for what he'd threatened: legal entreaty to keep me off his property. All because of Mr Cantwell. As if a piece of paper would keep me off. We played tennis while he was away. I made it clear that Mr Cantwell and Dr Gill were heartily welcome. Everyone knew, of course, about the impending clash. But I carried on my business. I drew the women as they washed and dried the fish. I listened to them talk. Carmel Lahey had a two-year-old she kept in a little round basket, right on the flake. I mean, the thing could have fallen over.

Emily Edwards: Look at the weather.

Rachel Dobie: Yes, it'll keep up.

Carmel Lahey: How's the fish.

Rachel: Fish be good. Not sour at all.

Not burning is it.

Emily: Just feel it.

Looks burnt.

Feel it.

Carmel: So we'll keep it out then.

We got how many of us.

Emily: With or without Mr Kent.

The women giggled and posed coyly.

Rachel: There's enough to bring it in.

Emily: Yes. We'll bring it in tomorrow.

How many weeks it been out now.

Three weeks.

34

It was fish fish fish. Everything now devoted to fish, night and day. It had rained.

I said, The rain will be good for the gardens.

Tom Dobie: Yes, it'll make them jump up.

His hands were raw from hauling nets. He wore mitts to bed, he said, with pieces of raw liver in the fingers, just to soothe them.

I went again to Dr Gill. To make sure he was on board. He laughed at Hearn. Put him in my buggy, he said, take him into my shop. We'll fix him up, we'll give him a fright.

35

I watched my wife roll out some pastry.

Dont make it too thin.

If you think my pastry's thin, you can ask how I like it. Second, no one's asked you to diagnose a problem with the pastry. I am very happy with it.

No, it's too thin.

Kathleen fell out of love with me because of a perceived meanness. She thought that to raise children one needed a gentleness and a discipline. And all I had was the discipline. She had said, Dont do anything to Hearn. Build another court.

If there was another decent stretch of land, then yes.

She was adding flour to the rolling pin. She stroked the flour over the barrel of the pin.

I love your hips, Kathleen.

My hips are your hips.

Kathleen's figure. She had a high tight bum. There was a ledge to it. I put my thumbs on the small of her back. She rolled out the pastry.

You shouldnt stretch it.

I slipped my hand under her dress. Her legs were warm. She had such a high metabolism. She was always hot.

Just bend over.

Kathleen moved her feet away from the counter.

I got behind her and then knelt behind her. The children were with Emily.

Keep rolling the pastry.

She picked up the pastry with the belly of the rolling pin, then laid it on the floor of the pie pan. She piled in blueberries and sugar. I felt flour on my hands. I pushed my head into her. She was taking a second lump of pastry to roll out. I pulled away layers of her underclothes. I pulled them down over one leg and she lifted the leg. As she did this she threw flour on the counter. She pretended she was alone.

I nuzzled into her. I licked her.

It's tangy, I said. It's mildly sour.

She opened her legs. I licked. I licked her asshole. She flinched and I held her ass. I opened up her asshole with my thumb and licked her some more.

She pulled me up by the hair.

I turned her around.

Sit up on the counter. Sit on the pastry.

I put a hand behind her head. So her head wouldnt bang against the cupboards.

36

Word got around about what we had planned for Hearn. The town was turned out at the railroad station to watch. It wasnt something I wanted. I did not want to shame Hearn. I wanted to frighten him. I had Gill with me, but a private event had turned public. It reminded me of headlines in the *Sunday Times*: President to meet Pope to approve Vatican sanctions. When I see those lines I think, Why doesnt the president just mail the pope a newspaper. Save himself the trip. Perhaps

Hearn's hearing what I had in mind was enough. I couldnt tell.

Hearn alighted from the train and took a puzzled look at the crowd before I smoothly bent him in a headlock. I dug my chin into a blue eye. I ground the heel of my fist in his bald ear. It was pantomime but forceful. Rocky was delighted. I directed Hearn to Dr Gill's buggy.

Me: You all set?

I'm good to go.

But the doctor panicked when he saw how red Hearn's face was, and he drove off without us. Fucker, I thought.

I have a huge, passive man in a headlock. I am two miles from town.

Improvise. I heard applause.

I shifted Jim Hearn's head, like a rudder, towards the railroad station office. The crowd had jammed the wicket and the office door. I didnt know what to do. But I had to have a performance. When you have an audience you must perform.

Me: Youre a swine, Hearn. Youre a tiny giant. Youre a perfidious, two-faced, gutless wonder. And having killed many a scoundrel in my life, I am thinking of adding you to the list.

The ticket agent waded in. We'll have no murdering in here today, Mr Kent.

37

They loved what had happened to Hearn. I was celebrated. Hearn was not liked, I realized. They were eager to play tennis.

I taught Tony Loveys how to serve. Jim Hearn stayed in his pharmacy. I thought that was it, a lesson learned. I even felt sorry for the man. I thought about going to him, but a bit of time should pass first. I might give him a drawing. I wanted to make amends, but it's true I was enjoying the attention. It provided zest to work. I got up at five, walked to the brook nude, hauled up some water. Listened to the dawn chorus. I had a coffee and worked in the studio. I was stoked with ambition and drive. But every time I entered that studio, it was as if I opened a small drawer in an oak cabinet and slipped in a burlap sack that contained my humour. The drawer was a river in which I drowned my humour. It was as if funniness would cancel out serious art. So I banished my humour. And yet I was very careful not to damage that little bag, because I wore it in life. It was my relief. After work, after the workshop of serious labour, I whistled for the burlap sack and the cabinet drawer opened and out pounced my lightheartedness.

How ambition bled playfulness from my work.

I look back on it now and I see how romantic it was. How industrial my art had become, and how measured. It was full of effort. Technique appeared all over the surface, and where was I? Where was the personal?

I have many smaller niggling grievances, but this large, erasing ambition still seems the only evidence left — when it was the small life that really runs things. It is this small life I believe in now: the overall accumulation of disparate events. I believe in the hybrid, I'm convinced that new things come from the merging of tradition and new thought. I had ambition back then and a big heart, and I was ruthless and could laugh. I was mischievous, but I was hard too. I believed in acting on desire. I still do.

I cut the children's hair. And the next day the hair looked shorter. It's as if hair carries around the memory of its long-hairedness for a day. And then sleep and then the short hair wins out. This is true: a new thing will come about and fail. And then the new thing will win. New things fail, then prevail.

If you get the right rhythm you can love almost anything. Because it involves life and youre in love with life. The reason I could have children is that the predictable drudge of their inevitable growing up never swamped the joy I had at how things looked and how they behaved. I did not shrivel at the thought of inevitability. Death is part of life and children are a sly inheritance. At least that's the persuasion I come from. I know I will die, I have to die. I'm an old man now, and I'm convinced that I will die. Death spurs me on. It's a simple logic, especially since my children are not like me.

Gerald Thayer once said to me, I'm afraid of dying. He was afraid, he said, that there might be a life after death. He was afraid that he believed there might be a God. He did not want it. He could not bear the thought of living again, after death. Seventy years, yes. But forever? It depressed the hell out of him. A short life excited him. He thought that when Hobbes said life was nasty, brutish, and short, he meant the last quality as a relief. I've thought the opposite. That even though life is mean and harsh, it's still better than nothing.

38

Tom Dobie came with a constable. There was a written griev-
ance. Jim Hearn had pressed charges.

Is he serious?

Constable: It is hard to know the mind of a gull.

I didnt hurt him.

Kathleen: You humiliated him.

Constable: And he knows the law.

Tom: Perhaps you were too hard on him.

The thing is, if Dr Gill had not abandoned me.

Tom: It was funny while you had a man of the town alongside.

But when it was just me against Hearn.

And now that the constable had visited, I noticed people were
slightly formal around me. They felt Hearn a fool, but still what
right did I have to make a public fool of him. I was an outsider. I
lived apart from the community, in that house along the headland. I had complained more about the loss of my toolbox than
the loss of the *Southern Cross*. I heard this openly spoken —
voices travel well over water and in darkness at night. I had
ordered all that coal. It was a show of wealth and that had bothered them. They thought my figurehead above the door
outrageous. And wasnt I trying to rile up the fishermen to form a
union? How quickly a mood can shift. Perhaps I was a little arrogant. Yes, I see now how they saw my spirit as arrogance. And
maybe I was. Even Kathleen was uncomfortable in town — but
only when she was with me. The women were quiet around her.
But there was nothing I could do to turn this impression. I wanted

to work but found their suspicions hard to ignore. It goaded me.
I asked Bud Chafe. I said, What's up? And he laughed.
Nobody's that fond of Hearn, he said. Let it blow over.

I visited the Pomeroys and the Bartletts. They were still the
same. They saw the humour. But most of the men were with
the fishery now, and I was noted for my apparent lack of industry. Who the hell was I? If only they knew what we lived on.
Sixty-five dollars a month and the allowance from my mother.
Then it struck me. I was living under the same conditions as
the fishermen. I had created my own personal truck system. I
was living on credit and was beholden to my agent, Charles
Daniel, for a price he had fixed. What kind of fool was I. I was
tearing my hair out at my own folly. If I was to rail against the
merchants and encourage the men to unionize, I needed to set a
better example. It was Kathleen who hit on a solution.

Why dont you, she said, sell shares in your work.

I sat at my desk and thought of that. Shares.

Instead of a monthly stipend from Charles Daniel, I'd draw
up shares. I'd sell futures. I would stake my reputation and sell
shares in my ability to make art. I had arrived at capital — the
future lay in creating equity, not debt.

I designed the artwork for a single share in Rockwell Kent,
worth a hundred dollars. I wrote to Charles Daniel to cancel
our arrangement. I included the original share in Rockwell Kent
and asked him to make a print run of two hundred. My estate, I
wrote, will be worth twenty thousand dollars. Charles, you can
acquire a share a month and send me a hundred dollars instead
of sixty-five.

39

Painting is a solitary and isolating work. What did that Kent fellow do in his house all day? If a farmer saw me up in his fields, painting his cows and his hills, he no longer waved to me. He seemed annoyed at my presence, as though by giving me leave to use his property to stand and paint on, he was guilty of fraternizing with a strange and corrupting influence.

So I decided to get out of there for a while. There was a floater heading down to prosecute the Labrador fishery. Niner Harris was going aboard with his mother and father. Rupert had said I could stay at their quarters in Turnavik. Would that be okay, Kathleen? Perhaps she alone could begin to build up goodwill. Now that the vegetarian socialist was away. She could have Emily help her with the children. Emily did not seem to mind the talk. And Tom Dobie, if anything occurred to the house of a physical nature, was on alert to help out. Yes, go, she said. She knew that to deny me would make me sulk, would make me judge her as limiting me. She did not allow me to go because she loved my leaving, she just feared the consequences of my feeling stymied.

It was the great Labrador fishery and I thought I should document it. I should see fishermen at work on the sea. I brought paper and brushes and ink and paint.

I took a boat down there and planned to stay a week in Turnavik. To hell with this, is what I thought. I dont have to be in Brigus all the time.

40

There was a storm out of Conception Bay and we went below the *Industry*'s deck. On board the floater — a fifty-ton schooner — they ate tinned beef, potatoes, pickles, and a good mustard in a cruet. I was feeling a little seasick and stuck to tea.

Bit shy of feeding, said one, an old, well-built man in a colourful cloth bathrobe, filling his pipe. You could tell he was of a different class, even from his shoes.

Yes, I said.

Because of the storm.

Is it true, I said, that Newfoundlanders like to point out the obvious?

If you feel like feeding the gulls, he said, that door is quickest to the gunwale.

Thank you, I said.

He was a judge, this man. A member of the floating court, he said, on his way to mete out justice along the Labrador coast. Almost eighty years of age. Come along, he said, let's get some air.

He lit his pipe and passed it to me. Prowse was his name. He took me on a tour of the deck and then below deck. The men, he said, they make their way down the Labrador to stations along the coast, including Bartlett's station at Turnavik. You know Bartlett.

Yes, I said. I'm staying in Brigus.

He pointed out that the dories on the port side were painted buff yellow with a green trim, the dories on the starboard side grey with red trim. So the fisherman who slipped out to fish would know by the colour of his boat which side of the schooner to come to if he had to get aboard quickly. If a swell rose.

41

Because of the storm we decided to lie to in Harbour Grace. Twenty-five thousand Newfoundlanders, Prowse said, migrate to Labrador each spring. Some, the livyers, stay all year. They live the winter in shacks on flour, tea, and molasses.

All hands aboard the *Industry*, he said, are Christian. Except you and the sailmaker.

I go to church, I said.

Yes, and he smiled.

Is it that obvious I'm not religious.

Let's say an independent mind stands out.

The ninety crew aboard the *Industry* were permanent. They caught green fish. The fish were laid in salt in the holds of the boat. Sometimes a salt banker would come by and more salt purchased. If the fishing was good.

Belowdecks we checked out the quarters. Most of the hold was salt. On top of the salt was bedding and luggage. We found Niner Harris and his parents, Mag and Mose. They were stationers and late in the season. They were to join Mag's brother in Turnavik. They shared a bunk on top of the salt — their faces just inches from the beams and planking of the deck above them. A piece of sailcloth divided them from the next bunk. They cooked and washed on deck but slept and changed down here.

Mose Harris, joking, We came aboard to get away from you, Kent.

We passed a coper selling tobacco and alcohol to the fishermen. Illegal, Prowse said, but done openly and freely. The rum and gin then sold in shebeens onshore.

Aboard at night the dark was devoted to stars.

Prowse, looking up: Made in vain.

Me: I wonder about that — is it all in vain.

I'm speaking of the Milky Way, he said. They call it the maiden vein.

We slept at anchor along the Labrador coast. Anchorage was marked by a naked man on the shore. In the evenings the officers fished for salmon near the mouth of a river. We had salmon for lunch. The king of fish, Prowse said.

We stopped into Cartwright for the day, and he invited me to court. You might find these cases sad but interesting.

I took a seat in back so I could leave if I got bored. A man was brought before the judge and admitted he was a ship's captain. He was in charge of a vessel outside Lloyd's security. The claim by him was that his ship had foundered and was wrecked on the rocks off Blanc Sablon. Insurance was received, the ship sold. It was sold back to him.

This is all true, your Honour, and legal.

The charge, Prowse read, is that you intentionally wrecked the ship.

It had been a bad season with no fish, your Honour.

Yes, but your crew says you forced them to ram the ship onto a shoal.

I hardly rammed it, sir. A bit of misfortune. She was put up on a low-tide sunker.

You claimed the ship was beyond repair.

He shrugged.

You claimed she was played out, got your money to compensate for a poor season. You bought her back and salvaged her.

That's about how it's done, sir.

Prowse's head in his big hands. Crew claims you bought the vessel for a dollar.

I tendered the only bid, your Honour.

I bet you did. You had her careened, and then sailed home in her.

That is correct, your Honour.

Prowse fined the captain seventy dollars. He seized the ship and gave it to Lloyd's. Not for a moment did the captain think he had done something wrong.

The next case was against an entire southcoast community. There had been a true shipwreck the winter before. A salt banker had been trapped in a galloping surf and crushed on a reef. The crew in the frozen sea, hanging to the bowsprit. They wrapped themselves in canvas. They held on to chopped-down masts. And while they drowned and perished of hypothermia, a small gang from the town had rowed out in a chain of dories and stripped the banker of plates and silver and manila rope and tobacco. They had gathered spoons and money and a mantel clock while the salt dissolved around them. They had pushed survivors aside for the booty. This was the charge against four-teen residents of the town. There had been one survivor, and this was his testimony. The man was helped into the stand, for he had lost both his hands and one leg. He said they had been at sea for months. Had sailed from Cadiz and meant to land in St John's with a load of salt. There was smallpox on board, and beriberi. There was scurvy, he said, typhus, lice, nervous exhaustion, and venereal disease. There was blood poisoning and influenza. There was hypothermia, he said, and frostbite and gangrene. Then this storm. Our rudder, he said, holding up one handless wrist, was sheered off, and a makeshift one cut away. We didnt put up a stitch of canvas. We were pushed north, away from St John's. We saw the birds of Funk and then the island, but we couldnt hold the island, so Captain told us to better crack on sail. We hove west like that for a day. Captain figured it was an emergency, so we lowered the colours and turned them upside down. That's what they saw.

Prowse: Did you see them?

We got in close to a rough shop.

Please explain.

We fell victim to a canal effect, your Honour. A change in pressure, it pushes your vessel towards the land. So we got sucked up onto these here rocks. That's when I saw them coming out in small boats. We was hoping yet to free ourselves. The masts were cut down, both to raise the level of the deck and to offer the crew something if we had to abandon ship. We tossed over the salt too, to lighten her. Hoping she'd come off the rocks. But her jawbones were broke, so we covered her with a sail to see if the water could be stopped from reaching the engines. I climbed into the shrouds and saw it all as they come out in their boats. We thought they come to help us.

The shrouds.

What gives the mast lateral support. The men, your Honour, were clinging to the chopped-down masts. Some were rolling under and losing their grip. All they had to do was throw a line made into a loop. A man in water will reach with his weakest hand and can often not hold on to a rope.

You saw the death of one mate.

Yes, before they were through with him they stripped him of his clothing. They appeared pleased with his death.

They knew the man.

He was from there. One often hates the mate.

You stayed above in the rigging.

I had bread and salt pork in a handkerchief. When I saw what they done to the mate, well, I stayed up there. The ship was doomed.

Youve been after having three operations to amputate hands and one leg.

My genitalia just recently was removed. Your Honour, my hands rotted off during the seventeen weeks I spent here. The man in charge would not agree to ferry me to St John's. They was hoping I'd perish. I was put into a cold hut downwind from town.

After the people left the ship, what did you do.

I went down aboard her and made a raft of some planks. I put my feet in a box meant for ship's papers. I found a hen basket with four hens dead in it. I paddled to a fellow shipwreck, who was in a broken boat. We found a barrel of cider. We were to use a hoop off the cider barrel to repair the boat. But neither of us had the strength to turn the boat over. We had to paddle ashore up to the chest in water. He perished then. I kept on. Seventeen weeks, sir, without proper treatment.

A woman came up to testify. She was gaunt and open around the eyes. She looked insane and starved and determined and sorry but vexed with a dilemma. You could tell she knew starvation well, and she was intimidated by the formality of court. I thought she too must be a survivor, but she was one of the fourteen on trial.

Is the charge before you accurate, Judge Prowse asked.

She replied, bitterly: Why did they have to go up on the rocks. And tempt us like that?

The way she said it. There was nothing more to be said.

The judge sought me out and stood me a drink.

I have a confession, he said.

He'd heard all about me. American painter in the hinterland. He joked about the romance of it. I love experts, he said. Regardless of the field. Except experts in poverty.

He shook his head. They are that poor, he said, that they are lured by the misfortunes of others. And imagine being that man, perched in a mast, having climbed as far as he is able. He looks down at the world.

I dont know how you do it.

Sometimes, in my line, there is levity too.

He'd just done a trial in St Anthony. There was a stabbing. On the stand a witness who described the murder. Kept addressing Prowse as me old trout. Bailiff cautioned him, said, Call him your Honour. Then Prowse asked if there was anything else the witness wished to say. There was nothing left on the books. But the witness said, No, your Honour me old trout, except perhaps what I heard the man say after stabbing Vince.

What was that.

After he stabbed Vince, the man he was terrified. He said, What's I gonna do.

Pause.

That's it. That's all the accused said?

Yes, your Honour me old trout.

Okay.

Except for what Vince said back to him. Vince, he said, holding in his guts, he says, What's you gonna do? What's *I* gonna do?

Judge Prowse and I slugged back our drinks.

I told him about my charge in Brigus. He smiled. Oh, I know all about that one, he said. That's how I heard about you. Got your file right here.

He had been assigned the case.

Back on board that night I heard Mose Harris say: I plan to spend most of this summer drunk. When youre married the best thing you can ask for is a fight.

42

We left Prowse in Cartwright and continued on to Turnavik. On our way we fell into a pack of drift ice. The ice was not stationary. The ice had a destination. Our floater tried to find a path through it. It pushed pans of ice away. But looking at the icefield ahead you felt the pattern was not random. You could feel an intention. The ice was inanimate, yet it had purpose. By nightfall the ice had knitted firmly together and grown thicker. It was not a purpose that was on a human scale of geography or time. The ice had taken us prisoner and was leading the floater to some ice-logical rendezvous.

I thought this was summer.

Mose Harris: It's awful weather all right.

He said we could be stuck like this for a day or a week. The captain asked if some of us wouldnt mind going overboard and chopping at the ice. I was happy to. We used poles to push away the ice pans. The floater moved ahead half a boat length and we marched up to the next set of pans. We did this for three hours, and when we looked at the shore we saw we hadnt made any progress. The ice had drifted south as we were pushing north.

The ice grew coarse and bunched around the floater. It broke and clawed in giant fingernails. The ice contained greens and browns and blacks. The floater listed to starboard. The ice buckled and crunched around the hull.

Jesus, Mose said. I never seen anything like it for the season.

There was a raft of ice on the starboard side. A white wall pressed against the engines. The ship lacked the beams and sheathing for ice work. The captain was calm, just making sure his lifeboats were in order. There seemed to be a shared humour about the fluke of it all. Mose said, about the ice, I have seen a dog's jaws carry a duck egg for miles and then crush it in a second.

A column of ice from a mile off bore through the ice pans as if looking for something to eat. It was heading directly for us. The engine sounded like a tired heart.

Time to scuttle her.

The crew unloaded tons of food, loose wood, dogs, tents, crates of ammunition, petrol, coal, alcohol, rigging, sails, kitchen supplies. We got to free her out, Mose Harris said. He had been on one boat like this when they chopped the masts down. To make the boat less top-heavy. He said it felt like they were chopping into the skull of the ship.

I could not believe I had spent a day in court listening to this very kind of ordeal. It made me anxious for looters, though we could not see land. I was happy that we could not, but then worried about how we'd get home. We had drifted many miles into ice-clogged sea. Which was worse.

The crew stepped off the ship and winched over the nested dories. A sail was spread across a gunwale. Men on the ice and men on board held the sides of the sail. We lifted one of the dogs and let it slide down. Nine dogs this way. The dogs were delighted.

The ice became bony and indifferent. If you scraped away the top layer of white snow crust, all the ice was black. It was an odd find, like parting an animal's white coat to see a dark pigment.

The weather grew bad.

We built a wall of snow and sat leeward. Mose Harris gave me some advice. Keep ahold of a gaff stick. If you wake up this night and find yourself on an ice pan, floating away, you'll have something to burn. Make shavings off your stick. Better yet if you get a seal. Cut strips of fat and drip on the shavings.

As if I'm going to discover a seal.

If one comes handy, hit him with your gaff, hit him with the service end and make sure he dont sink. Watch out for the sun, he'll scald the eyes out of your head, and dont be fooled by the blue drop. You'll see houses and ships on it. If it snows you won't hear a ship's whistle if youre windward.

I think, Mose, youre enjoying this.

We kept a watch for five days, but never had to sleep on the ice. One night from the deck we watched the horizon flash. Mose called it an ice-blink, beyond the blue drop. On the morning of the fifth day the ice relaxed. It lost its determination and eased back. The space around the floater gently filled with cold sea water. It had squeezed its hands together for five long days making a plan, and now it released us. The captain ordered the stores back on board. Hoist the spanker, he said. That'll make her smarter.

We were safe but lost. The captain took a shot of the sun with his sextant and brought it down to kiss the sea. Then he pointed us in a direction that he knew would make us hit land. A coper sailed close by. We waved him over.

Where are we? our captain shouted.

You got the Cook map aboard?

Yes.

Well, look at the *E* in Newfoundland. Youre right under the *E*.

43

What I like about the name Newfoundland: how many other places are named so repetitively, redundantly. Yes, it is land. Yes, we found it. And yes, it is new. The only place that has new in it that does not refer to an older place. After Ireland it was England's first colony. When so much land is named after benefactors. No one got the nod for this one. Perhaps no one wanted the responsibility. But Bartlett and Peary named things in worse places than this. Peary named an entire mountain range after Jenny Starling's father: Crocker Land. And a thing imagined can never be fully unimagined. And Newfoundland, its descriptor telling of time, discovery, and substance.

We put in at Turnavik. The nose of our steamer curled in to the pier. There were many rocks the ship had to manoeuvre around. Sunkers, Mose Harris called them. Lethal to sailors.

Me: I guess the skipper knows where every rock in the harbour is.

Mose Harris: No. But he knows where theyre not.

As we docked there was a hymn in the air. From a distance a brass band. I could not see the band. There were blubber barrels on the stagehead and Inuit women pounding out the hard blubber. Then, on the hill, this unfinished church. Mose Harris said, That's the Moravian mission. Moravians, I said. Did you know that when Tolstoy was a kid, his older brother told him they would all be ant brothers? He'd misheard the word *Moravian*, which sounds like *ant* in Russian.

Mose: Yes boy. Right on.

Then I saw them. Standing in the rafters of this unfinished church. Figures dressed in sealskin, playing big polished brass instruments. They swayed at the hips. A tuba and cymbals. They were Inuit women and men welcoming us to Turnavik.

I think, I said to Mose, I'm being converted.

Children stood in a barrel without ends, tipping it. Dogs running amok, dogs that had leapt from the floater into the sea before it reached the wharf. Dogs sick of being on the water.

The stagehead filled with livyers. Looking for supplies, for family and friends. This is where the Harrises put in.

Mose: We've been fishing out of Turnavik since I was eleven years old.

And this is Bartlett's station?

This is where he parks the *Morrissey*.

And where he docked the *Roosevelt*. To pick up fifty pairs of sealskin boots, and whale meat for the dogs, on their way to find Crocker Land. This is where they returned, five years later, and made their claim by wireless for the pole.

They use hook and line, no traps. Mag, she does the cooking. We have a room, just an ordinary fishing room. More of a summer resort, Mose Harris said. We have a dwelling house and salt store that we share with Baxter Hodge. You can stay with us if you like.

I said Rupert Bartlett was taking care of me.

Well yes, you'd want to stay with Rupert.

But I'd love to see you work.

I walked with them to the brother-in-law's fishing rooms. Baxter Hodge. Their stage was about sixty feet long and sixteen feet wide. A fair-sized stage. It was rundown. Can't afford to keep her up, Baxter Hodge said. But the salt store was in good repair. The men shook hands.

Baxter Hodge said he came down on the *Kyle* and in the fall he'll leave the boat on the stages. Just turn her over and pile some boughs and longers over her. He left Brigus in mid-June. They had their boat in the davits of the *Kyle*. Last year, Baxter said, we got two hundred and ninety quintals of fish. That almost paid our account. It would have paid, but my fish got mixed in with some cullage aboard the coaster that we was shipping to St John's on. I wasnt too happy about that. I make good fish and there they were loading it in with cullage. I wanted to have it placed in piles, and so I had a kick with the captain about this.

Captain Bob?

Yessir that cunt.

Mose: Be easy, boy.

Mag: Rupert's easier. Rupert's here now.

Baxter: I give Bartlett my fish and it was to be subject to the St John's prices. I wanted that to appear on my receipt. After they culled my fish I had roughly a quintal left over. A man who broke his arm on one of the steamers asked us for some fish to help him out — it is customary for us to help one another out down there if we can do it. I gave him this extra hundred pounds or so. and a man aboard the *Hesperus* told me that he sold that same quintal of fish in St John's for forty cents more than what I got. If I had got the extra forty cents a quintal, I would have been able to pay my account.

44

I stayed with Rupert Bartlett. He oversaw the operation. In his office there were photographs of animals arranged by frozen taxidermy. Polar bears in the moment of swiping the shoulder off his brother, Bob. Peary's head inside the tusks of a walrus, like he was planning a jailbreak. Peary spearing a char, letting it freeze on the ice, shattering it, then eating the chunks like they were pink strawberries. I wanted to be with the men. I was excited by the work of labourers. Paperwork bored me. So I went with Mose and Baxter and Niner Harris and helped them land twenty-three barrels of fish in a day. Then we split it and washed it before nightfall. One day's work. Enough fish to last a family a year. We were all cleaned up by seven oclock and then a man came in and told Mose he could have thirteen quintals more. We took it and by nine-thirty it was all stowed away. Then we had a drink of rum.

A good fisherman, Baxter Hodge said, can do a lot in one day.

I'm realizing the very same.

That is, a fisherman who understands his work. Lots of men go fishing just for something to do. They are not real fishermen. Use makes master of any trade.

Judge Prowse had told me that there might be much demand for Labrador fish this year, and that the Bartletts werent taking a big risk outfitting. The demand would come if there was a European war.

Baxter: You met the judge?

Mose: He was right chummy with him all the way down the shore.

We left him, I said, in Cartwright.

Youre a ballsy one.

I asked Baxter Hodge what he thought of Labrador fish this summer.

I am afraid to say anything, he said. It may be all right — in fact, I really do not know enough to say anything just now. It might not be worthwhile touching it. Whether the market is going to be any better during the next six months you cannot say. It cannot be any worse. If there is less fish caught, it should be better still.

The next day was Sunday and I walked up to the new church with Rupert. Inside there were Bibles in the pews, but all the covers had been torn off. I asked about this. Dogs, Rupert said. They came charging down that hill last winter. They were ploughing mad through the snow. Made a beeline to the church and dove straight through a window like it was open. They took over the church, starved out of their minds. There were dogs with Bibles in their mouths, the whites of their crazy eyes, reeling drunken-like over the pews. Dogs madly tearing the covers off with their back teeth. They ate everything leather in the place.

I asked about the Dobies. Yes, Rupert said. That was an awful case. That winter was too bad to talk about.

He showed me the house where it had happened. The house was empty now. No windows and no door. Inside, the hearth and the roof open above it. No chimney. There never was a chimney, Rupert said, just a wooden funnel. Along the walls were benches to sleep on. Where Robert Dobie had shot himself.

I said goodbye to the Harrises. Mose was talking to an Inuk named Anasqasi. Her three young sons. The sons looked tall, something strange in their faces. They looked like me. There was a young black man too. I took Mose Harris aside. How did he end up here. That's Henson's child, Mose said. Matthew Henson? He nodded. And Anasqasi's boys? Those are Peary's.

I stared at their faces, their height. I've met Peary and you could see parts of Peary breaking out on the faces. Eruptions of cheekbone and eyelid and earlobe.

The American men, Mose Harris said, they all took on Inuit wives. Even the black man, Henson.

Me: And Bartlett?

Mose laughed. No, Bartlett stayed true.

Stayed true. To who.

That's a good question. He never had no time for women. They were three years in Greenland.

What Henson wrote: On this day the son of Ethiopia, the sons of Asia and of Europe, stand here representing humanity at the top of the earth.

In Peary's book: I felt almost nothing. It all seems so commonplace.

45

I bought my wife a sealskin coat. I bought it from the Greenland Eskimo Anasqasi, a beautiful woman who convinced me that Greenland was a place I had to visit. I confess I did not spend every night under Rupert's roof. When I went to see the Eskimo coats I stayed over. I ate with Anasqasi's family. I was exhilarated with their language, their faces and eyes. The texture of their hair and how we spoke in sign language, their humour. I was fascinated, and when I'm so entranced I forget the rest of the world. I wanted to absorb Anasqasi's world for the short time I had.

I was not watching the time, and then the time came to retire. They assumed I would stay, and I spent the night with Anasqasi.

Did Rupert know this? Perhaps. And I was not happy that he would have to bear the burden of this information. He liked my wife. He did not wish to be complicit in my behaviour. He was happy when the steamer arrived to take me home. I'll see you soon, he said. A telegram had arrived. His brother was safe. He'd found the *Karluk* survivors. He was steaming back to Turnavik to pick up Rupert and the *Morrissey*.

It took us another ten days, owing to ice and fog, to sail back to Brigus. Judge Prowse boarded again at Cartwright. He was consoling a man with a broken leg whom he'd met below deck. He'd given up, Prowse said.

The man was fifty-one years old now and first went fishing when he was twelve. I can't recall, the man says, a summer when we didnt come away with a voyage of fish. I was twenty-six years old when I left my father and went for myself. It's a hard thing for a man to give up what he is used to. A man that got any kind of fair play at the Labrador fishery, there's no better way of making a living.

46

I came back to Brigus. The children were there with Emily Edwards. Kathleen stood over me as I tugged off my boots. She pushed me up against the door to my studio. She said, Rockwell Kent, I'm pregnant.

I kissed her. I stroked her stomach. I put a hand under her heart. I have a coat for you.

She loved the coat and the fact that I'd thought of her. There was a moment when we recognized each other and pushed away the ordinariness of pretending to live original lives. And in the background Emily Edwards on the floor with the children.

Kathleen was a tall woman. Dark hair and quiet. But a surprise, like this pushing against a door, her heel lifting out of her slipper. This ability to deliver a secret. She told me once that she didnt like people. And that stuck. Even after, when I realized that what she meant was a type of people. She did not enjoy artists. Or ideas. She was not swayed by words that a particular time conveyed to be the truth. She was too aware of prejudice. But she enjoyed talking to Mrs Pomeroy about hens. Or the children with bits of nature. She admired Emily Edwards for both her brashness and how she cultivated a true sense of the seasons and the mystic nature of the sea and wind.

I loved Kathleen for this graceful disposition. She sat with her back slightly erect. I watched her take steps and it was as if each time her foot landed it was to feel the texture of the step in the sole of her shoe. Every move was considered. We married and my love for this movement lasted three years. It's true that I marvelled that foot-testing for three years. We call that early love. And then those same mannerisms began to annoy me. Why does she always look like she is entering cold water.

Gerald, a shit disturber. A woman at a party had said, There are no men. Gerald: Kent has left his wife. The woman was interested. So interested that Gerald had to retract: It's not true.

But the idea was planted. A lazy lie takes on a bit of the truth. It was the same with Alma. The reason she left Gerald. He'd had a tightening in his chest. He'd said, Call an ambulance. He was working upstairs. What? A cab, call a cab.

They went to the hospital. There was a man waiting with a pitchfork in his chest. George started to describe his symptoms in metaphorical terms, but as soon as Alma said her husband was having chest pains they took him in. They studied his body for thirty minutes. He was okay. A heart attack, the doctor said, feels like a vise clamp on your chest. It crushes you.

But as they went home Alma thought about how she'd felt during that moment of fear. She'd thought, I've wasted my life. I havent lived enough.

Her attitude changed. And while she stayed with Gerald, she could not love him. So she left him. Perhaps for men it is not such a blow: years later Gerald found his way back to Jenny Starling.

Alma said to me after she left Gerald: Funny thing is this — if he had a chest pain now I'd think, Why didnt I stick it out with him. Why did I go so easily.

So in a way, Gerald's joking at a party about Kathleen and me being finished, well, that precipitated the thought of finishing. We like to coddle the thought of ending things, even if those things are good. It's the nature of sabotaging one's own happiness. Jenny Starling's husband had left her. Luis Starling. Before they'd married Luis had said, The next woman I'm with will be the one. Jenny had believed he meant her. But Luis Starling was describing the woman after Jenny.

After Kathleen had left me, that's when Gerald and Jenny got together. Jenny said to me: I dont see what the problem is. Youve got me. Youve got me like this and the rest of the world too. Would you really be happy with me and two children and nothing else? Because you'd have to be faithful. See, I'm not going to do anything to hurt Gerald. I love Gerald and —

Yes, I said. I'm not saying anything about your predicament.

It's not a fucking predicament.

Okay, your choice.

Kent, why do you have to see it that way? This is the situation. This is the way it is.

Oh, so that's different from a predicament.

When I married Kathleen, my friends had quietly complained of her. And when I first moved to Brigus, she'd stayed with Gerald and Alma in New York. She received but did not exude. And Gerald had felt drained as one is drained after visiting a hospital. Except I had brought them the hospital. She was a ward.

But she was good with the children and now we would have a fourth.

Are you happy? she said. She was three inches from me.

It's terrific, I said.

47

I was ordered into Judge Prowse's temporary offices. He'd put on a dickey and his robes. His rooms were bare of ornament. Sun through high small windows. A cold woodstove and a pale oak desk.

Sir, you have been charged with assault.

He said it formally. And I realized he was being a professional now.

It was a prank, Judge. No one was hurt. Someone should have been hurt, but they werent.

You will come to a hearing?

I would find a hearing fascinating.

Fine. He got up and hung up his robes. You do any hunting.

I have been known to accompany hunters.

Well, come on then.

The Judge borrowed a rifle from Bob Bartlett's father. It looked long and dubious. A gun to shoot seals with, William Bartlett said. We took it to a gravel basin to sight it in. I drew a portrait of Jim Hearn with antlers on the side of a wooden crate, paced off fifty yards, and fired three rounds. A bullet at fifty yards will hit the same target at two hundred yards, Prowse said, such is the trajectory of a rifled bullet. The sights were top-notch.

Mr Pomeroy had told Prowse that several caribou had been visiting the gardens and munching the tops of his turnips. If we got up at dawn and cruised down there.

I was up at five oclock and I walked down to wake up Prowse. He was putting a leg into his tweed knickers. He looked like an Austrian skier.

There is something cold and reluctant in my bones about getting up in the dark. But the thing is, it's terrific to choose to get up early. This has to do with control, of course. In deciding what one wants to do.

Prowse loaded the rifle and we strolled out to the back acre of Pomeroy's garden.

Want to carry that, son?

The word surprised me. I hadnt thought of the judge as much older than me. If your father dies while youre young he takes the standard with him and you forget to age. Or else you grow up immediately and bypass the idea of aging. So here was the judge, calling me son. I knew that he meant the word as an affectionate one. But it made me think that I was with a man who could be my father. That I was learning to hunt.

The rifle in one hand felt heavy and powerful. The sky was dark but promising. I stared at tree stumps. I picked out the rows of turnip and potato. I lifted the barrel and loaded the magazine. It made a loud metal shunking.

Prowse pointed at something. He gestured for me to give him the gun.

I stared at this flatness, this quiet stillness. Nothing moved. The bushes were heavy with dew.

Prowse: Just past that flash of marsh.

A smudge. The smudge was what caught your eye. I looked for the smudge and some tree branches moved across the far shore of the bog. The branches were not branches. They were antlers, and three quiet caribou jogged up to the edge of the garden and halted. They were alive and silent.

Prowse levelled the rifle on them. Then he knelt on one knee. He lowered the rifle.

We moved up with them. When they moved we moved. Then they heard us. Prowse sighted them again. And they trotted on. Suddenly he ran. He got far ahead of me and they froze. The first light was banking off their flanks.

We tracked them like this for another twenty minutes, a little deeper into the woods. I wasnt sure if Prowse was really considering a shot. He froze when they froze. He was enjoying this mimicry. I was breathing hard from the false shots of adrenaline. There was nothing in the world for me now except Prowse and these caribou.

We were a good hundred yards away from the three of them. But a clear shot. Prowse raised the stock of the rifle to his cheekbone. He levelled it at the neck of the stag. Then he let out a little whistle. A loud crack. Something struck my bare hand — it was the bright brass casing of the bullet. It had ejected from the chamber and struck me. It was hot.

Nothing.

Damn ya, he said.

He reloaded. The caribou turned their necks to look at us, curious. I realized then that Prowse was eighty years old and probably half blind. He squeezed out a second crack and the back of the stag slumped down.

You got him.

I got him.

He knelt down and I came up to him. I waited for his advance. He put a hand on my shoulder.

Just wait.

He patted my shoulder and laid his back on the brush, the rifle across his knees. He chuckled. He was delighted with himself. He just lay there for a minute, then he got up.

Let's get a bit of kindling from under that brush.

Why'd you whistle?

Theyre skinny when theyre front on. You have to make them turn their head.

We collected some old dry boughs and built a fire. Prowse

walked to a brook and came back with a wet kettle. It made the fire hiss. We flaked out there in the fresh sun. The bushes full of dew then drying out. Water bubbled out the spout.

Now a cup of tea.

We drank the tea. About twenty minutes had gone by. Prowse then got up. There was nothing to see.

He was up by that birch stand, wasnt he.

I thought he was over by the brook more.

We walked towards the far end of the bog. The stag lay there on his side, his big white belly exposed.

If someone shot you, he said. And he started running after you. What would you do.

I'd run.

You got to give the animal time to die. Give him peace and he won't run far. He'll sit down and rest and end up bleeding to death. He won't even know it happened till he closes his eyes.

But as we got closer the caribou jerked his neck and lifted a hoof. It was a wild, thrashing hoof motion near my head. It could have slit my throat.

Prowse put the rifle to its ear and squeezed. A crackling as if the world had broken. He opened the breach and handed the gun to me. Dont lose it, he said.

He removed his pack. He plunged a knife into the caribou's neck and rummaged through the neck to bleed him.

Help me get him on his back.

He put a front leg over the antler tines, to get him balanced. Then slit through the hide to the breastbone and down to the penis sheath. He avoided puncturing the gut. In the pack was a small saw — a tenon saw. He handed it to me.

You know how to handle one of these fellows.

Me: I'm afraid I've only accompanied hunters.

Saw through the chest.

We had to work fast. The bright stomach and organs spilled up. They were fresh and clean. I worked deep into the body and scraped at the pelvic bone. I sliced with the knife some hitches to the chest. The organs were warm. The hoofs were black blades. Four bits to a hoof. This gutting was getting to me.

Did I tell you I was vegetarian?

No one's asked you to eat anything.

The neck and chest were open now. Prowse cut through the windpipe and slit a hole in. He pushed a finger through and hauled the windpipe down. It was like hauling an inner tube out of a bicycle rim. The guts followed. He stopped, shifted his feet, and carved deep down into the chest, loosening it all. He sliced the diaphragm.

There's a bit of pelvic bone, he said, that needs to be sawed through.

Green intestines pushed up like links of sausage. He carved around the anus and sloughed the guts out. I helped him. They poured out over the caribou's side. The guts were outside the body now. The body was gutted.

How quickly an animal can be reduced to meat. Essence rubbed out. This should be a time for mourning, for prayer, and yet all we can do is rush to get this great animal out of the morning heat.

Prowse sliced down between the second and third ribs. Then sawed through the backbone. He cut off the head. Now there were two halves. He removed an inch of fur from the backbone.

Then tipped up the rear half and I sawed down through the marrow of the vertebrae. The bone was warm and pliable and peeled away from the saw. We did the same to the front half.

Want the antlers?

I chopped out the antlers. Fragments of skull splintered like coconut. I was crazed now with the butchery. I turned back to the organs to rescue the heart. The heart was a small pyramid and it covered the platter of my hands.

My watch was smeared in blood. It was nine oclock in the morning and we were done. The whisky-jacks arrived to peck at the guts. Prowse handed me a green apple and we sat and ate apples. The green against the blood on my fingers.

So what are you going to do with your half?

Pardon?

Of the meat. If youre not going to eat it.

I'm just your scout, Prowse. I'm your labour for getting this animal out.

Give some meat to Hearn.

Youre a very forgiving judge.

We each hoisted a quarter on our backs and walked it out. We used the leg as a lever, hide side on our shoulders, draping an arm over the ankle.

Handy, isnt it? The leg.

We went back for the other half. Then we hung the quarters in the Pomeroy shed. Mrs Pomeroy was happy for us and delighted with the meat. She inspected it thoroughly. You did a good job with it.

I explained that I was giving a quarter of the meat to Tom Dobie. Of course, she said. I want Tony Loveys and George

Browiny and Dr Gill and Marten Edwards and the Bartletts, I
want them all to get a steak or a roast. I want anyone who wants
one except Jim Hearn.

She laughed at that. The judge, he likes to get a bit of gam-
ing in.

The next morning he showed me how to skin the meat. I
peeled the velum off the antlers. Tom Dobie took a quarter for
his mother. A good meal of fresh, he called it. He brought it
over in his wheelbarrow.

48

Kathleen made a picnic. She packed a suitcase with French
glasses and English plates. It was the day of my hearing. She
chose the small forks and a bottle opener. She had a thermos of
cocoa and there were five sandwiches. We were each to have a
sandwich and I would finish the crusts of the children's. I like
the crust, as long as there's a bit of something still stuck to the
bread. I like the remnants of things.

We decided to make it into an adventure. The family, in a
chain of hands, walked over the Pomeroy fields to Bunker's Hill
and built a cairn. The stones had a streak of quartz in them like a
salt lick. I stood on the cairn. This is our naked man, I said. We
have climbed the highest unclimbed peak in the world.

Rocky: Uppy uppy.

Me: Okay downy downy.

When we ate the sandwiches, I opened Kathleen's sandwich
and sprinkled salt on her tomato. We both love salt. I did not know

she was watching me. But then I saw her lift the bread off mine and rub her fingers above my slice of tomato. Salt. Yes, it was things like this that made me love her. And perhaps I looked at her in a way that made her feel I was promising things. And when you promise someone and they love you, they will trust you.

She ambled off into some bushes, and I watched her. She had on a sage top and a dusky blue skirt. She was camouflaged. All you could see was the sunlight catching a stream of her urine, arcing down behind her. She was only partly crouched. I said, You look like a caribou. Then she stuck her arms out in front of her, still peeing. A pregnant caribou.

The courtroom was the telegraph office, the very place the offence had happened. The Pomeroys and the Bartlett sisters, Tom Dobie, my supporters. People had brought their own kitchen chairs. Then Prowse entered and sat on the desk. Mr Rockwell Kent — he pointed at me — you are accused of phys-ically assaulting James Hearn.

Hearn: And threatening me, your Honour.

Let me read the charges, Hearn. What do you plead, Mr Kent?

I plead rowdyism. I plead a temporary bout of insanity. I will admit to a headlock, and I admit to calling Hearn a misbe-gotten viper and a hell-born stygian monster.

Prowse ordered Hearn to the stand.

Hearn: He near tore off my head, your Honour. I still got a crink. He threatened me and was entirely unusual.

Prowse: Less theatrics please, Hearn.

Why are you calling me Hearn and him Mr Kent?

Shut up, Hearn.

While Hearn was testifying I drew a cartoon of him. I strained my eyes at him until he looked at me, then I furiously drew his figure.

I whispered that his fly was down. He buttoned up, turned red, and sat down.

Kent, less out of you too. Now, your defence?

I admit to a little wrestling, your Honour. I admit to wanting to pull every tooth from Hearn's head. I confess generously to many desires, but I state emphatically that nothing unusual occurred. Except a good fright.

He threatened to kill me.

I did bark at him.

You barked at him.

And I meowed at him.

Did you say you wanted to kill Mr Hearn?

Yes.

And I paused. There was muttering amongst the crowd.

And then I said I wanted to cook him. And eat him.

That got a laugh.

Prowse: Mr Kent, are you rolling your eyes at the plaintiff?

Me: No, your Honour. I'm just rolling my eyes.

Prowse: And where did the offence take place.

Hearn: By the wicket, sir.

Hearn pointed at the wicket. This confused the judge.

Prowse: How far was this wicket from, say, the front door.

We all looked at Judge Prowse. Then Prowse realized that this very room was the scene of the incident. But even with this realization he refused to bend his mind over to considering the room a fair enough model to indicate the action of the crime. He tried not to look at the wicket. As if the hearing could be unbiased only as long as the setting remained theoretical and the incident summoned only through language. But now we were all looking at where I stood and where Hearn had been when I choked him.

Prowse: Never mind. I'd say there's a good fifteen feet between —

And he waved at the wicket and the door.

And that's when he attacked you?

Hearn: That's when he went savage.

Prowse: Dont be childish, Hearn. He put you in a headlock.

Hearn: He went aboard me. That man is a disgrace to the artistic profession.

Me: That's not fair, your Honour. I would be a disgrace to any profession, and I'd like to point out that —

Be steady, Mr Kent, we won't be needing a lecture from you.

Me: And you won't be hearing one. I get paid for my lectures.

This made him nod his head.

Prowse: The entire affair, I rule, has been in the nature of a practical joke. I find the defendant guilty and fine you five dollars. Or thirty days in jail. Now let's get some partridge hunting in, shall we.

There was a roar and a heartiness. I asked, Does Hearn get any of the money?

Prowse: Not a penny.

Then, I said, I'll pay the fine.

I offered the bailiff the five dollars then and there. I made a show of it to the crowd. They were silent from the sight of so much money so easily handed over. Straight from my pocket. As Bartlett informed me later, a mistake.

49

Charles Daniel's next letter included a cheque for sixty-five dollars. Not a hundred. He explained. The idea of shares in an artist, he said, is unheard of. The selling off of future work, it was a pyramid scheme. He preferred to stick with the monthly stipend, and I was still under contract. I am keeping, he wrote, the original share for its artistic merit. It is a rather beautiful piece of paper. But if I persisted, he would honour the scheme and print the two hundred shares. However, he would not like to invest. He wrote, Perhaps you need some time to change your own mind.

This is how a conversation would go with my agent. In New York he would call on me and say, Did you paint today.

Yes.

Did you paint every day this week.

Yes, every day, Charles.

Every day.

Yep.

Every single day you painted.

That's right.

Didnt miss a day.

No, not a one.

So if I said to a prospective buyer, Rockwell Kent paints every day of the week, I wouldnt be telling a lie.

You'd be right on the ball.

Every day.

Okay, maybe not every day.

Not every day?

I might have missed a day.

Oh, so one day you didnt paint.

Correct.

Wouldnt have been today.

No, I painted today. Youre looking at me painting as we speak.

But you didnt paint all week.

Well, except for one day.

Now that's one day you didnt paint, right? Not one day you painted.

I painted six out of the last seven goddamn days.

But youre not consistent with that.

That's right.

Though you did paint today.

Christ yes look at me.

I had been painting a portrait of the family. I wrote Charles Daniel back and thanked him for the money. Youre making a big mistake about the shares, I wrote. I wanted them printed. Gerald Thayer would see to it. Then I told him about compulsion. Because I was looking through Kathleen's photos for an object to paint. This is new, this painting from photos. Usually I paint the rooms and light I live in. But I dont find these rooms, so far, paintable. I had done some landscapes, but nothing vivid. I wasnt ready for landscapes. So I came across this picture Kathleen had taken of us amongst the birch trees near the Bartletts'. Rockwell is leaning up to me, Kathleen has our little Kathleen in the air. There is joy here, and something edenic. I have spent maybe three days painting it. This is what I get out of painting. First, the cropping. The composition. I like figuring that out. For this painting I inserted the curtain of hills of Brigus. And the colour. I can spend a lot of time looking at the shadow falling on the ground and wonder what that colour is. I love isolating the colour from the rest of the scene and saying, Actually it's a panel of blue and green with a speckle of orange. And then finding it in the oils. All of that, Charles, has little to do with art. It has more to do with my joy at mimicry. But tonight another thing crept in. I realized that I was in love with the family I was painting. I had fallen in love with them. I would do anything for them. I was so grateful that Rockwell was leaning up to me in the picture. I spent a long time on his shoulders. Getting the colour right on his back. There was light reflecting off his body. He was willing to let me help him. I had his trust. I was painting trust. Not only that, but the three days of painting our bodies embracing, those three days of devoting myself to that pagan image, it felt a bit like prayer. It felt that I was making trust come true. That I was honouring it. Strange, isnt it. I was painting my devotion to family, to Kathleen, to the town of Brigus, which was our home. I was painting what I loved.

50

The thing about Monhegan. Gerald Thayer pushed me to go there. And that is where Jenny was. Gerald said to me, I can't do anything with Jenny. I promised my father I'd be good.

Me: Your father? What about your goddamned wife.

Gerald: What I mean is.

But it's true. He was more loyal to, or felt the honour of, Abbott Thayer. He did not want to let him down.

We were drinking at the Green Dolphin with his father and Alma. I was on my way to Monhegan. There was live music. I said to Gerald: How come a big pool of beer keeps following you around?

This, Kent, is the reason right here why I quit liquor. Because if I get to the next level shit will happen.

He was looking over at his wife, Alma, flirting with Abbott Thayer.

What has she got, he said, for paunchy, pretentious, bespectacled men?

She's working on a whole new morality, Gerald. It's not based on appearance, attitude, or perfect vision. It's bigger than both of us.

Gerald: I asked my wife if she'd ever sleep with you. Alma said no and I said why not, youre such a good lay.

Me: If I thought we could still be friends, I'd sleep with her.

Gerald: If I thought you could adore me, I'd sleep with you.

Me: I'm not happy that your father's gone to the bar.

He's singing "Lakes Be a Bunch of Trees" to Alma.

He's singing "Lakes of the Pontchartrain." But yes, he's singing it to Alma.

Neither of us brought up the issue of her having slept with Gerald's father.

Gerald: I'm miserable. And I'm too embarrassed to get up and go home. You can't hear anything for that brass section in the corner.

Me: Sit closer.

Gerald: All this laughter, and nothing's funny.

We slugged down our drinks.

Kent, I would tell you the meaning of life, but it would take forty-three books to write it all down.

Forty-three books, you figure. Tell me, Gerald, did Jesus ever ask for help?

He asked the disciples to pray with him.

I mean did he ever ask anyone to make him a sandwich or let someone know he needed a hand.

Gerald shook his head. We were looking at Alma's bright legs moving from Abbott Thayer to the band.

That gesture doesnt look like an equal and opposite attraction.

Shut up.

Gerald: Unlike my wife I dont do that end of town.

Me: Your father's the sexiest man here, and I'm going home with him.

Coming from you, Kent, that's okay, I can handle that.

Alma came over. I just saw the most beautifulest band.

Gerald: Youre drunk.

Oh fuck off. I mean, I love you, baby.

Dont be calling me baby.

Me: Gerald, dont be nasty.

Alma: There was a tuba and a tumpet.

God you smell.

Me: Gerald.

Did I say tumpet. Maybe there was. There was a tumping thing. Kent, she said, tell me about my husband. I have no idea what he's like.

51

There's a telegram, George Browiny said. He'd come into Chafe's with it. Bud Chafe read it. Charlie's coming home, Bud said. Bob Bartlett has him aboard the *Morrissey*. They'll be here tomorrow afternoon.

There was a time in Charlie Chafe's honour. The men filled their clay pipes and poured rum and Bartlett's mother had a barking pot made spotless. The daughters cooked up a scoff of ham and hard tack out on the garden. The guests climbed the eleven stairs to Bartlett's Hawthorne Cottage and filled the house and spilled into the gardens. We waited for the *Morrissey* to come. Outside, three tables were joined together, with table-cloths extending to the kitchen window. White china and the silver placings. Emily Edwards played bright piano in the parlour. The small children were arranged on the front steps by Rupert, each holding a bunch of wildflowers, while Kathleen took their picture. For once it wasnt a sad homecoming: Bartlett was bringing Charlie Chafe home.

Tom Dobie: If you want to see an ornament, come look.

The *Morrissey* rounded the rocks of Red Head. Bob Bartlett at the wheel in a fedora and a raglan. Rupert keeping something at bay in the hold. They skimmed into port with Charlie Chafe waving. They anchored off Molly's Island.

Tom: He's got a water bear aboard.

They anchored there, and Tom Dobie and I prepared a skiff.

We're coming aboard, Bud Chafe said.

We rowed Bud and Alice out to the island. Charlie had been gone two years. As we came alongside Charlie jumped down into the skiff and Bud Chafe put his hand on Charlie's forehead. Then we got aboard and saw what the Bartletts had in the hold: a polar bear. Bob was wrestling near the neck of the polar bear. It wore a collar and a hundred feet of chain. He had a pole to its neck as it climbed out of the hatch. The pole had a hook attached to the collar. We pushed the bear over the side. The bear tumbled in the water and whipped its head up to the surface. Buoyant. It shook its head. Bartlett prodded it with the pole.

Tom Dobie: He doesnt know his own mind, that bear dont. Or maybe he's a her.

Bartlett: I named her Maureen, after an old girlfriend of mine.

Rupert was holding a cat. A survivor of the *Karluk*, he said. They left a seal carcass for the bear. They had three hundred pounds of walrus meat. Every bit of it good to eat, Bartlett said later. Ate the same thing myself. Then we all came ashore and we walked up to the Bartlett house.

Charlie Chafe, mobbed by his two sisters.

Charlie, youre older.

He had gone through a severe anguish. A physical strain. A short-lived but terrific hardship that coats the youthful body with an arthritic veneer, a shell that protects the other life — that allows that other far different but certainly less distinguished life to emerge. Charlie Chafe laughed at it. I need to keel out for a spell, he said. And then flaked out on a daybed in the parlour. I'm like a busted wire, he sighed, like I been hit with electricity. We partied on.

Bartlett got the bear off Greenland. The fellow who named Greenland, he said, must have been in the real estate business. First they'd noosed a male polar bear, madder than a march hare. It got away and beelined home to tell it all to the missus. Missus came out and that's who we ended up with. A feisty one for sure, women usually are.

52

Charlie: I served the men their meals. I never served gentles before. I polished boots and fed sled dogs. I'm only twenty, he said. I'd never been out of Conception Bay. Me and Captain the only Newfoundlanders on board the *Karluk*, hey, Captain Bob.

Bartlett: There was this cat. And a Newfoundland pony.

Emily: I love the smell of horseshit.

Charlie: Let's hear James Murphy's "Song of the Apples."

Emily sneezed.

Me: You just wet my entire hand.

At least no one's said I'm loud.

Me: Been meaning to tell you, Emily. Youre wet and loud.

She twisted herself on the piano stool. Come here, she said, and I'll give you a smack between the eye and the ear where you can't lick it.

She stared with all of her youth into my bare eye.

Dont tempt me.

A shudder went through me, for I knew I was tempted. I went outside. I exhaled. I looked at the bear out on the island. A wild, white, chained element. I rubbed my arms. It was as if Emily's vigour had splashed upon me. Rupert and Kathleen sitting on the bottom step. Rupert was pointing at something, their shoulders touched, and then she pointed at the same thing. I went back inside to the Artic Room. Charlie Chafe was holding forth.

Charlie: We lived on a spit of land and we did not know how long Bartlett would be. We forked into three parties like Bartlett told us. We had nine dogs and the cat. In the third month a man shot himself from an episode of panic. The boys in one party died from the canned meat. Only Kuraluk had a good aim. Whenever we ate seal or walrus we felt better.

Tony Loveys: You were gone so long we thought you learnt the huskimaw.

Charlie: I was on the hand of it. I became pretty primitive, I got to say. I understand now the desire for raw meat.

Bartlett: You relaxed into coarse mannerism.

Boys, it was the most efficient manner to live by.

Bartlett: I call them coarse now, but at the time you were refined to the predicament.

I looked out the window just as Rupert and my wife went for a walk.

Me: Yes, this is true of all time and place.

On a hunt with the sled Charlie lost the trail and a storm picked up. He staggered about with the dogs all evening until he found one of the shelters he'd built in a pressure ridge two months previous. He huddled in this but did not sleep: I was afraid to sleep. My foot was frozen and my teeth were hackering. I watched myself wiggle the foot. I cursed myself for not paying attention to the foot. I packed the dogs around me.

In the morning the storm continued and the dogs howled about the sled. He unleashed the dogs and let them go, except for one. He chained his wrist to this dog, it was the dog he trusted most. The dog pulled him through the snow. For six hours he staggered after the dog. By then he'd gone ice blind. It was like having sand in your eyes, he said. He prayed that the dog would catch a scent.

After six hours, that dog he crested a ridge and there, in a bowl of snow, was home.

Charlie had three operations on his heel, the gangrene carved away with a pocketknife. The gangrene was fresh and bubbly and gas rose from it, a good sign it was the wet gangrene. The wet is what you wanted.

They had to improvise. And when a ship came by they took it. Charlie: They had been looking for us and then we knew Captain Bob was safe. Only then. We met Skipper Bob in the Bering Sea. We transferred over and Bartlett had new clothes for us.

Me: You look in fine shape.

We didnt know Bob had made it, he said again. Until this ship picked us up.

There were tears in Charlie Chafe's eyes, and Bob Bartlett put an avuncular hand on his shoulder. It was Charlie he had wanted to see alive, to bring him home to Brigus. He was only twenty. He had been eighteen when he left.

I went outside and found Rupert and Kathleen with our children, picking black currants. I heard Rupert say, Come on over here Kath.

He called her Kath. The polar bear watched us, a prisoner on Molly's Island.

Do I have anything to worry about here?

This made Kathleen furious.

53

I was worried about the size of the house. About raising four youngsters in it. Tom Dobie said the Pomeroys had thirteen children in that house, and I could not believe it. Thirteen, I said. Where did they put them all. Tom: Well, not all at once. The first half-dozen was gone into the world by the time the last half-dozen rolled in.

He was down by his flake, collecting the fish to store. Bartlett aboard the *Morrissey* mending rope. Tom Dobie: You spread the fish and then carry it to the store. And goodbye to that.

Bartlett was aboard the *Morrissey* night and day. He preferred it to his own bedroom. My sweetheart, he said, the *Morrissey*. She's so handsome. He kept an eye on the bear and they stayed for eight days. And then Bartlett took the bear down to New York, for a zoo. The cat stayed at Hawthorne and lived under the stove.

An American expedition, he said, theyve just come back from Greenland. Theyve combed the area north of Greenland. Spent four years looking. Mapped every square mile and figured out, mathematically, that no Crocker Land exists.

A hoax?

Not a hoax, Bartlett said, I saw it. A range of mountains to the northwest. Clear as those hills behind us. But it must have been rafted ice. We wanted to see land. We needed it.

54

Bob Bartlett made me a tomato sandwich. Fresh tomatoes from his garden, fresh bread from his sister. He cut thick slices of tomato and we sat down to the sandwiches. Nothing beats a tomato sandwich, he said.

You know what I miss most, I said. My mouth is starving for corn.

It's a marvel isnt it, corn.

Fresh raw corn. It looks manufactured. It's a colour so pale it's almost no colour.

It's a colour that warrants the study of colour.

I wanted to strip yellow ears of corn from a green field. To tear the intelligent skins away and eat the baby kernels.

You should, he said, go berry picking.

And that's what this mouth did. It discovered the fall berries and the fruit of apple trees. It wasnt all bad. It was not all dead food.

We went berry picking. The side of the hill full of berry pickers. I heard a voice call out, Have you filled your empter yet? Tom and Emily. The small bucket that you empty into the large one. My family all bent to the industry of berries, young love in the hills.

55

Bartlett heard about the Hearn affair. He was anxious about it. It vexed him. He asked about the fine and I told him how I'd paid it. That is when he told me what he'd heard. That I had plenty of money. You cross-hackled him and then became a man who can pay a five-dollar fine right there in court. What kind of man is that. You want to be a man of the people, Bartlett said. But scenes like that divorce you from them. High-learnt and full of money. They cannot help looking at you as different.

I said I so much wanted to fit in, to be invisible. To merge.

Not all men, he said, are destined to blend in. It's not always a matter of choice. Do me a favour, he said, and stop paying for things in front of people. Get credit at Chafe's. Pay him discreetly at the end of the month.

END

THE BIG WHY

I am a lonely American in this dismal little
British colony. The thought of the land is
stupefied by dogma.

— Rockwell Kent
letter to the *New Republic*, 1915

1

Then the war came. I took it as a personal insult. That the world was intruding upon the life I was living. Small union jacks were tilted out of bedroom windows. It was autumn. The war was a surprise — most of us did not know that it would come. But when it did we were alert to it and, of course, within minutes what was unforeseen had become inevitable. I saw men act differently. They became men who knew they had to absorb war. Women were knitting grey socks as if they had always knitted grey socks. As if war were a season for which knitted socks were mandatory.

There were meetings. The word *crucial* was used. And *effort*. The word *deploy*. I guess there were orders from elsewhere trickling down to small communities like Brigus, but all I saw were the local executions of work. Now excess muscle must be devoted to the war push. This was aggressively agreed upon. I am speaking of the men in charge here — in the fishermen and their families I saw little change. There was no genuine rise in patriotic zeal. But they were attentive. They were on call to duty. They were obedient, though they were not won over by nationhood. The men signed a sheet that committed them to the war, until it ended, or for no longer than a year. That seemed reasonable. These men were used to signing on to positions of a year or more and going foreign. The assumption that it would be less than a year made the thought of being a soldier a novelty.

I was concerned about this signing up. I went to Billy Cole's to see the boys. Tony Loveys, Charlie Chafe, and bald Patrick Fardy. I kept away from Fardy. They were drinking rum. I ordered a bottle. Billy Cole lifted a plank in his kitchen floor and pulled up a string. On the end of the string a dusty bottle. I asked if they felt loyal to England. Did they really want to join a European war. Didnt it have more to do with economic interests than a true evil that had to be quashed. Where was the badness. Who was being suppressed. Werent they, the soldiers, werent they the ones who would be most afflicted?

They were obliging me. They nodded. They were not keen. But the fishery would be over soon, and sure a stint in the army with proper wages. A winter in Europe. A trip across the ocean? It all sounded like a change in the weather, and what the hell, cheers to that.

2

We went to church. And I asked to sing — I sang a Schubert tune. During the middle of it there was a clearing of throats. I sang louder. I sang in a more guttural way. Murmurs.

I looked at Kathleen, her face in her hands.

No one said a word except Bartlett.

Fine tune, he said. But next time, surely to God you know a song using the King's English.

I wanted to express, I said, how lovely the culture is of the country we're about to destroy.

Did you know, Bartlett said, that that very culture has submarines off the coast here? If ever a supply boat heads for England, I'm sure there'll be Schubert aplenty sung beneath the waves.

There was talk of a submarine. Idling in Conception Bay. It had sunk three frigates heading out of St John's harbour. There were rumours that Germans were coming ashore at night, raiding farms for fresh potatoes and carrots. A lady in Cupids swore she saw three men in military costume make off with her cow. Two young lads spied some foreigners in a dinghy collecting water from a falls into the ocean.

3

Emily Edwards, teaching the children how to play Catching Thirds and Hidey Hoop. They played Hoist Your Sails and Run, a version of hide-and-seek. The child in Emily mixed with the element of adult supervision. The youth in her and the fresh authority of her, they mixed to create a surplus. This surplus engaged the corner of my eye. I did not want to be tempted. I refused to think about it and I did not say anything to Kathleen. I kept the thought at a distance, a garden of cold roses. I used to say everything, now I'm circumspect. I will halt an inquiry. For instance, I wanted to ask Jenny Starling — this was years later — what she thought of Gerald's writing. But then I remembered that they have a relationship now. And that she loves him.

And I did not want my question to be construed as doubt in his worth. Some people, and those some are many, believe that when you ask a question, it is for reasons that are not altruistic. They will turn your words. I used to be this way. I turned inquiry into bad motive. I believed people held opinions of me, judgments, when they did not. They might have said snarky things, but that is not the same as holding an opinion. The snarky statement is made, and it flies through the air like a sneeze and lands in a foreign ear. It is this ear that makes the judgment. And passes it on. So rumour goes. How furious I am about fixed opinion now, when I know so much is taken from overheard moments of thought.

So I kept my attraction to Emily to myself. There would be no pronouncement from the stage built in the front of my brain, a stage where words could be issued like a press release, words that pretended raw emotion was dispassionately considered. I would will the gut attraction away.

Gerald Thayer could lecture, but I knew him. I told him of walking in after a poetry reading when he was answering questions from the audience, and he said there is a word for that. When you enter at the climax. A Latin word. But he could not remember it. It began with an *A*. This is learned. He knew he conveyed an ignorance while at the same time attempting learnedness. The learnedness was not earned and his only authority was over his body language. His ignorance was betrayed to an eye like mine.

Gerald's father had a refined appearance, well kept, except for his neck. Abbott Thayer's hair grew out coarsely and there was something angry and Scottish about the back of his neck.

The very blind part of his body betrayed a rawness. Whereas Gerald was less self-conscious and his neck was smooth and tame.

4

Kathleen: Rockwell?
  I'm working.
  There's a man at the door.
  Do we owe him money.
  He's a constable.
  It was nine in the morning. It was the man who had brought my court summons during the Hearn affair. He was sizing up the outside of the house. Abbott Thayer once told me that, with everyone, there is an unusual quality of light. And if I remark on that quality it will make the person stand out for you. This constable. He is inspecting the outside of my house. The edge of the summons, he's scraping it against the bottom of his nose. His nose is yellow, and the cut of his hair is dark and precise. Yes, his colouring is clipped and neat. He isnt happy with his prospects, with the event before him, for the results of the event are not predictable. He is the type of man who does not celebrate the unknown. He shook my hand, he leaned around me.
  So you work there, Mr Kent.
  I shut the door.
  Yes.
  Mind if I have a look.

Yes.

You do mind.

Yes.

Cosy house you got here.

We find it pleasant.

Just we've had a complaint, sir. Silly one. But youve caused a bit of a stir. It was you, sir, who had that row with Mr Hearn?

The constable was pretending we hadnt met before. He took out a small notebook.

Hearn had a row with me, I said.

Man of the people are you, Mr Kent.

Pardon?

Wouldnt share a field, is that right?

I took him to the gate and explained the Hearn affair. I am happy to share all things, I said. It was Hearn who wished to possess. However, I'm quite over it, I said.

I opened the gate.

There was some thought, Mr Kent, that you might not be fully behind the effort.

The effort. I'm *E* for effort.

To fight the Germans.

I will fight no Germans.

So you oppose England.

I'm dead against the war.

But surely the British position is just.

The man was poised with a pencil to his notepad.

The British, I said, make a good condiment. Beyond that I see little to recommend the British. You spell condiment with an *i*.

But surely you dont support the Germans.

I am a supporter of great culture, I said. Have you read Bach? Listened to Goethe?

You know you look a bit like a German.

How can you respond to that? I bid my apologies, excusing myself from a longer interview by having to tend to my pregnant wife.

I watched him walk up the path, past the Pomeroys'. He waved to Old Man Pomeroy. And then Old Man Pomeroy had him over.

Kathleen: What was that about?

I'm not sure.

5

When the war began the trees lost their leaves. And I thought, Why trees, why green, why the futility of it. I was caught up in the belief of progress, and now I saw turmoil. There was chaos. I read about entropy. If you left a pile of bricks and time was infinite, then a moment would arrive when the bricks, through random change, would form a wall. That was my thought. But this is not true. The bricks, without work injected into the system, will become a simpler structure. They prefer to turn to dust. I saw the world now starved of energy from the sun. It was turning to dust. It was returning to a simpler form. It was becoming nostalgic. Nostalgia can be good. It is incorrect to think of nostalgia as merely the pain one feels in returning to home. Memory never matches the reality of home. Nostalgia is the friction between home itself and the memory of home. A friction that turns time to dust.

All my life I've wanted to strip sentimentality from nostalgia and be left with the hearkening. With the strange newness of return.

6

I spoke to Bartlett about the constable. He was surprised.

He came from St John's?

I think perhaps a branch from Conception Bay.

The one from Harbour Grace, Bartlett said. Who came about the Hearn affair.

Same fellow. But it had more to do with my view on the war. He said I looked like a German.

Well, you were born there.

I was born in New York.

I thought I heard you had a bit of German.

I like Germans.

So do I. Look, I wouldnt worry about it. They have nothing to do in Harbour Grace. They are a curious bunch down there. Their interest will wane.

But something about it dispirited me. I walked back to my little house with no electricity and no running water. I wrote to my mother. Please send a copy of my birth certificate. It had come to that. Cramped with three children and another one on the way. At least that child will be a Newfoundlander. My life was beautiful in ways but also old-fashioned. I was a modern man living an old-fashioned life. I was trying to blend the two and it seemed a bad idea. It was never a good idea — dont let anyone tell you otherwise. It was never a good place to be. I thought I could disappear in Brigus and lead a pure, natural life, free of suspicion. But I was misguided. My motives were not true. I didnt just want to live here, I wanted its customs to inform my work and make it unique. I wanted to make my name in Brigus. I was using the culture. I was exploiting it. And what I was creating is not what happened here.

There may be no reason. Or there are no reasons. Reasons may be an idea.

7

I had mustered up good faith with my wife and now I began a ten-year decline of mortgaging. I began to trade on good faith. We sat in the garden eating crabapples from Pomeroy's garden. They were hard but edible. I left my core on my wrist and Kathleen picked it up and ate it. I liked that she ate the cores of fruit. She ate it and looked at me.

Are you wondering, I asked, about the faith I have.

I'm thinking of the love I pour into you.

Youre hoping I might repay it.

Occasionally there's an instalment.

It's not a personal thing, Kathleen. I'm not trying to be mean about loving you, only avoiding disappointment.

The way I figure it, Rockwell, is youre working in the space between wanting to be in love and leaping into the act of loving.

I loved her, and yet the ease of that love was crumbling. I was realizing that there was another Rockwell Kent. Or an agent that acted on my behalf. I lay awake at night and stared at the corner of the window, where the light bordered on the dark room. It reminded me of a window of childhood, when my father was alive. I would hear him in his study. Some precise sounds that happened on the face of his desk. There is something to be said about the desperation to be loved that affects those who've lost a parent. But what surprised me was my realizing that I wasnt in charge of what I'd been reminded of. It's one thing to decide to think of childhood, another for that remembrance to come upon you without your asking. And this happened to me, I realized, all day long. Some intuitive agent was making connections for me. I sensed this was the agent too that checked my ability to love. I wanted to love my wife. The desire for love was there, but the agent would deny it. If you are upset with what I'm writing then obviously we have different tastes about what gets written down.

The thing is, since she was pregnant she was less interested in sex. Well, that was one brutish thing. There are often about eight things. But for most of us, brutish things are the hardest to overcome.

8

Tom Dobie came over and said, There's always a piece of fog there. Right on the turn.

He had signed up. Him and Charlie Chafe and Tony

Loveys. Patrick Fardy had tried, but what can you do with only one leg. Rupert Bartlett an officer.

I didnt think you were old enough.

I'm only one day under.

You feel a loyalty.

No, Tom said. I feel a money.

He rubbed his hands, It's a jacket colder tonight.

Yes, I said. It's a keen day.

Could I look after Smoky. Yes. He was worried about Emily. Would I keep an eye on her. Would I help her and her father out. It's not help, I said. She's helping us.

Good, he said. That is all good.

9

Then they left.

We walked Tom Dobie, Charlie Chafe, and Tony Loveys to the train. We're six weeks, Tom Dobie said, in St John's under Rupert Bartlett, then we're shipped to Scotland. We're only backup.

It is this expectation that is important to write about, as expectations always are. Emily refused to walk with them.

Last I saw of her, Tom said, was this morning. She gave me this letter. I'm not to open it until St John's.

The three young men were under Rupert's command. They were forming a Newfoundland battalion.

Charlie, I said, you havent been home a month.

It's all right. We'll be back full of money in the spring.

The night before, Bob had thrown a party for them. I'd begged them not to go. No one is forcing you, I said, there is no conscription. But they laughed at me. It was money, they said again. It's just a stint overseas.

We waved to the flat train windows as they slipped by. Even though I was only fifteen years older than Tom I felt like a father to him. We walked back together without the young men.

Kathleen: Rupert showed me the weigela.

Me: That will have pleased him.

She knew I was kidding. Though she understood I had ambivalent feelings about a man in uniform being touched by my wife.

I had said to Tom, What about Emily.

We'll marry in the summer, he'd said.

What if the war's not over.

Then I'll get leave.

Why not marry her now.

It can wait till the summer.

I did not want Emily Edwards unmarried.

10

I said, Let's take the children and go for a swim.

Kathleen: There's fish guts in the harbour.

We'll go up towards the naked man. We'll take Smoky.

There is a small stretch of sand near the naked man. Lying on mats, the sand drifting on the mats. Our children testing the water. It was September, perhaps the last good day to swim.

Our feet pushing the mats into the sand. As though the sand was a wet thing. Kathleen's back to me. The sand on her back. The grit lets me know her back is there.

I was wearing a hat. I lay down, the hat on my face. I put a stone in the crown of my hat. To keep the wind from blowing it.

Kathleen: Youre funny.

Because it's me?

We read as the children swam. I thought of their surfaces, housing for marrow then muscle and tendon. Then blood and nerve. If we built children from early promise. And had I married wholeheartedly.

I moved my arms and legs to change the shadow, to give parts of my skin rest from the sun. I said, I have to retrieve my arm. Or, I have to have my arm back. Pins and needles. Kathleen moved. Her face was full of colour.

Kathleen: I need to pee.

Me: Go for a swim.

She was still wearing her bandanna. I watched her scrubbing sand off her legs in water up to her arms. You could not tell that she was pregnant. The children rolled in the sand like dogs. Sand printed on their feet and calves. They looked like birthmarks, or tattoos, as though they wore socks made of sand.

She returned, cold and wet and happy. Smoky snapping after her on his three legs.

We must take care of Emily.

Smoky will remind us.

The waves drove in over themselves. They pushed in from the Atlantic. But then that's not true. The fact is, it's the same width of water that drives itself to shore over and over. It is the energy of the wave that moves through the water. That pounds itself senseless on the shore. A line of water constantly beaching. It must be different water. The pounding must turn it into something else.

11

Dear Gerald. What's good about listening to people who are out of the artistic loop, and who have strong oral skills and are unconscious of it — Tom Dobie — is that they will say original things, things you know arent from books but from their uncles or grandparents. If I write these down they will sound new, and new in print. Originals.

Love, Rockwell.

ps: Stop beating your wife.

The full moon. Remember that a full moon is only half the moon. I am suspicious of anyone who tells me theyve seen everything. You can only ever see half of a thing — hence the stupidity of abstract art. You see the palm of the hand or you see the back of the hand.

I said this to Jenny Starling in Monhegan: When's your birthday.

December.

And I thought, Oh good. I won't have to deal with it. That was the full story of us.

12

There was worry about salt. The Germans were torpedoing the salt bankers from Cadiz. And sailing crews had thought their worries were only with the half-starved people of Labrador.

One doryload is a ton of salt, Bob Bartlett said.

The fishermen were taking the livers now, and they were out trolling squid for bait. I went out with Marten Edwards for the squid. While hauling in the lines he kneeled over the gunwale to piss. I watched him pass his hands through the stream of urine.

You look like youre doing that on purpose.

It's to get the sting, he said, of the ink out of my hands.

We hooked into a spot and Marten yelled to Patrick Fardy to come out. He left his fish splitting and rowed out. Marten Edwards: In the first part of the year, the yield of cod oil is not so good. Much more oil during the trap season. August and September is the right time to get a good yield from cod livers. And right now is when the squid usually come in.

It takes three and a half gallons of cod livers to make one gallon of refined oil.

13

There was quiet with the men gone to war. Less industry by the water. The fishing season was done, the dried fish up to be culled. Bud Chafe had a culler come in for St John's. The women were not happy. Bim fish, Emily said. There was some choice, but most of the fish had spoiled and was fit only for the Barbados. They would not have enough to pay off their credit at Chafe's. Never mind, Bud said. Next year will be better.

I painted. I finished touching up the painting of my family. It summed things up for me. I called it, simply, *Nude Family in a Landscape*. It was innocent, it lacked cynicism. It voiced a domestic heroism. I rolled up the canvas and built a wooden box for it. I brought the painting to George Browiny, the shipping agent. As I walked with it I thought of it under my arm, rolled into itself. It epitomized my love, the direction I wanted to go in. I was happy with the tone of it. I thought, Charles Daniel will see now the reason I left New York.

I passed some of the younger boys, who were piling together wood for a bonfire. One had stolen a barrel used for cod livers. That'll burn nicely, I said.

I had the painting rolled and wrapped, sitting in its open box. I felt I had something of worth. A painting of joy, a celebration. Something to confirm my decision to be here. I had sent Charles Daniel my *House of Dread* and he had not been impressed. This was the one. I had filled out the customs forms. All I needed was George Browiny's signature. I opened the box.

George Browiny stared at the sealed tube.

Can you unroll it, please.

It's a painting.

I'd like to have a look at it.

It wouldnt be something you'd like.

I'm not interested in gawking at its artistic merit.

What tone was that. I can tell you what it is, I said.

I prefer to see things for myself.

Feel it, I said. Weigh it. It's canvas, it's a painting.

The content of the picture.

I thought about that. I thought about George Browiny's reason as a customs agent. His tone wasnt one of aesthetic curiosity. It was aggressive. It made me feel private.

It's a very beautiful painting, I said. And it's a delicate thing of a private nature.

Kent, I just have to see if it *is* a painting.

I'm telling you it's a painting. It's a roll of canvas. What else could it be?

He did not answer.

I am here, I said, because I'm bound legally to be here to get your signature.

There was a pause. I wanted the pause to make him uncomfortable. But he was unflappable.

So that you can verify, I continued, that I, Rockwell Kent, am signing the customs form. I am signing.

Just let me slit her up the side, Mr Kent.

The man unfolded a pen knife. He began to slice the paper and I pulled the tube away from him. I was furious.

You have no right, I said.

I could have slit his throat.

Very well. That is all very well.

So you'll confirm the signature.

I will confirm what I suspect.

Which is.

Let's not get into it, Kent.

I want to know what I've confirmed.

He wrote a note in a ledger. And I read it, upside down: RK refuses inspection.

What the hell was that. The thing is this. When I left, and I saw the perfidious gutless wonder Jim Hearn go in, I heard George Browiny talk to him. I waited outside the door. I heard him say, In the service of Germany. A war map or something.

A war map!

Kathleen: Just ignore it.

She was so upset by this. She wanted me to back down. To be meek. Meekness made fury rise behind my cheekbones. What enraged me: that my love of German culture should be construed as a love for German political ambition. And what's more: that my painting should be considered evidence of spy activity.

A war map, I said again.

If you'd shown it to him.

I could not. It would have been a violation. It would have ruined everything.

She was against me. She liked Hearn. He was a good pharmacist and a generous man. She said, You judge people too quickly.

Me: The only judgment going on is your judgment that I judge. And their judgment of me. The only person not judging is me. And now I have to write a letter of complaint to the postmaster in St John's — about George Browiny. And another to the chief inspector about that constable. It's intolerable.

As if all I had to do there was write letters.

14

It's you again.

Constable: My name is Bishop, sir. May as well call me Bishop. Seems I'll be here now and again.

What can I help illuminate today.

The notebook. He is flipping to a fresh page.

Is it true you were, earlier this month, enticing men to refuse His Majesty's service?

I looked at him. I am often enticing men, I said. You will have to be more precise.

You were at the Bartlett house. There were enlisted men.

That was a private party.

I thought about that night, the farewell party for Tom Dobie and the boys. We had been drinking. I expressed my scepticism that a war between the European powers would benefit the working class.

Is it true sir, that you purchased seven tons of coal.

Would you like to buy some? It's all in that shed.

I already took the liberty of peering into the shed, sir. There seems not much over three tons left, sir.

I do apologize for that, Bishop. I have been recklessly burning it. Also, I said, I plan to use some of it later on in the children's Christmas stockings.

You will be serving a meat dish.

Pardon?

There is talk of your not eating animals.

Talk to Judge Prowse and you will see to what regard I hold animals.

May I ask, Mr Kent, if this is a religious house?

Do you see a cross in the bell tower?

I see a figurehead above your door. Can you explain that?

This is a house of pagan worship, so yes, mark me down as religious.

I saw him actually write that down.

And you not only sing but can speak in German?

Das ding an sich.

A fine day to you, Mr Kent.

15

I got into the habit of writing letters and wrote many of them. I wrote to the *St John's Mail and Advocate*. I wrote one for the *New York Evening Mail*. I wrote Rufus Weeks and Gerald Thayer in New York. I wrote to Judge Prowse too. I wrote the chief inspector in St John's about his constable's inquiries. I looked up the U.S. consul in St John's and complained to him. I decided to write three letters every morning for a week. Twenty-one letters in all. There was a war on, but I spent my energy clarifying my indignity. I supported the mail effort. I sent a few rich letters to the New York papers. I suspected that my mail was being read, so I larded them with provocative claims. I wanted a German submarine to blow this tiny British enclave to smithereens.

It made me think, though. About spying. What it is to be a spy. I *was* a spy of sorts. My witnessing of this town. My paintings of it. My own family. They were not altogether flattering portraits. When you involve yourself in the private lives of others it can disenchant you with your world. But you do not speak of it, though you may be inspired by it. It's true that some of the work betrayed a despair about my married life. And perhaps I had begun to lose my wife through this portrayal. You begin to paint a life that you have not openly admitted to, and those who love you suddenly see your secret life exposed. They realize what your undisclosed life is, and that youve been a spy all along.

I cut Rocky's hair and I saved the clippings. Then we went down to the beach to watch the bonfire the boys had built. It was November fourth. A spark landed on Rocky's finger and made him cry. We strolled back home, the bonfire licking light on all the darkness. I made an aristocratic moustache out of the clippings of Rocky's hair. I carved a small gun of wood and painted it black. I put on what I thought of as my German shirt and I posed like the kaiser.

Kathleen, take my picture.

I'm not going to assist you.

Then give me your camera. Show me where your camera is. I bought you that camera.

She pointed to a drawer.

I decided to risk developing the film in St John's. I wanted the Likeliness Shop to feel awkward. But when I went in the photographer, Mr Wilansky, was professional. He hunched over the prints with me. Look here, he said. Were you looking for the spoof.

I was trying my best, I said.

You see, the background is what gives it away: children on the floor, a blurred wife. I could have made you into a convincing German, he said. And pointed to his studio.

Youre a man of good taste.

Look after yourself, Mr Kent.

I sent the films to Rufus Weeks in New York and he was delighted. He forwarded an article that mocked the bigotry and stupidity of the people here. I had a supporter in New York! The writer, a man unknown to me, said it was obvious the police had it in for me. The writer quoted me as desiring to be shot or cleared.

I thought that all this would make them cower. That they would lick their wounds, see how mistaken they were, and retract and apologize.

Some hope.

16

I moved about applying stealth to situations while my wife made herself open to change. Most things change, though some things are constant. The glass confounds the moth, the net strangles the gill. Kathleen stayed in one place and picked things out of the air as they floated past. I was in the fields, chasing butterflies. Often I chased things to her. Rupert, for instance.

I dont think he even knew it. My wife was unaware of any-thing forming. Anything illicit. Let us be clear: nothing happened between them. But I saw a spark of the primrose. I saw the way the threads wound about them. Both too good and innocent for anything like seduction to be in the air. I saw that. I was the sinful agent. It was my suspicion that could have led them to badness, that planted the thought in their minds. Sometimes a sin arises against the good intentions of both parties. I believe in agents independent of our souls that travel about looking to cause wreckage.

17

I wrote a letter to the prime minister. I copied it to Judge Prowse. I told them of my plight. How a cultured man was being oppressed. I demanded an apology and an investigation. I did not want any more visits from stupid policemen.

I wrote to Rufus Weeks. Please keep me informed, I wrote, about the ties between government, industry, and the military. I am under scrutiny. My fondness for German culture, my pacifist stance, my atheism, even my vegetarianism are under assault.

When I came back from the post office, Constable Bishop was trying to persuade my wife to let him in.

Just one more thing, Mr Kent. You refused a shipping agent's inquiry into a package?

I refused his curiosity. I know my rights under the postal system.

While it is not mandatory for Mr Browiny to look at the contents of every parcel, under the War Act he is allowed to use his discretion.

I preferred to not give him the lurid satisfaction of seeing the contents. It would tarnish them. I did not want his mug to see what I had made. It would have been like having to strip to my drawers.

I suppose a look around is out of the question.
That is the first sensible thing youve said.

I was innocent. I was falsely accused. I know I've been an asshole about many things, but to pervert the effort of my painting,
to consider it an act of espionage, well, this disappointed me. It
vexed me that something so symbolic of my resolve to be good
was being considered evidence of my double life.

18

Fall turned to winter. I was furious and immobilized. I did not
like going into town. When Emily came to help with the children I lost myself in my studio. Kathleen felt ill with the
pregnancy. She did not feel sexual. Part of me did not mind this.
I did not mind embracing the ascetic life. I wanted to focus on
work. I wanted to train myself to defeat this suspicion of my
motives. I felt it important not to back down. To back down
was to admit that I was doing something wrong. Instead my
pride rose up. I was reckless with pride. There is nothing worse
than a proud stoic.

Then the snow came. Old Man Pomeroy in a red sleigh
laughed, pulled by his little daughter, Grace. He had this laugh
— on one hand it was nice, I wanted to support the laugh. But
now the sounds of the harbour were aggravating me. To me it
was a colonial laugh that I derided. I tried to turn it around, to
make the laugh pure again, as I'm sure it was. It was the laugh
of a man being pulled around in a red sleigh by a girl. I was

corrupted, and a wave of resentment poured over the dike I had built. I walked into Brigus and bought a small can of red paint at Chafe's. Bud Chafe served me, but he no longer joked with me. I was just money now. I walked back and took out one of my old brushes. I painted the chest and profile of an eagle on my studio door. It was a German eagle with a serious brow. Beneath this I wrote, in Gothic type, BOMB SHOP.

19

We spent the Christmas season alone. We had the children. We snowshoed and tobogganed and on Christmas day we visited the Bartletts. We were surprised that they were having a party. We're going to blow the pudding out of the pot, Bartlett said. He took the shotgun to the door and fired it off when the figgy duff came out of the oven. George Browiny played chin music. He made up these words, and he hummed while the children danced in the inside room. My children dancing with the other children. Then a crowd of mummers came in, one riding a hobby horse. The snock of the cloth horse's jaws — it had iron nails for teeth.

Come in, Bartlett said, and get yourself a plate of gear.

We had to guess the mummers, as the men were dressed in women's clothes and the women wore bed sheets and gauze over their faces. They spoke by inhaling, aspirating their words. There was a tot of rum when they were all guessed — Marten Edwards and Carmel Lahey and Emily Edwards and Bud Chafe and Rose Foley. Bud Chafe had an accordion. Give us a fiddle,

Bartlett said. And Bud Chafe started up the accordion and Rose Foley sang.

We ate and the children chased the cat and Eleanor told them not to cram it. There was a big feed of salt beef and cabbage and turnip and pease pudding. Then Bob Bartlett walked us home and came in for a drink. He laughed at my German eagle. You know, he said, where the name Brigus comes from?

I did not.

They say it's from the French for *brigues*. Which means intrigue. Let me know if youre forming a cabal, I might join.

We had a drink as Kathleen put the children to bed. Youre as stubborn, he said, as a log.

I no longer feel welcome, I said, in town.

He took a drink. Queer taste, he said.

It's Jagermeister. A fine German liquor sent as a Christmas joke by my good friend Gerald Thayer in New York.

I've met him.

Of course you have.

Your wife's cousin.

I nodded and he drank it off.

It's good not to marry too far, he said.

Yes, you should know who youre marrying. Their people.

Was the bottle tampered?

Opened, yes, by our good man the shipping agent.

I'll have a stain more, he said. To George Browiny.

We drank it all. He stayed and we drank everything. Kathleen went to bed and then we followed. I woke up with Bob Bartlett in my bed. He was nuzzled into me. Kathleen on the other side. He was an elegant sleeper, a man used to close quarters. I got up and let them sleep together. I looked out at the new snow over Brigus. I walked down to the brook for water. On the way back I noticed, in front of the house, a slight white mound. Like beaten egg white. And then a cracking through of the white, of yellow fur on the black guard hairs like butterscotch, and a dog breaking out of the meringue to hunch and shake the snow off his shoulders. Tom's three-legged dog.

Come here Smoky boy.

He bounded over gleefully, he hurled himself against my knees.

Abandoned, are you?

I went back inside and made coffee. Then I brought the coffee upstairs. The two of them, back to back. I liked it.

20

New Year's Eve was our wedding anniversary, six years. And in the early new year I decided to write Jenny Starling. We were out of money. I thought that the money we'd given Jenny, to raise George, a portion could be returned. Now that he was dead. I wrote this letter. A month later I wrote again. I asked, more officially, that the money I had given towards our child's support be sent to us. Jenny wrote back. She was agreeable to this, but her husband, Luis, was not. She was back with Luis Starling. As if he needed the money. So I got a Boston lawyer, and went there myself to attend the trial. This may sound a little mean, but we were broke and I felt Jenny wasnt hurting.

Luis Starling did not like me. In his eyes I had had an affair with his wife. They were estranged then but not divorced. They were off and on and I had come between them. For Luis, the money we'd given Jenny was compensation for his grief. And now, with the death of George, he felt astonished that I should be sniffing at the perimeter, looking for reimbursement.

I visited the grave of my son. I had never seen him. Kathleen had refused it — when he's older, she said. When we have to introduce him to his other family. And perhaps that is part of the guilt Kathleen had about his death. The cemetery was pretty. Jenny had made a triangular headstone with a roof, so you could put a candle in there. Your grandfather, George, died of typhoid on a ship at sea. I was not much older than you. The captain telegraphed to ask permission to bury him. Your grandmother refused it. To be buried in water. If you must, cremate him. Return his ashes.

After the verdict, in my favour — a portion of the total — I visited Gerald in New York. It was two in the morning. I was flush with money.

I said this to Gerald as we walked to the bar: The weather is mild.

His eyes slid over, under his straw boater. He delivered a punch to the ribs.

Gerald: We're not gonna start describing the weather, are we?

We had a drink in a bar called the Aloha Room. It was a favourite of Gerald's, with red swag lamps, a peacock feather in a vase. We lifted a glass to my dead son. The candles were lit with a blowtorch and the paintings had unnecessary texture. As soon as we sat down the table next to us left.

Me: We clear rooms, you and I.

Gerald, eyeing the waitress: I can give her five dollars and she'll —

Me: They'll kick us out.

Gerald: The Aloha Room is not gonna tell you to leave. That's a sunny joke. Works well outdoors, but not in a room.

Me: The alcohol room.

So what about Jenny?

We've discussed this.

We have?

At the Green Dolphin. She's holding a riding crop and wearing a Roosevelt mask.

Gerald: It takes too much effort to say the word *effortlessly*.

Me: The word *inexhaustible* exhausts me.

Gerald: I avoid words that end in an apostrophe. That a word should be owned by a word to come. Have I said I'm at odds with nature? Annuals, for instance. Now that's an aggressive stance towards civilization.

Me: I would count you, Gerald, amongst my allies if I ever waged a war on mediocrity.

Your letters make you sound like Saint Sebastian. But I dont see the arrow wounds.

The arrows didnt kill Sebastian. He was still alive, so they beat him up.

What kind of man would it take to beat up a saint with a chestful of arrows.

He wasnt a saint at the time of the beating.

A window behind us was open. I leaned over and closed it.

That's something the younger generation doesnt have, Kent — that ability to do something.

Close a window?

Not only the ability but the gumption.

Youre too easily impressed, Gerald.

All we're doing, Kent. Is assembling the dark and light. That woman of mine, she will divorce well.

Is that what they say of Alma?

That's what I'm saying.

I got up to piss. There were pitchers full of lime and lemon wedges sitting in a sink of crushed ice. A coal heater glowing orange. When I returned, Gerald: How could you urinate and wash your hands so fast?

His hands locked, and then he looked into his hands. The palms. Where the fingers lock in that ladder of knuckles.

Gerald: My father's book. Do you know theyre using it now?

Who's using it.

Our beautiful war department.

Theyre going to make our boys look like animals?

They'll have dark spots on top and light on the bottom.

Little fuzzy ears would be excellent camouflage.

My father is now — do you know where he is? He is in the West Indies. Abbott Thayer is looking for a flamingo. He wants to lie in a marsh at dusk and see if it disappears against the setting sun.

Your father is pretending he is an alligator.

He wants to go unnoticed.

Well, may he blend in. I certainly havent.

You dont get it. For him it's all to do with blending in. But the flamingo, he's trying to find a mate. It's all about sex.

I stared hard at Gerald. Is that, I said, what the world boils down to? Camouflage and flare?

We raised our glasses to camouflage and flare.

Gerald: I got drunk so fast I'm gonna shit my bed tonight.

Me: Do you think we drink too much?

It's not a problem, yet. And if we drank this beer all the time we wouldnt drink so much.

The beer you'll end up sipping like scotch.

It's not very good, but it'll get you drunk.

Another round. But I could see that Gerald was losing it. He was concerned with his weight.

Me: If youre heavy stay heavy.

So you think consistency is the plan.

You shouldnt change your body, Gerald. If you put on weight then lose it then put it on again, that's worse than maintaining the weight. That's how you live a long life.

You live a long life, Gerald said, by achieving a poise.

And we drank to that.

That woman over there, he said. She's got that baby fat and a want.

Youre married, Gerald.

He wheeled to me: Dont fuck with me, Kent, or I'll put on more weight.

He said theyre close to separating. Alma's alienation is on a deep level. Gerald: Am I building up the alienation, or is it as serious as all that.

Me: That's a pretty damn unhappy thought.

I've had a lot of difficulty with the children, Kent. I think they came too soon. My work is so important and it takes up a lot of time.

You guys dont spend time well together.

I smoke cigarettes, one every other day.

We both looked at the woman. We were reminded of Jenny.

Me: Dont you love getting your asshole licked?

It's nice. It's been a while. But I'll tell you what's nicer, Kent. And that's the spot between your asshole and the bag of your balls. To have a woman's tongue lick you there. Lick you like a cat.

Me: The thing most people have trouble with is loving themselves.

No, it's not, he said. It's allowing love to move them. Accepting the risk.

He wanted to bicycle home. He wanted to steal a bicycle.

Me: Youre gonna perambulate.

That's not a word you hear very often in here. You hear paramedic, but. Jesus, let's get out of here.

As we passed the woman he said this: Your earrings remind me of the lamps in Barcelona.

On our way back to his house he said, I think I might have syphilis.

I looked at the gleam on his coat buttons.

The rim of my foreskin. It has a puckered-eyelid look to it. I can't remember if it always looked like that.

Me: Do you want me to look at it.

I'd like you, yeah. Let's dart in here.

I watched his hands unbuckle his pants. The weather was growing worse. He heaved out a generous cock.

Jesus that's some bit of dangle.

Just look at the crown.

I think that's the way it looks, but my God youre a horse.

He said his legs had got skinny since he'd stopped bicycling.

We walked back to Gerald's as a snow began to blow. It quickly turned into a blizzard. In the cold of winter, Gerald said, the buildings in a city are like hardwood trees that have lost their leaves.

Then we were sunk into a heavy dark. We had gone blind.

The power grid, Gerald said. The power's out. The whole damn city. Look at Brooklyn. Come on, let's walk down to the Hudson.

We walked to the river and out onto a wooden pier where large ferries stood moored and lit up. We witnessed the snow melt into the dark water. I admire, Gerald said, these bright ships with their independent light.

Theyre like floating towns.

We appreciated these city-states, and Brooklyn joyfully lit in the distance, while at our back the cold buildings stood mouthless, black, perplexed.

I was thinking about Jesus, he said, and if he ever asked for help. And there is one time. He asks this woman for a glass of water.

Because he's thirsty?

He's parched. But with Jesus you have to watch it. Because he's cunning. He's always looking for moments to preach.

Yes he never really talks except with an ulterior motive. Living water. He tells her about the living water.

When we got back to Gerald's I took a bath. I bent my knees at the faucets and let my ears sink under the suds. The sizzle of suds. I listened for the subway. For the shunk of heavy steel shuttling through underground passages. It comforted me, that intelligent transportation. Then I crashed on his couch. In the morning I saw him on his bed. His shoes still on. Alma was not around. I made coffee. The children came downstairs and I made them eggs. When Gerald got up, it was like a shell of him. His eyes opening up, his lips a crease. Barely alive. He grabbed a tin of oatmeal. Keeps me regular, he said. Then brightened. It's not a dump, it's an event.

There was a note on the table. His eyes blinking back flashes of wet. He was holding the note.

I hate it when my wife asks mechanical engineers to go to California with her. Tell me, last night, were there white tablecloths?

What?

At the Aloha.

Yes Gerald.

That's me, isnt it, five-star. I'm so fucking five-star.

21

The children went to school and we had lunch in the restaurant we'd first met Jenny Starling in. You cannot love without hating, Gerald said. And hating hard. It has to do with someone you love leaving you.

He was thinking of Alma. I wondered who was leaving me. My father had left. And since then I had done the leaving. Everything that had happened to me was because of my choosing. And now this rebellion in Brigus. It was beyond my control, and it made me resentful.

I had a rosebud from my mother's greenhouse. To bring back to Kathleen, I said. My mother had picked it. She pulverized the stem to allow it to preserve better. To retain water. She loved Kathleen.

I told this to Gerald and he said, I can't understand the lack of repercussions youre facing. You seem to be getting away with it.

With what, I said.

With willing your life and hang the consequences.

I told him, then, of how it had come to be that I was considered a German spy. It all began, I said, with my attempt to blame the wrong man for the seal hunt. Then there's been suspicion about the coal I bought. They seriously think that I have tools to make a bomb. That I'm supplying a German submarine. That I'm painting war maps. That I have money.

I said, But why do repercussions have to be negative? Why can't I enjoy the positive fallout.

Pause.

You know, Gerald said. And you havent been at all deceitful. I think that's an interesting point.

The one thing I havent mentioned, I said, is a woman.

He liked to hear this.

I said her name. Emily.

Yes, I know her, Gerald said. It was as if it didnt interest him. She loves your work.

You dont know her.

I know the type. Yeah. And I can tell from your eyes that youve slept with her.

I have not slept with her.

He laughed at me. I hated this laugh. His laugh knew that I was trying to be a greater man than I was. His laugh said, You will sleep with her.

Our job, Gerald said, is to marry our selfishness with our goodness. Poise. You hurt people, Kent, you betray them. Not because you want to, but because of an abundance of desire.

Which is another word for joy. How can that be wrong?

You have curiosity.

I dont want to be a hypocrite. I dont want to value art over life.

Gerald: Or the other way around.

Exactly.

If they were separate, then you could justify your struggle of conscience.

Me: I wouldnt *have* a struggle of conscience.

This whole discussion, this lifelong thing you have, it's all about you being at pains to justify the betrayals youve committed in the name of art.

But I havent separated them.

Maybe not, but the very curiosity that makes your art good is what gets you into trouble domestically.

Art does not justify personal betrayal.

So theyre separate. Or the personal wins out.

I'm trying to find a balance.

You make it sound like some equilibrium between joy and joylessness.

Well, that's my character, Gerald.

Your character, not your art, is what has burdened you with having to cope with your own betrayal.

Thank you, Gerald, for that rationalization.

Well, someone without your sexual drive doesnt have to deal with it.

Are you saying that I am passionate and sensual?

I'm stressing the reverse: if Kathleen is congratulating herself on having more restraint than you, then that's false. Her fidelity doesnt mean she has more willpower. Just less drive.

I dont think she's congratulating herself. I think she's hurt.

You want to live your life well, Kent. So that you dont have to be discreet. So youre not racked with guilt.

Discretion is a vain pursuit.

There's no need for secrets when youre a man with a clear conscience. All of this worry about doing the right thing becomes irrelevant when there's nothing to hamper the free expression of yourself.

22

I met up with Rufus Weeks. Let's meet, he said, at the Bankers Club.

I'll wear my cufflinks, I said.

The Bankers Club is on Broadway. It's the hub of the
world's finances. I took the elevator to the thirty-fourth floor.
Rufus dining at a corner window. He was a runt of a man with a
lot of contempt. His contempt was his fuel. It made him unlike-
able. Even though his argument was just (avoid war), his
motives were not mine. He had investments, he was an interna-
tionalist. Rufus Weeks did not want his countries ruined, either
by war or by freedom: his businesses prospered because they
was no competition. Yes, you stared at this man's small, expensive coat and smelt a meanness. Who would want to be run by a
man like Rufus Weeks. It was a shame that a good cause (revolution) had to be ruined because of a man like him. But the truth
is, the cause would never have had motion without a man like
him. Look at me. What had budged in Newfoundland because
of me.

Kent, he said. He smiled, but he did not get up. His smile
was a lifting of lips from his teeth.

23

I took the *Glencoe* back to St John's. I realized I was living in the
age of the shift from sail to steam. I was witnessing the decline
of a way of life. Brigus was an old seaport that had promised to
dominate but was losing out to St John's.

St John's. It was Valentine's Day when I arrived. I was alone
in the world of love. At least, I felt alone. I delivered a copy of
my birth certificate to James Benedict, the U.S. consul. When
you carry your birth certificate you feel alone. The thing is,

we're all very much alike in the core of our bones. We're alone and it's Valentine's Day. At least, that's how you feel if you have the luxury to feel it. It's true that all my life I've given myself the space to think that thought. It's a brave thought and I've always admired courage.

There had been a fire near the harbour. A stationery supply store. They think it was sabotage, by German sympathizers. A wooden building full of paper. Flames climbed over the backs of shorter flames, up to a hundred feet. The windows burst with the heat. Ships tied to the finger piers let loose their hawsers and anchored out in the harbour. The ships did this manoeuvre without fear. They were intelligent ships. They were ships used to avoiding fires, but even so one burnt to the waterline from a cinder. As a ship burns it rises in the water. Barrels of cod oil stacked at the docks, frozen in a casing of snow, melted and then exploded as the fire ate through the oak to the oil. A spray of oil and fire lit up patches of harbour. The cold, indifferent masts of the ships in the harbour. All over the city that night, bits of paper floated down. I picked one up: a singed greeting card, a burnt heart.

Have I said how unimpressed I was with that soot-begrimed, sordid city? It teemed with poverty and squalor. Its steep hills and the clutter of ships' rigging at the wharves could be termed picturesque, if the eye held no communication with the heart. It was a city built on the belief that no one would be staying long. A permanent tent city made of wood. I stayed only the one night.

I made a visit on Judge Prowse. I thought I could persuade him to weigh in and influence what was happening to me. I received a warm welcome at his home. He was big and jovial and aggressive, in the last year of his life. I'm having a little dinner party, Prowse said. Would you join us.

His house had high ceilings, and that space up there above my head made me feel rich and lavish. I began to tell him of the situation, but he cut me off.

We are discussing the war, he said. Come in.

In the dining room he introduced me to John Bartlett, an uncle of Bob's. He was wearing gloves. He was known as Follow-on John. I met his wife, and then the sealing captain Abram Kean.

So youre the spy in Brigus, he said.

And youre the cause of a hundred widows.

Kent.

Prowse took me aside. That's not right, he said.

We walked into the parlour. I can't behave with that man, I said. I came here only to clear my name.

You havent heard the reports, Prowse said, of the cruiser *Dresden*. It is to enter St John's harbour and force our surrender. Kean and John Bartlett here are to sink two ships out by the Narrows. To trap that cruiser in the harbour. Then we'll destroy it. Forgive us, but we think that action is rather heroic. Your situation, Kent, I hesitate to even compare your situation. We are well aware of it and frankly you are the limit. Do yourself a favour and drag your tail in the dirt. I've been dogged in helping you here. Show them youre licking your wounds. Let them think youve been a bull-nosed arsehole and want forgiveness.

I said that was the last thing I'd ever do. I was tooth and nail, and I had a few more things to write and decree and deride. If that was —

Prowse cut me off again. He laid a light finger on my chest. For three months, he said, I've been softening Morris and Squires towards you. Yes, the prime minister himself. And what have you done in those three months? Write letters, be flagrant and snotty and arrogant and half a fool.

Prowse turned to look at me and something changed in him.

I've just decided, Kent. I'm done with you, do you hear? If youre to let your arrogance lead you, then go ahead and find yourself friendless. I have helped and by God I'm done helping you. The one thing I cannot do is prevent the residents of Brigus from reciprocating the contempt that you have so emphatically expressed for them.

And with that I realized I was on my own.

24

I heard myself using a snotty tone to Judge Prowse. I was put off by it. But then wondered where snottiness comes from. It comes from an attempt to be funny and companionable. And this striving stems from a sense that one is not secure or confident — it's a lack of confidence. That one feels smaller than the world one is trying to keep up with. So a snotty tone is saying, I dont feel I'm good enough.

25

Kathleen: How was Gerald?

Me: He's great, he's. I saw Alma too, briefly. And she said, Yeah, I know he's great, but I have to deal with him.

Kathleen: Meaning the whole package.

I was standing in the doorway, stretching, naked. It was February and I was celebrating my first full year here.

Alma was away having this affair with a mechanical engineer. And all Gerald could think of was the afternoon he spent in the mechanical engineer's kitchen. The engineer had a set of kitchen chairs that were beautiful. Gerald envied the chairs. And that the mechanical engineer had arrived at them probably with no exertion. The mechanical engineer doesnt even know that the chairs are beautiful. That is the thing with attractive people: they dont know that they are surrounded by things of beauty. As soon as youre made aware of what is talented about you, that self-consciousness degrades your attractiveness.

Kathleen: I know that man.

What man.

The mechanical engineer.

What is a mechanical engineer.

Anyway I've met him. He's got a face that attracts, perhaps. Which is different from an attractive face. That cultured pout suits a man whom Alma might fall for. Handsome hair.

And some hair?

I said handsome hair.

Me: He's a redneck, this mechanical engineer. He builds bridges. He's taking the hat out of Manhattan. He's the man with the tan. It wouldnt be beyond him to tell a joke about rape. Have you seen his bridge? Alma and I walked over it. He took us over it and Alma had to comment. My God, he spoke about these gods streaming from the clouds over his bridge. So she said to him, Perhaps these references could be better put to a spiritual work.

That's pretty funny.

Me: Alma's said a few things in her time.

Like.

She once said to me, Your arse looks big.

She said that?

No, she said, Those pants, Kent, dont make you as small as you are from behind.

Speaking of which. I wish you wouldnt stand naked like that for all the world to see.

The world can't see us.

Well then the children. They're getting too old to see their father buck naked.

26

I told Kathleen what happened with Prowse. I was wondering how it had come to that. She turned, livid.

Kathleen: It's always the way with you, isnt it.

This is what poisoned my wife. Why are things this way instead of another. Why is this the life we're living and not another.

I am a believer in planting seeds. But I dont want to be held accountable if those seedlings come to quarrel. It is true that I'd like to make over the world entirely touched by me. Influenced by my opinion. The difference between intention, predilection, and accident. It's like a meandering footpath that some bright person decides to straighten out to its destination. It says, This is the way. There is intention here, intention is paramount. But of course, something gets lost: the meandering.

27

Green. Spring. The colour of water in a white enamel basin. I was not comparing. It was what I was looking at when I realized that I was resigned. I was shoring up defences rather than growing. Why was I here. I was looking into a white tub full of brook water. What I could capture from the brook as my second spring thawed the shell of ice covering it. The brook, like water plunging out of a glass bottle. I knelt there naked with my tub and dipper. I filled the tub. Then I saw her. She was standing up by the gate. I pretended not to see her. I wanted her to see me naked. For some reason I wanted that. Perhaps it was the privacy. I wanted Emily Edwards to see how little privacy we had. I stood and faced her. I held the tub and dipper. I looked down at the brook. The brook is heard more than seen. Without its sound it was calm and green, like water in a white basin. I have never understood brooks, or the capacity of hills to contain water. Could all this water be above me. I let Emily Edwards note my backside as I walked back to the house.

The volume of emotions. Desire is spoken of, by those who suggest they know, as a flame that devours and grows hungrier.

But there is no answer to any vice. Sometimes desire can be sated and puts itself out. Sleeping with Emily would douse the spirit to sleep with her. I knew this, in my case, to be true. I could be better to Kathleen after sleeping with Emily. I'd be more in love with my wife. I am not advocating this to all — there is no blanket for all — I am just warning you against those who would repress desire.

28

Kathleen was troubled with the pregnancy and Dr Gill recommended a clinic in St John's. Youre to have a boy, he said. I'm never wrong, I'll even write it down. And we watched him write it in his notebook. We got Emily to look after the children and we took the train into town. The clinic advised us to keep Kathleen there. She was upset by this. Frightened to stay on her own.

Think of it as a time of peace.

Back in Brigus the children were driving me mad. Emily helped and I merely glanced at her.

There was the seal hunt, even with the war, and there was the industry of net mending and the painting of boats. Then it would be lobster and a summer in Labrador or the cod fishery in Conception Bay. The flakes would be built and the fish dried. I had seen this seasonal activity the year before, and now I did not give a shit about it. No one was letting me have a place in it. I was an outsider and not to be trusted. I missed my one true friend, Tom Dobie. I had let him down, I thought. I had promised him a union, but I was not the man to help Coaker. I felt I had had a hand in Tom's decision to sign up early. I stopped looking at the harbour. I hated the town. I passed my days drawing and walking and eating and looking after the children. I was horny and hateful. I had not had sex in five months. For how much longer could I be good?

The church was having its annual fundraiser. But this time it was to help purchase cloth for uniforms.

Rocky: Can we do the Anther Panther and the Wonderbird?

Yes. But you and your sister and the children must organize it.

After a week I went back to St John's to visit my wife. I took her out to dinner. I analyzed her face. I studied the surfaces of it. I did not look into her head. I allowed her the secret life.

As we left she said, Your coat.

As I'd put it on, the vents of my coat had passed over a diner's table. A corner had slipped across his plate of pork and mashed potatoes. There was something green and glistening. I'm sorry, I said. But they were annoyed. The diner and Kathleen. And this irritated me. I was annoyed, not at myself but at the proximity of the tables, and even at the diner's encroachment on my right to don outerwear. It pissed me off and I was not apologetic. It was the world's fault, especially this British enthusiasm for war. The way the world was. I wanted the world to alter itself and fit me like a size-forty suit.

We went to the theatre. In the play was a wedding. And I thought, This is the only sacrilege. It would be fine to pretend a love scene on stage. But a marriage is the words. The words are spoken. And so it is not a real minister, but the words are real. The bride and the groom must speak them. And how can you speak them without diluting their spirit? They should be words spoken only during the ceremony. How some people do not say the name of God.

I said, Let's make love.

Kathleen: Right now I'm not interested in you.

Then let's forget it.

29

I was driven out of my mind.

Bob Bartlett: Take Emily. Take her.

So Emily Edwards came to look after the children for longer stretches of time. She could stay in the house while I travelled again to St John's and got Kathleen set up in a house for pregnant women. Prowse recommended a midwife — a woman, he said, who knew them all in Brigus.

On the train back to Brigus I prayed. I prayed to be absolved. To have this nagging ferocity of spite lifted. I sat angrily. I was the essence of anger. That train was methodically dragging me back to a house of domestic banality, in a town that either ignored me or treated me with suspicion. I wrote a letter to the St John's paper. I said I wanted to be exonerated from all charges. Either that or put up against a wall and shot.

Emily was good with the children. She had this unconscious thing. She did not know she was beautiful. She was always seeing things that were the most fabulous things, or a person who was the most handsome or a food that was the best thing she'd ever tasted. She made my heart light. Her mouth, it was her tongue. Her tongue kept licking the words she'd just said.

Her mouth was full of saliva, she kept swallowing as if everything she said was delicious and tasty. Things were always the
best they had ever been, and she pronounced it all on her last
breath. As if this would be the last thing she'd say, this declaration. The thing is, I believed her.

Was I hoping to be good? My wife. I'm a man who crumples
money in his pocket. It appears from my pocket. To pay for the
theatre tickets I rummaged in the lining of my pockets to peel off
bills. I've already said I'm sure my father never had a wallet.
Does it feel to you that I am troubled by my father?

My father wrote notes in books. Years after his death my
mother would stumble on a note in the margin or on a book-
mark. I can see her now, standing, face down, reading a note
from my father. It was part of the reason why she could not
move on.

30

I wrote to Kathleen on my birthday. My birthday is the first day
of summer. How a year ago I had such hopes for this place.
Now Gerald's pear tree was struggling below us. And I was
accepting that this was a doomed venture. I had snuffed out
my ecstatic bliss at being alive in the world. I had turned thirty-
three, the age of crucifixion, and had failed at my own private
goal. I wrote, How fearfully old.

Emily was new to cooking, so she got Mrs Pomeroy to bake
a cake. And they came down. Emily took me by the wrists and
kissed me on the cheek. Happy birthday, she said. The children

helped me blow out the candles. The sides of Emily's mouth full of delight. She wanted me to be having a good time. Then she stroked her own belly and felt the cuff of the lemon cardigan she wore over her light dress. She liked to touch herself, as if straightening the contours of her own body. I had seen her backlit in the sun, rubbing her breasts through the dress out of the enjoyment of having them touched in the sunlight.

I dont think she ever knew I would look at her that way. But that night, after the children were put to bed, I pulled out a bottle of whisky and we started on that. I think she felt, because I was an outsider, that she could confess. Even though I'd planned to live there, I was living in this house on the far end of town. It was like a confessional. I decided, too, to admit all. It was my birthday. This night would be the beginning of our confessing. I dont, she said, understand Tom Dobie. She wasnt sure he loved her. She wasnt sure he found her attractive. Was she ugly.

No, I said. You are very very beautiful.

I said that sometimes men have a hard time reassuring loved ones. And then it becomes hard to express all the love one has through the accepted channels of wife, children, friends. It's difficult, I said, to ignore the possibility of a lover.

Emily was intrigued by this. I wasnt answering her and yet she wanted to be loved.

Tom, she said, does not make me feel lovable.

She was direct about it. She wanted to have a man. She knew this. She was waiting for Tom Dobie. She said his name because she realized that she had said *a man*. She didnt say, I want Tom Dobie. She did not know if Tom would. We've been close, she said. I wanted him to, but he wouldnt. He was reluctant and yet he won't marry me. He's only promised me something later. But how long will he be away?

She loves him more for it, the possibility that he could be killed.

Did you love Stan Pomeroy?

What me and Stan had. We were just fooling about.

Tom was mad about it.

Emily: He was good about it. I find him so beautiful to look at.

The fact of Tom Dobie made it easier for us to be intimate. It was as if we both knew we would have Tom Dobie as a border. But our love for him brought us closer too. I cannot speak for what she thought of Kathleen.

Me: Your name. It's a good name. Famous people have the double initial, Emily Edwards. Harry Houdini. Jack Johnson. Bob Bartlett.

Charlie Chafe, she said. Your wife.

Kathleen Kent. I hadnt thought of it. She was Kathleen Whiting.

My name would be Emily Dobie if I married Tom.

You could keep it. My friend Gerald's wife kept hers.

We drank and I watched her press herself against the table. The whole top half of her body leaning over the table to be close to me. Her arms gesturing were a mere inch away from my own. We drank. We drank until I thought of her clothes as the skin of a peeling thing. Her clothes would pull away easily, as if they were something she couldnt choose to put on again. Once the clothes were off, they would be off. They would dry up, and blow away. They would no longer be clothes.

You know youre gorgeous, dont you.

Emily: Youre the gorgeous one.

I think youre the — youre young, your arms are golden. Your face. I said, My wife and I, we've not.

I could not say it.

There's a grey area between my wife and me.

Emily listened to this. It made her uncomfortable. So she did have Kathleen between us and I had just tested her.

I have an understanding with my wife, I said.

Emily was not beautiful in the conventional sense.

I think I should go, she said.

31

She came by the next day and took the children. She was cheery. It was as if nothing had been said. We had a picnic with the children out by the naked man. And then she left after putting them to bed. But the next day she lingered. I have wine, I said. Why dont we.

I dont feel beautiful, she said. That's the main thing. I can't get over that. I'm not convinced.

She had emptied her wine. And her face had descended into the wine glass, so that her chin was resting in it.

We went over it again. She loved my convincing her.

What was it you meant about your wife.

I have slept around on my wife. My wife knows this. She understands. It isnt something dreadful.

It sounds dreadful.

You can get used to anything.

It decided things for her. When I took her up the narrow stairs that night I was stunned that I was with the body of that face. That face's body was against my own. It was a lie about my wife and both of us felt the wrong in it. We did not face each other. It began in the narrow stairs. We made the movements that are like stairs. I held Emily with her back to me. It was as if we were not making love because we were not in a room, though it turned the stairs into a room. A place on your way to another place.

In the bed it was both of us facing the same direction. She said, This bed. This was my mother's bed. She was thinking of her mother as we lay there. The bed from Marten Edwards. Can we just lie here, she said. This is nice.

32

I wrote again to Prime Minister Morris. Prowse had been speaking to him. Since he'd seen Kathleen pregnant Prowse had been pleading my case. If only for her sake and not mine. I thought that if the prime minister could weigh in. Perhaps things could be salvaged.

I wrote to Kathleen. I wrote, You are no longer the cousin of Gerald Thayer. You are nobody's cousin. You are Kathleen Kent and you are you and I am your husband. I have been with you so long that you remind me of no one but yourself. Do you feel the same.

Yes she felt the same.

33

What Emily told her father, Marten Edwards. That she had to take care of the children. That often the children woke up at night and needed consoling. That the painter needed his sleep. It was her duty. This was how Emily Edwards explained the sleeping over. We made a false bed for her on the chaise longue. It is odd to think that it wasnt my sleeping with Emily that contributed to our expulsion. More, it was my disinterest in my children. That was chalked up as another heartless Germanic affliction.

She was lying in bed and I saw her back in the hall mirror. I decided to talk to her while looking there. At first she spoke to the room, then she said, Come out from behind the wall.

How did you see me behind the wall.

Then her eyes found me in the mirror. Youre casting a shadow.

I'm not used to being with someone who can find me in the mirror.

Well, we're a lot alike. Does that disappoint you?

I dont know what it does.

Oh surely you must know what it does.

I felt at least two things. Yes, I felt disappointment. But I felt that of course she knew. She's a quick looker like me. Youre open to looking at all surfaces and angles, even those in mirrors.

I'm open to the possibilities of where I might find you.

If you werent, I may think you oblivious.

Is that what you thought of your other girlfriends?

When Emily left, her footsteps shifted from the open door to bouncing off the ceiling through the window. The sound was like a tiny high cracking of timbers, the sound insects make when eating.

34

I want you on your knees.
    Do you want me on my hands and knees?
    Me: Your hands and knees. I want you looking down.
    Look.
    Yeah.
    Emily: I'm so dark.
    Yeah youre dark.
    Look.
    You want me to compare.
    Well just look at my skin on your skin.
    You sound proud or something.
    I'm noticing how brown I am. Just look at our arms.
    Emily, I want you looking down. What I want is I dont want you to see me. I want it to be a surprise to you that I'm over you, that I'm —
    Entering me.

35

What was I doing. Was I trying to broaden my wife's expressions? Did it excite me to pain her, to see pain track Kathleen's forehead. I was making her big, or breaking her. Gerald had told me that I did not know composure. Kent, he said, you can't understand harmony. It irritates you, for you cannot possess it. You want to turn harmony over and watch it struggle.

I knew that Kathleen had given herself over to me, every ounce. Even her eyelids were mine. I was not a man who could give himself over, and so there was the difference in power. To love is to be vulnerable to hurt.

Gerald had said, If you do not speak of some desires, and even acts you are ashamed of, it is better in the long run.

Me: Can you diminish the extent of your desire?

Gerald: If you allow desire room to live, you may develop a habit, or at least a proclivity.

36

Emily and I took the children for a drive into Carbonear. We borrowed Mackinson's horses and cart. It made me understand the cleft in my ass. Along the way we passed an internment camp. There were about seventeen German POWs digging posts. Stop a second. I jumped on the cart bed. I waved my arms and, in German, yelled: The kaiser is winning the war! It will not be long now!

They looked around, confused. One man blew a gob of

snot. So I yelled it again. Then they cheered heartily, waving their spades.

It was our last night together. I should have sent her away. After we made love I told Emily this was the end. When youre being good, she said, it's not that youre being good to that person. Youre being good to the spirit of that person.

Me: Youre too loyal to a belief.

Tom's being away had made her lose hope. It had made her not care. She wanted to enjoy something. She wanted to see what kind of repercussions could come from obvious wrong.

37

This time Constable Bishop walked over with an officer from St John's. I heard them while we were in my studio. We were naked and we had surprised each other. So much for the last time. The children were upstairs, unattended. I dressed and closed the studio door on Emily and invited the men in. The officer merely stood there while Bishop asked me his fresh questions. Is it true, he said, that you were seen Thursday last saluting prisoners of war and encouraging them to escape.

Was I seen?

Did you do it.

I met a few Germans and I enjoy speaking German.

Would it be possible to inspect your house.

That would not be appropriate. The house is a mess. I'm embarrassed by the house. My wife is in St John's and I am not much of a homemaker.

Your children are upstairs.

They have a nanny.

A Miss Edwards.

That is so.

She is upstairs.

She is in the house.

Perhaps then just your studio.

That would be even less likely.

Could you tell us the meaning of this eagle and the words *Bomb Shop*.

A man is allowed to write anything he wants on his house.

The house belongs to the Pomeroys.

Has Mr Pomeroy complained?

He has not, but he did say we could go through his house.

The foundation and all that stands above it belong to the Pomeroys. The studio I built myself, at my own expense. It is mine and I can write on it whatever I wish and bar entry to whomever I choose. I've certainly learned one thing well from Sniffles Hearn.

But what is it you intend by writing such a flagrant thing.

Why, flagrancy of course.

Mr Kent, if I can talk freely.

As a matter of fact, I'd prefer it if you didnt talk freely. I'd like you to feel as caged with your talk as I feel walking about this town. If anyone is spying, Mr Bishop, it is this community. On me. The reason I chose this house was for privacy. And privacy is the last thing I am receiving.

Did you visit St John's recently.

It was the officer speaking now.

I passed through, on my way back to Brigus.

Is it true that you met with William Coaker.

I tried my best, but the man was busy.

And while in New York you were seen with a Mr Rufus Weeks.

Do you have anything in that notebook on Rufus?

I have never met the man, so no, there is nothing about him in here.

Rufus, I said, is an old chum.

Our regards to your wife, sir. We hear youre expecting a puff-up in your house.

Let me walk you to the gate.

When I came back in Emily had dressed and taken the children down to the naked man.

38

I went to St John's. Kathleen had had the baby. A little girl.

Barbara.

And when I saw her I knew I would not tell Kathleen about Emily. All thoughts of Emily were gone. I loved my wife. I was saturated in love for this woman who had given me this child. When my father died, my mother had been pregnant with my sister, Dorothy. I thought of this during Kathleen's pregnancy. The birth of my memory came with my father's death. And in a sense, my father was born to me out of his death. He became a fixed notion that could not be altered. I wanted to stay alive and volatile for the sake of Barbara. So she'd know you could be anything, change yourself, become new.

Kathleen was not well enough to come home. I'm going to rest up in St John's.

Okay, I said. You two stay here.

I visited Prime Minister Morris. Yes, he'd received my letter. He looked indifferent. He was studying a model of a pulp mill. It had been set up on the floor of his office, the roof on hinges, and it was open. He received a lot of letters.

There was a folder on his desk.

What do you think of newsprint, Kent?

I've been known to read papers.

And write for papers.

That too.

We have a number of your letters. To the New York papers and papers here. Youve created quite a little stink, havent you.

It was not I who created it. I've merely reacted to false allegation. Something I hoped you might help to alleviate.

Morris was piling tiny wooden logs into a heap beside a model vat inside the open head of the pulp mill. He was hardly listening to me.

They are wanting to build this on the west coast of the island, he said. The largest pulp mill in the world. That's a tremendous number of New York newspapers. What do you think of that?

Your *they* is telling.

Pardon.

I think *you* should build it.

Lovely.

I mean the government. The people should own it.

Youre opposed to private ownership.

Of the forests and oceans, yes.

He collected up a handful of the pulp logs. He held them as though they were the facts one could know in the world. I'm surprised, Morris said, that youre in my office instead of William Coaker's.

If he were the prime minister I'd be there.

Look, Kent. This trouble in Brigus. Can you make up with a few people? We know there is nothing to the spy allegations. It is all rather hilarious. But once a file is in the hands of the bureaucrats, it's hard to extinguish. A folder never grows thinner. He touched something in his pocket. Paper, you know?

We shook hands. I left him to his pulp mill.

39

I took the train back to Brigus. Every toe in my fingers was tapping. I promised myself to stay away from Emily. I wanted to force myself to be good. I told her it had to stop. Was she relieved? I had convinced her that she was beautiful. That a man could enjoy her. But she was not looking forward to the complications of Kathleen's return. I'm not sure she was convinced that my wife, even if she knew, would be able to accept it. But then, Kathleen was a woman from New York and they had other arrangements in big cities.

I wrote Kathleen once a day. I drew her landscapes. I had

Rocky and little Kathleen draw postcards. I staved off desire —
deprivation made me feel good.

I saw Dr Gill. I told him of the girl.

As I predicted, he said.

I'm sorry, you said a boy.

He looked puzzled. Then fished a notebook from his bag.
He turned through the pages. No, see here, he said. I wrote it
down: a girl.

There it was. And then he laughed. That's my little trick, he
said. I say the one and I write down the other.

So youre right a hundred percent.

Dont tell anyone.

It was July before Kathleen and the baby could travel. I went
to meet them when it was safe to return. I held Barbara. It was
going to be good. I loved the child. I remembered the promise
that children bring. I thought that perhaps it could work out. We
had a true Newfoundlander in the family. We showed the baby
to the children and Emily had the place spotless.

You must raise her up, Emily said. Stand on a chair.

I stood on a kitchen chair with Barbara. Emily and Kathleen
staring up at me. For a second Emily touched my knees.
Kathleen saw the look Emily gave me.

Emily: Okay, that'll be good luck for her.

She said she'd be off now. And Kathleen knew.

What type of man are you.

Her frozen face.

You are a burden, she said. In the end the weight of you.

It's all over, I said. It was a small thing six weeks ago. It has
been stopped for a long time.

I cannot fathom you. Can you call her back.

You know this of me.

I keep praying, though. I keep thinking you will become more like me. Call her.

Kathleen, can you not say anything to her?

You want me to pretend.

Nothing can come — you'll just make her feel bad.

I wouldnt want to make anyone feel bad. Not this pure girl.

Look. It's my fault.

She gripped her head to keep it all in. The force in her hands, pressing down.

You pulverize me, Kent. You love that word, and that is what you do to me.

She gave me a mad look.

You want everything and yet you know you can't have everything. For to have it all excludes a deepening of anything. There is a limit in me.

I have a powerful will and you have a powerful heart.

We paused and there was a moment of tenderness. Kathleen released the agony in her skull. She exhaled. She was about to do something silly. A soft-shoe routine.

So you think, she said, that it's okay for my friends to sleep with you.

No it's not okay.

That I shouldnt take it personally.

There was something about Emily that was the hired help. How respectful.

You know I find a lot of people attractive.

I wish. I wish that at least you'd just find distant women

attractive. It wouldnt be so bad if they werent in the same god-damn town.

She swore. It took a lot out of her to swear. I wanted to say I was sorry. I wanted to beg. I loved Kathleen, I loved her integrity and her long arms. The ferocity of her hurt pained me. But also, her anger and her outrageous wishes made me say that I hated the predicament. I hate this, I said.

What if I found Gerald Thayer attractive. Or if I fucked Rupert Bartlett.

Gerald is your cousin. Then I said it: Could you please not swear?

For that was what I hated. The jarring of goodness with a malevolent, ill-used force.

I think that's what I'll do.

She was white-hot with anger.

Rupert is not going to sleep with you, I said. And Gerald's your cousin. I did not know what I was arguing. I had lost my footing, and I did not know where she was or who she was. She had become unknowable. The thing is, we're all unknowable, but usually we mask it. Now her unknowableness had surfaced.

Kathleen: So youre saying your friends are more principled.

Well, for one thing Gerald's my best friend, and Rupert is not a sexual man. But in general, yes, I'm saying men are more principled.

You have to be the most arrogant — that is such bullshit. I could have had something with Rupert.

Well okay, sleep with Rupert, but I dont want to hear about it. And if I do hear about it, I won't embarrass him.

What had I been saying? What was the root of the fight?

That is so civil, she said. Really. Youre such a swell guy, Kent. So where did you fuck her.

Kathleen, that is an endless road that road.

Oh it is endless, I know. So not only in our bed but over the kitchen table. I bet the children had to eat their breakfast on top. You fuck.

Please dont swear.

And in that little room and on the kitchen floor. Did you fuck her in all the unusual places where youve fucked me? Have you so little imagination?

Kathleen.

And in the bed that was her mother's. That's very good, Rockwell. You at least. Well, what did you do with the children. She was supposed to be with the children, so did you hire someone else to look after the children while you, or did they just listen in their rooms upstairs. Oh you ingrate, and I suppose the whole town knows.

Kathleen, this is important. No one must know of this. If they knew, that would be it for here.

You remind me of a man in a towel who is staring as his house burns down. I was having a bath — that's what he says.

She beat her arms against me. She punched me in the neck. She caught a knuckle in my eye. I held my hands up. I took the flurry. I let her flail against me, whip me until she was exhausted. Then she sat down in a chair and caught her breath. She made a concentrated effort to be unapproachable. We stared at parts of the room, as quiet as individuals. She said, It all comes down to what kind of honesty can you dredge up. And am I legitimizing what you did with Emily.

She reminded herself that I didnt mislead her. That she had always known what I was like.

I will not argue with you, I said, or defend my case.

I handed her a glass of water and she drank it. I was standing there, saying nothing. She was waiting for me to say something. She got up and opened a window and it was chilly. I thought that this predicament, if we let time pass without talking about it, would sizzle away and be over with. It is never the case, though. Something is usually said later and it makes the thing harder to take. It makes it bigger because it is deliberated on. This time, though, it would be different. I was a new man. This time was to be the first moment of a new length of time. But there it sat, someplace above the back of her mouth, in her head. It was like an inert material, a grain of a new type of insulation. We both refused to speak — as the room got colder. This time, I thought, she will be able to get over it without saying anything more about it. She is too weary. I have made her weary.

40

I walked down to the naked man. I was an asshole. I knew that part of my assholeness came from the fact that I was unrepentant. I just wanted to go away and sit with it. I enjoy feeling sorry for myself. I'd had this fight with Kathleen and the children were going nuts and I had to be on my own. I sat there and lit the hurricane lamp. I leaned back against the cairn of rocks and listened to it hiss. It made the night darker — light does that. The dark also makes things louder. Behind me the house all intense, the four tiny bright windows of a family. I had made that. I had willed it and I was strangling the juice out of it. I stretched out my knees, my knees ached. I could feel the heat coming out of the land. The wind swung around. It was warm off the land and then cold off the water. It just swung right around. My light fluttered. I had to shade it, so I leaned up against the naked man. All the lights of the town now. As if there were a dial and it was being turned up just a notch a minute. Waves now. The tide is down and the bare black rock. The crest of a white wave over the rock, creamy and fizzing. Little boats up on the slipway. This was the littoral zone, where so much of the work of the world happens. A few small boats were coming in. You could hear the oarlocks groaning. An oil lamp lit in the bow. Idling in. A painter thrown to the stagehead. The oars drawn up, clunking on the gunwales. Something happening in the dark. Now standing. Now the flash of the sides of fish being pitchforked up. Having to connect shreds of sound and light to a story. Fresh, stiff fish. Pushed around by feet. Into a barrel. Slow, the work is slow and long and constant. A storeroom lit now and they'll work in there until three in the morning. I stand and I take up my lantern. I swing it in their direction. I swing it as if it's a toast to their work. I want them to know that I am acknowledging them. I take the path back up to the tight and tiny lights of my will being done.

41

I wore the scarf that was my wife's. I wore it the way I've seen women wear scarves. You double it, wrap it around your neck, then thrust the two ends through the loop and tighten. I was soaking my feet in a tub of hot water and scraping my soles with a German knife. Kathleen had put the children to bed. I formed a sludge of grey along the edge of the blade. Dunk and scrape. I had a sore nose too, and I was pushing eczema cream into my nostrils. It was all I had. And I noticed how deep and cavernous is the nostril cavity.

They want us to leave.

Kathleen listened. She knew this.

Me: What do you think.

I think it's hilarious. They want you to leave for being a spy. When all you are is unfaithful.

I was listening to Schumann's "Traumerei" over and over. It was making me say sentences that ended with *and yet*. I will love you until the cows come home, Kathleen, and yet. I am alive with the spirit of grace and generosity, and yet. I will commit and be driven and centred and empty myself and never lie, and yet.

This conviction as I soaked my feet in a tub of slurry.

Happiness, she said. It is a difficult, complicated place to attain.

Me: It is easier to be unhappy.

And so we shy away from the complication that might foster happiness.

You do. You become simple in the depth of your tenacity to endure, and so become sad.

Kathleen looked at me in the tub. You look like you just got out of bed, she said. You look more like yourself now. I mean, when you were younger.

Right now, I said, youre more like me than yourself.

Because I'm looking at you with a cold eye.

Yes, it's something across the eyes. It's not bad. I've got the same look. You look like youre thinking: Oh, this is where I'm at and this is new and I'm resolved to where I'm at.

Kathleen: Everything seems more me than I am.

Regret is hoping backwards.

Kathleen: There is a difference between the fact of the matter and the truth of the matter.

An ironic distance, I said.

Kathleen: A sense of humour is important in any serious thing you do. If you can joke about something youre involved in, then it's working.

Me: Are you saying it's working?

She smiled at me.

We should leave, then.

I'm not interested in fighting them, Rockwell. Not after this.

You mean after Emily.

She nodded.

Then we'll leave.

42

What I heard at Billy Cole's window. Patrick Fardy: Did you see our man out on the point night before last.

Jim Hearn: Yes, with that bug light. Did you read it.

Patrick: What was it, Morse.

Hearn: It was Morse, boy, right up on the clay scrape.

What was he saying.

It was in German.

You what. You think.

Oh I knows it, he was right by the naked man.

It makes sense, dont it. That map. The bomb shop. Got to be.

Did you hear what he shouted out in Carbonear?

So he was signalling a submarine.

For sure he was.

He's a Kraut through and through that one.

And paid. Who goes around flashing five-dollar bills.

She tried, but even good, kind Kathleen found that her humour wavered and up pulsed anger. And as her anger grew her love dispersed in little ships. Her anger stole her love of me away. I could see her complexion drain of love.

43

When my father died my mother became a different person. It was a gradual thing. At first she was the mother still. And she did the things she'd always done. Perhaps it wasnt until I was a teenager that she began to do the things that she would not have done under his eye. She was freed up to be herself. She was not expecting this. We all, I think, imagine a decade after the death of a spouse. When we're seventy. A spread of solo years, not too long a spread. When we will wing out in a new bloom. Just a junior partner to the rest of your life. There is childhood and being a new adult and then there is marriage — the grounded living — and then the separation at death and the permission to be wild in a breeze or a calm pool. So for a time my mother, in her thirties, maintained my father's ways. We moved into her aunt's house for financial reasons. It's not that we didnt have money, we just didnt have enough to maintain a standard that my father would have assumed. We had to keep the appearance of a good living even when Father was dead.

44

Tom Dobie came home on leave to marry Emily Edwards. They found out he was only seventeen. He looked stronger and he had enjoyed the time away. He wore his uniform and they both had white roses pinned to their hearts. Emily in white gloves. A gorgeous day. The morning had been rainy, so Bartlett said, Let's burn a shoe. He was happy about the wedding. You dont want to marry, he said again, too far.

Tom Dobie, as he stood by his bride: Youre short.

Emily: I'm not.

Tom: I didnt realize you were so short.

She: I'm in a dip is what. You stand in it.

And so they moved over a foot. And Emily grew three inches. When the minister asked them to be faithful. They pronounced the word as fateful. They all did, bride, groom, and minister. I wondered if they thought that was their pledge, to be fateful.

Tom's mother was ill in bed. So they walked over to the house in Frogmarsh. They climbed the stairs, Emily and Tom, and sat on the corner of the bed so Rachel Dobie could see them. From a drawer in a night table, she passed them an English silver coin.

Tom Dobie was in town five days. He heard about my troubles. He spoke to Emily's father, Marten. And Marten drew up a petition. Tom: Marten Edwards composed it. We got all the Bartletts to sign it, as have the Pomeroys and Dr Gill. We said you was a spirited man who loves culture. That youre stubborn yes, but not a German spy. The idea of you involved in espionage. No, this is what Marten wrote: It is highly improbable that Kent, as a socialist, has any particular regard for the kaiser or the military aristocracy of Germany. I'm sorry for your troubles, Kent.

Tom shook my hand like a gentleman. Formal.

And then he was sent back to St John's.

45

Fate is something you cannot avoid, destiny is something you choose. A wedding is public, a marriage private. This book, consider it my marriage to the world. All I have written before this, a wedding.

At my wedding. I was nonchalant. Sauntering into the church, taking in the heads and shoulders. The men had rounded top hats. I walked down the aisle and up the green stairs. I walked up all the stairs, shook hands with the minister, doffed my hat, set it down, and stepped back to meet my bride. I was not supposed to take all the steps, but I wanted to take in the steps. I have never left a stair unstepped, and I have never been patient. I had broken the rules of the ceremony and that is me: bigger than ceremonies, wanting to recreate them in my image. I stood there, rolling on my feet, waiting. I looked back on the guests. They giggled at my easygoingness. There's a nervous groom, Gerald Thayer said. There were men holding women's purses and men, afterwards, giving children money. And then my bride arrives decked out in a fabric the colour of ecru. A reception in a canvas tent, in case of rain. It's sunny, so it offers shade. I want more dancing. What I want is more of a good time, and I want a good time on my behalf, sponsored by me. I do not want a time paid out like some debt of sociability.

46

Bob Bartlett came with the news. He told Constable Bishop he'd deliver it. It was a telegram from Prime Minister Morris. Youve been told to leave by the end of the month, he said. You have seventeen days.

Well, thank you, I said. Youre not put out at being seen with me.

I'm not ashamed to visit a prisoner, he said.

The children began to cough. You realized that the coughing was regular. And then small fits of choking. As if they were being politely strangled. Their mouths were full of phlegm and we called the doctor. They had a fever but then the fever passed. Dr Gill couldnt see anything wrong. It was just a cold, he said.

A cold. They got a little better and then they grew worse. I was not going to have any more dead children on my hands. I refused it. When they coughed their cheeks and temples bloomed in colour. First red, then blue. Is that green. Yes, Kathleen theyre green. Theyre not getting oxygen.

Rocky vomited and little Kathleen's face was puffy. They looked at us as if they did not know why they were being punished. Clara wheezing, and thankfully Barbara was spared of any symptoms. I called Dr Gill again. But by the time he arrived they seemed fine enough.

We listened to the children cough, anticipating their coughs. Urging them to stop. It was as if they were coughing as much as they could on one breath. Just exhaling. Not inhaling. Every single molecule of air out of their lungs. And then this dreadful sound like something being sucked down a sink. Kathleen: It's whooping cough. That's what this is.

We got another telegram then, the final word, from the governor: YOU MUST LEAVE. We must. No later than the end of the month.

I wrote a terse response. I was fit when it came to writing. I said that if they didnt mind, two of my children had the whooping cough and could they postpone our expulsion.

We packed. I tallied a list of the expenses I'd put into the house. I was thinking damages.

The U.S. consul, James Benedict, wired us that they'd offered a reprieve. But by now we had decided to go. Kathleen tried to book berths aboard the *Florizel*. She was told that the family needed a permit to leave the country, otherwise they would not allow us on board. I wrote to the immigration chief and had George Browiny, who seemed polite with a kind of remorse now, send it:

> May I render some humble assistance to the government in the performance of its present humanitarian work by begging you kindly to permit us to obey the government's orders. The six Kent suspects are unanimous in their desire to depart.

We bade adieu to the Bartletts, to the Pomeroys, and in St John's to James Benedict and Judge Prowse. It was a rushed farewell. In Brigus I watched Marten Edwards walk out to us. There was something in his face, full of conviction and dignity. He was red in the face. I thought it might be that his daughter had spoken of what had happened. I had thought *that*, if anything, would have been the reason for our expulsion. Marten Edwards came up to us with stiff, angry hands. I am, he said, awful sorry. Youre the finest kind, Kent. My daughter loves you and your wife — he nodded seriously at Kathleen — and your children. She will miss the children and I will miss you both. Emily is not with me, for she is feeling poorly, he said. She's missing Tom and now your departure.

He shook our hands vigorously, Kathleen was touched. He gave the children each a five-cent piece and then abruptly left, as if he had a lot of work to do.

Bob Bartlett said we'd miss his birthday. He was turning forty in two weeks. He accompanied us to St John's, he played with the children. He saw us off in St John's harbour. The siren blew. The hawsers slackened, and we were drawn aboard. We were off. It was only then, with the hard Atlantic wind punishing our faces, that I appreciated how Bob Bartlett and Marten Edwards had taken time to see us off. How Prowse had tried his best. But as the gap of seething water widened in our wake, I, sadly, had no hope or thought of ever seeing Newfoundland again.

47

We arrived in New York like immigrants. No, we had left New York as émigrés and returned as exiles. Our children had not seen the city from this angle. Yes, it felt like my dream of a Newfoundland life had been attached to them, and now a new one was to begin in a foreign land. But this was where they were from. My life with Kathleen was near an end, but I loved my children.

I took my son for a walk. I would travel with my son. There is a good church in New York that we visited — I liked it because the rain off the copper eavestroughs had painted the ears of the gargoyles green. The church had been under renovation for ten years. Buildings rust, I told Rocky, even when theyre being built. My son cannot remember the church without scaffolding. First one spire, then the other. All his life there had been a leg of scaffolding. I wanted the city to remove all scaffolding for one day, to restrain the repair of roofs in general. For the sides of houses to be finished with paint. For boats to remain untended. For gardens left unmowed. I would like to take a photograph of the city with no industry of repair. For a city is unlike a woods. We think a city finished and modern and alive. When it is a dead thing. A city presents an identity, whereas we have an identity at the end of our lives, in hindsight. Nature too. Sometimes I will look at the back of a yard and see the mature trees and think: Finally, it has come into its own, this yard.

I explained to Rocky that hidden in the belly of the Statue of Liberty is an Eiffel Tower. Her raised heel is the root of permanent internal scaffolding. All of her weight is on one leg, a trick they learned from the caryatids in Athens. The left leg holding her right arm above. To the east, the other bookend, the Brooklyn bridge. And between them, the Flatiron Building. All fenestration. St John's, I said, was a city that, a century before, had promised to be larger than New York. There were projections. There were plans and anticipation and investment. There was the consideration of a world of commerce and growth that would take place on that cold, foggy island in the north, a way station into North America that did not pan out. Someone had folded a map down the middle of the Atlantic, I said. They saw that Europe and America sat on top of each other. And Newfoundland is like England, a little island off the American coast. There was a promise, a potential, a world that did not get born.

But Manhattan — this other island, nestled in the armpit of the Eastern Seaboard — this bloom grew and flourished and you are the one, Rocky, who will compare. You will grow up during a war and a revolution in Russia. You will see me work with Rufus Weeks, work and fail at a change here at home. It was difficult to realize that once you have returned home you can still be looked upon as an alien and a menace. You wanted to be different, Gerald Thayer said to me. You wanted to avoid repetition, and yet here youve gone and done the same thing. The truth is, people want home to stay the same as well. To always repeat.

48

We lasted another five years. As Kathleen said, everything takes five years. Then we separated. It was her decision. After three months apart we arranged a day of reconciliation. The day was ten days away. I had it marked and kept thinking about it. I was excited by it. I wanted the family together. I thought it could work. And then Kathleen called. She wanted to meet earlier, to relieve the pressure. How about tomorrow. I said tomorrow was bad, but how about now. And she said okay. I could come over.

It was closing on four oclock. I knocked on the door that used to be my door. I had never had a reason to knock on it. The only thing new was the lock.

The children were with Kathleen's parents. Kathleen was wearing a lavender skirt, clingy, with a thin dark top. She looked great. She told me that she wanted to be alone for a year. That when she weighed returning to me or being on her own — the prospects looked dim.

Kathleen: I should want to be with you, not resigned to it.

We sat at the kitchen table. She by the wall. And I took it in. I said, Youre looking at me now with the same attention you gave me when I was young. That intimacy I offered, that flirting. That sense of openness, that willingness to talk and listen.

Kathleen: That same power was the power that undid us.

I did not realize that the force you trained upon me, Kathleen, you would then shift to others. The very same sly wooing you laid upon me you could just as easily manoeuvre onto someone else. I did not understand you were a wooer. I had thought I was the thing, rather than the wooing act being the thing.

She was seeing a man named Finney.

But now I know these things, Kent.

We've spent three months apart, Kathleen, and I want us to try it. Have you thought about it.

Yes, and I dont.

Why not.

Because it will offer false hope.

Just tell me you dont love me. Do you love me?

She shook her head.

So you dont love me. And you dont think you could.

Pause.

Me: Youre sure of that.

A nod from Kathleen.

She was in the place of wordlessness. When she's most wordless, that is when I want to talk the most.

Me: How can you be so sure.

Kathleen: I'm happy now. I dont want to return to that. I'm afraid of it.

But I love you. And I dont believe you dont love me.

Kathleen: Well, it's true.

It was six oclock now. She had to get a train.

Okay, Kathleen. But you dont need to say you dont love me.

Okay.

She sat there with me for a long time, maybe another hour. Even though she was the one crying she knew I needed comfort. In fact her crying was a comfort.

I said, I wish I'd been nicer to you.

Kathleen: I feel it's my fault.

That's odd.

Yes, it's odd.

Everything we said was well-thought, considered. True, apologetic. It grew dark and I lit a candle. Her phone rang quietly. She did not like a loud phone.

She got up from the cushioned chair near my old studio. And we hugged. She wore the amber ring I'd given her a hundred years ago and on her other hand a copper ring. Finney. She had some makeup. I asked if she'd lie down with me. And she did. We both cried. I said it felt as if something was drowning. As if we were drowning it. She was wrong, we had a good thing. I reminded her that we had children with little Kathleen and Rockwell faces, our own goddamn names. I said, pulling up, So we're not going to grow old together.

She did not react.

I said, I hadnt realized I was harming you. I loved you and thought that was enough.

She listened.

I can change. I dont want to be an angry man. I can be so bullish.

Kathleen: I dont want the things I love to be made angry at by you.

She said this into the open faces of her hands. She was talking about her life. The way I criticized the things she enjoyed.

I do have a meanness. But I wondered if there was a way for Kathleen to call me on it. To say, That hurts. Yes, she said. But she hadnt been able to do that in the past. And that was why she felt not big enough for me.

Me: What I've realized is that you can't just say what you want. You have to consider the other person. I thought you could just be who you are.

I lay there with Kathleen. Our children with her parents. There was an old man next door, cleaning his soffits with a broom from the upstairs balcony. The sound exactly like the mailman opening the lid on a mailbox. As if he was continuously delivering mail. He had been doing it all afternoon and now at night.

I miss, I said, how you brush your hair into a paper bag and then put the hair in the compost. I miss how you spread water on your thighs to stop static cling.

When I was younger, she said, people'd stand next to me. They said they could feel the heat coming off me.

She had to be on a train. She had to get the children. We sat on a bench outside. I'm plunged in love with you. I dont want to move on. I want you in my life.

Kathleen was very kind about this.

She did not like how I interacted with the world. She found it abrupt. And tough to watch without judging me. The strength in my correction of things. She needed softer language. Some people, she once said, can argue to win a point. I dont need it.

All of this is pushing the inside out. Or what we do is push the outside in. Kathleen had a gentle, private centre. I didnt care for it then, but I see the beauty of it now. In hindsight. I didnt appreciate the delicate restraint. Or anything hidden. We have mountains only because the seas are pursing their lips.

49

I noticed that Rocky wasnt good at figuring out, at the traffic lights, what was red and what was green. A doctor gave him a dot-pattern test. It's a simple test for colour-blindness. Which is only, the doctor said, the inability to differentiate between shades of colour. As if that was a small thing. The son of a painter. It's true it never bothered Rocky. And what did he do but study vision. We built a lab. Rocky grew up to work in spectroscopy, the analysis of materials. I said to him, Why. Why this. He said, It's science, Dad.

But it's not artful.

He was offended. Dad, he said, I'm tired of the surfaces of art. I'm interested in the spirit within. I spin electrons. I disperse energy. I deflect ions into thin slits and measure current. I study emissions and the absorption of different wavelengths. The nucleus of every element, it carries a charge. And I study that charge. I tell it where to go. I'm involved in chemical noise, in magnetic resonance. If that is not interesting, Dad. If you dont think that's important.

It is important, son. Youre studying light and pigment. Youre inside them. And as you say, I'm only on the surface of them.

He got it from his mother, the colour-blindness. A weak X chromosome.

50

A year after my divorce I saw Jenny Starling. In New York. I was living alone, I said. I hardly saw the children. Jenny could tell I was lonely. She had left Luis Starling for good and had married Gerald Thayer. We met near my apartment during the last days of December. I had missed her birthday. She said Kathleen had offered me adoration and stability.

These are the things one looks for, Jenny said, when one is aggressive and wants babies.

I realized then that it was not Kathleen but me who'd wanted children. It was me with the pattern and a fixed life. I wanted both the conventional and the exotic.

Jenny: You were impressed with talent, and yet when youre impressionable, it means you can also be embarrassed. It is always better if one is not vulnerable to embarrassment.

Jenny said my irises were betraying me.

It had rained all morning. All the light from the world drained out to fight the rain.

Gerald told me that if ever I saw you I could fuck you but not kiss you.

Me: Jesus.

Jenny: What do you think of that.

Me: I dont know what to think.

Jenny: I can't figure out where Gerald is these days. He's all over the map.

Alma used to say the same thing.

We were in the car the other day and he told me to pull over. He'd pissed in his pants.

Was he, what was it.

He was anxious. He said it just came over him.

He should get that checked out.

She took my hand. Are you going to invite me up?

Jenny.

I showed her up. My apartment was a place to crash. I was spending most of my time on a small farm in Ausable Forks.

Jenny: Do you think people a century ago had similar thoughts to what they have today?

Me: Probably.

It's just their public comportment that changes.

Society, I said, was more polite and mannered.

But the inner life remains the same.

Yes, the inner life.

Just fuck me hard, she said. Will you do that?

Jenny. What's wrong with you.

And then I gave up. I pushed her into the bedroom. I pressed her into the mattress. I fucked Jenny Starling in an angry way. I said I'm going to break a bone, Jenny. And you'll have to go to the hospital.

The bad hospital.

I thought about this. It will be the hospital where the janitor shits on you.

Where the doctors in white cloaks walk around with their big cocks hanging out.

That's the one.

They fuck the patients in packs. They have swollen veiny cocks.

Here's one now. He's wiped the shit off your ass and he's got a clipboard that he smacks you in the head with.

I rammed her hard in the cunt.

We fucked like this until she came. I pushed against the flex of her pelvis. Then we dressed and stood at the window and looked at the cold city. It rained a little more. Do you want to go outside?

Jenny wore my green jacket. We walked to a little wet park. She said she didnt know that men thought that way. She had talked to a few women about fantasies. Gerald, she said, likes to make love gently. She said Gerald is a blend of arrogance and insecurity. And his arrogance, like yours, covers up his insecurity.

You like the illicitness.

The degradation comes as a release.

We sat there in the park until she was hungry. I held her hand a little. Then we walked back to my apartment. We ate cherries while I cooked dinner. And I hugged her as she left. She was on the edge of staying. But I suggested she should go. Her boyish nice feet. She said, Youve gotten conservative and youre hard-working and you smell like soap.

I smiled at this. Then she said, I decided to say something that did not belong within the assumptions we have of each other.

I was rolling out pastry when she came back.

Are you making pie for me?

I always make pie at Christmas.

And there I was, thinking.

Happy birthday, Jenny.

I forgot your coat.

She reached her arms around my neck and kissed me. Blue eyes. She had a snaggly tooth. Sometimes, when her mouth relaxed, her lips rested raggedly, like an animal after it yawns. She was beautiful, sexy, and alive.

I put the pie in and we got back into bed. We got into bed in a tired, comfortable way.

Do you want more of the bad hospital?

No.

I had painted the bedroom red, but only one coat. The white primer had showed through. You could see the roller marks and the white like skin through a dark stocking. But the roughness appealed. It was not what I'd intended to do in painting the room. I was to be thorough and then had reconsidered thoroughness. There was something indicative of my thrust in the world, this rough colour. I was attracted to that which wasnt methodical. To what was fleeting.

I went down to the lobby with Jenny, and then watched her walk away into the night. It was the last time I saw her. She had a buoyant step. I liked her shoulders — from behind she reminded me of Emily Edwards. There was a resilience in Jenny's gait, a resilience that made me understand that there are some women in the world you never have to worry about.

51

You are, Kathleen said, a man who cannot look at a woman without contemplating the sexual. Youre awake to it. Youre a scallop with its shell lip unlocked, considering, a tendril out, testing. And now, looking back, and knowing, at least having a sense of how things lie, it's safe to say that Bob Bartlett was a man who could not give in to his sexual side.

I would bump into him here and there and stand him a drink. A man devoted to the North. He often spoke of the trouble with women. The women in his life. I'm a teetotaller, he'd say, as I poured him one. At least, back home I am. Which was true, for I knew him in both places. He did not drink in Newfoundland. But in New York, in those deadly years of the thirties and forties, Bob Bartlett drank. I've seen him boast, as he drank, that he's never touched alcohol. And in the next breath recalls falling in love with a woman in England. But did I ever see him come on to a woman?

Bob Bartlett was, as they used to say then, inverted.

I have seen Bartlett in the Explorers Club, drinking Guatemalan rum on the house, telling stories of Peary, polar bears, and shipwrecks. I have walked him home, to his room in the Murray Hill Hotel, and listened to him complain of the ignominy of it all, that he must exchange these delicious stories for a meal and a drink. He did not use the word *ignominy*. He said *wrong*. The wrong of it all. I join a circle of men, he said, and they begin to goad me into a Peary recollection. It is a fall of dignity. It is degrading.

But this was all decades after, when Bartlett had been reduced to making coin off his name. It's one thing to lecture and another to find yourself holding a glass of whisky, realizing you are the embodiment of the word *regaling*. To regale is fine, as long as the tone of your regaling is not the reason youve been invited. If your story has honourable rather than cynical intentions. The dinner and the salad and then desserts and coffee and then the nod over to the map room, the wooden cork smacking out of the neck of twelve-year-old whisky, and the interlude that signalled it was Captain Bob's time. The fat cigars.

He did it and the worst part was the agreeing. A man retains the structure of integrity, even after he has sold off the shelves of goods that integrity insisted should never be sold. And so Bob Bartlett walked about as a proud shell of a man. And that was when he drank. He drank as a youth and he drank in his forties. There was a ten-year period in the Brigus house, under his mother, when he drank nothing. And it was this period of life that he tried to spread over his entire life. It was his ideal of the good man, and he wanted to construct himself ideally. Maybe all men do. Perhaps that is our downfall.

52

It was nine years later in New York City. Tom Dobie had come to work on the Manhattan skyline. He looked me up. He assumed I would want to see him and he was right. I can forget people, but if you return to my mind and have made an impression, then I am eager to see you.

I was working on salvaging a life with wife number two, Frances. I had come into my own as an artist. I had commissions, I was writing a book about my travels with my son in Alaska, and I felt I deserved the acclaim. I had incorporated myself and severed my ties with Charles Daniel. I was making a lot of money, but I worked hard for it.

Tom Dobie: I been working with Jim Cole of Colliers. Jim he invented the safety belt and safety wire for ironworkers. They love us cause we got experience climbing tall masts of ships in storm. I'll work this winter, then return to Brigus in summer to fish. That's why they call us Fish here in New York.

You want a drink?

Yes let's get a drink.

He was much older now. He shaved, but he had two patches of shadow on his cheekbones. His beard, if he let it grow, would start right under his eyes.

We walked down the road and dogs barked deep into properties. Up ahead a white truck with the words AM BUT ONCE painted on the back doors. I thought, So true. We are but once. We are but once, I said aloud, and Tom Dobie agreed with the tone, not knowing what I meant. And as we got closer I saw what the doors on the truck really said: AM BUL ANCE.

How's Coaker?

He's minister of marine and fisheries.

His party is the government?

His party, Kent, won eight seats.

This did not explain how he could be in government.

It's a minority government. Coaker says it's the proper thing.

So he's become one of them. Did the regulations go through.

No sir the exporters are not regulated. But salt fish is on the decline.

Refrigeration.

Yes, that's the key. Theyre doing away with salt fish. It's too much time and work.

I believe it will make a comeback.

That's an old-fashioned thought, he said. You got to use the freezer.

We reached the Green Dolphin and we both ordered beer. I asked him about Emily.

You havent heard.

I'm just asking about your wife.

She was pregnant, Tom Dobie said. That's why we married. I was glad about it, he said, but I knew it wasnt mine.

She was pregnant when you got married.

When I got home from the army.

You were too young. When they sent you back.

They sent me back because of Emily.

But it wasnt yours.

Well I was happy to give her the breeze. See I've never been interested in that sort of thing, with women. Never really got into it. So she was pregnant and that looked good — I got leave from the army and we was both going into St John's for work. We were to work until Christmas and then go back to Brigus for the winter. That was the end of my leave from the army. I'd be eighteen then and they'd ship me over. Emily got a berth aboard a schooner bound for Harbour Grace. The *Neptune*, her uncle captains her. She put on salt fish and cod oil. The schooner was going to put in at Brigus. I had more time so I took the train.

Anyway they left harbour and two days later this storm came over us. Knocked everything out of the water. We didnt hear from the *Neptune*. Never heard nothing. Two weeks went by and six schooners were lost. Then a third week and a boat come into St John's. She'd heard the *Neptune*'s danger bell out on the water. Gave her fresh water. The captain said they were fine — they were going slow for St John's. But then there were hurricane winds. Two months solid of nothing but storm. I wrote up the anxiety notice for the paper. Tony Loveys aboard her too. Gave her up for lost. We were all grieving. We been through some tough times there in Brigus.

Then we heard, we got a telegraph from Scotland. *Neptune* safe in Oban port.

Scotland?

She had crossed the entire Atlantic. I got a telegraph from Tony Loveys, he was bosun on board. Emily was alive, he said. But she was in hard shape. During the crossing they'd thought she would die for sure. She admitted she was pregnant. Her fingernails turned black. They decided they'd have to keep her on deck, wrapped in a sail for three days, but after that, if no sign of land, they were to bury her in the sea.

She was wrapped up in a sail.

No, boy — that was if she perished. But she hung on.

And they spotted land. It was the *Hesperus* towed them in.

The crew made arrangement for passage back to Newfoundland aboard the *Nova Scotia*. The doctor decided it'd be wiser for Emily to stay on, what with the war and all. She was halfway through the pregnancy. So she stayed. She stayed with this Scottish family, and that's where she met this man.

Me: You never wondered who the father was.

Tom: She loved me, but she'd gone and done something.

And this Scottish fellow.

I think she thought this might be a good thing. He'd been married, he was an older man. His wife died early. Emily had the baby. I hope he takes good care of her.

Tom looked at me then, So youve done all right.

I've prospered. But not because the kaiser came through.

Still waiting for your Iron Cross.

Tom said that after the war he left Newfoundland and he's been working foreign ever since. Now with the scaffolding. Remember Stan?

Stan Pomeroy, yes.

I never even told Emily the truth there. That Stan liked her.

I think we all knew that.

It got me riled. All I wanted was a life with Emily. And yet it felt wrong. I couldnt figure it out. It wasnt until he was dead that I figured something out. Did you know that? When he perished, do you know what we did? We had him, me and Tony Loveys, we had him in the twenty-five-foot skiff. It was rocking with fish, fish in the skirts and the vees, and me and Tony we'd never witnessed the like. Stan's body in the middle of the cod trap. We hauled him aboard and Tony was bawling. I told him to roll out the canvas sail from the cuddy across the loose fish and the gangboard. Now put Stan's body on it. Strip off his shirt and haul off his boots. His wet trousers. We got him naked. And I got naked too. I stripped down to nothing and I told Tony Loveys to do the same. Jesus Christ do it, I said. Now lie down like I'm doing. We got to warm him up. Get on the other side of him. Hold him close, push your heat into him. Rub his hands, rub his legs. But his back is solid cold, Tony said. I said, Hold yourself, Tony. Can you imagine being Stan? Lying there with the two of us buck naked around you. Youre probably just ears by then. Listening to the likes of me calling to you, rubbing your chest, pressing you.

The thought of it, I said, makes me want to get up and move.

Yes, you want to achieve less the image of a corpse.

It's alarming, I said.

It jolts you alive, Kent. It woke me up. I watched Stan's mouth, I waited for breath. But no breath. Just the chill in his body. I was turning cold too, and Tony Loveys got up out of it and pulled his clothes back on and stood over us, shivering and yelled his frigging lungs out, Get us back home out of it. He was hysterical, and all I could think of was Stan Pomeroy.

You loved him.

We were young men, Kent.

53

A few years later I returned to Newfoundland for a weekend. This was after my second divorce and I was on my way to Greenland on board the cutter *Direction*. It was not a planned stop. We hauled in for repairs and fresh provisions. I looked up Tom Dobie. He was working in a slaughterhouse. I found him having a smoke outside the building. A cow beside him. It wasnt much of an operation. He shook my hand — I noticed he was missing an index finger. He finished the cigarette. He savoured it, measuring out his puffs. Then he took the cow in by a rope through a ring in its nose. I went in to watch. Inside, a basin and a rut in the floor. He tied the cow to a ring set in the floor so its head was low. Took a pistol and fired right into the forehead. The cow shuddered, buckled immediately, and went down. Tom shoved a twelve-inch length of bamboo cane into the hole the bullet had made and wiggled it about. The cow went berserk, working out all of its reflex actions. He hoisted its rear legs onto two hooks and yanked the cow to the ceiling, its nose an inch from the ground. He sharpened a knife on a strop and skinned the entire carcass, even the face. The eyes bulging out of its hideless face. He slit the belly and chest and out plopped all the organs on the floor. A splash of blood whipped across the gutter. He whistled and a boy came down a hallway with a wheelbarrow. The boy tipped the wheelbarrow and had all the organs in the wheelbarrow in four shovelfuls. Then whisked on. Tom used a saw and cut the cow in half down the middle. And there were the two halves of a dead cow ready to hang. The butchering took about ten minutes. He went out for another smoke.

I asked him about the pistol. It's not a real gun, he said. It has a .22 cartridge inside that fires and the vacuum pushes a steel pin into the cow's head.

He was in hard shape. We went and had a drink near the finger piers. Tom Dobie said to me, If I had three hundred and fifty dollars, I could economize and get along on that to supply myself.

He'd been looking around St John's and sizing things up.

Take oil clothes. A fisherman has to pay four dollars a suit for oil clothes. If a man had the money he could buy flour bags and have them made out of that. Flour bags are the very best thing you could make oil clothes from. They'd last you for three years. I could make them for sixty cents, and then the oil costs about one dollar, but you'd have a number-one suit. Mother knitted my underwear and I dont waste very much. Take a pair of rubber boots. Theyre worth three dollars. In the fall we have to pay four dollars for them.

Last year he worked the salmon racket. And it was a failure.

Salmon, he says, have a magnetic pulse in their heads. They swim on the north side of the bays. No fish in the middle of the bay, five hundred feet of water.

He did not make five cents at the salmon. It was after the fifth of August by then and he had to go back to Brigus. Mother set out six barrels of seed potatoes last year and we got forty-five barrels. But this year we only got sixteen barrels because of the canker. Total failure. Mother, she got to look after everything while I'm away. Cabbage, turnips. Also beets. Last year she had to cut three thousand hay and stow it away for the season.

They had four sheep and one horse last year, but they had to sell them all and last year Tom Dobie had to sell his cart wheels. Two hundred and fifty dollars, that would get them through the winter.

He'd been to the lighthouse department, but they had nothing to offer him. He'd been to the department of postal and telegraphs and been told they had more men than they needed.

If I only had a chance I could get along. If someone would back a note for me at the bank, I would come home in November and pay it all back and have a little for myself.

I asked if he'd been on the dole.

When the prime minister gave the dole I took the shovel and went over to Bell Island and worked there. I bid there two years and later on went to New York. That's when I saw you. I followed a horse there for a bit and then got onto the big steel. Afterwards I came home and got a job in construction.

Now he was laying brick and digging foundations and working at this here slaughterhouse.

Yes sir, until after Christmas and then I'm going home.

I heard they might open up another ore mine.

Well there's three hundred idlers there now and they will get the first of the work.

And what about the fishery.

I dont have much edge for it.

Are you a believer in motor boats?

Oh yes. But I recall when rowing was the only means to go fishing. Sure when you were out in Brigus that's how we done it. They got more time to fish now since they have the six-horsepower coaker. You can get there much quicker than by rowing, and you can remain out until half an hour before night-fall. When you had oars you had to leave after dinner to get in. Of course gasoline is high and quite an expense in the motor boat.

You think a man without a motor boat can compete with a man owning one?

No. Not very well. When I first met you, I was — what? — sixteen. I didnt know what the world was. I thought the world was mine. But I had a limited vision because of the poverty of my family and the small view they had of the world's offerings.

Me: The very opposite is true of me. I had reduced circumstances, but I expected the world. I came from a family used to the world. Because of my background I was used to expecting, and expecting puts you in a position to receive.

Youre sitting there saying that, he said, with a big shit-eating grin.

Youre misreading my face. I'm not pleased about it.

Youre excited by it.

Tom, I want to back your note.

Out on the hill, as our cutter left port, the sheep's laurel blanketed the slopes like small pink popcorn. Warm wind, but it was still cold off the land. Carrots were up, beet leaves, turnip, peas. The comfrey too, in big stands, as though someone, just below the surface, was grasping it in handfuls. The hopeful vegetables. I was leaving all this, tended.

54

I spoke to Kathleen before she died. She had become, after our divorce, more religious. She had become more herself and rebelled against my atheism. But her private Christianity, over thirty years, had ground her down. And now she had cancer.

Is Jesus still your saviour?

Kathleen: I couldnt say. Except that he's not a comfort any longer. I'm shedding skins. I'm losing a lot of friends. I'm honest with people now. I might have to get some new friends. I'm interested in different kinds of people now.

What kind.

Well, there's not many around here. A lot of the things that I thought were me arent me. I'm sick of a bunch of the old stuff. You helped me. What I'm really interested in is art and writing by women. I was looking at my bookshelf and thought, Who wants to read it? The fundamentalist, one-way dogma has to go. Though I still believe in immortality. The integrity of our personhood. I definitely experience a spiritual reality that I hope will translate into immortality. I've had an injured state of mind and been annihilated. And now I wonder why people must be so relentlessly themselves. You, for instance. Were a bulldozer.

Yes. But why couldnt you just let it not affect you.

I wanted to be with someone who was forgiving.

I could see the kindness in that now.

In the end, she said, it's all about repercussions. The sum of your acts, and your concern for or indifference towards those who have loved you. The question is not have you been loved, but have you loved.

55

The thing is, I am a man of ambiguity. But I portrayed assurance. I had to convey that. Give it off. I did not want anyone to sense a whiff of doubt.

I have become a public man living a quiet country life. I have a dairy farm. My house in Ausable Forks burnt down and I rebuilt it. I will defeat entropy. I love hosting parties and my neighbours put up with me. When youre a little more famous, your neighbours will submit. But my friends are New York friends. I have given up on marrying myself to the rural as if it were the only truth. My only belief now is that if you keep moving, perhaps the laws of nature will forget how old you are.

When I was eighty-six, I received a strange letter. The envelope said Office of the Premier, Province of Newfoundland, Canada. The premier, a Mr Smallwood. What a fine letter. He'd felt compelled to write me, he said, for in compiling facts for his *Encyclopaedia of Newfoundland*, he had discovered my fifty-year-old correspondence with the government of Newfoundland, his government. He was shocked by the treatment I'd received. He'd been prepared, he said, to write a letter of apology to my son or daughter. He was then mightily pleased to hear that I was still alive, happily living out my time in Upstate New York. He wrote:

> Would you come back here? Would you be this Government's guest on a visit back to Newfoundland, including Brigus? Please forgive us for past injuries, and please be magnanimous enough to be our guest some time at your convenience.
>
> With assurances of my highest regard,
>
> Joseph R. Smallwood

I was stunned.

And vindicated. The premier had read my correspondence and was shamed. They wanted me to return.

56

And so the next summer I returned, with my third wife, Sally. I have lived with Sally for longer than I did my first two wives put together. And yet there are events in youth that form you so strongly that a mere year can live within you for the rest of your life. Part of me has always regretted the failure of my Newfoundland plans. That is the reason for this book. To discuss openly the very events that caused my will to be rebuked.

We flew into St John's in the dark. There was trouble with the plane's braking. The runway slick with rain. There was a family in the seats beside ours. A girl held a goldfish bowl in her lap — she had held it the entire flight. One goldfish. We touched down and veered, lurching a little to one side. We skidded along the tarmac, until the tarmac ended. The highway lights through the dark trees. The plane pushing its wings a little into the woods. Then we stopped. I was pleased to be with Sally — I have learned in old age the grace of how to be a good husband. I thought, If we die here on this tarmac in Newfoundland, it will have been a good life. I will have died where I once thought I would die. We looked at each other and prayed there would be no fire. The intercom and then the pilot, Welcome to St John's. We heard sirens, the flash of emergency vehicles in the dark, the applause of the passengers, the happy goldfish, but we used the stairs down to the ground. It was woods. Behind us, a line of idling taxis perched at the end of the runway, their low beams shining in our faces, fire trucks in the distance. The taxis had beaten the fire trucks, to take us to the terminal. The rain began again and we sat in a taxi. It is nice, Sally said, in the rain, to sit in a car.

In the morning I saw that St John's was a nicer-looking town. Still a bit roughed up, but not so sordid. I met the premier. There were photographers. The papers were interested in my story: I was the famous spy of Brigus. They call it Kent Cottage now, Smallwood said, but not after you. It's named after the place in England.

The premier was tanned. He had just returned from Cuba. He had met with Castro. I like, he said, island nations.

I have met the man, I said. I hear doves land on him.

We made a film, Smallwood said. I should show it to you sometime.

We visited the government buildings, the university, and the new shopping mall. Smallwood was proud of it, and he had a right to be proud. It was not picturesque, but can you expect people to live in squalor just so you can have good material for paintings?

It might look a little less pretty, I said, but it's healthy and functional.

The city was modern. We drove to Brigus. We passed a boot factory and a building where they produced chocolates.

We've got to get the people off fishing, Smallwood said. That's stone age. We have mining and hydro, paper mills and shipbuilding. There's chemicals and oil refining and agriculture and logging.

It's satisfying, I said, to see the Old World transformed.

I like to cast aside old allegiances.

Me: Losers imitate winners.

We stopped near Frogmarsh. Me and Sally, the premier and his wife. Smallwood's wife was called Clara, the same as my daughter. I told them about the war map, which was the painting of my nude family. They knew all about it. Even so, I was looked on with admiration, and I realized that my great age granted me a certain respect. I had known Prowse, for instance. They were talking to a man who had spent time with Judge Prowse.

I looked for the Dobie house. A trail down to a valley where the damson plums grew wild. Apples too. Morning glories and a field of hemp nettle like lavender. A boat jigging for cod, its red side looking blue in the shadows. The first thing I noticed was that all the fences were gone.

What do they do to keep out the cows.

Smallwood: There are no cows, Kent. Did away with the cows. We have a central dairy now, in St John's. Supplies all the Avalon. Got a lovely creamery too, makes butter out of petroleum.

The plum trees were wild and tall. You could see how they framed three sides of a house that did not exist — a ghostly perimeter of a house long gone. This, I said, was the Dobie house.

We walked behind the plums and found a rock wall. In the front field the high grass covered a garden that had a corrugated ripple.

A young man lived here, I said. A fine young man who helped me once.

Old potato drills. There were fields now. Long, wide fields. All the fences had rotted, the houses fallen in or moved.

Resettled, Smallwood said. We got rid of a lot of poverty. There was a lot of that all along this shore. The shore was rotten with it. But Brigus will survive. Brigus has old money.

The Bartlett house. Who lives there now.

The spinster Eleanor.

Bob Bartlett's sister?

Yes she's still around. Of course you knew her.

Eleanor came out to meet us.

Well chop the beam, she said. You must be going up for ninety years of age.

We had not known each other well, but she was polite and friendly. Could she hug, she asked, the German spy who lived down the path?

I just came by, I said, to remind you to put in the tulips.

Oh, tulips, she said. Theyre no good for flowers.

We walked down Rattley Row to the far shore. There was exactly half a house. Sliced in two like a dollhouse. It was the Pomeroys'. Someone had zipped through the middle with a chainsaw, had used the wood to build a shed. The frame of the house and the bedrooms upstairs all tilted. But the roof still solid, and the floors too.

Not a nail used in her, Smallwood said. Tight as a drum.

Me: What a house that was.

Smallwood: Theyre a bit savage, hey. With culture.

I'd say.

You got to live now with a bucket of keys.

We walked down the lane to my house. It had been maintained, and not renovated. It looked pretty good, except that the figurehead was gone. An elderly man had lived there after me. A polite English professor who was a Sunday painter. The brook was the same, though the trees around it had grown. The trees had changed. Gerald's pear tree had survived, and it was magnificent. I leaned over and picked one. It was hard, but I ate it anyway.

A Gerald pear, I said.

Sorry?

A friend of mine.

Smallwood: I've heard of a Bartlett pear.

That's funny.

I pointed to the shed. That's where I painted my German eagle.

They laughed at that. They all knew the story.

We went inside. There was propane now. The old stoves and fireplaces were gone. Replaced by modern kerosene heaters. The rooms were tiny. Six people had lived here, I said. It was strange to see my third wife in here.

I was born, Sally said, the year you lived here.

Smallwood: Will I put the kettle on?

Yes, I said.

We took the kettle and I found the dipper hung at the brook by the gate. You still had to do that.

57

I believe Kierkegaard: It is in your power to review your life, to look at things you saw before, from another point of view. Kierkegaard thought that he was quoting Marcus Aurelius, but he got it wrong. Aurelius wrote: To recover your life is in your power. Look at things as you used to look at them, for in this lies the recovery of your life.

58

It is not enough to have been loved. One must have loved. To love is to give yourself over. It is to realize trust. Trust is not something you can acquire. You cannot train yourself. There is no fitness class to trust. You must cultivate love and push love towards the seeds of what interests you. Give out the heart. If you do this, then you will have lived. And you will be loved. Those who kill themselves are often well loved. Gerald Thayer was loved. He was an exuberant man. A man of life. But there was a weight to him, and in late fall, on his way to meet me, that weight stopped him. I was on my farm in the Adirondacks. He'd hit a wall, he said. He'd left Jenny. He had family money, but he had no work. He was thrilled by his children. I take it as an accident. As an evening that overtook. I think it surprised him — he was a man who had never broken a bone in his body. But on his way here, he was driving. On his way, in a small town in Upstate New York, he stopped for the night. I have been to this small town. I have seen that time of year, when the light is a constant pale grey. It is past fall, the trees and fields are bare and all that's promised is a long absence of anything with buds. It happened there, in his hotel room, at dusk. It is a mournful time, that part of the world and that season. The season, the scene, the air are all favourable to numbness and isolation. He did not arrive in Ausable Forks and then Alma called to tell me. After all those years it was Alma Wollerman. Alma had been in his passport. He had his passport with him. Alma called to tell me. Gerald's gone.

Sometimes the people bursting with life feel they dont deserve it. What they feel is the fact that they havent managed to throw themselves into the joy of devotion. They have not placed themselves in servitude. They have always led and therefore have never experienced the love that comes from admiration, from not being in charge, from not having the light shine upon one's acts.

59

I saw Bob Bartlett soon before he died. He was seventy and in rough shape. He had just accepted an award for marine service. He had been in the wilderness for thirty years, living at Murray Hill and singing for his supper. Then this award, a medal from the National Geographic Society. It was in late April, and the first creamy magnolia blossoms were pushing out, the size of the top joint of your thumb. I passed a butcher in white, rubber boots on, blood on his shirt, carrying a bicycle wheel. He reminded me of Tom Dobie. And inside, when Bob Bartlett rose in his dinner jacket, they all stood around him, applauding. I saw his face. Bob's face looked out at them with astonishment. That he had achieved this acclaim. But there was something else in his face as well: a satisfaction, an appreciation. It looked as though he was saying to himself, I deserve this.

He had no good work and he was drinking. After the First World War he took a bit part in a Hollywood movie, *The Viking*. A romance set during the seal hunt. The first talking film, Bartlett said, shot outside the United States, and they shot it in Newfoundland.

I showed it, he said, to the sealers in Brigus. They were extras in it. I took them down one night to the government wharf and sat them there. I had Tom Dobie unfurl the mainsail on the *Morrissey*, and I projected the movie on it. What a sight — the sealers sitting on the wharf to watch themselves copy over ice pans up on the sail. It was a fine thing.

We were drinking at the Explorers Club. There was a woman with a blue spot on her lip watching us. She was finding the clasp on the back of her necklace. Bartlett saw me look at her.

He was writing a memoir. He thought that could be a ripping good yarn. He wanted to know if I'd ever read Siegfried Sassoon's memoir.

It's a good diary, he said. Of the war — it's what my brother must have felt. There's a scene, Bartlett said, where he's describing a bath. He says that his memories of how the water was poured into the vat may not be of much interest to anyone, but for him it was a good bath and it's his own story he's trying to tell.

Bartlett let out a little laugh.

When he said that, Kent, I realized that I've never told my own story. I've told a public story. And here Sassoon is, just attempting to show the war's effect on a solitary-minded young man.

But it's still a public story, I said. It's not his real, deep-down personal, gut-truth story.

The thirties, he said, were hard. Peary had found him work investigating the condition of ships. During the Second World War he made hydro measurements in uncharted channels aboard the *Morrissey*. It was this patronage that made Bartlett change his mind about Peary.

They worked the *Morrissey* north through straits and channels near Baffin Island. They gauged their depth and breadth for the U.S. Navy. Bartlett was by then a citizen of the United States, and he was part of the merchant marine. Once he came across a U-boat — it sizzled to the surface in front of them. The *Morrissey* full of American sounding equipment, enough to make them prisoners of war.

How far off's that icefield.

It'll take us twenty minutes, sir, to wend back into that.

Okay, direct our bow towards that sub.

Sir.

Get me some fish. Bring up some good fish and let's start waving. Just wave to them. Be delirious.

They waved and a sailor manning the gunning tower studied them through binoculars. They waited for the *Morrissey* to come alongside. Then the captain and a naval officer who knew English. You are a fishing boat.

Youre welcome to this. We havent seen a soul in months.

You are American.

No, sir, Newfoundlanders.

They took the fish. They thanked Bartlett. I was just, he said, a regular seafaring man.

So what youre saying is that you supplied a German submarine.

Good one, Kent.

As they quartered and sailed off, Bartlett noticed another sailor come up onto the U-boat's gunning tower. He was holding a birdcage. In the cage a linnet. To think of a bird in a submarine. He was giving it some air.

I knew it was a linnet for the tune it sang. Did you know, Kent, that they pluck the eyes out of a linnet when it's young. To make it sing like that.

I guess the linnet never knows it's under water.

He was going home to Brigus, he said. His mother, his best girl, had passed away. This seemed to bring him much sadness. He said, Youve moved inland, I hear.

I have had a dairy farm, I said, in the Adirondacks for thirty years.

So youre off the water.

I nodded.

Augustine, Bartlett said, thought the land baptized. It is the seas that have no faith.

Me: I went to the sea to live but ended up inland.

I guess, he said, you moved to the sea to be a pagan. But in the end, Kent, youre a good Christian man.

He seemed upset, so I asked him. I wanted to tell him that I loved him. I asked him if he felt he was loved. He thought about this. He was very drunk.

I decided to get very drunk with him. Then he told me this. This was in the last year of his life. His mother had wanted him to be a minister: a Wesleyan Methodist minister. She had pounded it into him until his father had said, You can't forge steel, Mary, in a cold fire. He'd wanted to marry. This woman he'd met in England. But he felt it safer to stay single. He wanted to be a sealing captain, like his father. This too he failed at. He lucked into work in the North. He knew he liked living on boats. So his goal became to stand at the north pole.

Are you brave enough, he said, to be yourself, to explore your deep self.

Me: One is only ever oneself.

Well, that's good, because everyone else is taken.

He laughed at that, cheered it, and called for another round.

For me, the difficulty was curbing myself to be with others.

For thirty years Bob Bartlett remained a virgin. For twenty years he wiggled the arses of vessels through pack ice. At thirty-three he got to stand eighty miles from the north pole. And that was it. From then on, it's been downhill.

A few years ago, he said, I met this man in New York. A married man, much younger than me. And we got into it. We got into everything. We'd been to a bar where a man was aloft, his legs in straps, and you could go over to him. You could manoeuvre his thighs and stand between them. The man did this, and fucked him from behind. I watched the man do this. It was a strange new world, it was. We went back to my room at the Murray Hill Hotel and got into it. The man guided me. I ended up with my fist in the man. I had my hand up the man's rectum. The man showed me how to follow the course of the large intestine to the solar plexus.

He slugged back his drink, then pushed it along the bar with a finger inside the glass.

Can I call you Rockwell?

It's far too late to stand on formalities, Bob.

I could feel the man's heart beat, he said. And then, You believe that? I know. It's hard to believe.

We continued drinking. Bob Bartlett's hands, one on the zinc counter, the other gripping a new glass of whisky. The very hand. I noticed that his thumb had a blackened nail.

The question is not, he said, were you loved. Or did you love. Or did you love yourself. Or did you allow love to move you, though that's a big one. Move you. The question, Rockwell, is did you get to be who you are. And if not, then why. That, my friend, is the big why.

60

Thing is, I've lived my life by ideas. I've been governed by them. I learned what I thought was the just life and applied those ideas to my conduct. I saw monogamy as a good thing, so I strove for monogamy. I disregarded my inner hunch. There is the life that is acted out, and then there is the secret life. But I do not advocate a merger between the secret life and the willed one. I do not believe bad men should confess to their badness and find ways to reroute badness into socially constructive ways. Let the badness be bottled up. Let it remain unexplored. There is something to be said for repression. To have a secret does not mean one is living a lie. A hand is played out and a hand is kept close to the chest. What is wrong in living the double life? Why praise the open one? Why risk feelings? Why risk the embarrassment that may come from revealing them? What is so wrong with discretion? Why not withhold emotion? So much is said without saying anything, and so much harm is done through confession and openness.

One can be known without revelation. The whole point of revelation is that it comes from the inside. It blooms inwardly. The biblical stories of visions are not meant to be seen with the outer eye.

I imagined what Gerald might say: that often this leads to hypocrisy. You live at odds with your ideals. You spend your life trying to find out what other people think of you, and then you get old and moribund. Youre old and repetitious and you realize the world is getting younger. The opposite of suddenly, Gerald said once, is over time. And over time one realizes a change has occurred. This appears to people as some kind of conversion. It carries the odour of spirituality. I have tried, Gerald said, to represent things with an exact correspondence to the real. You have too, Kent. You have managed to uncover something, rather than perform a feat. Your life has been the feat. Your art, he said, is plain but imbued with spirit. Your friends are interesting. It is your life, not your art, that will last. In a sense, none of us, Kent, had a religion. In another sense, we were all the most religious people in the world.

But what are you to do when what youve struggled for your whole life seems like the most obvious thing in the world. Art is all about expanding the world, making it possible to think new things. Living well will infuse your work with an exuberance. But what do you do when you hit your limit? When your art is no longer new.

Gerald: When youre unhappy, you dont have a sense of privacy. You tell everyone you meet how you feel and what you think. When youre in that place, you must achieve a poise between revelation and secrecy.

That poise. The privilege of someone who is well balanced.
Then the question of discretion becomes irrelevant, because
youre living your life well.

ACKNOWLEDGMENTS

Some of Rockwell Kent's books inspired this novel, including his autobiography, *It's Me, O Lord*; the travel book *N by E*; some collected essays on art and living, *Rockwellkentiana*; and his chapbook, *After Long Years*. Captain Robert A. Bartlett's autobiography, *The Log of Bob Bartlett*, was helpful too.

I plundered many books on Newfoundland to supply colour and detail to *The Big Why*. For instance, the scene of the boys out rabbit-catching and the image of Tom Dobie and his father breaking through river ice were prompted by passages from *Little Nord Easter* by Victor Butler.

The description of Bob Bartlett projecting the film *The Viking* on a ship's sail is borrowed from a documentary by Victoria King.

Curatorial comments from two art catalogues proved very helpful: *Rockwell Kent: The Newfoundland Work* by Gemey Kelly, and *Distant Shores: The Odyssey of Rockwell Kent* by Constance Martin.

The idea that a private journal contrasts in tone and intimacy from a published memoir is a point that Ronald Rompkey makes in his books on Eliot Curwen and Wilfred Grenfell.

I also stole, from his *Labrador Odyssey*, the description of the living quarters on board a freighter bound for Turnavik.

A notable source of unpublished material was Mark Ferguson, especially his thesis, "Making Fish" (Folklore Department, Memorial University, St John's). David O'Meara provided the Sexday anecdote.

I thank Claire Wilkshire, Larry Mathews, and Martha Sharpe for reading and commenting on early versions of this manuscript. I thank Christine Pountney for her wise suggestions and imaginative leaps, which make this novel more interesting to read.

A hearty thank you to my agent, Anne McDermid.

I wrote this book wondering what Lisa Moore would think of it.

I am grateful to the Canada Council for the Arts, the Ontario Arts Council, and the Toronto Arts Council for funding during the long haul. The Civitella Ranieri Foundation was also very kind to me.

For a full list of acknowledgments and an author's note on the writing method, please visit the House of Anansi Press web site at www.anansi.ca and click on *The Big Why*.

I thank you Edgar Saltus.